Philip Massinger, Thomas Coxeter

The Works of Philip Massinger
Vol. 2. Containing The Renegado. The Picture. The Fatal Dowry. The Emperor of the East. The Maid of Honour.

ISBN/EAN: 9783337344917

Printed in Europe, USA, Canada, Australia, Japan

Cover: Foto ©Andreas Hilbeck / pixelio.de

More available books at **www.hansebooks.com**

Philip Massinger, Thomas Coxeter

The Works of Philip Massinger

Vol. 2. Containing The Renegado. The Picture. The Fatal Dowry. The Emperor of the

East. The Maid of Honour.

II

THE

WORKS

OF

PHILIP MASSINGER.

VOLUME the SECOND.

CONTAINING,

The RENEGADO.
The PICTURE.
The FATAL DOWRY.
The EMPEROR OF THE EAST.
The MAID OF HONOUR.

LONDON:

Printed for T. DAVIES, in *Ruffel-Street*, *Covent-Garden*.
MDCCLXI.

THE
RENEGADO.

A

TRAGI-COMEDY.

As it hath been often Acted, by the Queen's
Majesty's Servants, at the private Play-house in
Drury-Lane, in the Year 1630.

By PHILIP MASSINGER.

Vol. II. A

TO THE

RIGHT HONOURABLE

GEORGE HARDING,

Baron *Barkley*, of *Barkley* Caſtle, and Knight
of the Honourable Order of the BATH.

My good Lord,

TO *be honoured for old Nobility, or Hereditary Ti-*
tles is not alone proper to yourſelf, but to ſome
few of your Rank, who may challenge the like
Privilege with you : But in our Age to vouch-
ſafe (as you have often done) a ready Hand to raiſe the de-
jected Spirits of the contemned Sons of the Muſes; ſuch as
would not ſuffer the glorious Fire of Poeſy to be wholly ex-
tinguiſhed, is ſo remarkable, and peculiar to your Lordſhip,
that with a full Vote, and Suffrage it is acknowledged, that
the Patronage, and Protection of the dramatic Poem, is
yours, and almoſt without a Rival. I deſpair not therefore,
but that my Ambition to preſent my Service in this Kind, may
in your Clemency meet with a gentle Interpretation. Confirm
it, my good Lord in your gracious Acceptance of this Trifle;
in which if I were not confident there are ſome Pieces wor-
thy the Peruſal, it ſhould have been taught an humbler
Flight ; and the Writer (your Countryman) never yet made
happy in your Notice, and Favour, had not made this an
Advocate to plead for his Admiſſion among ſuch as are
wholly, and ſincerely devoted to your Service. I may live
to tender my humble Thankfulneſs in ſome higher Strain;
and, 'till then, comfort myſelf with hope, that you deſcend
from your Height to receive

Your Honour's commanded Servant,

PHILIP MASSINGER.

A 2

Dramatis Personæ.	The Original Actors,
Asambeg, Viceroy of *Tunis*.	JOHN BLANYE.
Muſtapha, Baſha of *Aleppo*.	JOHN SUMNER,
Vitelli, a Gentleman of *Venice* diſguis'd.	MICHAEL BOWIER.
Franciſco, a Jeſuit.	WILLIAM REIGNALDS,
Anthonio Grimaldi, the Renegado.	WILLIAM ALLEN.
Carazie, an Eunuch.	WILLIAM ROBINS.
Gazet, Servant to *Vitelli*.	EDWARD SHAKERLEY.
Aga.	
Capiaga.	
Maſter.	
Boatſwain.	
Sailors.	
Jailor.	
Three *Turks*.	
Donuſa, Neice to *Amurath*.	EDWARD ROGERS.
Paulina, Siſter to *Vitelli*.	THEO. BOURNE.
Manto, Servant to *Donuſa*.	

The Scene, Tunis.

THE

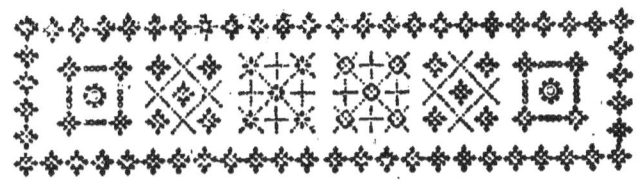

THE
RENEGADO.
A
TRAGI-COMEDY.

ACT I. SCENE I.

Enter Vitelli *and* Gazet.

Vitelli.

YOU'VE hir'd a Shop, then?
  Gaz. Yes, Sir; and our Wares
(Though brittle as a Maidenhead at fixteen)
Are fafe unladen; not a Chryftal crack'd,
Or China Difh needs fod'ring; our choice Pictures,
As they came from the Workman, without Blemifh;
And I have ftudied Speeches for each Piece,
And in a thrifty Tone, to fell 'em off,
Will fwear by *Mahomet*, and *Termagant*,
That this is Miftrefs to the great Duke of *Florence*,
That Neice to old King *Pepin*, and a Third
An *Auftrian* Princefs by her *Roman* Nofe,
How e'er my Confcience tells me they are Figures
Of Bawds and common Courtefans in *Venice*.
  Vitel. You make no Scruple of an Oath, then?
  Gaz. Fye, Sir!
'Tis out of my Indentures; I'm bound there

To

To fwear for my Mafter's Profit, as fecurely
As your Intelligencer muft for his Prince,
That fends him forth an honourable Spy
To ferve his Purpofes.   And, if it be lawful
In a Chriftian Shopkeeper to cheat his Father,
I cannot find but, to abufe a *Turk*
In the Sale of our Commodities, muft be thought
A meritorious Work.
  Vitel. I wonder, Sirrah,
What's your Religion?
  Gaz. 'Troth, to anfwer truly,
I would not be of one that fhould command me
To feed upon poor *John*, when I fee Pheafants
And Partridges on the Table: Nor do I like
The other that allows us to eat Flefh
In Lent though it be rotten, rather then be
Thought fuperftitious, as your zealous *Cobler*,
And learned *Botcher* preach at *Amfterdam* [1]
Over a Hotchpotch.   I'd not be confin'd
In my Belief, when all your Sects, and Sectaries
Are grown of one Opinion; if I like it,
I will profefs myfelf,—in the mean Time
Live I in *England*, *Spain*, *France*, *Rome*, *Geneva*,
I'm of that Country's Faith.
  Vitel. And what in *Tunis?*
Will you turn *Turk* here?
  Gaz. No: So I fhould lofe
A Collop of that Part my *Doll* enjoin'd me
To bring home as fhe left it: 'Tis her Venture,
Nor dare I barter that Commodity
Without her fpecial Warrant.
  Vitel. You're a Knave, Sir;
Leaving your Roguery, think upon my Bufinefs:
It is no Time to fool now——

1 ——— *As your zealous Cobler*
  And learned Botcher preach at Amfterdam
  Much about this Time the Low Countries were infefted with a fuperftitious Crew of Puritans and Fanatics, and the Perfons here alluded
to, were perhaps the moft noted: A Cobler and a Taylor.

Remember

Remember where you are too: Though this Mart-time,
We are allowed free Trading, and with Safety.
Temper your Tongue and meddle not with the *Turks*,
Their Manners, nor Religion.

 Gaz. Take you Heed, Sir,
What Colours you wear. Not two Hours fince there
 landed
An *English Pirate*'s Whore with a green Apron,
And, as fhe walk'd the Streets, one of their Muftis
(We call them Priefts at *Venice*) with a Razor
Cuts it off, Petticoat, Smock and all, and leaves her
As naked as my Nail; the young Fry wond'ring
What ftrange Beaft it fhould be. I 'fcap'd a Scouring
My Miftrefs' Bufk Point, of that forbidden Colour
Then ty'd my Codpiece, had it been difcover'd
I had been capon'd.

 Vitel. And had been well ferv'd.
Hafte to the Shop, and fet my Wares in order
I will not long be abfent?

 Gaz. Though I ftrive, Sir,
To put off Melancholy, to which you are ever
Too much inclin'd, it fhall not hinder me
With my beft Care to ferve you.   [*Exit* Gazet.

    Enter Francifco.

 Vitel. I believe thee.
O welcome, Sir! Stay of my Steps in this Life,
And Guide to all my bleffed Hopes hereafter!
What Comfort, Sir? Have your Endeavours profper'd?
Have we tir'd Fortune's Malice with our Sufferings?
Is fhe at length, after fo many Frowns,
Pleas'd to vouchfafe one cheerful Look upon us?

 Fran. You give too much to Fortune, and your
 Paffions,
O'er which a wife Man, if religious, triumphs.
That Name Fool's Worfhip, and thofe Tyrants, which
We arm againft our better Part, our Reafon,
May add, but never take from our Afflictions.

    A 4   *Vitel.*

Vitel. Sir, as I am a finful Man, I cannot
But like one fuffer. [a]

Fran. I exact not from you
A Fortitude infenfible of Calamity,
To which the Saints themfelves have bow'd, and fhew
They're made of Flefh and Blood : All that I challenge
Is manly Patience. Will you, that were train'd up
In a religious School, where divine Maxims
Scorning Comparifon with moral Precepts
Were daily taught you, bear your Conftancy's Trial,
Not like *Vitelli,* but a Village Nurfe,
With Curfes in your Mouth ? Tears in your Eyes ?
How poorly it fhows in you.

Vitel. I am fchool'd, Sir,
And will, hereafter, to my utmoft Strength
Study to be myfelf.

Fran. So fhall you find me
Moft ready to affift you : Neither have I
Slept in your great Occafions fince I left you :
I have been at the Viceroy's Court, and prefs'd
As far as they allow a Chriftian Entrance.
And fomething I have learn'd that may concern
The Purpofe of this Journey.

Vitel. Dear Sir, what is it ?

Fran. By the Command of *Afambeg,* the Viceroy :
The City fwells with barbarous Pomp and Pride
For the Entertainment of ftout *Muftapha*
The *Bafha* of *Aleppo,* who, in Perfon,
Comes to receive the Neice of *Amurah*
The fair *Donufa* for his Bride.

Vitel. I find not
low this may profit us.

---

[a] *Sir, as I am a finful Man, I cannot.*
But like one fuffer.
In *Macbeth* we have a fine Expreffion like this.
   Difpute it (fays *Malcolm*) like a Man.
   Malcolm, I fhall do fo :
   But I muft alfo feel it as a Man.
                              The Rev. Mr. *Dodd.*

Fran.

Fran. Pray you, give me Leave.
Among the reft that wait upon the Viceroy,
(Such as have under him Command in *Tunis*)
Who, as you've often heard, are all falfe Pyrates,
I faw the Shame of *Venice* and the Scorn
Of all good Men : The perjur'd *Renegado*,
Antonio Grimaldi.
　Vitel. Ha! his Name
Is Poifon to me.
　Fran. Yet again ?
　Vitel. I've done, Sir!
　Fran. This debauch'd Villain, whom we ever thought
(After his impious Scorn done in St. *Mark*'s
To me as I ftood at the holy Altar)
The Thief that ravifh'd your fair Sifter from you,
The virtuous *Paulina*, not long fince
(As I am truly given to underftand)
Sold to the Viceroy a fair Chriftian Virgin,
On whom, maugre his fierce and cruel Nature
Afambeg dotes extremely.
　Vitel. 'Tis my Sifter :
It muft be fhe ; my better Angel tells me
'Tis poor *Paulina*. Farewell all Difguifes!
I'll fhow in my Revenge that I am Noble.
　Fran. You are not mad ?
　Vitel. No, Sir ; my virtuous Anger
Makes ev'ry Vein an Artery, I feel in me
The Strength of twenty Men ; and, being arm'd
With my good Caufe to wreak wrong'd Innocence,
I dare alone run to the Viceroy's Court
And with this Poignard, before his Face,
Dig out *Grimaldi*'s Heart.
　Fran. Is this religious ?
　Vitel. Would you have me tame now ? Can I know
　　my Sifter
Mew'd up in his Seraglio, and in Danger
Not alone to lofe her Honour, but her Soul ?
The Hell-bred Villain by too, that has fold both
To black Deftruction, and not hafte to fend him

To

To the Devil his Tutor? To be patient now,
Were, in another Name, to play the Pander
To th' Viceroy's loose Embraces, and cry Aim
While he by Force, or Flattery compels her
To yield her fair Name up to his foul Lust,
And after turn *Apostate* to the Faith
That she was bred in.

Fran. Do but give me Hearing,
And you shall soon grant how ridiculous
This childish Fury is.   A wise Man never
Attempts Impossibilities : 'Tis as easy
For any single Arm to quell an Army,
As to effect your Wishes.   We come hither
To learn *Paulina*'s Faith, and to redeem her :
Leave your Revenge to Heaven.   I oft have told you
Of a Relique that I gave her, which has Power
(If we may credit holy Mens Traditions)
To keep the Owner free from Violence :
This on her Breast she wears, and does preserve
The Virtue of it by her daily Prayers.
So, if she fall not by her own Consent
(Which it were Sin to think) I fear no Force.
Be, therefore, patient; keep this borrow'd Shape,
Till Time and Opportunity present us
With some fit Means to see her; which perform'd,
I'll join with you in any desperate Course
For her Delivery.

Vitel. You have charm'd me, Sir!
And I obey in all Things :—Pray you, pardon
The Weakness of my Passion.

Fran. And excuse it.
Be cheerful, Man; for know that good Intents
Are, in the End, Crown'd with as fair Events.

[*Exeunt.*

SCENE

SCENE II.

A Room.

Enter Donufa, Manto, Carazie.

Don. Have you feen the Chriftian Captive,
The great Bafhaw is fo enamour'd of?
Manto. Yes, an't pleafe your Excellency.
I took a full View of her, when fhe was
Prefented to him.
Don. Is fhe fuch a Wonder,
As 'tis reported?
Manto. She was drown'd in Tears then,
Which took much from her Beauty; yet, in fpite
Of Sorrow, fhe appear'd the Miftrefs of
Moft rare Perfections; and, though of low Stature,
Her well-proportion'd Limbs invite Affection:
And, when fhe fpeaks, each Syllable is Mufic
That does inchant the Hearers.—But your Highnefs,
That are not to be parallel'd, I never yet
Beheld her Equal.
Don. Come, you flatter me;
But I forgive it. We, that are born great,
Seldom diftafte our Servants, though they give us
More than we can pretend to. I have heard
That Chriftian Ladies live with much more Freedom
Than fuch as are born here. Our jealous *Turks*
Never permit their fair Wives to be feen
But at the public Bagnios, or the Mofques;
And even then veil'd, and guarded. Thou, *Carazie,*
Wert born in *England*; what's the Cuftom there
Among your Women? Come, be free and merry:
I'm no fevere Miftrefs; nor haft thou met with
A heavy Bondage.
Car. Heavy? I was made lighter
By two Stone Weight, at leaft, to be fit to ferve you.
But to your Queftion, Madam; Women in *England*,

For

For the moſt Part, live like Queens. Your Country
    Ladies
Have Liberty to hawk, to hunt, to feaſt;
To give free Entertainment to all Comers,
To talk, to kiſs: There's no ſuch Thing known there.
As an *Italian* Girdle. Your City Dame,
Without Leave, wears the Breeches, has her Huſband
At as much Command as her 'Prentice; and, if Need be,
  Can make him Cuckold by her Father's Copy.
    Don. But your Court-Lady?
    Car. She, I aſſure you, Madam,
Knows nothing but her Will; muſt be allow'd
Her Footmen, her Coach, her Uſhers, her Pages,
Her Doctor, Chaplains; and, as I have heard,
They're grown of late, ſo learn'd, that they maintain
A ſtrange Poſition, which their Lords with all
Their Wit cannot confute.
    Don. What's that, I pr'thee?
    Car. Marry, that it is not only fit, but lawful
Your Madam there, her much Reſt, and high Feeding
Duly conſider'd, ſhould, to eaſe her Huſband
Be allow'd a private Friend. They have drawn a Bill
To this good Purpoſe; and, the next Aſſembly,
Doubt not to paſs it.
    Don. We enjoy no more
That are of the *Ottoman* Race, though our Religion
Allows all Pleaſure. I am dull:—Some Muſic.
Take my Chapins off. [3] So, a luſty Strain— [*A Galliard.*
Who knocks there?
    Manto. 'Tis the Baſhaw of *Aleppo,*
Who humbly makes Requeſt he may preſent
His Service to you.
    Don. Reach a Chair.—We muſt
Receive him like ourſelf, and not depart with
One Piece of Ceremony State, and Greatneſs,
That may beget Reſpect, and Reverence
In one that's born our Vaſſal. Now admit him.

    [3] *Take my Chapins off.*
Chapin (*Spaniſh*) a high Cork-heel'd Shoe.

Enter

Enter Muſtapha, *puts off his yellow Pantofles.* [4]

Muſta. The Place is ſacred, and I am to enter
The Room where ſhe abides, with ſuch Devotion
As Pilgrims pay at *Meccha*, when they viſit
The Tomb of our great Prophet.
   Don. Riſe, the Sign
That we vouchſafe your Preſence.
                    [*The Eunuch takes up the Pantofles.*
   Muſta. May thoſe Powers,
That rais'd the *Ottoman* Empire, and ſtill guard it,
Reward your Highneſs for this gracious Favour
You throw upon your Servant. It hath pleas'd
The moſt invincible, mightieſt *Amurath*,
(To ſpeak his other Titles would take from him)
That in himſelf does comprehend all Greatneſs,
To make me the unworthy Inſtrument
Of his Command. Receive, divineſt Lady,
                    [*Delivers a Letter.*
This Letter, ſign'd by his victorious Hand,
And made authentic by th' imperial Seal.
There when you find me mention'd, far be it from you
To think it my Ambition to preſume
At ſuch a Happineſs, which his pow'rful Will
From his great Mind's Magnificence, not my Merit
Hath ſhower'd upon me. But, if your Conſent
Join with his good Opinion and Allowance
To perfect what his Favours have begun,
I ſhall in my Obſequiouſneſs and Duty
Endeavour to prevent all juſt Complaints,
Which Want of Will to ſerve you may call on me.
   Don. His ſacred Majeſty writes here that your Valour
Againſt the *Perſian* hath ſo won upon him,
That there's no Grace, or Honour in his Gift
Of which he can imagine you unworthy;

---

[4] Pantofles *(French)* Slippers; it is a Cuſtom with the *Turks* to be
bare footed whenever they appear before any of the royal Blood.

                                        And,

And, what's the greateft you can hope, or aim at,
It is his Pleafure you fhould be receiv'd
Into his Royal Family—Provided,
(For fo far I am unconfin'd) that I
Affect and like your Perfon.   I expect not
The Ceremony which he ufes in
Beftowing of his Daughters, and his Neices.
As that he fhould prefent you for my Slave,
To love you, if you pleas'd me; or deliver
A Poignard on my leaft Diflike to kill you.
Such Tyranny and Pride agree not with
My fofter Difpofition.   Let it fuffice
For my firft Anfwer, that thus far I grace you.

                        [*Gives him her Hand to kifs.*

Hereafter, fome Time fpent to make Enquiry
Of the good Parts, and Faculties of your Mind
You fhall hear further from me.
    Mufta. Though all Torments
Really fuffer'd, or in Hell imagin'd
By curious Fiction, in one Hour's Delay
Are wholly comprehended : I confefs
That I ftand bound in Duty, not to check at
Whatever you command, or pleafe to impofe
For Trial of my Patience.
    Don. Let us find
Some other Subject; too much of one Theme cloys me:
Is't a full Mart?
    Mufta. A Confluence of all Nations
Are met together : There's Variety too
Of all that Merchants traffic for.
    Don. I know not.—
I feel a Virgin's Longing, to defcend
So far from my own Greatnefs, as to be,
Though not a Buyer, yet a Looker on
Their ftrange Commodities.
    Mufta. If without a Train
You dare be feen abroad, I'll difmifs mine.
And wait upon you as a common Man,
And fatisfy your Wifhes.

                                        Don.

Don. I embrace it.
Provide my Veil; and at the Poſtern Gate
Convey us out unſeen.—I trouble you.
Muſta. It is my Happineſs you deign to command me.
[*Exeunt.*

S C E N E III.

A Shop diſcovered, Gazet *in it.*

Franciſco *and* Vitelli *walking by.*

Gaz. What do you lack? Your choice *China* Diſhes,
your pure *Venetian* Chryſtal of all Sorts, of all neat and
new Faſhions, from the Mirror of the Madam, to the
private Utenſil of the Chamber-Maid; and curious Pic-
tures of the rareſt Beauties of *Europe:* What do you
lack, Gentlemen?
Fran. Take heed, I ſay; howe'er it may appear
Impertinent, I muſt expreſs my Love,
My Advice, and Counſel. You are young,
And may be tempted; and theſe *Turkiſh* Dames,
Like *Engliſh* Maſtiffs, that increaſe their Fierceneſs
By being chain'd up from the Reſtraint of Freedom,
If Luſt once fire their Blood from a fair Object,
Will run a Courſe the Fiends themſelves would ſhake at,
To enjoy their wanton Ends.
Vitel. Sir, you miſtake me:
I am too full of Woe, to entertain
One Thought of Pleaſure, though all *Europe's* Queens
Kneel'd at my Feet, and courted me: Much leſs
To mix with ſuch, whoſe Difference of Faith
Muſt, of Neceſſity, (or I muſt grant
Myſelf forgetful of all you have taught me)
Strangle ſuch baſe Deſires.
Fran. Be conſtant in
That Reſolution, I'll abroad again,
And learn, as far as it is poſſible,
What may concern *Paulina.* Some two Hours
Shall bring me back.

Vitel.

Vitel. All Bleſſings wait upon you ! [*Exit* Franciſco.
Gaz. Cold Doings, Sir! a Mart do you call this?
  'Slight!
A Pudding-Wife, or a Witch with a Thrum Cap,
That ſells Ale under-ground to ſuch as come
To know their Fortunes in a dead Vacation,
Have, ten to one, more Stirring.
 Vitel. We muſt be patient.
 Gaz. Your Seller by Retail ought to be angry
But when he's fingering Money.

  Enter Grimaldi, *Maſter, Boatſwain, Sailors, Turks.*

 Vitel. Here are Company ;
Defend me, my good Angel, I behold
A Baſiliſk!
 Gaz. What do you lack ? What do you lack ? Pure
China Diſhes, clear Chryſtal Glaſſes, a dumb Miſtreſs
to make Love to ? What do you lack, Gentlemen ?
 Grim. Thy Mother for a Bawd ; or, if thou haſt
A handſome one, thy Siſter for a Whore ;
Without theſe, do not tell me of your Traſh ;
Or I ſhall ſpoil your Market.
 Vitel. —Old *Grimaldi ?*
 Grim. 'Zounds, wherefore do we put to Sea, or ſtand
The raging Winds aloft, or piſs upon
The foamy Waves, when they rage moſt ? Deride
The Thunder of the Enemy's Shot, board boldly
A Merchant's Ship for Prize, though we behold
The deſperate Gunner ready to give Fire
And blow the deck up ? Wherefore ſhake we off
Thoſe ſcrupulous Rags of Charity, and Conſcience,
Invented only to keep Churchmen warm,
Or feed the hungry Mouths of famiſh'd Beggars ;
But, when we touch the Shore, to wallow in
All ſenſual Pleaſures.
 Maſter. Ay, but, Noble Captain,
To ſpare a little for an After-clap
Were not Improvidence.

         Grim.

Grim. Hang Confideration :
When this is fpent, is not our Ship the fame?
Our Courage too the fame, to fetch in more?
The Earth, where it is fertileft, returns not,
More than three Harvefts, whilft the glorious Sun
Pofts through the Zodiack, and makes up the Year:
But the Sea, which is our Mother, (that embraceth
Both the rich *Indies* in her out-ftretch'd Arms)
Yields every Day a Crop, if we dare reap it.
No, no, my Mates! let Tradefmen think of Thrift,
And Ufurers hoard up; let our Expence
Be, as our Comings in are, without Bounds;
We are the *Neptunes* of the Ocean,
And fuch as traffick, fhall pay Sacrifice
Of their beft Lading. I'll have this Canvas
Your Boy wears lin'd with Tiffue, and the Cates
You tafte, ferv'd up in Gold; though we caroufe
The Tears of Orphans in our *Greekifh* Wines,
The Sighs of undone Widows paying for
The Mufick bought to chear us; ravifh'd Virgins
To Slav'ry fold for Coin to feed our Riots.
We will have no Compunction.

Gaz. Do you hear, Sir?
We have paid for our Ground.

Grim. Hum!

Gaz. And hum too,
For all your big Words, get you farther off,
And hinder not the Profpect of our Shop,
Or ———

Grim. What will you do?

Gaz. Nothing, Sir — But pray
Your Worfhip to give me Handfel.

Grim. By the Ears;
Thus, Sir; by the Ears.

Mafter. Hold, hold! ———

Vitel. You'll ftill be prating?

Grim. Come, let's be drunk: Then each Man to his
Whore.

—'Slight, how you look! you had beft go find a Corner

To pray in, and repent. Do, do, and cry.
It will fhew fine in Pirates.   [*Exit* Grimaldi.
    Mafter. We muft follow ;
Or he will fpend our Shares.
    Boatfw. I fought for mine.
    Mafter. Nor am I fo precife but I can drab too :
We will not fit out, for our Parts.
    Boatfw. Agreed.   [*Exeunt Mafter, Boatfwain, Sailors.*
    Gaz. The Devil gnaw off his Fingers! If he were
In *London* among the Clubs, up went his Heels
For ftriking of a 'Prentice.   What do you lack ?
What do you lack, Gentlemen ?
    1 *Turk.* I wonder how the Viceroy can endure
The Infolence of this Fellow.
    2 *Turk.* He receives Profit
From the Prizes he brings in ; and that excufes
Whatever he commits.—Ha! what are thefe ?

            Enter Muftapha, Donufa, *veil'd.*

    1 *Turk.* They feem of Rank and Quality ; obferve 'em.
    Gaz. What do you lack ? See, what you pleafe to
buy ; Wares of all Sorts, moft honourable Madona.
    Vitel. Peace, Sirrah! Make no Noife : Thefe are not
            People
To be jefted with.
    Don. Is this the Chriftians Cuftom
In the vending their Commodities ?
    Mufta. Yes, beft Madam!
But you may pleafe to keep your Way, here's nothing
But Toys, and Trifles, not worth your obferving.
    Don. Yes, for Variety's Sake. Pray you fhew us,
            Friends,
The chiefeft of your Wares.
    Vitel. Your Ladyfhip's Servant ;
And, if in Worth or Title you are more,
My Ignorance plead my Pardon.
    Don. He fpeaks well.
    Vitel. Take down the Looking-Glafs.——Here is a
            Mirrour   Steel'd

Steel'd fo exactly, neither taking from,
Nor flattering, the Object, it returns
To the Beholder, that *Narciffus* might
(And never grow enamour'd of himfelf)
View his fair Feature in't.
   Don. Poetical too!
   Vitel. Here *China* Difhes to ferve in a Banquet,
Though the voluptuous *Perfian* fat a Gueft.
Here Chryftal Glaffes, fuch as *Ganymede*
Did fill with Nectar to the Thunderer,
When he drank to *Alcides*, and receiv'd him
In the Fellowfhip of the Gods; true to the Owners.
Corinthian Plate ftudded with Diamonds,
Conceal oft deadly Poifon : This pure Metal
So innocent is, and faithful to the Miftrefs
Or Mafter that poffeffes it ; that rather
Than hold one Drop that's venomous, of itfelf
It flies in Pieces, and deludes the Traitor.
   Don. How movingly could this Fellow treat upon
A worthy Subject, that finds fuch Difcourfe
To grace a Trifle!
   Vitel. Here's a Picture, Madam!
The Mafter-piece of *Michael Angelo*,
Our great *Italian* Workman.——Here's another,
So perfect in all Parts, that, had *Pygmalion*
Seen this, his Prayers had been made to *Venus*,
T' have given it Life, and his carv'd Iv'ry Image
By Poets ne'er remember'd. They are, indeed,
The rareft Beauties of the Chriftian World,
And no where to be equal'd.
   Don. You are partial
In the Caufe of thofe you favour, I believe;
I inftantly could fhew you one, to theirs
Not much inferior.
   Vitel. With your Pardon, Madam,
I am incredulous.
   Don. Can you match me this ?   [*Unveils herfelf.*
   Vitel. What Wonder look I on! I'll fearch above,
And fuddenly attend you.   [*Exit* Vitelli.

Don. Are you amaz'd ?
I'll bring you to yourſelf.   [*Breaks the Glaſſes.*
Muſta. Ha! what's the Matter!
Gaz. My Maſter's Ware ?—We are undone!—O
ſtrange!
A Lady to turn Roarer, and break Glaſſes!
'Tis Time to ſhut up Shop, then.
Muſta. You ſeem mov'd.
If any Language of theſe Chriſtian Dogs
Have call'd your Anger on, in a Frown ſhew it,
And they are dead already.
Don. The Offence
Looks not ſo far. The fooliſh paltry Fellow
Shew'd me ſome Trifles, and demanded of me,
For what I valu'd at ſo many Aſpers,
A thouſand Ducats. I confeſs he mov'd me;
Yet I ſhould wrong myſelf, ſhould ſuch a Beggar
Receive leaſt Loſs from me.
Muſta. Is it no more?
Don. No, I aſſure you. Bid him bring his Bill
To-morrow to the Palace, and enquire
For one *Donuſa :* That Word gives him Paſſage
Through all the Guard; ſay there he ſhall receive
Full Satisfaction. Now when you pleaſe ——
Muſta. I wait you.
                    [*Exeunt* Muſtapha, Donuſa, 2 *Turks.*
1 *Turk.* We muſt not know them.—Let's ſhift off,
              and vaniſh.
Gaz. The Swine's-Pox overtake you : There's a Curſe
For a Turk that eats no Hog's Fleſh.
Vitel. Is ſhe gone ?
Gaz. Yes : You may ſee her Handy-work.
Vitel. No Matter :
Said ſhe aught elſe ?
Gaz. That you ſhould wait upon her,
And there receive Court Payment; and, to paſs
The Guards; ſhe bids you only ſay, you come
To one *Donuſa.*
Vitel. How! remove the Wares.

                                        Do

Do it without Reply.   The Sultan's Niece !
I have heard, among the Turks for any Lady
To fhew her Face bare, argues Love, or fpeaks
Her deadly Hatred. What fhould I fear ? My Fortune
Is funk fo low, there cannot fall upon me
Aught worth my fhuning.—I will run the Hazard.—
She may be a Means to free diftrefs'd *Paulina*.—
Or, if offended, at the worft, to die 5
Is a full Period to Calamity.   [*Exeunt.*

The End of the Firft Act.

☒:☒☒☒☒☒☒☒☒☒☒☒☒☒☒☒☒☒☒☒☒☒☒:☒

A C T II.   S C E N E I.

A Room.

Enter Carazie, Manto.

Car. **I**N the Name of Wonder, *Manto*, what hath my
            Lady
Done with herfelf fince Yefterday ?
Manto. I know not.
Malicious Men report we are all guided
In our Affections by a wand'ring Planet :
But fuch a fudden Change, in fuch a Perfon,
May ftand for an Example to confirm
Their falfe Affertion.
Car. She's now pettifh, froward :
Mufick, Difcourfe, Obfervance tedious to her.
Manto. She flept not the laft Night; and yet prevented
The rifing Sun, in being up before him.
Call'd for a coftly Bath, then will'd the Rooms

5 ———————— *To die*
Is a full Period to Calamity.

Maffinger makes ufe of thefe Words on a fimilar Occafion in the
Roman Actor. See the latter Part of the firft Scene, in Act 5.

Should

Should be perfum'd; ranſack'd her Cabinets
For her choiceſt, richeſt Jewels; and appears now
Like *Cynthia* in full Glory, waited on
By the faireſt of the Stars.

Car. Can you gueſs the Reaſon,
Why the *Aga* of the *Janizaries*, and he
That guards the Entrance of the inmoſt Port,
Were call'd before her?

Manto. They are both her Creatures,
And by her Grace prefer'd. But I am ignorant
To what Purpoſe they were ſent for.

Enter Donuſa.

Car. Here ſhe comes,
Full of ſad Thoughts: We muſt ſtand farther off.—
What a Frown was that!

Manto. Forbear.

Car. I pity her.

Don. What Magick hath transform'd me from my-
Where is my Virgin Pride? How have I loſt   [ſelf?
My boaſted Freedom? What new Fire burns up
My ſcorched Entrails? What unknown Deſires
Invade, and take Poſſeſſion of my Soul,
All virtuous Objects vaniſh'd? Have I ſtood
The Shock of fierce Temptations, ſtop'd mine Ears
Againſt all *Syren* Notes Luſt ever ſung,
To draw my Bark of Chaſtity (that with Wonder
Hath kept a conſtant and an honour'd Courſe)
Into the Gulf of a deſerv'd ill Fame?
Now fall unpitied? And, in a Moment
With mine own Hands dig up a Grave to bury
The monumental Heap of all my Years,
Employ'd in noble Actions? O my Fate!
—But there is no reſiſting. I obey thee,
Imperious God of Love, and willingly
Put mine own Fetters on, to grace thy Triumph:
'Twere therefore more than Cruelty in thee
To uſe me like a Tyrant. What poor Means

Muſt

Muſt I make uſe of now? And flatter ſuch,
To whom, till I betray'd my Liberty,
One gracious Look of mine would have erected
An Altar to my Service. How now, *Manto!*
My ever careful Woman, and *Carazie*
Thou haſt been faithful too.

Car. I dare not call
My Life mine own, ſince it is yours; but gladly
Will part with it, when e'er you ſhall command me;
And think I fall a Martyr, ſo my Death
May give Life to your Pleaſures.

Manto. But vouchſafe
To let me underſtand what you deſire
Should be effected, I will undertake it,
And curſe myſelf for Cowardice if I paus'd
To aſk a Reaſon Why.

Don. I'm comforted
In the Tender of your Service, but ſhall be
Confirm'd in my full Joys, in the Performance.
Yet, truſt me, I will not impoſe upon you
But what you ſtand engag'd for, to a Miſtreſs;
Such as I have been to you. All I aſk
Is Faith, and Secrecy.

Car. Say but you doubt me,
And, to ſecure you, I'll cut out my Tongue
I am *libde* in the Breech already.

Manto. Do not hinder
Yourſelf by theſe Delays.

Don. Thus then I whiſper
My own Shame to you. O that I ſhould bluſh
To ſpeak what I ſo much deſire to do!
And further— *[Whiſpers, and uſes vehement Actions.*

Manto. Is this all?

Don. Think it not baſe;
Although I know the Office undergoes
A coarſe Conſtruction.

Car. Coarſe? 'Tis but procuring
A Smock Employment, which has made more Knights,
In a Country I could name, then twenty Years

Of

Of Service in the Field.

Don. You have my Ends.

Manto. Which fay you have arriv'd at, be not wanting
To yourfelf, and fear not us.

Car. I know my Burthen :
I'll bear it with Delight.

Manto. Talk not, but do. [*Exeunt* Carazie, Manto.

Don. O Love! what poor Shifts thou doft force us to?
[*Exit* Donufa.

SCENE II.

Enter Aga, Capiaga, *Janizaries.*

Aga. She was ever our good Miftrefs, and our Maker,
And fhould we check at a little Hazard for her,
We were unthankful.

Cap. I dare pawn my Head,
'Tis fome difgufed Minion of the Court,
Sent from great *Amurath*, to learn from her
The Viceroy's Actions.

Aga. That concerns not us;
His Fall may be our Rife: Whate'er he be,
He paffes through my Guards.

Cap. And mine—provided
He give the Word.

Enter Vitelli.

Vitel. To faint now, being thus far,
Would argue me of Cowardice.

Aga. Stand—the Word—
Or, being a Chriftian, to prefs thus far,
Forfeits thy Life.

Vitel. Donufa.

Aga. Pafs in Peace.   [*Exeunt* Aga, *and* Janizaries.

Vitel. What a Privilege her Name bears!
'Tis wond'rous ftrange!
If the great Officer
The Guardian of the inner Port deny not.—

Cap.

Cap. Thy Warrant.—Speak,
Or thou art dead.
Vitel. Donufa.
Cap. That protects thee; without Fear, enter.
So—Difcharge the Watch.   [*Exit* Vitelli, Capiaga.

SCENE III.

Enter Carazie, Manto.

Car. Though he hath paft the *Aga*, and chief Porter,
This cannot be the Man.
Manto. By her Defcription, I am fure it is.
Car. O Women, Women!
What are you? A great Lady dote upon
A Haberdafher of fmall Wares!
Manto. Pifh! thou haft none.
Car. No; if I had I might have ferv'd the Turn:
This 'tis to want Munition, when a Man
Should make a Breach and enter.

Enter Vitelli.

Manto. Sir! you're welcome:
Think what 'tis to be happy, and poffefs it.
Car. Perfume the Rooms there, and make Way.
Let Mufic's choice Notes entertain the Man,
The Princefs now purpofes to honour.
Vitel. I am ravifh'd.   [*Exeunt.*

SCENE IV.

A Room of State.

A Table fet forth, Jewels and Bags upon it : Loud Mufic.

Enter Donufa, *takes a Chair; to her* Carazie, Vitelli,
Manto.

Don. Sing o'er the Ditty, that I laft compos'd
Upon my Love-fick Paffion : Suit your Voice

To

To the Mufic that's plac'd yonder, we fhall hear you
With more Delight and Pleafure.

    Car. I obey you.   [*Song.*

    Vitel. Is not this *Tempe,* or the bleffed Shades,
Where innocent Spirits refide? Or do I dream,
And this a heavenly Vifion? Howfoever,
It is a Sight too glorious to behold
For fuch a Wretch as I am.   [*Stands amaz'd.*

    Car. He is daunted.

    Manto. Speak to him, Madam! cheer him up, or you
Deftroy what you have built.

    Car. Would I were furnifh'd
With his Artillery, and if I ftood
Gaping as he does, hang me.

    Vitel. That I might ever dream thus.   [*Kneels.*

    Don. Banifh Amazement:
You wake; your Debtor tells you fo, your Debtor:
And to affure you that I am Subftance,
And no aerial Figure, thus I raife you.
Why do you fhake? My foft Touch brings no Ague;
No biting Froft is in this Palm; nor are
My Looks like to the *Gorgon*'s Head, that turn
Men into Statues: Rather they have Power
(Or I have been abus'd) where they beftow
Their Influence (let me prove it Truth in you)
To give to dead Men Motion.

    Vitel. Can this be?
May I believe my Senfes? Dare I think
I have a Memory? Or that you are
That excellent Creature, that of late difdain'd not
To look on my poor Trifles.

    Don. I am She.

    Vitel. The Owner of that bleffed Name, *Donufa,*
Which, like a potent Charm, although pronounc'd
By my prophane, but much unworthier Tongue,
Hath brought me fafe to this forbidden Place,
Where Chriftian yet ne'er trod?

    Don. I am the fame.

                            Vitel.

Vitel. And to what End, great Lady, pardon me,
That I prefume to afk, did your Command
Command me hither ? Or what am I, to whom
You fhould vouchfafe your Favours; nay, your Anger?
If any wild or uncollected Speech
Offenfively deliver'd, or my Doubt
Of your unknown Perfections, have difpleas'd you,
You wrong your Indignation, to pronounce
Yourfelf my Sentence : To have feen you only,
And to have touch'd that Fortune-making Hand,
Will with Delight weigh down all Tortures, that
A flinty Hangman's Rage could execute,
Or rigid Tyranny command with Pleafure.

Don. How the Abundance of Good, flowing to thee,
Is wrong'd in this Simplicity : And thefe Bounties,
Which all our Eaftern Kings have kneel'd in vain for,
Do by thy Ignorance, or wilful Fear,
Meet with a falfe Conftruction. Chriftian! know
(For till thou art mine by a nearer Name,
That Title though abhorr'd here, takes not from
Thy Entertainment) that 'tis not the Fafhion
Among the greateft and the faireft Dames,
This *Turkifh* Empire gladly owns, and bows to
To punifh, where there's no Offence ; or nourifh
Difpleafures againft thofe, without whofe Mercy
They part with all Felicity. Pr'ythee be wife,
And gently underftand me ; do not force her,
That ne'er knew aught but to command, nor e'er read
The Elements of Affection, but from fuch
As gladly fu'd to her, in the Infancy
Of her new-born Defires, to be at once
Importunate, and immodeft.

Vitel. Did I know,
Great Lady, your Commands; or, to what Purpofe
This perfonated Paffion tends, (fince 'twere
A Crime in me deferving Death, to think
It is your own) I fhould, to make you Sport,
Take any Shape you pleafe t' impofe upon me;
And with Joy ftrive to ferve you.

Don.

Don. Sport? Thou art cruel,
If that thou canſt interpret my Deſcent,
From my high Birth and Greatneſs, but to be
A Part in which I truly act myſelf.
And I muſt hold thee for a dull Spectator
If it ſtir not Affection, and invite
Compaſſion for my Sufferings. Be thou taught
By my Example, to make Satisfaction
For Wrongs unjuſtly offer'd. Willingly
I do confeſs my Fault; I injur'd thee
In ſome poor petty Trifles; thus I pay for
The Treſpaſs I did to thee. Here—receive
Theſe Bags ſtuff'd full of our Imperial Coin;
Or, if this Payment be too light, take here
Theſe Jems for which the ſlaviſh *Indian* dives
To th' Bottom of the Main: Or, if thou ſcorn
Theſe as baſe Droſs (which take but common Minds)
But fancy any Honour in my Gift
(Which is unbounded as the *Sultan*'s Power)
And be poſſeſt of't.
Vitel. I am overwhelm'd
With the Weight of Happineſs you throw upon me:
Nor can it fall in my Imagination,
What Wrong I e'er have done you; and much leſs
How like a royal Merchant to return
Your great Magnificence.
Don. They are Degrees,
Not Ends, of my intended Favours to thee,
Theſe Seeds of Bounty I yet ſcatter on
A Glebe I have not try'd:—But, be thou thankful,
The Harveſt is to come.
Vitel. What can be added
To that which I already have receiv'd,
I cannot comprehend.
Don. The Tender of
Myſelf.—Why doſt thou ſtart! and in that Gift
Full Reſtitution of that Virgin Freedom
Which thou haſt rob'd me of. Yet, I profeſs,
I ſo far prize the lovely Thief that ſtole it,

That,

That, were it poſſible thou couldſt reſtore
What thou unwittingly haſt raviſh'd from me,
I ſhould refuſe the Preſent.
  Vitel. How I ſhake
In my conſtant Reſolution! and my Fleſh,
Rebellious to my better Part, now tells me,
As if it were a ſtrong Defence of Frailty.
A Hermit in a Deſert, trench'd with Prayers,
Could not reſiſt this Battery.
  Don. Thou an *Italian?*
Nay more, I know't, a natural *Venetian,*
Such as are Courtiers born to pleaſe fair Ladies,
Yet come thus ſlowly on?
  Vitel. Excuſe me, Madam,
What Imputation ſoe'er the World
Is pleas'd to lay upon us: In myſelf
I am ſo innocent, that I know not what 'tis
That I ſhould offer.
  Don. By Inſtinct I'll teach thee,
And with ſuch Eaſe as Love makes me to aſk it.
When a young Lady wrings you by the Hand—thus;
Or with an amorous Touch preſſes your Foot
Looks Babies in your Eyes, plays with your Locks,
Do not you find, without a Tutor's Help,
What 'tis ſhe looks for.
  Vitel. I am grown already
Skilful i' th' Myſtery.
  Don. Or, if thus ſhe kiſs you,
Then taſtes your Lips again.——
  Vitel. That latter Blow
Has beat all chaſte Thoughts from me.
  Don. Say ſhe points to
Some private Room, the Sun Beams never enters,
Provoking Diſhes paſſing by to heighten
Declined Appetite, active Muſic uſhering
Your fainting Steps, the Waiters too as born dumb,
Not daring to look on you. [*Exit, inviting him to follow.*
  Vitel. Though the Devil
Stood by, and roar'd, I follow : Now I find,

That

That Virtue's but a Word, and no fure Guard,
If fet upon by Beauty, and Reward.   [*Exeunt*.

SCENE V.

Enter Aga, Capiaga, Grimaldi, *Mafter*, *Boatfwain*, &c.

Aga. The Devils in him, I think.
Grim. Let him be damn'd too.
I'll look on him, though he ftar'd as wild as Hell;
Nay, I'll go nearer to tell him, to his Teeth,
If he mends not fuddenly, and proves more thankful,
We do him too much Service.   Wer't not for Shame,
    now,
I could turn honeft and forfwear my Trade,
Which, next to being truft up at the Main-yard
By fome low Country Butter-box, I hate
As deadly as I do fafting, or long Grace
When Meat cools on the Table.
    Cap. But take Heed,
You know his violent Nature.
    Grim. Let his Whores
And Catamites know't; I underftand myfelf,
And how unmanly 'tis to fit at home
And rail at us, that run abroad all Hazards:
If ev'ry Week we bring not home new Pillage,
For the fatting his Seraglio.

Enter Afambeg, Muftapha, Aga.

Aga. Here he comes.
Cap. How terrible he looks?
Grim. To fuch as fear him:
The Viceroy *Afambeg!* were he the Sultan's felf,—
He'll let us know a Reafon for his Fury,
Or we muft take Leave without his Allowance,
To be merry with our Ignorance.
    Afam. Mahomet's Hell

Light

Light on you all—you crouch, and cringe now. Where
Was the Terror of my juſt Frowns, when you ſuffered
Thoſe Thieves of *Malta*, almoſt in our Harbour,
To board a Ship, and bear her ſafely off,
While you ſtood idle Lookers on ?
  Aga. The odds
I' th' Men and Shipping, and the ſuddenneſs .
Of their Departure yielding us no Leiſure
To ſend forth others to relieve our own,
Deter'd us, mighty Sir.
  Aſam. Deter'd you; Cowards ?
How durſt you only entertain the Knowledge
Of what Fear was, but in the not Performance
Of our Command ? In me great *Amurath* ſpake ;
My Voice did eccho to your Ears his Thunder,
And will'd you, like ſo many Seaborn-Tritons,
Arm'd only with the Trumpets of your Courage,
To ſwim up to her, and, like *Remoras*
Hanging upon her Keel, to ſtay her Flight
'Till Reſcue, ſent from us, had fetch'd you off.
You think you're ſafe now ; who durſt but diſpute it,
Or make it queſtionable, if this Moment [6]
I charg'd you from yon hanging Cliff, that glaſſes
His rugged Forehead in the neighbouring Lake,

[6] ————— *If this Moment.*
I charg'd you from yon hanging Cliff, &c.
In *Hamlet* we have an Image that bears ſome Reſemblance to this,
  ————— The dreadful Summit of the Cliff
That beetles o'er his Baſe into the Sea ;
                       Act 1. Scene 4.

And in the *Lady Errant*, a Tragi-Comedy, by Mr. *William Cart-
wright*, I remember a Paſſage, which though not ſimilar to the above,
I ſhall for its Beauty and Elegance here tranſcribe.

  ————— Haſt thou read
Of any Mountain, whoſe cold frozen Top
Sees Hail i' th' Bed, not yet grown round, and Snow
I' th' Fleece, not carded yet, whoſe hanging Weight
Archeth ſome ſtill deep River, that for Fear
Steals by the Foot of't without Noiſe.
               . Act 1. Scene 4.
                           To

To throw yourfelves down headlong ? Or like Faggots
To fill the Ditches of defended Forts,
While on your Backs we march'd up to the Breach ?
 Grim. That would not I.
 Afam. Ha ?
 Grim. Yet I dare, as much
As any of the Sultan's boldeft Sons,
(Whofe Heaven, and Hell, hang on his Frown, or Smile,)
His warlike *Janifaries.*
 Afam. Add one Syllable more,
Thou doft pronounce upon thyfelf a Sentence
That, Earthquake-like, will fwallow thee.
 Grim. Let it open ;
I'll ftand the Hazard : Thofe contemned Thieves
Your Fellow-Pirates, Sir ! the bold *Maltefe*
Whom with your Looks you think to quell, at *Rhodes*
Laugh'd at great *Solyman's* Anger : And, if Treafon
Had not delivered them into his Power,
He had grown old in Glory, as in Years,
At that fo fatal Siege ; or ris'n with Shame
His Hopes and Threats deluded.
 Afam. Our great Prophet !
How have I loft my Anger, and my Power ?
 Grim. Find it, and ufe it on thy Flatterers :
And not upon thy Friends that dare fpeak Truth,
Thefe Knights of *Malta* but a Handful to
Your Armies that drink Rivers up, have ftood
Your Fury at the Height, and with their Croffes
Struck pale your horned Moons ; thefe Men of *Malta*
Since I took Pay from you, I've met and fought with ;
Upon Advantage too. Yet, to fpeak Truth,
By th' Soul of Honour, I have ever found them
As provident to direct, and bold to do,
As any train'd up in your Difcipline :
Ravifh'd from other Nations.
 Mufta. I perceive
The Lightning in his fiery Looks, the Cloud
Is broke already.
 Grim. Think not, therefore, Sir,

          That

That you alone are Giants; and fuch Pigmies
You war upon.

Afam. Villain, I'll make thee know
Thou haft blafphem'd the *Ottoman* Power, and fafer
At Noon-day might have given Fire to St. *Mark*'s,
Your proud *Venetian* Temple.—Seize upon him;—
I am not fo near reconcil'd to him,
To bid him die: That were a Benefit
The Dog's unworthy of, to our Ufe confifcate
All that he ftands poffefs'd of: Let him tafte
The Mifery of Want, and his vain Riots,
Like to fo many walking Ghofts, affright him
Where e'er he fets his defperate Foot. Who is't
That does command you?

Grim. Is this the Reward
For all my Service, and the Rape I made
On fair *Paulina?*

Afam. Drag him hence,—he dies,
That dallies but a Minute.

Boatfw. What's become
Of our Shares now, Mafter?

Grimaldi, *drag'd off, his Head covered.*
Maft. Would he had been born dumb:
Patience, the Beggar's Cure, is all that's left us.

[*Exeunt Mafter and Boatfwain.*

Mufta. 'Twas but Intemperance of Speech, excufe
him——
Let me prevail fo far. Fame gives him out
For a deferving Fellow.

Afam. At *Aleppo*
I durft not prefs you fo far: Give me Leave
To ufe my own Will and Command in *Tunis*,
And, if you pleafe, my Privacy.

Mufta. I will fee you
When this high Wind's blown o'er. [*Exit* Muftapha,
Afam. So fhall you find me
Ready to do you Service. Rage, now leave me;
Stern Looks, and all the ceremonious Forms
Attending on dread Majefty, fly from

C   Transformed

Transformed *Afambeg*.   Why fhould I hug
[*Plucks out a gilt Key.*
So near my Heart, what leads me to my Prifon?
Where fhe, that is inthral'd, commands her Keeper,
And robs me of the Fiercenefs I was born with.
Stout Men quake at my Frowns; and, in Return,
I tremble at her Softnefs.   Bafe *Grimaldi*
But only nam'd *Paulina*, and the Charm
Had almoft choak'd my Fury, e'er I could
Pronounce his Sentence.   Would, when firft I faw her,
Mine Eyes had met with Lightning, and, in Place
Of hearing her inchanting Tongue, the Shrieks
Of Mandrakes had made Mufic to my Slumbers:
For now I only walk a loving Dream,
And, but to my Difhonour, never wake;
And yet am blind, but when I fee the Object,
And madly dote on it.   Appear bright Spark
[*Opens a Door*, Paulina *difcovered, comes forth.*
Of all Perfection! any Simile,
Borrow'd from Diamonds, or the faireft Stars
To help me to exprefs, how dear I prize
Thy unmatch'd Graces, will rife up, and chide me
For poor Detraction.
    Pau. I defpife thy Flatteries:
Thus fpit at 'em, and fcorn 'em; and, being arm'd
In the Affurance of my innocent Virtue,
I ftamp upon all Doubts, all Fears, all Tortures
Thy barbarous Cruelty, or, what's worfe, thy Dotage
(The worthy Parent of thy Jealoufy)
Can fhow'r upon me.
    Afam. If thefe bitter Taunts
Ravifh me from myfelf, and make me think
My greedy Ears receive angelical Sounds;
How would this Tongue tun'd to a loving Note,
Invade, and take Poffeffion of my Soul
Which then I durft not call mine own!
    Pau. Thou art falfe;
Falfer then thy Religion.   Do but think me
Something above a Beaft; nay more, a Monfter,
                                        Would

Would fright the Sun to look on, and then tell me,
If this bafe Ufage, can invite Affection.
If to be mew'd up, and excluded from
Human Society; the Ufe of Pleafures;
The neceffary, not fuperfluous, Duties
Of Servants to difcharge thofe Offices,
I blufh to name.

    Afam. Of Servants? Can you think
That I, that dare not truft the Eye of Heaven
To look upon your Beauties; that deny
Myfelf the Happinefs to touch your Purenefs,
Will e'er confent an Eunuch, or bought Handmaid,
Shall once approach you?—There is fomething in you
That can work Miracles, or I am couzen'd;
Difpofe and alter Sexes. To my Wrong,
In Spite of Nature, I will be your Nurfe,
Your Woman, your Phyfician, and your Fool;
'Till, with your free Confent, which I have vow'd·
Never to force, you grace me with a Name
That fhall fupply all thefe.

    Pau. What is't?

    Afam. Your Hufband.

    Pau. My Hangman, when thou pleafeft.

    Afam. Thus I guard me
Againft your further Angers.—

    Pau. Which fhall reach thee;
Though I were in the Center.
                          [*Puts too the Door, and locks it.*

    Afam. Such a Spirit,
In fuch a fmall Proportion I ne'er read of;
Which Time muft alter:—Ravifh her I dare not;
The Magic that fhe wears about her Neck,
I think, defends her, this Devotion paid
To this fweet Saint, Miftrefs of my foure Pain,
'Tis fit I take mine own rough Shape again.
                                [*Exit* Afambeg.

SCENE VI.

Enter Francifco, Gazet.

Fran. I think he's loft.
Gaz. 'Tis ten to one of that;
I ne'er knew Citizen turn Courtier yet,
But he loft his Credit, though he fav'd himfelf.
Why, look you, Sir! there are fo many Lobbies,
Out-offices, and Difputations here
Behind thefe *Turkifh* Hangings, that a Chriftian
Hardly gets off but circumcifed.

Enter Vitelli, Carazie, Manto.

Fran. I'm troubl'd
Troubled exceedingly.—Ha! what are thefe?
Gaz. One by his rich Suit fhould be fome *French* Am-
    baffador:
For his Train, I think they are *Turks.*
Fran. Peace!—be not feen,
Cara. You are now paft all the Guards, and undif-
    cover'd
You may return.
Vitel. There's for your Pains:—Forget not
My humbleft Service to the beft of Ladies.
Manto. Deferve her Favour, Sir! in making Hafte
For a fecond Entertainment.
Vitel. Do not doubt me;   [*Exeunt* Carazi, Manto.
I fhall not live till then.
Gaz. The Train is vanifh'd:
They've done him fome good Office, he's fo free
And liberal of his Gold. Ha! do I dream?
Or is this mine own natural Mafter?
Fran. 'Tis he;
But ftrangely metamorphos'd. You have made, Sir,
A profperous Voyage; Heaven grant it be honeft!
I fhall rejoice then too.

Gaz.

Gaz. You make him blufh.
To talk of Honefty: You were but now
In the giving Vein, and may think of *Gazet*
Your Worfhip's 'Prentice.

Vitel. There's Gold: Be thou free too,
And Mafter of my Shop, and all the Wares
We brought from *Venice*.

Gaz. Rivo then.

Vitel. Dear Sir!
This Place affords not Privacy for Difcourfe;
But I can tell you Wonders: My rich Habit
Deferves leaft Admiration; there's nothing,
That can fall in the Compafs of your Wifhes
Though it were to redeem a thoufand Slaves
From the *Turkifh* Gallies, or at home to erect
Some pious Work, to fhame all Hofpitals
But I am Mafter of the Means.

Fran. 'Tis ftrange.

Vitel. As I walk, I'll tell you more.

Gaz. Pray you a Word, Sir!
And then I will put on. I have one Boon more—

Vitel. What is't? Speak freely.

Gaz. Thus then: As I am Mafter
Of your Shop, and Wares, pray you, help me to fome
Trucking,
With your laft fhe Cuftomer; though fhe crack'd my beft
Piece,
I will endure it with Patience.

Vitel. Leave your prating.

Gaz. I may: You have been doing; we will do too.

Fran. I am amaz'd, yet will not blame, nor chide you,
'Till you inform me further: Yet muft fay,
They fteer not the right Courfe, nor traffick well,
That feek a Paffage, to reach Heaven, through Hell.
[Exeunt.

The End of the Second Act.

C 3   A C T

Enter Donufa, Manto.

Don. WHEN faid he, he would come again?
Manto.   He fwore,
Short Minutes fhould be tedious Ages to him,
Until the Tender of his fecond Service,
So much he feem'd tranfported with the firft.
  Don. I'm fure I was. I charge thee, *Manto,* tell me,
By all my Favours, and my Bounties, truly,
Whether thou art a Virgin; or, like me,
Haft forfeited that Name.
  Manto. A Virgin, Madam?
At my Years, being a Waiting-Woman, and in Court
      too?
That were miraculous. I fo long fince loft
That barren Burthen, I almoft forget
That ever I was one.
  Don. And could thy Friends
Read in thy Face, thy Maidenhead gone; that thou
Hadft parted with it?
  Manto. No, indeed: I paft
For current many Years after; 'till, by Fortune,
Long and continued Practice in the Sport
Blew up my Deck: A Hufband then was found out,
By my indulgent Father, and to the World
All was made whole again. What need you fear, then,
That at your Pleafure may repair your Honour?
Durft any envious, or malicious Tongue,
Prefume to taint it?
  Don. How now?

Enter

|*Enter* Çarazie.

Car. Madam, the Bashaw
Humbly desires Accefs.
Don. If it had been
My neat *Italian*, thou hadst met my Wishes.
—Tell him we would be private.
Car. So I did;
But he is much importunate.
Manto. 'Best difpatch him;
His ling'ring here, elfe, will deter the other
From making his Approach.
Don. His Entertainment
Shall not invite a fecond Vifit.—Go,
Say we are pleas'd.

Enter Muftapha.

Mufta. All Happinefs.
Don. Be fudden.
'Twas faucy Rudenefs in you, Sir, to prefs
On my Retirements; but ridiculous Folly
To wafte the Time, that might be better fpent,
In complimental Wifhes.
Car. There's a Cooling
For his hot Encounter.
Don. Come you here to ftare?
If you have loft your Tongue, and Ufe of Speech,
Refign your Government: There's a Mute's Place void
In my Uncle's Court, I hear, and you may work me
To write for your Preferment.
Mufta. This is ftrange!
I know not, Madam, what Negleft of mine
Has call'd this Scorn upon me.
Don. To the Purpofe ——
My Will's a Reafon, and we ftand not bound
To yield Account to you.
Mufta. Nor of your Angers,

C 4

But

But with erected Ears, I should hear from you
The Story of your good Opinion of me
Confirm'd by Love, and Favours.

    Don. How deserv'd?
I have consider'd you from Head to Foot,
And can find nothing in that Wainscot Face, [7]
That can teach me to dote; nor am I taken
With your grim Aspect, or toadpole-like Complexion.
Those Scars you glory in, I fear to look on;
And had much rather hear a merry Tale
Than all your Battles won with Blood and Sweat,
Though you belch forth the Stink too, in the Service,
And swear by your Mustachios all is true.
You're yet too rough for me: Purge and take Physick,
Purchase Perfumers; get me some *French* Taylor,
To new-create you; the first Shape you were made with
Is quite worn out: Let your Barber wash your Face too,
You look, yet, like a Bugbear to fright Children;
Till when I take my Leave —Wait me, *Carazie.*

                   [*Exeunt* Donusa *and* Carazie.

  Musta. Stay you, my Lady's Cabinet-Key!
  Manto. How's this, Sir?
  Musta. Stay, and stand quietly, or you shall fall, else;
Not to firk your Belly up, Flounder-like, but never
To rise again.   Offer but to unlock
These Doors that stop your fugitive Tongue (observe
And, by my Fury, I'll fix there this Bolt   me)
To bar thy Speech for ever.—So.—Be safe, now,

---

   7 *And can find nothing in that Wainscot Face.*

  The abusive Terms contained in this Speech, and its Impropriety
in the Mouth of a Princess, must render it very disgustful to every
Reader conversant with the more refined Language of our modern
Poets.
   However, in some measure to defend *Massinger*: he is not the only
Poet guilty of such ill Manners: *Homer* makes his "Heroes of
Old, in rating each other, very free with the mutual Terms of *Dogs,
Cowards, Villains,* &c. In the *Odyssey* we have *impudent Bitch*; and
Jupiter, if I mistake not, pays exactly the same Compliment to his
Royal Consort in the *Iliad.*"   *The Rev. Mr.* SPENCE.

And

And but refolve me (not of what I doubt,
But bring Affurance to a Thing believ'd)
Thou mak'ft thyfelf a Fortune ; not depending
On the uncertain Favours of a Miftrefs,
But art thyfelf one.   I'll not fo far queftion
My Judgment, and Obfervance, as to afk
Why I am flighted, and contemn'd ; but in
Whofe Favour it is done.   I, that have read
The copious Volumes of all Women's Falfhood,
Commented on by the Heart-breaking Groans
Of abus'd Lovers ; all the Doubts wafh'd off
With fruitlefs Tears, the Spider's Cobweb Veil
Of Arguments, alledg'd in their Defence,
Blown off with Sighs of defperate Men, and they
Appearing in their full Deformity :
Know that fome other hath difplanted me,
With her Difhonour.   Has fhe giv'n it up ?
Confirm it in two Syllables.
    Manto. She has.
    Mufta. I cherifh thy Confeffion thus, and thus,
                                    [*Gives her Jewels.*
. Be mine. — Again I court thee thus, and thus :
Now prove but conftant to my Ends.
    Manto. By all ——
    Mufta. Enough ; I dare not doubt thee.   O Land-
        Crocodiles,
Made of *Ægyptian* Slime, accurfed Women !
But 'tis no Time to rail : Come, my beft *Manto.*
                                    [*Exeunt.*

SCENE II.

Enter Vitelli, Francifco.

Vitel. Sir, as you are my Confeffor, you ftand bound
Not to reveal whatever I difcover
In that Religious Way : Nor dare I doubt you.
Let it fuffice, you've made me fee my Follies,
And wrought, perhaps, Compunction ; for I would not
Appear an Hypocrite : But, when you impofe

                                    A Pe-

A Penance on me, beyond Flesh and Blood
To undergo, you must instruct me how
To put off the Condition of a Man;
Or, if not pardon, at the least, excuse
My Disobedience. Yet, despair not, Sir;
For, though I take mine own Way, I shall do
Something that may hereafter, to my Glory,
Speak me your Scholar.
 Fran. I enjoin you not
To go, but send.
 Vitel. That were a petty Trial;
Not worth one, so long taught, and exercis'd
Under so grave a Master. Reverend *Francisco!*
My Friend, my Father! in that Word, my All!
Rest confident, you shall hear something of me
That will redeem me in your good Opinion,
Or judge me lost for ever. Send *Gazet*
(She shall give Order that he may have Entrance)
To acquaint you with my Fortunes.   [*Exit* Vitelli.
 Fran. Go, and prosper.
Holy Saints guide and strengthen thee! Howsoever,
As my Endeavours are, so may they find
Gracious Acceptance.

Enter Gazet, Grimaldi, *in Rags.*

 Gaz. Now, you do not roar, Sir;
You speak not Tempests, nor take Ear-rent from
A poor Shop-keeper. Do you remember that, Sir?
I wear your Marks here still.
 Fran. Can this be possible?
All Wonders are not ceas'd then.
 Grim. Do, abuse me,
Spit on me, spurn me, pull me by the Nose!
Thrust out these fiery Eyes, that Yesterday
Would have look'd thee dead.
 Gaz. O save me, Sir!
 Grim. Fear nothing!
I'm tame, and quiet; there's no Wrong can force me
           To

To remember what I was. I have forgot,
I e'er had ireful Fiercenefs, a fteel'd Heart,
Infenfible of Compaffion to others:
Nor is it fit that I fhould think myfelf
Worth mine own Pity.—Oh!

Fran. Grows this Dejection
From his Difgrace, do you fay?

Gaz. Why he's cafhier'd, Sir!
His Ships, his Goods, his Livery-Punks confifcate:
And there is fuch a Punifhment laid upon him,
The miferable Rogue muft fteal no more,
Nor drink, nor drab.

Fran. Does that torment him?

Gaz. O, Sir!
Should the State take Order to bar Men of Acres
From thofe two laudable Recreations,
Drinking and Whoring, how fhould Panders purchafe,
Or thrifty Whores build Hofpitals? 'Slid! if I,
That, fince I am made free, may write myfelf
A City-Gallant, fhould forfeit two fuch Charters,
I fhould be fton'd to Death, and ne'er be pitied
By th' Liveries of thofe Companies.

Fran. You'll be whip'd, Sir!
If you bridle not your Tongue, Hafte to the Palace,
Your Mafter looks for you.

Gaz. My quondam Mafter,
Rich Sons forget they ever had poor Fathers:
In Servants 'tis more pardonable — As a Companion,
Or fo, I may confent: But, is there Hope, Sir!
He has got me a good Chapwoman? Pray you write
A Word or two in my Behalf.

Fran. Out, Rafcal!

Gaz. I feel fome Infurrections.

Fran. Hence!

Gaz. I vanifh.   [*Exit* Gazet.

Grim. Why fhould I ftudy a Defence, or Comfort,
In whom black Guilt, and Mifery, if balanc'd,
I know not which would turn the Scale? Look upward
I dare not; for, fhould it but be believ'd

That

That I (dy'd deep in Hell's moſt horrid Colours)
Should dare to hope for Mercy, it would leave
No Check or Feeling, in Men innocent
To catch at Sins, the Devil ne'er taught Mankind yet.
No! I muſt downward, downward; tho' Repentance [8]
Could borrow all the glorious Wings of Grace,
My mountainous Weight of Sins would crack their Pi-
And ſink them to Hell with me.   [nions,
  Fran. Dreadful! hear me,
Thou miſerable Man!
  Grim. Good Sir! deny not
But that there is no Puniſhment beyond
Damnation.

                Enter Maſter and Boatſwain.

  Maſter. Yonder he is: I pity him.
  Boatſw. Take Comfort, Captain: We live ſtill to
          ſerve you,
  Grim. Serve me? I am a Devil already.—Leave me! [9]
Stand farther off! you're blaſted, elſe, I've heard
Schoolmen affirm, Man's Body is compos'd
Of the four Elements; and, as in League together
They nouriſh Life, ſo each of them affords
Liberty to the Soul, when it grows weary
Of this fleſhy Priſon.—Which ſhall I make Choice of?

---

  [8] *No, I muſt downward, downward, though Repentance*
      Could borrow all the glorious Wings, &c.
  The Beauty of this Paſſage is inimitable, and truly original: *Shakeſpear* has, indeed many that are ſimilar to it; but none that can be brought in Competition.

  [9] ———————— *Leave me:*
      Stand farther off! you're blaſted elſe,
  Whenever the Mind is harraſſed by the Stings of Conſcience, or the Horrors of Guilt, the Senſes are liable to infinite Deluſions, and ſtartle at hideous imaginary Monſters. The Poet, who can touch ſuch Incidents with happy Dexterity, and paint ſuch Images of Conſternation, will infallibly work upon the Minds of others.
                                    The Rev. Mr. SMITH.

                                                        The

The Fire ? No ; I fhall feel that hereafter.
The Earth will not receive me.—Should fome Whirl-
Snatch me into the Air, and I hang there,   [wind
Perpetual Plagues would dwell upon the Earth,
And thofe fuperior Bodies, that pour down
, Their cheerful Influence, deny to pafs it
Through thofe vaft Regions I have infected.
The Sea, I, that is Juftice, there I plow'd up
Mifchief as deep as Hell : There, there I'll hide
This curfed Lump of Clay : May it turn Rocks
Where Plummet'sWeight could never reach the Sands! ¹⁰
And grind the Ribs of all fuch Barks as prefs
The Ocean's Breaft in my unlawful Courfe.
I hafte then to thee : Let thy rav'nous Womb,
Whom all Things elfe deny, be now my Tomb !
                                    [*Exit* Grimaldi.
Mafter. Follow him, and reftrain him.
Fran. Let this ftand
For an Example to you.   I'll provide
A Lodging for him, and apply fuch Cures
To his wounded Confcience, as Heaven hath lent me.
He's now my fecond Care ; and my Profeffion
Binds me to teach the Defperate to repent,
As far as to confirm the Innocent.   {*Exeunt.*

S C E N E III.

Enter Afambeg, Muftapha, Aga, Capiaga.

Afam. Your Pleafure ?
Mufta. 'Twill exact your private Ear ;
And, when you have receiv'd it, you will think
Too many know it.   [*Exeunt* Aga, Capiaga.
Afam. Leave the Room ; but be

    ¹⁰ *Where Plummet's Weight could never reach the Sands !*
So in *Shakefpear,*
      " Where Fathom-Line could never touch the Ground."
                    HENRY IVth, ıft Part, Act ı. Scene 3.

                                        Within

Within our Call.——Now, Sir, what burning Secrets
       brings you
(With which it feems you are turn'd Cinders)
To quench in my Advice, or Power?

  Mufta. The Fire
Will rather reach you.——

  Afam. Me?

  Mufta. And confume both;
For 'tis impoffible to be put out,
But with the Blood of thofe that kindle it:
And yet one Vial of it is fo precious,
It being borrow'd from the *Ottoman* Spring,
That better 'tis, I think, both we fhould perifh
Than prove the defp'rate Means, that muft reftrain it
From fpreading farther.

  Afam. To the Point, and quickly:
Thefe winding Circumftances in Relations
Seldom environ Truth.

  Mufta. Truth, *Afambeg?*

  Afam. Truth, *Muftapha.* I faid it, and add more!
You touch upon a String that to my Ear
Does found *Donufa.*

  Mufta. You then underftand
Who 'tis I aim at.

  Afam. Take Heed, *Muftapha;*
Remember what fhe is, and whofe we are.
'Tis her Neglect, perhaps, that you complain of;
And, fhould you practife to revenge her Scorn,
With any Plot to taint her in her Honour,——

  Mufta. Hear me.

  Afam. I will be heard firft; there's no Tongue
A Subject owes, that fhall out-thunder mine.

  Mufta. Well, take your Way.

  Afam. I then again repeat it,
If *Muftapha* dares with malicious Breath
(On jealous Suppofitions) prefume
To blaft the Bloffom of *Donufa*'s Fame,
Becaufe he is deny'd a Happinefs
Which Men of equal, nay, of more Defert,

                    Have

Have fu'd in vain for—

Mufta. More?

Afam. More. 'Twas I fpake it,
The Bafhaw of *Natolia*, and myfelf
Were Rivals for her; either of us brought
More Victories, more Trophies, to plead for us
To our great Mafter, than you dare lay claim to;
Yet ftill, by his Allowance, fhe was left
To her Election: Each of us ow'd Nature
As much for outward Form, and inward Worth,
To make Way for us to her Grace and Favour,
As you brought with you. We were heard, repuls'd;
Yet thought it no Difhonour to fit down
With the Difgrace; if not to force Affection
May merit fuch a Name.

 Mufta. Have you done, yet?

 Afam. Be, therefore, more than fure, the Ground, on
  which
You raife your Accufation, may admit
No underminding of Defence in her:
For if with pregnant and apparent Proofs,
Such as may force a Judge, more then inclin'd,
Or partial in her Caufe, to fwear her guilty;
You win not me to fet off your Belief:
Neither our ancient Friendfhip, nor the Rites,
Of facred Hofpitality (to which
I would not offer Violence) fhall protect you.
—Now when you pleafe.

 Mufta. I will not dwell upon
Much Circumftance; yet cannot but profefs,
With the Affurance of a Loyalty
Equal to yours, the Reverence I owe
The Sultan, and all fuch his Blood makes facred:
That there is not a Vein of mine, which yet is
Unemptied in his Service, but this Moment
Should freely open, fo it might wafh off
The Stains of her Difhonour. Could you think?
Or, though you faw it, credit your own Eyes?
That She, the Wonder and Amazement of

Her Sex, the Pride, and Glory of the Empire,
That hath difdain'd you, flighted me, and boafted
A frozen Coldnefs, which no Appetite,
Or Height of Blood could thaw, fhould now fo far
Be hurry'd with the Violence of her Luft,
As, in it burying her high Birth and Fame,
Bafely defcend to fill a Chriftian's Arms ?
And to him yield her Virgin Honour up ?
Nay, fue to him to take't.

 Afam. A Chriftian ?

 Mufta. Temper
Your Admiration :—And what Chriftian, think you ?
No Prince difguis'd ; no Man of Mark, nor Honour ;
No daring Undertaker in our Service,
But one, whofe Lips her Foot fhould fcorn to touch,
A poor Mechanick Pedlar.

 Afam. He ?

 Mufta. Nay, more ;
Whom do you think fhe made her Scout, nay, Bawd,
To find him out, but me ? What Place makes Choice of
To wallow in her foul and loathfome Pleafures,
But in the Palace ? Who the Inftruments
Of clofe Conveyance, but the Captain of
Your Guard, the *Aga*, and, that Man of Truft,
The Warden of the inmoft Port ?—I'll prove this ;
And, though I fail to fhew her in the Act,
Glu'd like a neighing Gennet to her Stallion,
Your Incredulity fhall be convinc'd
With Proofs I blufh to think on.

 Afam. Never yet
This Flefh felt fuch a Fever.—By the Life
And Fortune of great *Amurath*, fhould our Prophet
(Whofe Name I bow to) in a Vifion fpeak this,
'Twould make me doubtful of my Faith.—Lead on ;
And, when my Eyes, and Ears, are, like yours, guilty,
My Rage fhall then appear ; for I will do
Something ;—but what, I am not yet determin'd.

            [*Exeunt.*

         SCENE

SCENE IV.

Enter Carazie, Manto, Gazet.

Car. They're private to their Wiſhes.

Manto. Doubt it not!

Gaz. A pretty Structure this! a Court do you call it?
Vaulted and arch'd: O! here has been old jumbling
Behind this Arras.

Car. Pry'thee let's have ſome Sport
With this freſh Codſhead.

Manto. I am out of Tune,
But do as you pleaſe. My Conſcience,—Tuſh! the Hope
Of Liberty does throw that Burthen off;
I muſt go watch, and make Diſcovery.   [*Exit.*

Car. He's muſing,
And will talk to himſelf; he cannot hold;
The poor Fool's raviſh'd.

Gaz. I am in my Maſter's Clothes;
They fit me to a Hair too; let but any
Indifferent Gameſter meaſure us Inch by Inch,
Or weigh us by the Standard, I may paſs:
I have been prov'd, and prov'd again, true Metal.

Car. How he ſurveys himſelf.

Gaz. I've heard, that ſome
Have fool'd themſelves at Court into good Fortunes,
That never hop'd to thrive by Wit i' th' City,
Or Honeſty i' th' Country. If I do not
Make the beſt Laugh at me. I'll weep for myſelf,
If they give me Hearing.—'Tis reſolv'd—I'll try
What may be done. By your Favour, Sir! I pray you,
Were you born a Courtier?

Car. No, Sir; why do you aſk?

Gaz. Becauſe I thought, that none could be prefer'd,
But ſuch as were begot there.

Car. O, Sir! many;
And, howſoe'r you are a Citizen born,
Yet if your Mother were a handſome Woman,

And ever long'd to fee a Mafk at Court,
It is an even Lay, but that you had
A Courtier to your Father; and I think fo,
You bear yourfelf fo fprightly.

    Gaz. It may be;
But pray you, Sir! had I fuch an Itch upon me
To change my Copy, is there Hope a Place
May be had here for Money?

    Car. Not without it;
That I dare warrant you.

    Gaz. I have a pretty Stock,
And would not have my good Parts undifcover'd,
What Places of Credit are there?

    Car. There's your *Beglerbeg.* [11]

    Gaz. By no Means that; it comes too near the Beg-
       gar;
And moft prove fo that come there.

    Car. Or your *Sangiack.* [12]

    Gaz. Saucy Jack? Fie! none of that.

    Car. Your *Chiaus.* [13]

    Gaz. Nor that.

    Car. Chief Gardener!

    Gaz. Out upon't!
'Twill put me in Mind my Mother was an Herb-woman,
What is your Place, I pray you?

    Car. Sir! an Eunuch.

    Gaz. An Eunuch? Very fine! I Faith! an Eunuch!
And what are your Employments? Neat and eafy.

    Car. In the Day, I wait on my Lady, when fhe eats,
Carry her Pantofles, bear up her Train;
Sing her afleep at Night, and, when fhe pleafes,
I am her Bedfellow.

      [11] *There's your* Beglerberg.
(i. e. Lord of Lords) a chief Governor of a *Turkifh* Province.
      [12] Or your *Sangiack.*
A *Turkifh* Governor of a City or Province.
      [13] Your *Chiaus.*

   An Officer in the *Turkifh* Court, who performs the Duty of an Ufher,
and alfo an Ambaffador to foreign Princes and States.

                               Gaz.

Gaz. How? Her Bedfellow?
And lie with her?
Car. Yes, and lie with her.
Gaz. O rare!
I'll be an Eunuch, though I fell my Shop for't,
And all my Wares.
Car. It is but parting with
A precious Stone or two. I know the Price on't.
Gaz. I'll part with all my Stones; and, when I am
An Eunuch, I'll fo tofs and towfe the Ladies;
Pray you help me to a Chapman.
Car. The Court-Surgeon
Shall do you that Favour.
Gaz. I am made! an Eunuch!

Enter Manto.

Manto. Carazie, quit the Room!
Car. Come, Sir! we'll treat of
Your Bufinefs further.
Gaz. Excellent! an Eunuch!   [*Exeunt.*

S C E N E. V.

Enter Donufa, Vitelli.

Vitel. Leave me, or I am loft again : No Prayers,
No Penitence, can redeem me.
Don. Am I grown
Old, or deform'd, fince Yefterday?
Vitel. You are ftill,
Although the fating of your Luft hath fullied
Th' imaculate Whitenefs of your Virgin Beauties,
Too fair for me to look on : And, though Purenefs,
The Sword with which you ever fought, and conquer'd,
Is ravifh'd from you by unchafte Defires,
You are too ftrong for Flefh and Blood to treat with,
Though Iron Grates were interpos'd between us,
To warrant me from Treafon.

Don. Whom do you fear ?

Vitel. That human Frailty I took from my Mother,
That, as my Youth increas'd, grew ftronger on me:
That ftill purfues me, and, thought once recover'd,
In Scorn of Reafon, and, what's more, Religion,
Again feeks to betray me.

Don. If you mean, Sir!
To my Embraces, you turn Rebel to
The Laws of Nature, the great Queen, and Mother
Of all Productions, and deny Allegiance,
Where you ftand bound to pay it.

Vitel. I will ftop
Mine Ears againft thefe Charms, which, if *Ulyffes*
Could live again, and hear this fecond Syren,
Though bound with Cables to his Maft, his Ship too
Faften'd with all her Anchors, this Inchantment
Would force him, in Defpite of all Refiftance,
To leap into the Sea, and follow her;
Although Deftruction with outftretched Arms,
Stood ready to receive him.

Don. Gentle Sir;
Though you deny to hear me, yet vouchfafe
To look upon me. Though I ufe no Language
The Grief for this unkind Repulfe will print
Such a dumb Eloquence upon my Face,
As will not only plead, but prevail for me.

Vitel. I am a Coward: I will fee and hear you;
The Trial, elfe, is nothing; nor the Conqueft,
My Temperance fhall crown me with hereafter,
Worthy to be remember'd. Up, my Virtue!
And holy Thoughts, and Refolutions arm me,
Againft this fierce Temptation! give me Voice,
Tun'd to a zealous Anger, to exprefs
At what an Over-value I have purchas'd
The wanton Treafure of your Virgin Bounties,
That in their falfe Fruition heap upon me
Defpair and Horror—That I could with that Eafe
Redeem my forfeit Innocence, or caft up
The Poifon I receiv'd into my Intrails,

From

From the alluring Cup of your Enticements,
As now I do deliver back the Price, [*Returns the Casket.*
And Salary of your Lust! or thus uncloth me
Of Sin's gay Trappings, (the proud Livery
     [*Throws off his Cloak and Doublet.*
Of wicked Pleasure) which but worn, and heated
With the Fire of Entertainment and Consent,
Like to *Alcides'* fatal Shirt, tears off
Our Flesh, and Reputation both together,
Leaving our ulcerous Follies bare, and open
To all malicious Censure.

 Don. You must grant,
If you hold that a Loss to you, mine equals,
If not transcends it. If you then first tasted
That Poison, as you call it, I brought with me
A Palat unacquainted with the Relish
Of those Delights, which most (as I have heard)
Greedily swallow; and then the Offence
(If my Opinion may be believ'd)
Is not so great; howe'er, the Wrong no more
Than if *Hippolitus* and the Virgin Huntress,
Should meet and kiss together.

 Vitel. What Defences
Can Lust raise to maintain a Precipice
     [*A* sambeg *and* Mustapha *above.*
To the Abyss of Looseness? But affords not
The least Stair, or the fast'ning of one Foot,
To re-ascend that glorious Height we fell from.

 Musta. By *Mahomet* she courts him!

 Asam. Nay, kneels to him:
Observe the scornful Villain turns away too,
As glorying in his Conquest.

 Don. Are you Marble?   [*Kneels.*
If Christians have Mothers, sure they share in
The Tygress Fierceness; for, if you were Owner
Of human Pity, you could not endure
A Princess to kneel to you, or look on
These falling Tears which hardest Rocks would soften
And yet remain unmov'd. Did you but give me

A Tafte of Happinefs in your Embraces,
That the Remembrance of the Sweetnefs of it
Might leave perpetual Bitternefs behind it?
Or fhew'd me what it was to be a Wife,
To live a Widow ever?

Enter Capiaga, Aga, *with others,*

Afam. She has confeft it ;—
Seize on him, Villains! O the Furies!
  Don. How ?—   [Afambeg *and* Muftapha *defcend,*
Are we betray'd?
  Vitel. The better ; I expected
A *Turkifh* Faith.
  Don. Who am I, that you dare this?
'Tis I that do command you to forbear
A Touch of Violence.
  Aga. We already, Madam,
Have fatisfied your Pleafure further than
We know to anfwer it.
  Cap. Would we were well off;
We ftand too far engag'd, I fear.
  Don. For us?
We'll bring you fafe off.   Who dares contradict
What is our Pleafure?

Enter Afambeg, Muftapha.

  Afam. Spurn the Dog to Prifon!
I'll anfwer you anon.
  Vitel. What Punifhment
So e'er I undergo, I'm ftill a Chriftian [*Exit with* Vitel.
  Don. What bold Prefumption's this? Under what Law
Am I to fall, that fet my Foot upon
Your Statutes and Decrees?
  Mufta. The Crime committed
Our *Alcoran* calls Death.
  Don. Tufh! who is here,
That is not *Amurath*'s Slave, and fo unfit
To fit a judge upon his Blood?

                                          Afam.

Afam. You've loft
And fham'd the Privilege of it ; rob'd me too
Of my Soul, my Underftanding, to behold
Your bafe, unworthy Fall from your high Virtue.

   Don. I do appeal to *Amurath.*

   Afam. We'll offer
No Violence to your Perfon, 'till we know
His facred Pleafure ; 'till when, under Guard
You fhall continue here.

   Don. Shall ?

   Afam. I have faid it.

   Don. We fhall remember this.

   Afam. It ill becomes
Such, as are guilty, to deliver Threats
Againft the innocent.   [*The Guard leads off* Donufa.
I could tear this Flefh now,
But 'tis in vain ; nor muft I talk, but do :
Provide a well man'd Galley for *Conftantinople :*
Such fad News never came to our great Mafter.
As he directs ; we muft proceed, and know
No Will but his, to whom what's Ours we owe. [*Exeunt.*

The End of the Third Act.

A C T IV.   S C E N E I.

Enter Mafter, Boatfwain.

Mafter. **H**E does begin to eat ?
Boatf.   A little, Mafter :
But our beft Hope for his Recovery is, that
His Raving leaves him ; and thofe dreadful Words,
Damnation, and Defpair, with which he ever
Ended all his Difcourfes are forgotten.

   Mafter. This Stranger is a moft religious Man, fure
And I am doubtful, whether his Charity

In the relieving of our Wants, or Care
To cure the wounded Conscience of *Grimaldi*
Deserves more Admiration.

    Boatf. Can you guess
What the Reason should be, that we never mention
The Church, or the high Altar, but his Melancholy
Grows, and increases on him?

    Master. I have heard him
(When he gloried to profess himself an Atheist,)
Talk often, and with much Delight and Boasting,
Of a rude Prank he did e'er he turn'd Pirate,
The Memory of which, as it appears,
Lies heavy on him.

    Boatf. 'Pray you, let me understand it.

    Master. Upon a solemn Day, when the whole City
Join'd in Devotion, and with barefoot Steps
Pass'd to S, *Mark*'s, the Duke and the whole Signiory,
Helping to perfect the religious Pomp
With which they were received; when all Men else
Were full of Tears, and groan'd beneath the Weight
Of past Offences (of whose heavy Burden
They came to be absolv'd and freed,) our Captain,
Whether in Scorn, of those so pious Rites
He had no Feeling of, or else drawn to it,
Out of a wanton, irreligious Madness,
(I know not which) ran to the holy Man,
As he was doing of the Work of Grace,
And, snatching from his Hands the sanctify'd Means,
Dash'd it upon the Pavement.

    Boatf. How escap'd he?
It being a Deed deserving Death with Torture.

    Master. The general Amazement of the People
Gave him Leave to quit the Temple, and a Gondola,[14]
(Prepar'd, it seems, before) brought him aboard,
Since which he ne'er saw *Venice.* The Remembrance
Of this, it seems, torments him; aggravated

---

[14] ———— *And a* Gondola.

A *Venetian* Wherry-Boat.

With a ſtrong Belief, he cannot receive Pardon
For this foul Faɕ, but from his Hands, 'gainſt whom
It was committed.

Boatſ. And what Courſe intends
His heavenly Phyſician Reverend *Franciſco,*
To beat down this Opinion ?

Maſter. He promis'd
To uſe ſome holy and religious Fineſſe,
To this good End ; and, in the mean Time, charg'd me
To keep him dark, and to admit no Viſitants ;
But on no Terms to croſs him.—Here he comes.

Enter Grimaldi *with a Book.*

Grim. For Theft, he that reſtores treble the Value, [15]
Makes Satisfaɕion ; and, for want of Means,
To do ſo, as a Slave, muſt ſerve it out,
'Till he hath made full Payment.—There's Hope left
    here ;
Oh ! with what Willingneſs would I give up
My Liberty to thoſe that I have pillag'd ;
And wiſh the Numbers of my Years, though waſted
In the moſt ſordid Slavery, might equal
The Rapines I have made ; 'till with one Voice,
My Patient Sufferings might exaɕ from my
Moſt cruel Creditors, a full Remiſſion,
An Eye's Loſs with an Eye, Limbs with a Limb ; [16]
A ſad Account !—yet, to find Peace within here,
Though all ſuch as I have maim'd, and diſmember'd

---

[15] *For Theft, he that reſtores treble the Value, makes Satisfaction,* &c.

This, and the following Part of this Speech alludes to the Law of *Moſes :* As in *Exodus* we read, " If a Man ſhall ſteal an Ox or a Sheep, " and kill it, or ſell it, he ſhall reſtore five Oxen for an Ox ; and four " Sheep for a Sheep.—If he have nothing, then he ſhall be ſold for " his Theft."   Cap. 22. Ver. 1, 3.

[16] *An Eye's Loſs with an Eye, Limbs with a Limb.*

Theſe are common Expreſſions both in the Old, and in the New Teſtament.

In

In drunken Quarrels, or o'ercome with Rage,
When they were giv'n up to my Power, ftood here now,
And cry'd for Reftitution ; to appeafe 'em,
I'd do a bloody Juftice on myfelf;
Pull out thefe Eyes, that guided me to ravifh
Their Sight from others ; lop thefe Legs, that bore me
To barbarous Violence ; with this Hand cut off
This Inftrument of wrong, 'till nought were left me,
But this poor bleeding limblefs Trunk, which gladly
I would divide among them.—Ha! what think I

Enter Francifco *in a Cope like a Bifhop.*

Of petty Forfeitures ! in this reverend Habit,
(All that I am turn'd into Eyes) I look on
A Deed of mine fo fiend-like, that Repentance,
Though with my Tears I taught the Sea new Tides,
Can never wafh off: All my Thefts, my Rapes
Are venial Trefpaffes, compar'd to what
I offer'd to that Shape; and in a Place too,
Where I ftood bound to kneel to't.   [*Kneels.*
    Fran. 'Tis forgiven ;
I with his Tongue (whom in thefe facred Veftments
With impure Hands thou did'ft offend) pronounce it ;
I bring Peace to thee ; fee, that thou deferve it
In thy fair Life hereafter.
    Grim. Can it be ?
Dare I believe this Vifion? Or hope
A Pardon e'er may find me ?
    Fran. Purchafe it
By zealous Undertakings, and no more
Twill be remembered.
    Grim. What celeftial Balm
I feel now pour'd into my wounded Confcience !
What Penance is there I'll not undergo ;
Though ne'er fo fharp and rugged, with more Pleafure
Than Flefh and Blood e'er tafted! fhew me true Sorrow,
Arm'd with an Iron Whip, and I will meet
The Stripes fhe brings along with her, as if

                                        They

They were the gentle Touches of a Hand
That comes to cure me.   Can good Deeds redeem me?
I will rife up a Wonder to the World,
When I have giv'n ftrong Proofs how I am alter'd,
I that have fold fuch as profefs'd the Faith
That I was born in, to Captivity,
Will make their Number equal, that I fhall
Deliver from the Oar; and win as many
By the Clearnefs of my Actions, to look on
Their Mifbelief, and loath it.   I will be
A Convoy for all Merchants; and thought worthy
To be reported to the World hereafter
The Child of your Devotion, nurs'd up,
And made ftrong by your Charity, to break through
All Dangers Hell can bring forth to oppofe me:
Nor am I, though my Fortunes were thought defperate,
Now you have reconcil'd me to myfelf,
So void of worldly Means, but, in Defpight
Of the proud Viceroy's Wrongs, I can do fomething
To prove, that I have Power; when you pleafe try me,
And I will perfect what you fhall injoin me,
Or fall a joyful Martyr.
   Fran. You will reap
The comfort of it; live yet undifcover'd,
And with your holy Meditations ftrengthen
Your Chriftian Refolution; e'er long,
You fhall hear further from me.
   Grim. I'll attend   [*Exit* Francifco.
All your Commands with Patience;—come, my Mates!
I hitherto have liv'd an ill Example;
And as your Captain led you on to Mifchief;
But now will truly labour, that good Men
May fay hereafter of me, to my Glory,
Let but my Power and Means hand with my Will,
" His good Endeavours, did weigh down his Ill."
                    [*Exeunt* Grimaldi, *Mafter, Boatfwain.*

Enter

Enter Francifco.

Fran. This Penitence is not counterfeit; howfoever
Good Actions are in themfelves rewarded;
My Travail's to meet with a double Crown,
If that *Vitelli* come off fafe, and prove
Himfelf the Mafter of his wild Affections.

Enter Gazet.

Oh! I fhall have Intelligence, how now, *Gazet!*
Why thefe fad Looks and Tears?
  Gaz. Tears, Sir? I have loft
My worthy Mafter. Your rich Heir feems to mourn for
A miferable Father, your young Widow
Following a bed-rid Hufband to his Grave,
Would have her Neighbours think fhe cries, and roars,
That fhe muft part with fuch a Goodman Do-nothing;
When 'tis, becaufe he ftays fo long above Ground,
And hinders a rich Suitor:—All's come out, Sir!
We are fmok'd for being Cunny-catchers; My Mafter
Is put in Prifon; his She-Cuftomer
Is under Guard too.—Thefe are Things to weep for;
But mine own Lofs confider'd, and what a Fortune
I have, as they fay, fnatch'd out of my Chops,
Would make a Man run mad.
  Fran. I fcarce have Leifure,
I am fo wholly taken up with Sorrow
For my lov'd Pupil, to enquire thy Fate;
Yet I will hear it.
  Gaz. Why, Sir! I had bought a Place,
A Place of Credit too, and had gone through with it:
I fhould have been made an Eunuch.—There was Ho-
    nour
For a late poor 'Prentice; when upon the fudden
There was fuch a Hurly-burly in the Court,
That I was glad to run away, and carry
The Price of my Office with me.
                                        Fran.

Fran. Is that all?
You've made a faving Voyage. We muſt think now,
Though not to free, to comfort fad *Vitelli* ;
My griev'd Soul fuffers for him.
    Gaz. I am fad too ;
But, had I been an Eunuch ——
    Fran. Think not on it.   [*Exeunt.*

SCENE II.

Enter Afambeg, *unlocks the Door, leads forth* Paulina.

    Afam. Be your own Guard : Obfequioufnefs and Ser-
Shall win you to be mine. Of all Reſtraint   [vice
For ever take your Leave : No Threats fhall awe you ;
No jealous Doubts of mine diſturb your Freedom :
No fee'd Spies wait upon your Steps. Your Virtue
And due Confideration in yourfelf,
Of what is noble, are the faithful Helps
I leave you, as Supporters to defend you
From falling bafely.
    Paul. This is wond'rous ſtrange !
Whence flows this Alteration ?
    Afam. From true Judgment,
And ſtrong Affurance : Neither Grates of Iron,
Hem'd in with Walls of Brafs, ſtrict Guards, high Birth,
The Forfeiture of Honour, nor the Fear
Of Infamy, or Punifhment, can ſtay
A Woman flav'd to Appetite from being
Falfe, and unworthy.
    Paul. You are grown fatyrical
Againſt our Sex. Why, Sir, I durſt produce
Myſelf in our Defence, and from you challenge
A Teſtimony that's not to be denied ;
All fall not under this unequal Cenfure.
I, that have ſtood your Flatteries, your Threats,
Bore up againſt your fierce Temptations ; ' fcorn'd
The cruel Means you practis'd to fupplant me,
Having no Arms to help me to hold out,

But Love of Piety, and conftant Goodnefs,
If you are unconfirm'd, dare again boldly
Enter into the Lifts, and combat with
All Oppofites Man's Malice can bring forth
To fhake me in my Chaftity, built upon
The Rock of my Religion.

    Afam. I do wifh
I could believe you ; but, when I fhall fhew you
A moft incredible Example of
Your Frailty in a Princefs, fu'd and fought to
By Men of Worth, of Rank, of Eminence ; courted
By Happinefs itfelf, and her cold Temper
Approv'd by many Years ; yet fhe to fall,
Fall from herfelf, her Glories, nay, her Safety,
Into a Gulf of Shame, and black Defpair ;
I think you'll doubt yourfelf, or, in beholding
Her Punifhment, for ever be deter'd
From yielding bafely.

    Paul. I would fee this Wonder ;
'Tis, Sir, my firft Petition.

    Afam. And thus granted ;——
Above you fhall obferve all.   [Paulina *fteps afide.*

       Enter Muftapha.

    Mufta. Sir, I fought you,
And muft relate a Wonder.   Since I ftudied
And knew what Man was, I was never Witnefs
Of fuch invincible Fortitude as this Chriftian
Shews in his Sufferings : All the Torments that
We could prefent him with to fright his Conftancy,
Confirm'd, not fhook it ; and thofe heavy Chains
That eat into his Flefh, appear'd to him
Like Bracelets, made of fome lov'd Miftrefs' Hairs,
We kifs in the Remembrance of her Favours.
I'm ftrangely taken with it, and have loft
Much of my Fury.

    Afam. Had he fuffer'd poorly,
It had call'd on my Contempt ; but manly Patience

                          And

And all-commanding Virtue, wins upon
An Enemy. I fhall think upon him. Ha!

Enter Aga *with a Black Box.*

So foon return'd ? This Speed pleads in Excufe
Of your late Fault, which I no more remember.
What's the Grand Signior's Pleafure ?
   Aga. 'Tis inclos'd here.
The Box too, that contains it, may inform you
How he ftands affected : I am trufted with
Nothing but this.—On Forfeit of your Head,
She muft have a fpeedy Trial.
   Afam. Bring her in
In Black, as to her Funeral : 'Tis the Colour
Her Fault wills her to wear ; and which, in Juftice,
I dare not pity.—Sit, and take your Place :
However in her Life fhe has degenerated,
May fhe die nobly ; and in that confirm
Her Greatnefs, and High Blood.

*A folemn Mufick. A Guard. The Aga, and Capi-Aga,
leading in* Donufa *in Black* ; *her Train borne up by* Carazie *and* Manto.

   Mufta. I now could melt ; —
But foft Compaffion leave me.
   Manto. I am affrighted
With this difmal Preparation. Should the enjoying
Of loofe Defires find ever fuch Conclufions,
All Women would be Veftals.   [*Afide.*
   Don. That you cloath me
In this fad Livery of Death, affures me
Your Sentence is gone out before, and I
Too late am call'd for, in my guilty Caufe
To ufe Qualification, or Excufe ——
Yet muft I not part fo with mine own Strength,
But borrow from my Modefty Boldnefs, to
Enquire by whofe Authority you fit

My Judges, and whose Warrant digs my Grave
In the Frowns you dart against my Life?

Asam. See here!
This fatal Sign, and Warrant! This, brought to
A General fighting at the Head of his
Victorious Troops, ravishes from his Hand
His e'en then conquering Sword: This shewn unto
The Sultan's Brothers, or his Sons, delivers
His deadly Anger; and, all Hopes laid by,
Commands them to prepare themselves for Heaven;
Which would stand with the Quiet of your Soul
To think upon, and imitate.

Don. Give me Leave
A little to complain: First, of the hard
Condition of my Fortune, which may move you,
Though not to rise up Intercessors for me,
Yet, in Remembrance of my former Life,
(This being the first Spot tainting mine Honour)
To be the Means to bring me to his Presence;
And then I doubt not, but I could alledge
Such Reasons in mine own Defence, or plead
So humbly (my Tears helping) that it should
Awake his sleeping Pity.

Asam. 'Tis in vain!
If you have aught to say, you shall have Hearing,
And in me think him present.

Don. I would thus then
First kneel, and kiss his Feet; and after, tell him
How long I'd been his Darling; what Delight
My infant Years afforded him; how dear
He priz'd his Sister, in both Bloods, my Mother;
That she, like him, had Frailty, that to me
Descends as an Inheritance; then conjure him,
By her blest Ashes, and his Father's Soul,
The Sword that rides upon his Thigh, his Right Hand
Holding the Scepter, and the *Ottoman* Fortune,
To have Compassion on me.

Asam. But suppose
(As I am sure) he would be deaf, what then
Could you infer?

                                    Don.

Don. I, then, would thus rife up,
And to his Teeth tell him, he was a Tyrant,
A moſt voluptuous, and inſatiable Epicure
In his own Pleaſures ; which he hugs ſo dearly,
As proper, and peculiar to himſelf,
That he denies a moderate lawful Uſe
Of all Delight to others. And to thee,
Unequal Judge, I ſpeak as much, and charge thee
But with impartial Eyes to look into
Thyſelf, and then conſider with what Juſtice
Thou canſt pronounce my Sentence. Unkind Nature !
To make weak Women, Servants; proud Men, Maſters.
Indulgent *Mahomet !* Co thy bloody Laws
Call my Embraces with a Chriſtian, Death ?
Having my Heat and *May* of Youth, to plead
In my Excuſe ? and yet want Power to puniſh
Theſe that with Scorn break thro' thy Cobweb-Edicts,'
And laugh at thy Decrees ? To tame their Luſts
There's no religious Bit ; let her be fair,
And pleaſing to the Eye, though *Perſian, Moor,*
Idolatreſs, *Turk,* or *Chriſtian,* you are privileg'd,
And freely may enjoy her. At this Inſtant,
I know, unjuſt Man ! thou haſt in thy Power
A lovely Chriſtian Virgin ; thy Offence
Equal, if not tranſcending mine: Why, then,
We being both guilty, doſt thou not deſcend
From that uſurp'd Tribunal, and with me
Walk Hand in Hand to Death ?

Aſam. She Raves ! and we
Loſe Time to hear her :—Read the Law.

Don. Do! do!——
I ſtand reſolv'd to ſuffer.

Aga. If any Virgin, of what Degree or Quality ſo-
ever, born a natural *Turk,* ſhall be convicted of cor-
poral Looſeneſs, and Incontinence with any Chriſtian,
ſhe is, by the Decree of our great Prophet, *Mahomet,*
to loſe her Head.

Aſam. Mark that ! then tax our Juſtice.

Aga. Ever provided, That if fhe, the faid Offender,
by any Reafons, Arguments, or Perfuafion, can win
and prevail with the faid Chriftian, offending with her,
to alter his Religion, and marry her, that then the
Winning of a Soul to the *Mahometan* Sect fhall acquit
her from all Shame, Difgrace and Punifhment whatfoever.

Don. I lay hold on that Claufe, and challenge from
The Privilege of the Law.   [you

Mufta. What will you do ?

Don. Grant me Accefs and Means, I'll undertake
To turn this *Chriftian Turk*, and marry him :
This Trial you cannot deny.

Mufta. O bafe !
Can Fear to die make you defcend fo low
From your high Birth, and brand the *Ottoman* Line
With fuch a Mark of Infamy ?

Afam. This is worfe
Than the parting with your Honour.—Better fuffer
Ten thoufand Deaths, and without Hope to have
A Place in our great Prophet's Paradife,
Than have an Act to After-times remember'd
So foul as this is.

Mufta. Chear your Spirits, Madam !
To die is nothing; 'tis but parting with
A Mountain of Vexations.

Afam. Think of your Honour,
In dying nobly you make Satisfaction
For your Offence ; and you fhall live a Story
Of bold heroic Courage.

Don. You fhall not fool me
Out of my Life : I claim the Law, and fue for
A fpeedy Trial; if I fail, you may
Determine of me as you pleafe.

Afam. Bafe Woman !
—But ufe thy Ways, and fee thou profper in 'em :
For, if thou fall again into my Power,
Thou fhalt in vain, after a thoufand Tortures,
Cry out for Death, that Death which now thou fly'ft from.
                                                 Unloofe

Unloofe the Prifoner's Chains.—Go! lead her on
'To try the Magick of her Tongue ——I follow : —
I'm on the Rack.——Defcend, my beft *Paulina*.

[Exeunt.

SCENE III.

Enter Francifco, *Jailor.*

Fran. I come not empty-handed ;—J will purchafe
Your Favour at what Rate you pleafe.—There's Gold.

Jailor. 'Tis the beft Oratory.   I will hazard
A Check for your Content.—Below there!

Vitel. Welcome!——   [Vitelli *under the Stage.*
Art thou the happy Meffenger, that brings me
News of my Death?

Jailor. Your Hand!   [Vitelli *pluck'd up.*

Fran. Now, if you pleafe,
A little Privacy.

Jailor. You have bought it, Sir ;
Enjoy it freely.   [*Exit Jailor.*

Fran. O, my deareft Pupil !
Witnefs thefe Tears of Joy: I never faw you,
'Till now, look lovely ; nor durft I e'er glory
In the Mind of any Man I had built up
With the Hands of virtuous and religious Precepts,
'Till this glad Minute.   Now you have made good
My Expectation of you.   By my Order !
All *Roman Cæfars*, that led Kings in Chains,
Faft bound to their triumphant Chariots, if
Compar'd with that true Glory, and full Luftre
You now appear in, all their boafted Honours,
Purchas'd with Blood, and Wrong, would lofe their
        Names,
And be no more remember'd.

Vitel. This Applaufe,
Confirm'd in your Allowance, joys me more
Than if a thoufand full-cram'd Theatres
Should clap their eager Hands, to witnefs that
The Scene I act did pleafe, and they admire it.

E 2   But

But thefe are, Father, but Beginnings, not
The Ends, of my high Aims. I grant t' have mafter'd
The rebel Appetite of Flefh and Blood,
Was far above my Strength; and ftill owe for it
To that great Power that lent it. But, when I
Shall make't apparent, the grim Looks of Death
Affright me not; and that I can put off
The fond Defire of Life (that, like a Garment
Covers, and cloaths our Frailty) haft'ning to
My Martyrdom, as to a heavenly Banquet,
To which I was a choice invited Gueft.
Then you may boldly fay, you did not plough,
Or truft the barren and ungrateful Sands
With the fruitful Grain of your religious Counfels.

Fran. You do inftruct your Teacher. Let the Sun
Of your clear Life (that lends to good Men Light)
But fet as glorioufly as it did rife,
Though fometimes clouded, you may write *nil ultra*
To human Wifhes.

Vitel. I have almoft gain'd
The End o' th' Race, and will not faint, or tire now.

Enter Aga *and* Jailor.

Aga. Sir, by your Leave (nay ftare not) I bring
        Comfort;
The Viceroy, taken with the conftant Bearing
Of your Afflictions; and prefuming too
You will not change your Temper, does command
Your Irons fhould be ta'en off. Now arm yourfelf
With your old Refolution : Suddenly

                    [*The Chains taken off.*
You fhall be vifited. You muft leave the Room too;
And do it without Reply.

Fran. There's no contending :
Be ftill thyfelf, my Son ! [*Exit* Francifco.

                                        Vitel.

Vitel. 'Tis not in Man

Enter Donufa, Afambeg, Muftapha, Paulina.

To change or alter me.

Paul. Whom do I look on?——

My Brother?——'Tis he!——But no more, my Tongue!
Thou wilt betray all.   [*Afide.*

Afam. Let us hear this Temptrefs:
The Fellow looks as he would ftop his Ears
Againft her powerful Spells.

Paul. He is undone elfe.

Vitel. I'll ftand th' Encounter——Charge me home.

Don. I come, Sir!   [*Bows herfelf.*
A Beggar to you, and doubt not to find
A good Man's Charity, which, if you deny,
You're cruel to yourfelf; a Crime a wife Man
(And fuch I hold you) would not willingly
Be guilty of; nor let it find lefs Welcome,
Though I (a Creature you contemn) now fhew you
The Way to certain Happinefs; nor think it
Imaginary or phantaftical,
And fo not worth th' acquiring, in refpect
The Paffage to it is not rough nor thorny;
No fteep Hills in the Way which you muft climb up;
No Monfters to be conquer'd; no Inchantments
To be diffolv'd by Counter-Charms, before
You take Poffeffion of it.

Vitel. What ftrong Poifon
Is wrap'd up in thefe fugar'd Pills?

Don. My Suit is,
That you would quit your Shoulders of a Burthen
Under whofe pond'rous Weight you wilfully
Have too long groan'd, to caft thofe Fetters off,
With which, with your own Hands, you chain your
      Freedom:
Forfake a fevere, nay, imperious Miftrefs,
Whofe Service does exact perpetual Cares,
Watchings, and Troubles; and give Entertainment

To one that courts you, whofe leaft Favours are
Variety, and Choice of all Delights
Mankind is capable of.

 Vitel. You fpeak in Riddles.
What Burthen, or what Miftrefs? or what Fetters
Are thofe, you point at?

 Don. Thofe, which your Religion,
The Miftrefs you too long have feiv'd, compels
To bear with Slave-like Patience.

 Vitel. Ha!

 Paul. How bravely
That virtuous Anger fhows!   [*Afide.*

 Don. Be wife, and weigh
The profperous Succefs of Things; if Bleffings
Are Donatives from Heaven (which, you muft grant,
Were Blafphemy to queftion) and that
They are call'd down, and pour'd on fuch, as are
Moft gracious with the great Difpofer of 'em,
Look on our flourifhing Empire, if the Splendor,
The Majefty, and Glory of it dim not
Your feeble Sight, and then turn back, and fee
The narrow Bounds of yours; yet that poor Remnant
Rent in as many Factions, and Opinions,
As you have petty Kingdoms; and then, if
You are not obftinate againft Truth and Reafon,
You muft confefs the Deity you worfhip
Wants Care, or Power to help you,

 Paul. Hold out now,
And then thou art victorious.

 Afam. How he eyes her!

 Mufta. As if he would look through her.

 Afam. His Eyes flame too,
As threat'ning Violence.

 Vitel. But that I know
The Devil, thy Tutor fills each Part about thee,
And that I cannot play the Exorcift
To difpoffefs thee, unlefs I fhould tear
Thy Body Limb by Limb, and throw it to
The Furies that expect it, I would now

Pluck

Pluck out that wicked Tongue, that hath blafphem'd
That great Omnipotency, at whofe Nod
The Fabrick of the World fhakes.   Dare you bring
Your juggling Prophet in Comparifon with
That moft infcrutable, and infinite Effence
That made this All, and comprehends his Work ?
The Place is too prophane to mention him
Whofe only Name is facred.   O *Donufa!*
How much in my Compaffion I fuffer,
That thou, on whom this moft excelling Form,
And Faculties of Difcourfe, beyond a Woman,
Were by his liberal Gift confer'd, fhould'ft ftill
Remain in Ignorance of him that gave it!
I will not foul my Mouth to fpeak the Sorceries
Of your Seducer, his bafe Birth, his Whoredoms,
His ftrange Impoftures ; nor deliver how
He taught a Pigeon to feed in his Ear;
Then made his credulous Followers believe
It was an Angel that inftructed him
In the framing of his *Alcoran.*   Pray you mark me.—
 Afam. Thefe Words are Death, were he in nought
  elfe guilty.
 Vitel. Your Intent, to win me
To be of your Belief, proceeded from
Your Fear to die.   Can there be Strength in that
Religion, that fuffers us to tremble
At that which every Day, nay, Hour, we hafte to ?
 Don. This is unanfwerable, and there's fomething tells
  me
I err in my Opinion.
 Vitel. Cherifh it!
It is a heavenly prompter ; entertain
This holy Motion, and wear on your Forehead
The facred Badge he arms his Servants with,
You fhall, like me, with Scorn look down upon
All Engines Tyranny can advance to batter
Your conftant Refolution : Then you fhall
Look truly fair, when your Mind's Purenefs anfwers
Your outward Beauties.
            Don.

Don. I came here to take you,
But I perceive an yielding in myſelf
To be your Priſoner.

Vitel. 'Tis an Overthrow,
That will outſhine all Victories. O *Donuſa!*
Die in my Faith like me; and 'tis a Marriage
At which celeſtial Angels ſhall be Waiters,
And ſuch as have been ſainted welcome us.
—Are you confirm'd ?

Don. I would be; but the Means
That may aſſure me ?

Vitel. Heaven is merciful,
And will not ſuffer you to want a Man
To do that ſacred Office, build upon it.

Don. Then thus I ſpit at *Mahomet.*

Aſam. Stop her Mouth :
In Death to turn Apoſtate! I'll not hear
One Syllable from any;—wretched Creature :
With the next riſing Sun prepare to die.
Yet Chriſtian, in Reward of thy brave Courage,
Be thy Faith right, or wrong, receive this Favour.
In Perſon I'll attend thee to thy Death;
And boldly challenge all that I can give,
But what's not in my grant, which is to live. [*Exeunt.*

The End of the Fourth Act.

'A C T V.　S C E N E I.

Enter Vitelli, Franciſco,

Fran. YOU'RE wond'rous brave, and jocund.
Vitel.　　Welcome, Father!
Should I ſpare Coſt, or not wear chearful Looks
Upon my Wedding Day, it were ominous,
And ſhew'd I did repent it ; which I dare not,
It being a Marriage, howſoever ſad

In

In the firſt Ceremonies that confirm it,
That will for ever arm me againſt Fears,
Repentance, Doubts, or Jealouſies, and bring
Perpetual Comforts, Peace of Mind, and Quiet
To the glad Couple.

Fran. I well underſtand you;
And my full Joy to ſee you ſo reſolv'd
Weak Words cannot expreſs.   What is the Hour
Deſign'd for this Solemnity?

Vitel. The ſixth;
Something before the ſetting of the Sun
We take our laſt Leave of his fading Light,
And with our Soul's Eyes ſeek for Beams eternal.
Yet there's one Scruple with which I am much
Perplex'd, and troubl'd, which I know you can
Reſolve me of.

Fran. What is't?

Vitel. This, Sir; my Bride,
Whom I firſt courted, and then won (not with
Looſe Lays, poor Flatteries, apiſh Compliments,
But ſacred, and religious Zeal) yet wants
The holy Badge that ſhould proclaim her fit
For theſe celeſtial Nuptials: Willing ſhe is,
I know, to wear it, as the choiceſt Jewel
On her fair Forehead; but to you, that well
Could do that Work of Grace, I know the Viceroy
Will never grant Acceſs.   Now, in a Caſe
Of this Neceſſity, I would gladly learn,
Whether in me a Layman, without Orders,
It may not be religious, and lawful
As we go to our Deaths to do that Office?

Fran. A Queſtion, in itſelf, with much Eaſe anſwer'd;
Midwives upon Neceſſity perform't;
And Knights that in the holy Land fought for
The Freedom of *Jeruſalem*, when full
Of ſweat, and Enemy's Blood, have made their Helmets
The Fount, out of which with their holy Hands
They drew that heavenly Liquor: 'Twas approved then
By the holy Church, nor muſt I think it now
In you a Work leſs pious.   *Vitel.*

Vitel. You confirm me;
I will find a Way to do it. In the mean Time
Your holy Vows affift me.

Fran. They fhall ever
Be prefent with you.

Vitel. You fhall fee me act
This laft Scene to the Life.

Fran. And, though now fall,
Rife a blefs'd Martyr.

Vitel. That's my End, my All.   [*Exeunt.*

SCENE II.

Enter Grimaldi, *Mafter, Boatfwain, Sailors.*

Boatf. Sir, if you flip this Opportunity,
Never expect the like.

Mafter. With as much Eafe now
We may fteal the Ship out of the Harbour, Captain,
As ever Gallants in a wanton Bravery
Have fet upon a drunken Conftable,
And bore him from a fleepy, Rug-gown'd Watch:
Be therefore wife.

Grim. I muft be honeft too,
And you fhall wear that Shape: You fhall obferve me,
If that you purpofe to continue mine.
Think you Ingratitude can be the Parent
To our unfeign'd Repentance? Do I owe
A Peace within here, Kingdoms could not purchafe,
To my religious Creditor, to leave him
Open to Danger, the great Benefit
Never remembred? No; though in her Bottom.
We could ftow up the Tribute of the *Turk*;
Nay, grant the Paffage fafe too; I will never
Confent to weigh an Anchor up, till he,
That only muft, commands it.

Boatf. This Religion
Will keep us Slaves and Beggars.

Mafter.

Mafter. The Fiend prompts me
To change my Copy : Plague on't, we are Seamen :
What have we to do with't, but for a Snatch, or fo,
At the End of a long Lent?

Enter Francifco.

Boatf. Mum. See, who is here?
Grim. My Father!
Fran. My good Convert! I am full
Of ferious Bufinefs, which denies me Leave
To hold long Conference with you : Only thus much
Briefly receive ;—a Day or two at the moft,
Shall make me fit to take my Leave of *Tunis,*
Or give me loft for ever,
Grim. Days, nor Years,
Provided that my Stay may do you Service,
But to me fhall be Minutes.
Fran. I much thank you :
In this fmall Scroll you may, in private read
What my Intents are; and, as they grow ripe,
I will inftruct you further : In the mean Time
Borrow your late diftracted Looks, and Gefture;
The more dejected you appear, the lefs
The Viceroy muft fufpect you.
Grim. I am nothing,
But what you pleafe to have me be.
Fran. Farewell, Sir!——
Be cheerful, Mafter! fomething we will do
That fhall reward itfelf in the Performance;
And that's true Prize indeed.
Mafter. I am obedient.
　　　　　[*Exeunt* Grimaldi, *Mafter, Boatfwain.*
Boatf. And I :—There's no contending.
Fran. Peace to you all.
Profper thou great Exiftence, my Endeavours,
As they religioufly are undertaken,
And diftant equally from fervile Gain,

Enter

Enter Paulina, Carzi, *and* Manto.

Or glorious Oftentation.—I am heard
In this bleft Opportunity, which in vain
I long have waited for.—I muft fhow myfelf!
O, fhe has found me! now if fhe prove right
All Hope will not forfake us.

   Paul. Farther off!
And in that Diftance know your Duties too!
You were beftow'd on me as Slaves to ferve me,
And not as Spies to pry into my Actions,
And after to betray me. You fhall find
If any Look of mine be unobferv'd,
I am not ignorant of a Miftrefs' Power,
And from whom I receive it.

   Car. Note this, *Manto.*
The Pride, and Scorn, with which fhe entertains us!
Now we are made her's by the Viceroy's Gift.
Our fweet condition'd Princefs, fair *Donufa*,
(Reft in her Death wait on her!) never us'd us
With fuch Contempt. I would he had fent me
To the Gallies, or the Gallows, when he gave me
To this proud little Devil.   [*Afide.*

   Manto. I expect
All tyrannous Ufage, but I muft be Patient;
And, though ten Times a Day, fhe tears thefe Locks,
Or makes this Face her Footftool, 'tis but Juftice.
                                        [*Afide.*

   Paul. 'Tis a true Story of my Fortunes, Father!
My Chaftity preferv'd by Miracle,
Or your Devotions for me; and, believe it,
What outward Pride fo e'er I counterfeit,
Or State to thefe appointed to attend me,
I am not in my Difpofition alter'd,
But ftill your humble Daughter, and fhare with you,
In my poor Brother's Sufferings.—All Hell's Torments
Revenge it on accurs'd *Grimaldi's* Soul,
That, in his Rape of me, gave a Beginning

                                            To

To all the Miferies that fince have follow'd.

Fran. Be charitable, and forgive him, gentle Daugh-
ter!
He's a chang'd Man, and may redeem his Fault
In his fair Life hereafter. You muft bear too
Your forc'd Captivity (for 'tis no better,.
Though you wear golden Fetters) and of him,
Whom Death affrights not, learn to hold out nobly;

Paul. You are ftill the fame good Counfellor.

Fran. And who knows,
(Since what above is purpos'd, is infcrutable)
But that the Viceroy's extreme Dotage on you
May be the Parent of a happier Birth
Than yet our Hopes dare fafhion.   Longer Conference
May prove unfafe for you, and me, however,
Perhaps for Trial, he allows you Freedom.
                                    [*Delivers a Paper.*
From this learn therefore what you muft attempt,
Though with the Hazard of yourfelf,—Heaven guard
    you,
And give *Vitelli* Patience; then I doubt not
But he will have a glorious Day, fince fome
Hold truly, fuch as fuffer, overcome.   [*Exeunt.*

S C E N E III.

Enter Afambeg, Muftapha, Aga, Capiaga.

Afam. What we commanded, fee perform'd; and fail
    not
In all Things to be punctual.

Aga. We fhall, Sir!   [*Exeunt* Aga, Capiaga.

Mufta. 'Tis ftrange, that you fhould ufe fuch Cir-
    cumftance
To a Delinquent of fo mean Condition!

Afam. Had he appear'd in a more fordid Shape
Then difguis'd Greatnefs ever deign'd to mafk in,
The gallant bearing of his prefent Fortune
A loud proclaims him noble.

                                         Mufta.

Musta. If you doubt him
To be a Man built up for great Employments,
And, as a cunning Spy, sent to explore
The Cities Strength, or Weakness, you by Torture
May force him to discover it.

Asam. That were base;
Nor dare I do such Injury to Virtue
And bold, assured Courage; neither can I
Be won to think, but, if I should attempt it,
I shoot against the Moon. He, that hath stood
The roughest Battery, that Captivity
Could ever bring to shake a constant Temper;
Despis'd the Fawnings of a future Greatness,
By Beauty in her full Perfection tender'd;
That hears of Death as of a quiet Slumber,
And, from the Surplusage of his own Firmness,
Can spare enough of Fortitude, to assure
A feeble Woman; will now, *Mustapha*, never
Be alter'd in his Soul for any Torments
We can afflict his Body with?

Musta. Do your Pleasure!
I only offer'd you a Friend's Advice,
But without Gall, or Envy, to the Man
That is to suffer.—But what do you determine
Of poor *Grimaldi?* The Disgrace call'd on him,
I hear, has run him mad.

Asam. There weigh the Difference
In the true Temper of their Minds. The one,
A Pirate sold to Mischiefs, Rapes, and all
That make a Slave relentless and obdurate;
Yet, of himself wanting the inward Strengths
That should defend him, sinks beneath Compassion,
Or Pity of a Man; whereas this Merchant,
Acquainted only with a civil Life,
Arm'd in himself, intrench'd, and fortify'd
With his own Virtue, valuing Life and Death
At the same Price, poorly does not invite
A Favour, but commands us do him right;
Which unto him, and her (we both once honour'd)

As

As a juſt Debt I gladly pay 'em—they enter;
Now ſit equal Hearers.   [*A dreadful Muſick at one Door.*

The Aga, *Janizaries*, Vitelli, Franciſco, Gazet *at the
other:* Donuſa, Paulina, Carazie, Manto.

   Muſta. I ſhall hear,
And ſee, Sir! without Paſſion; my Wrongs arm me.
   Vitel. A joyful Preparation! to whoſe bounty
Owe we our Thanks for gracing thus our Hymen?
The Notes, though dreadful to the Ear, found here
As our *Epithalamium* were ſung
By a Cæleſtial Choir, and a full Chorus
Aſſur'd us future Happineſs.   Theſe that lead me
Gaze not with wanton Eyes upon my Bride,
Nor for their Service are repaid by me
With Jealouſies, or Fears; nor do they envy
My Paſſage to thoſe Pleaſures from which Death
Cannot deter me.   Great Sir, pardon me!
Imagination of the Joys I haſten to
Made me forget my Duty; but, the Form
And Ceremony paſt, I will attend you,
And with our conſtant Reſolution feaſt you,
Not with courſe Cates, forgot as ſoon as taſted,
But ſuch as ſhall, while you have Memory,
Be pleaſing to the Palate.
   Fran. Be not loſt
In what you purpoſe.   [*Exit* Franciſco.
   Gaz. Call you this a Marriage?
It differs little from Hanging; I cry at it.
   Vitel. See, where my Bride appears! in what full Lu-
    ſtre!
As if the Virgins, that bear up her Train,
Had long contended to receive an Honour
Above their Births, in doing her this Service.
Nor comes ſhe fearful to meet thoſe Delights,
Which, once paſt o'er, immortal Pleaſures follow.
I need not, therefore, comfort, or encourage
Her forward Steps; and I ſhould offer Wrong

                           To

To her Mind's Fortitude, fhould I but afk
How fhe can brook the rough high going Sea,
Over whofe foamy Back our Ship, well rig'd
With Hope and ftrong Affurance, muft tranfport us.
Nor will I tell her, when we reach the Haven
(Which Tempefts fhall not hinder) what loud Welcome
Shall entertain us; nor commend the Place,
To tell whofe leaft Perfection would ftrike.dumb
The Eloquence of all boafted in Story,
Though join'd together.

 Don. 'Tis enough, my deareft?
I dare not doubt you; as your humble Shadow,
Lead where you pleafe, I follow.

 Vitel. One Suit, Sir!
And willingly I ceafe to be a Beggar;
And, that you may with more Security hear it,
Know, 'tis not Life I'll afk, nor to defer,
Our Deaths, but a few Minutes.

 Afam. Speak; 'tis granted.

 Vitel. We being now to take our lateft Leave
And grown of one Belief, I do defire
I may have your Allowance to perform it,
But in the Fafhion which we Chriftians ufe,
Upon the like Occafions.

 Afam. 'Tis allow'd of.

 Vitel. My Service: Hafte, *Gazet,* to the next Spring,
And bring me of it.

 Gazet. Would I could as well
Fetch you a Pardon; I would not run but fly,
And be here in a Moment.

 Mufta. What's the Myftery of this? Difcover it.

 Vitel. Great Sir! I'll tell you.
Each Country hath it's own peculiar Rites:
Some, when they are to die, drink Store of Wine,
Which pour'd in liberally does oft beget
A baftard Valour, with which arm'd they bear
The not to be declined Charge of Death
With lefs Fear, and Aftonifhment: Others take
Drugs to procure a heavy Sleep, that fo

        They

They may infenfibly receive the Means
That cafts them in an everlafting Slumber;
Others—O welcome!

Enter Gazet *with Water.*

Afam. Now the Ufe of yours?
Vitel. The Clearnefs of this is a perfect Sign
Of Innocence; and as this wafhes off
Stains, and Pollutions from the Things we wear,
Thrown thus upon the Forehead, it hath Power
To purge thofe Spots that cleave unto the Mind,
                    [*Throws it on her Face.*
If thankfully receiv'd.
    Afam. 'Tis a ftrange Cuftom!
    Vitel. How do you entertain it, my *Donufa?*
Feel you no Alteration? No new Motives?
No unexpected Aids that may confirm you
In that to which you were inclin'd before?
    Don. I am another Woman,—till this Minute
I never liv'd, nor durft think how to die.
How long have I been blind! yet on the fudden,
By this bleft Means I feel the Films of Error,
Ta'en from my Soul's Eyes.   O divine Phyfician!
That haft beftow'd a Sight on me, which Death,
Though ready to embrace me in his Arms,
Cannot take from me.   Let me kifs the Hand
That did this Miracle, and feal my Thanks
Upon thofe Lips from whence thefe fweet Words va-
        nifh'd
That freed me from the crueleft of Prifons,
Blind Ignorance, and Mifbelief: falfe Prophet!
Impoftor *Mahomet!*
    Afam. I'll hear no more;
You do abufe my Favours, fever 'em:
Wretch if thou hadft another Life to lofe,
This Blafphemy deferv'd it,—inftantly
Carry them to their Deaths.
    VOL. II.   F   *Vitel*

Vitel. We part now, bleft one !
To meet hereafter in a Kingdom, where
Hell's Malice fhall not reach us.

Paul. Ha ! ha ! ha !

Afam. What means my Miftrefs ?

Paul. Who can hold her Spleen,
When fuch ridiculous Follies are prefented ;
The Scene too made Religion ? O, my Lord,
How from one Caufe two contrary Effects
Spring up upon the fudden.

Afam. This is ftrange !

Paul. That which hath fool'd her in her Death, wins
    me,
That hitherto have bar'd myfelf from Pleafure,
To live in all Delight.

Afam. There's Mufick in this.

Paul. I now will run as fiercely to your Arms
As ever longing Woman did, borne high
On the fwift Wings of Appetite.

Vitel. O Devil !

Paul. Nay more ; for there fhall be no odds betwixt
    us,
I will turn *Turk.*

Gazet. Moft of your Tribe do fo,
When they begin in Whore.   [*Afide.*

Afam. You are ferious Lady ?

Paul. Serious :—But fatisfy me in a Suit
That to the World may witnefs that I have
Some Power upon you, and To-morrow challenge
Whatever's in my Gift ; for I will be
At your Difpofe.

Gazet. That's ever the Subfcription
To a damn'd Whore's falfe Epiftle.   [*Afide.*

Afam. Afk this Hand,
Or, if thou wilt, the Heads of thefe. I am rapt
Beyond myfelf with Joy.—Speak, fpeak, what is it ?

Paul. But twelve fhort Hours reprieve for this bafe
    Couple.

Afam. The Reafon, fince you hate them ?

Paul.

Paul. That I may
Have Time to triumph o'er this wretched Woman:
I'll be myfelf her Guardian.   I will feaft,
Adorned in her Choice and richeft Jewels,
Commit him to what Guards you pleafe.   Grant this,
I am no more mine own, but yours.

Afam. Enjoy it.
Repine at it who dares.   Bear him fafe off
To the Black Tower, but give him all Things ufeful;
The contrary was not in your Requeft.

Paul. I do contemn him.

Don. Peace in Death deny'd me?

Paul. Thou fhalt not go in Liberty to thy Grave,
For one Night a Sultana is my Slave.

Mufta. A terrible little Tyrannefs.

Afam. No more;
Her Will fhall be a Law.   'Till now ne'er happy.
[Exeunt.

SCENE IV.

Enter Francifco, Grimaldi, *Mafter, Boatfwain, and Sailors.*

Grim. Sir! all Things are in Readinefs; the *Turks*
That feiz'd upon my Ship ftow'd under Hatches;
My Men refolv'd, and chearful.   Ufe but Means
To get out of the Ports, we will be ready
To bring you aboard, and then (Heaven be but pleas'd)
This for the Viceroy's Fleet.

Fran. Difcharge your Parts,
In mine I'll not be wanting: Fear not, Mafter!
Something will come along to fraught your Bark,
That you will have juft Caufe to fay you never
Made fuch a Voyage.

Mafter. We will ftand the Hazard.

Fran. What's the beft Hour?

Boatf. After the fecond Watch.

Fran. Enough;—each to his Charge.

Grim. We will be careful.   *[Exeunt.*

SCENE V.

Paul. Sit, Madam! it is fit that I attend you;
And pardon, I beſeech you, my rude Language,
To which the ſooner you will be invited,
When you ſhall underſtand, no Way was left me
To free you from a preſent Execution,
But by my perſonating that, which never
My Nature was acquainted with.

Don. I believe you.

Paul. You will, when you ſhall underſtand I may
Receive the Honour to be known unto you
By a nearer Name.——And, not to rack you further,
The Man you pleaſe to favour is my Brother;
No Merchant, Madam, but a Gentleman
Of the beſt Rank in *Venice*.

Don. I rejoice in't,
But what's this to his Freedom? For myſelf,
Were he well off, I were ſecure.

Paul. I have
A preſent Means, not plotted by myſelf,
But a religious Man, my Confeſſor,
That may preſerve all, if we had a Servant
Whoſe Faith we might rely on.

Don. She, that's now,
Your Slave, was once mine; had I twenty Lives,
I durſt commit them to her Truſt.

Manto. Oh! Madam!
I have been falſe,—forgive me.—I'll redeem it
By any Thing, however deſperate,
You pleaſe t' impoſe upon me.

Paul. 'Troth theſe Tears,——
I think, cannot be counterfeit,—I believe her,
And if you pleaſe will try her.

Don. At your Peril;
There is no further Danger can look towards me.

Paul.

Paul. This only then—canſt thou uſe Means to carry
This bak'd Meat to *Vitelli?*

Manto. With much Eaſe;
I am familiar with the Guard; beſide,
It being known 'twas I that did betray him,
My Entrance hardly will of them be queſtion'd.

Paul. About it then.—Say it was ſent to him
From his *Donuſa:* Bid him ſearch the midſt of't,
He there ſhall find a Cordial.

Manto. What I do
Shall ſpeak my Care and Faith. [*Exit* Manto.

Don. Good Fortune with thee!

Paul. You cannot eat.

Don. The Time we thus abuſe
We might employ much better.

Paul. I am glad
To hear this from you.   As for you *Carazie!*
If your Intents do proſper, make Choice, whether
You'll ſteal away with your two Miſtreſſes,
Or take your Fortune.

Car. I'll be gelded twice firſt;
Hang him that ſtays behind.

Paul. I wait you Madam.
Were but my Brother off, by the Command
Of the doting Viceroy there's no Guard dare ſtay me;
And I will ſafely bring you to the Place
Where we muſt expeƈt him.

Don. Heaven be gracious to us. [*Exeunt.*

S C E N E VI.

Enter Vitelli, Aga, *and a Guard.*

Vitel. *Paulina* to fall off thus! 'tis to me
More terrible than Death; and, like an Earthquake
Totters this walking Building (ſuch I am)
And in my ſudden Ruin would prevent,
By choking up at once my vital Spirits,
This pompous Preparation for my Death.

But

But I am loft; that good Man, good *Francisco*,
Deliver'd me a l'aper, which till now
I wanted Leifure to perufe.   [*Reads the Paper.*
    Aga. This Chriftian
Fears not, it feems, the ne'er approaching Sun
Whofe fecond Rife he never mult falute.

Enter Manto *with the bak'd Meat.*

    1 *Guard.* Who's that?
    2 *Guard.* Stand!
    Aga. Manto ?
    Manto. Here's the Viceroy's Ring
Gives Warrant to my Entrance.   Yet you may
Partake of any Thing I fhall deliver;
'Tis but a Prefent to a dying Man
Sent from the Princefs that muft fuffer with him.
    Aga. Ufe your own Freedom.
    Manto, I would not difturb
This his laft Contemplation,
    Vitel. O, 'tis well!
He has reftor'd all, and I at Peace again
With my *Paulina,*
    Manto. Sir! the fad *Donufa*
Grieved for your Suff'rings, more than for her own,
Knowing the long and tedious Pilgrimage
You are to take, prefents you with this Cordial,
Which privately fhe wifhes you fhould tafte of,
And fearch the middle Part, where you fhall find
Something that hath the Operation to
Make Death look lovely,
    Vitelli. I will not difpute
What fhe commands, but ferve it.   [*Exit* Vitelli.
    Aga. Pr'ythee, *Manto!*
How hath the unfortunate Princefs fpent this Night
Under her proud new Miftrefs?
    Manto. With fuch Patience
As it o'ercomes the other's Infolence;
Nay, triumphs o'er her Pride.   My much Hafte now
                              Commands

Commands me hence; but, the fad Tragedy paft,
I'll give you Satisfaction to the full
Of all hath pafs'd, and a true Character
Of the proud Chriftian's Nature.   [*Exit* Manto.
    Aga. Break the Watch up.—
What fhould we fear i' th' midft of our own Strengths?
'Tis but the Bafhaw's Jealoufy.   Farewell, Soldiers.
                                        [*Exeunt.*

SCENE VII.

Enter Vitelli, *with the bak'd Meats above.*

Vitel. There's fomething more in this than means to
        cloy
A hungry Appetite,—which I muft difcover.
She will'd me fearch the midft.—Thus, thus I pierce it:
—Ha! what is this? A Scroll bound up in Pack-thread?
What may the Myftery be?   [*He reads the Scroll.*

    " Son, let down this Pack-thread, at the Weft Win-
" dow of the Caftle.   By it you fhall draw up a Ladder
" of Ropes, by which you may defcend, your deareft
" *Donufa* with the reft of your Friends, below attend
" you.   Heaven profper you!"   *Francifco.*

O beft of Men! he that gives up himfelf
To a true religious Friend, leans not upon
A falfe deceiving Reed, but boldly builds
Upon a Rock; which now with Joy I find
In reverend *Francifco,* whofe good Vows,
Labours, and Watchings in my hoped-for Freedom,
Appear a pious Miracle.—I come,
I come, good Man, with Confidence; though the De-
        fcent
Were fteep as Hell, I know I cannot flide
Being call'd down by fuch a faithful Guide.
                                        [*Exit* Vitelli.

SCENE

SCENE *the last.*

Afambeg, Muftapha, *Janizaries.*

Afam. Excufe me *Muftapha*, though this Night to me
Appear as tedious as that treble one
Was to the World, when *Jove* on fair *Alcmena*
Begot *Alcides.* Were you to encounter
Thofe ravifhing Pleafures, which the flow-pac'd Hours
(To me they are fuch) bar me from, you would
With your continu'd Wifhes ftrive to imp
New Feathers to the broken Wings of Time,
And chide the amorous Sun, for too long Dalliance
In *Thetis'* wat'ry Bofom.
    Mufta. You are too violent
In your Defires, of which you are yet uncertain,
Having no more Affurance to enjoy 'em
Than a weak Woman's Promife, on which wife Men
Faintly rely.
    Afam. Tufh! fhe is made of Truth;
And what fhe fays fhe will do, holds as firm
As Laws in Brafs that know no Change: What's this?
Some new Prize brought in, fure.—Why are thy Looks
                                     [*A Piece fhot off.*

So ghaftly.—Villain, fpeak!

Enter Aga.

    Aga. Great Sir! hear me,
Then, after, kill me.—We are all betray'd,
The falfe *Grimaldi* funk in your Difgrace,
With his Confederates, have feiz'd his Ship,
And thofe that guarded it ftow'd under Hatches:
With him the condemn'd Princefs, and the Merchant,
That with a Ladder made of Ropes defcended
From the black Tower in which he was inclos'd,
And your fair Miftrefs,—
    Afam. Ha!

                                                Aga.

Aga. With all their Train,
And choicest Jewels, are gone safe aboard,
Their Sails spread forth, and with a Fore-gale
Leaving our Coast, in Scorn of all Pursuit
As a Farewell they shew'd a Broad-side to us.
    Asam. No more.——
    Musta. Now note your Confidence!
    Asam. No more.——
O my Credulity! I am too full
Of Grief, and Rage to speak.——Dull heavy Fool!
Worthy of all the Tortures that the Frown
Of thy incensed Master can throw on thee
Without one Man's Compassion.   I will hide
This Head among the Desarts, or some Cave
Fill'd with my Shame and me; where I alone
May die without a Partner in my Moan.   [*Exeunt.*

F I N I S.

THE

PICTURE.

A

TRAGI-COMEDY.

As it was often prefented with good Allowance,
at the *Globe*, and *Black-Friers* Playhoufes, by
the King's Majefty's Servants. 1630.

WRITTEN

By PHILIP MASSINGER.

THE

PICTURE.

A

TRAGI-COMEDY.

As it was often presented with good Allowance,
at the Globe, and Blacke-friers Play-houses, by
the Kings Majesties Servants. 1630.

WRITTEN

PHILIP MASSINGER.

T O

My Honoured and Selected Friends

OF THE

Noble Society of the INNER TEMPLE.

IT may be objected, my not inscribing their Names, or Titles, to whom I dedicate this Poem, proceedeth either from my Diffidence of their Affection to me, or their Unwillingness to be published the Patrons of a Trifle. To such as shall make so strict an Inquisition of me, I truly answer, The Play, in the Presentment, found such a general Approbation, that it gave me Assurance of their Favour to whose Protection it is now sacred; and they have professed they so sincerely allow of it, and the Maker, that they would have freely granted that in the Publication, which, for some Reasons, I denied myself. One, and that is a main one; I had rather enjoy (as I have done) the real Proofs of their Friendship, than Mountebank-like boast their Numbers in a Catalogue. Accept it, noble Gentlemen, as a Confirmation of his Service, who hath nothing else to assure you, and witness to the World how much he stands engaged for your so frequent Bounties, and in your charitable Opinion of me believe, that you now may, and shall ever command,

Your Servant,

PHILIP MASSINGER.

Dramatis

Dramatis Personæ.	The Original Actors.
Ladiſlaus, King of *Hungary*.	ROBERT BENFIELD.
Eubulus, an old Counſellor.	JOHN LEWIN.
Ferdinand, General of the Army.	RICHARD SHARPE.
Mathias, a Knight of *Bohemia*.	JOSEPH TAYLOR.
Ubaldo, ⎱ Two wild Courtiers.	THOMAS POLLARD.
Ricardo, ⎰ tiers.	EYLARDT SWANSTONE.
Hilario, Servant to *Sophia*.	JOHN SHANUCKE.
Julio Baptiſta, a great Scholar.	WILLIAM PEN.
Honoria, the Queen.	JOHN TOMSON.
Acanthe, a Maid of Honour.	ALEXANDER GOFFE.
Sophia, Wife to *Mathias*.	JOHN HUNNIEMAN.
Coriſca, *Sophia*'s Woman.	WILLIAM TRIGGE.

Six Maſquers.
Six Servants to the Queen.
Attendants.

THE

THE
PICTURE.
A True Hungarian History.

ACT I. SCENE I.

Enter Mathias *in Armour*, Sophia *in a riding Suit*, Co-rifca, Hilario, *with other Servants.*

Mathias.

SINCE we muſt part, *Sophia*, to paſs further
Is not alone impertinent, but dangerous.
We are not diſtant from the *Turkiſh* Camp
Above five Leagues, and who knows but
    ſome Party
Of his Timariots, that ſcour the Country,
May fall upon us ?—Be now, as thy Name
Truly interpreted, hath ever ſpoke thee,
Wife, and diſcreet, and to thy Underſtanding
Marry thy conſtant Patience.
  Soph. You put me, Sir,
To the utmoſt Trial of it.
  Math. Nay, no Melting ;
Since the Neceſſity that now ſeparates us,
We have long ſince diſputed, and the Reaſons
Forcing me to it, too oft waſh'd in Tears.
I grant that you in Birth were far above me,
And great Men, my Superiors, Rivals for you ;
But mutual Conſent of Heart, as Hands
Join'd by true Love, hath made us one, and equal :
                      Nor

Nor is it in me mere Defire of Fame,
Or to be cry'd up by the publick Voice
For a brave Soldier, that puts on my Armour;
Such airy Tumours take not me. You know
How narrow our Demeans are, and what's more,
Having as yet no Charge of Children on us,
We hardly can fubfift.

    Soph. In you alone, Sir, [*]
I have all Abundance.

    Math. For my Mind's content,
In your own Language I could anfwer you;
You have been an obedient Wife, a right one;
And to my Power, though fhort of your Defert,
I have been ever an indulgent Hufband.
We have long enjoy'd the Sweets of Love, and though
Not to Satiety, or Loathing, yet
We muft not live fuch Dotards on our Pleafures,
As ftill to hug them to the certain Lofs
Of Profit and Preferment. Competent Means
Maintains a quiet Bed; Want breeds Diffention,
Even in good Women.

    Soph. Have you found in me, Sir,
Any Diftafte, or Sign of Difcontent,
For want of what's fuperfluous?

    Math. No, *Sophia*;
Nor fhalt thou ever have Caufe to repent
Thy conftant Courfe in Goodnefs, if Heaven blefs
My honeft Undertakings. 'Tis for thee
That I turn Soldier, and put forth, Deareft,
Upon this Sea of Action as a Factor,
To trade for rich Materials to adorn
Thy noble Parts, and fhew 'em in full Luftre.
I blufh that other Ladies, lefs in Beauty

---

[*] I am apt to think this Speech of *Sophia* ought to be read thus:

    Soph. In you alone, Sir,
I have all Abundance; for my Mind's content.

     Math. In your own Language I could anfwer you;
You have, &c.

And outward Form (but in the Harmony
Of the Soul's ravishing Musick, the same Age
Not to be nam'd with thee) should so out-shine thee.
In Jewels and Variety of Wardrobes;
While you (to whose sweet Innocence both *Indies*
Compar'd are of no Value) wanting these
Pass unregarded:

   Soph. If I am so rich, or
In your Opinion so, why should you borrow
Additions for me?

   Math. Why!—I should be censur'd
Of Ignorance, possessing such a Jewel
Above all Price, if I forbear to give it
The best of Ornaments. Therefore, *Sophia*;
In few Words know my Pleasure, and obey me,
As you have ever done. To your Discretion
I leave the Government of my Family,
And our poor Fortunes, and from these command
Obedience to you as to myself:
To the utmost of what's mine live plentifully;
And e'er the Remnant of our Store be spent,
With my good Sword, I hope, I shall reap for you
A Harvest in such full Abundance, as
Shall make a merry Winter.

   Soph. Since you are not
To be diverted, Sir, from what you purpose,
All Arguments to stay you here are useless.
Go when you please, Sir: Eyes, I charge you waste not
One Drop of Sorrow, look you hoard all up
Till in my widow'd Bed I call upon you,
But then be sure you fail not. You blest Angels,
Guardians of human Life, I at this Instant
Forbear t' invoke you, at our parting; 'twere
To personate Devotion. My Soul
Shall go along with you, and when you are
Circled with Death and Horror, seek and find you;
And then I will not leave a Saint unsu'd to
For your Protection. To tell you what
I will do in your Absence, would shew poorly;

My Actions fhall fpeak me; 'twere to doubt you,
To beg I may hear from you where you are;
You cannot live obfcure, nor fhall one Poft
By Night, or Day, pafs unexamin'd by me.
If I dwell long upon your Lips, confider
After this Feaft the griping Faft that follows,
And it will be excufable ; Pray turn from me,
All that I can is fpoken. ²　　　　　　　*Exit* Sophia,

　Math. Follow your Miftrefs.
Forbear your Wifhes for me ; let me find 'em
At my Return, in your prompt Will to ferve her.

　Hil. For my Part, Sir, I will grow lean with Study
To make her merry.

　Corif. Though you are my Lord,
Yet being her Gentlewoman, by my Place
I may take my Leave; your Hand, or if you pleafe
To have me fight fo high, I'll not be coy,
But ftand a tip-toe for't.

　Math. O ! farewel, Girl.

　Hil. A Kifs well begg'd, *Corifca.*

　Corif. 'Twas my Fee;
Jove, how he melts ! I cannot blame my Lady's
Unwillingnefs to part with fuch Marmulade Lips.
There will be fcrambling for 'em in the Camp;
And were it not for my Honefty, I cou'd wifh now
I were his leager Landrefs, I would find
Soap of mine own, enough to wafh his Linnen,
Or I would ftrain hard for't.

　Hil. How the Mammet twitters !
Come, come, my Lady ftays for us.

　Corif. Would I had been
Her Ladyfhip the laft Night.

---

　　² ————— *Pray turn from me ;*
　　All that I can is fpoken.

　　The foregoing Scene between *Mathias* and *Sophia,* though fhort,
is very beautiful: The Affemblage of Love and Grief at their parting, muft be very pleafing to every Heart that is capable of being
touched with Tendernefs.

　　　　　　　　　　　　　　　　　　　　　Hil.

Hil. No more of that, Wench

[*Exeunt* Hilario *and* Corisca.

Math. I am ſtrangely troubled: Yet why I ſhould
    nouriſh
A Fury here, and with imagin'd Food ?
Having no real Grounds on which to raiſe
A Building of Suſpicion ſhe ever was,
Or can be falſe hereafter ? I in this
But fooliſhly inquire the Knowledge of
A future Sorrow, which, if I find out,
My preſent Ignorance were a cheap Purchaſe,
Though with my Loſs of Being. I have already
Dealt with a Friend of mine, a general Scholar,
One deeply read in Nature's hidden Secrets,
And (though with much Unwillingneſs) have won him
To do as much as Art can to reſolve me
My Fate that follows — To my Wiſh he's come.

Enter Baptiſta.

Julio Baptiſta, now I may affirm
Your Promiſe and Performance walk together;
And therefore, without Circumſtance to the Point,
Inſtruct me what I am.
    Bapt. I could wiſh you had
Made Trial of my Love ſome other Way.
    Math. Nay, this is from the Purpoſe.
    Bapt. If you can,
Proportion your Deſire to any Mean,
I do pronounce you happy: I have found,
By certain Rules of Art, your matchleſs Wife
Is to this preſent Hour from all Pollution
Free and untainted.
    Math. Good.
    Bapt. In reaſon therefore
You ſhould fix here, and make no farther Search
Of what may fall hereafter.
    Math. O *Baptiſta !*
'Tis not in me to maſter ſo my Paſſions ;

I muſt

I muſt know farther, or you have made good
But half your Promiſe.—While my Love ſtood by,
Holding her upright, and my Preſence was
A Watch upon her, her Deſires being met too
With equal Ardour from me, what one Proof
Could ſhe give of her Conſtancy, being untempted?
But when I am abſent, and my coming back
Uncertain, and thoſe wanton Heats in Women
Not to be quench'd by lawful Means, and ſhe
The abſolute Diſpoſer of herſelf,
Without Controul or Curb; nay more, invited
By Opportunity and all ſtrong Temptations,
If then ſhe hold out ——

    Bapt. As no doubt ſhe will.

    Math. Thoſe Doubts muſt be made Certainties, *Bap-*
By your Aſſurance, or your boaſted Art   [*tiſta*,
Deſerves no Admiration. How you trifle ——
And play with my Affliction? I'm on
The Rack, till you confirm me.

    Bapt. Sure, *Mathias*,
I am no God, nor can I dive into
Her hidden Thoughts, or know what her Intents are;
That is deny'd to Art, and kept conceal'd
E'en from the Devils themſelves: They can but gueſs,
Out of long Obſervation, what is likely;
But poſitively to foretel that this ſhall be,
You may conclude impoſſible; all I can
I will do for you, when you are diſtant from her
A thouſand Leagues, as if you then were with her;
You ſhall know truly when ſhe is ſolicited,
And how far wrought on.

    Math. I deſire no more.

    Bapt. Take then this little Model of *Sophia*,
With more than human Skill limb'd to the Life;
Each Line and Lineament of it in the Drawing
So punctually obſerv'd, that, had it Motion,
In ſo much 'twere herſelf.

    Math. It is, indeed,
An admirable Piece; but if it have not

Some

Some hidden Virtue that I cannot guefs at,
In what can it advantage me?
  Bapt. I'll inftruct you,
Carry it ftill about you, and as oft
As you defire to know how fhe's affected,
With curious Eyes perufe it: While it keeps
The Figure it now has entire and perfect,
She is not only innocent in Fact,
But unattempted; but if once it vary
From the true Form, and what's now white and red
Incline to yellow, reft moft confident
She's with all Violence courted, but unconquer'd.
But if it turn all black, 'tis an Affurance
The Fort, by Compofition or Surprize,
Is forc'd, or with her free Confent, furrender'd.
  Math. How much you have engag'd me for this Fa-
    vour,
The Service of my whole Life fhall make good.
  Bapt. We will not part fo; I'll along with you,
And it is needful, with the rifing Sun
The Armies meet; yet, e'er the Fight begin,
In fpite of Oppofition I will place you
In the Head of the *Hungarian* General's Troop,
And near his Perfon.
  Math. As my better Angel
You fhall direct and guide me.
  Bapt. As we ride
I'll tell you more.
  Math. In all Things I'll obey you.   [*Exeunt.*

SCENE II.

Enter Ubaldo *and* Ricardo.

  Ric. When came the Poft?
  Ubal. The laft Night.
  Ric. From the Camp?
  Ubal. Yes, as 'tis faid, and the Letter writ and fign'd
By the General *Ferdinand.*
        G 3   *Ric.*

Ric. Nay, then fans queftion
It is of Moment.

Ubal. It concerns the Lives
Of two great Armies.

Ric. Was it chearfully
Received by the King?

Ubal. Yes, for being affured
The Armies were in View of one another;
Having proclaim'd a public Faft and Prayer
For the good Succefs, he difpatch'd a Gentleman
Of his Privy Chamber to the General,
With abfolute Authority from him
To try the Fortune of a Day.

Ric. No doubt then
The General will come on, and fight it bravely,
Heaven profper him : This military Art
I grant to be the nobleft of Profeffions;
And yet (I thank my Stars for't) I was never
Inclin'd to learn it, fince this bubble Honour, ³
(Which is indeed the Nothing Soldiers fight for,
With the Lofs of Limbs or Life) is in my Judgment
Too dear a Purchafe.

Ubal. Give me our Court-warfare :
The Danger is not great in the Encounter
Of a fair Miftrefs,

Ric. Fair and found together
Do very well, *Ubaldo*. But fuch are
With Difficulty to be found out ; and when they know
Their Value, priz'd too high. By thy own Report
Thou waft at Twelve a Gamefter, and fince that
Studied all Kinds of Females, from the Night-trader
I'the Street, with certain Danger to thy Pocket,

---

³ ——— *This Bubble Honour.*

In fpeaking of *Honour*, *Meffinger* feems to have had *Shakefpear* in his Eye: Thus, in *As you like it*,

> Seeking the *Bubble*, Reputation,
> Even in the Cannon's Mouth,

And in *Falftaff's* Catechifm, See the Firft Part of *Henry* IV. Act 5. Scene 2.

To the great Lady in her Cabinet,
That fpent upon thee more in Cullifes,
To ftrengthen thy weak Back, than would maintain
Twelve *Flanders* Mares, and as many running Horfes;
Befides Apothecaries and Chirurgeons Bills,
Paid upon all Occafions, and thofe frequent.

   Ubal. You talk *Ricardo*, as if yet you were
A Novice in thofe Myfteries.

   Ric. By no Means;
My Doctor can affure the contrary,
I lofe no Time. I have felt the Pain and Pleafure,
As he that is a Gamefter, and plays often,
Muft fometimes be a lofer.

   Ubal. Wherefore then
Do you envy me?

   Ric. It grows not from my Want,
Nor thy Abundance, but being as I am
The likelier Man, and of much more Experience,
My good Parts are my Curfes: There's no Beauty
But yields e'er it be fummon'd; and as Nature
Had fign'd me the Monopolies of Maidenheads,
There's none can buy till I have made my Market:
Satiety cloys me: As I live, I would part with
Half my Eftate, nay, travel o'er the World,
To find that only *Phænix* in my Search
That could hold out againft me.

   Ubal. Be not rap'd fo:
You may fpare that Labour, as fhe is a Woman,
What think you of the Queen?

   Ric. I dare not aim at
The Petticoat royal; that is ftill excepted:
Yet were fhe not my King's, being the Abftract
Of all that's rare, or to be wifh'd in Woman,
To write her in my Catalogue, having enjoy'd her,
I would venture my Neck to a Halter. But we talk of
Impoffibilities; as fhe hath a Beauty
Would make old *Neftor* young, fuch Majefty
Draws forth a Sword of Terror to defend it,
As would fright *Paris*, though the Queen of Love

Vow'd

Vow'd her best Furtherance to him.

Ubal. Have you observ'd
The Gravity of her Language mix'd with Sweetness ?
Ric. Then, at what Distance she reserves herself
When the King himself makes his Aproaches to her ?
Ual. As she were still a Virgin, and his Life
But one continued Wooing.

Ric. She well knows
Her Worth, and values it.

Ubal. And so far the King is
Indulgent to her Humours, that he forbears
The Duty of a Husband, but when she calls for't.

Ric. All his Imaginations and Thoughts
Are buried in her; the loud Noise of War
Cannot awake him.

Ubal. At this very Instant,
When both his Life and Crown are at the Stake,
He only studies her Content, and when
She's pleas'd to shew herself, Music and Masques
Are with all Care and Cost provided for her.

Ric. This Night she promis'd to appear.

Ubal. You may believe it by the Diligence of the King,
As if he were her Harbinger.

Enter Ladislaus, Eubulus, *and Attendants with Perfumes.*

Ladis. These Rooms
Are not perfum'd, as we directed.

Eub. Not Sir.
I know not what you would have ; I am sure the Smoak
Cost treble the Price of the whole Week's Provision
Spent in your Majesty's Kitchens.

Ladis. How ! I scorn
Thy gross Comparison.   When my *Honoria,*

---

⁴ *As she were still a Virgin and his Life*
       But one, &c.

This Passage I think would read better thus.
       As she were still a Virgin—His Life's
       But one continued Wooing.

Th'

Th' Amazement of the present Time, and Envy
Of all succeeding Ages, does descend
To sanctify a Place, and in her Presence
Makes it a Temple to me, can I be
Too curious, much less Prodigal to receive her?
But that the Splendour of her Beams of Beauty
Hath struck thee blind.

    Eub. As Dotage hath done you.

    Ladif. Dotage, O Blasphemy! is it in me
To serve her to her Merit? Is she not
The Daughter of a King?

    Eub. And you the Son
Of ours I take it, by what Priviledge else
Do you reign over us? For my Part, I know not
Where the Disparity lies.

    Ladif. Her Birth, old Man,
Old in the Kingdom's Service which protects thee,
Is the least Grace in her: And though her Beauties
Might make the Thunderer a Rival for her,
They are but superficial Ornaments,
And faintly speak her. From her heavenly Mind, ⁵
Were all Antiquity and Fiction lost,
Our modern Poets could not in their Fancy
But fashion a *Minerva* far transcending
Th' imagin'd one, whom *Homer* only dream't of:
But then add this, she's mine, mine *Eubulus*.
And though she knows one Glance from her fair Eyes
Must make all Gazers her Idolaters,
She is so sparing of their Influence,
That to shun Superstition in others,
She shoots her powerful Beams only at me.
And can I then, whom she desires to hold
Her kingly Captive above all the World,
Whose Nations and Empires if she pleas'd

    ⁵ *From her heavenly Mind*
    Were all Antiquity, &c.

  Maffinger abounds in these Allusions, and is very happy in them:
They must be very pleasing to every Reader of a poetical Turn.

                                 She

She might command as Slaves, but gladly pay
The humble Tribute of my Love and Service?
Nay, if I said of Adoration to her,
I did not err.

 Eub. Well, since you hug your Fetters,
In Love's Name wear 'em.　You are a King, and that
Concludes you wise.　Your Will a powerful Reason,
Which we that are foolish Subjects must not argue.
And what in a mean Man I should call Folly,
Is in your Majesty remarkable Wisdom.
But for me I subscribe.

 Ladis. Do, and look up,
Upon this Wonder.

Loud Musick, Honoria *in State under a Canopy, her Train*
   born up by Sylvia *and* Acanthe.

 Ric. Wonder? It is more Sir.

 Ubal. A Rapture, an Astonishment.

 Ric. What think you, Sir?

 Eub. As the King thinks, that is the surest Guard
We Courtiers ever lie at.　Was ever Prince
So drown'd in Dotage? Without Spectacles
I can see a handsome Woman, and she is so:
But yet to Admiration look not on her.
Heaven, how he fawns! and as it were his Duty,
With what assured Gravity she receives it!
Her Hand again! O she at length vouchsafes
Her Lip, and as he had suck'd Nectar from it,
How he's exalted! Women in their Natures
Affect Command, but this Humility
In a Husband and a King, marks her the Way
To absolute Tyranny.　So, *Juno*'s plac'd
In *Jove*'s Tribunal, and like *Mercury*
(Forgetting his own Greatness,) he attends
For her Employments.　She prepares to speak,
What Oracles shall we hear now?

 Hon. That you please, Sir,
With such Assurances of Love and Favour,

          To

To grace your Handmaid, but in being yours, Sir,
A matchlefs Queen, and one that knows herfelf fo,
Binds me in Retribution to deferve.
The Grace conferr'd upon me.

Ladif. You tranfcend
In all Things excellent, and it is my Glory,
(Your Worth weigh'd truly) to depofe myfelf
From abfolute Command, furrendering up
My Will and Faculties to your Difpofure:
And here I vow, not for a Day or Year,
But my whole Life, which I wifh long, to ferve you:
That whatfoever I in Juftice may
Exact from thefe my Subjects, you from me
May boldly challenge.   And when you require it,
In Sign of my Subjection, as your Vaffal,
Thus I will pay my Homage.

Hon. O forbear, Sir,
Let not my Lips envy my Robe: On them
Print your Allegiance often.   I defire
No other Fealty.

Ladif. Gracious Sovereign,
Boundlefs in Bounty!

Eub. Is not here fine fooling?
He's queftionlefs bewitch'd.   Would I were gelt
So that would difenchant him.   Though I forfeit
My Life for it I muft fpeak.—By your good Leave, Sir,
I have no Suit to you, nor can you grant one,
Having no Power.   You are like me, a Subject,
Her more then ferene Majefty being prefent.
And I muft tell you, 'tis ill Manners in you,
Having depos'd yourfelf, to keep your Hat on,
And not ftand bare as we do, being no King,
But a fellow Subject with us.   Gentlemen Ufhers,
It does belong to your Place, fee it reform'd,
He has given away his Crown, and cannot challenge
The Privilege of his Bonnet.

Ladif. Do not tempt me.

Eub. Tempt you, in what? In following your Example?

If

If you are·angry, queſtion me hereafter,
As *Ladiſlaus* ſhould do *Eubulus,*
On equal Terms. You were of late my Sovereign,
But weary of it, I now bend my Knee
To her Divinity, and deſire a Boon
From her more then Magnificence.

   Hon. Take it freely.
Nay, be not mov'd, for our Mirth Sake let us hear him.

   Eub. 'Tis but to aſk a Queſtion : have you ne'er read
The Story of *Semiramis* and *Ninus?*

   Hon. Not as I remember.

   Eub. I will then inſtruct you,
And 'tis to the Purpoſe. This *Ninus* was a King,
And ſuch an impotent loving King, as this was,
But now he's none. This *Ninus* (pray you obſerve me)
Doted on this *Semiramis,* a Smith's Wife,
(I muſt confeſs, there the Compariſon holds not,
You are a King's Daughter, yet, under your Correction,
Like her, a Woman) this *Aſſyrian* Monarch
(Of whom this is a Pattern) to expreſs
His Love and Service, ſeated her, as you are,
In his regal Throne, and bound by Oath his Nobles,
Forgetting all Allegiance to himſelf,
One Day to be her Subjects, and to put
In Execution whatever ſhe
Pleas'd to impoſe upon 'em. Pray you command him
To miniſter the like to us, and then
You ſhall hear what follow'd.

   Ladiſ. Well, Sir, to your Story.

   Eub. You have no Warrant, ſtand by; let me know
Your Pleaſure, Goddeſs.

   Hon. Let this Nod aſſure you,

   Eub. Goddeſs like, indeed; as I live, a pretty Idol!
She knowing her Power, wiſely made Uſe of it;
And fearing his Inconſtancy, and Repentance
Of what he had granted (as in Reaſon Madam,
You may do his) that he might never have
Powe: to recall his Grant, or queſtion her
For her ſhort Government, inſtantly gave Order
To have his Head ſtruck off.   *Ladiſ.*

Ladif. I'ft poffible?

Eub. The Story fays fo, and commends her Wifdom
For making Ufe of her Authority:
And it is worth your Imitation, Madam,
He loves Subjection, and you are no Queen,
Unlefs you make him feel the Weight of it.
You are more then all the World to him, and that, [6]
He may be Foe to you, and not feek change,
When his Delights are fated, mew him up
In fome clofe Prifon if you let him live,
(Which is no Policy) and there diet him
As you think fit to feed your Appetite,
Since there ends his Ambition.

Ubal. Devillifh Counfel.

Ric. The King's amaz'd.

Ubal. The Queen appears too, full
Of deep Imaginations, *Eubulus*
Hath put both to it.

Ric. Now fhe feems refolv'd:
I long to know the Iffue   [Honoria *defcends.*

Hon. Give me Leave,
Dear Sir, to reprehend you for appearing
Perplex'd with what this old Man, out of Envy
Of your unequal'd Graces fhowr'd upon me,
Hath in his fabulous Story faucily
Apply'd to me. Sir, that you only nourifh
One Doubt, *Honoria* dares abufe the Power
With which fhe is invefted by your Favour,
Or that fhe ever can make Ufe of it
To the Injury of you the great Beftower,
Takes from your Judgment. It was your Delight
To feek to me with more Obfequioufnefs,
Then I defir'd; and ftood it with my Duty

----

[6] *You are more than all the World to him, and that*
He may be Foe *to you,*

This is the reading of all the old Copies, but moft certainly falfe.
It ought to be
You are more then all the World to him, and that - - -
He may be fo *to you.*

Not

Not to receive what you were pleas'd to offer?
I do but act the Part you put upon me,
And though you make me perfonate a Queen,
And you my Subject, when the Play, your Pleafure,
Is at a Period, I am what I was
Before I enter'd, ftill your humble Wife,
And you my royal Sovereign.

    Ric. Admirable!

    Hon. I have heard of Captains taken more with Dan-
        gers
Then the Rewards, and if in your Approaches
To thofe Delights which are your own, and freely
To heighten your Defire, you make the Paffage
Narrow and difficult, fhall I prefcribe you?
Or blame your Fondnefs? Or can that fwell me
Beyond my juft Proportion?

    Ubal. Above Wonder!

    Ladif. Heaven make me thankful for fuch Goodnefs.

    Hon. Now, Sir,
The State I took to fatisfy your Pleafure,
I change to this Humility; and the Oath
You made to me of Homage, I thus cancel,
And feat you in your own.

    Ladif. I am tranfported
Beyond myfelf.

    Hon. And now to your wife Lordfhip,
Am I prov'd a *Semiramis?* Or hath
My *Ninus*, as malicioufly you made him,
Caufe to repent th' Excefs of Favour to me,
Which you call Dotage?

    Ladif. Anfwer Wretch.

    Eub. I dare, Sir,
And fay, however the Event may plead
In your Defence, you had a guilty Caufe;
Nor was it Wifdom in you (I repeat it)
To teach a Lady, humble in herfelf,
With the ridiculous Dotage of a Lover,
To be ambitious.

                            Hon.

Hon. Eubulus, I am fo,
'Tis rooted in me, you miſtake my Temper.
I do profefs myſelf to be the moſt
Ambitious of my Sex, but not to hold
Command over my Lord, ſuch a proud Torrent
Would ſink me in my Wiſhes; not that I
Am ignorant how much I can deſerve,
And may with Juſtice challenge.

Eub. This I look'd for;
After this ſeeming humble Ebb, I knew,
A guſhing Tide would follow.

Hon. By my Birth,
And liberal Gifts of Nature, as of Fortune,
From you, as Things beneath me, I expeēt
What's due to Majeſty, in which I am
A Sharer with your Sov'reign.

Eub. Good again !

Hon. And as I am moſt eminent in Place,
In all my Aētions I would appear ſo.

Ladiſ. You need not fear a Rival.

Hon. I hope not;
And till I find one, I diſdain to know
What Envy is.

Ladiſ. You are above it, Madam.

Hon. For Beauty without Art, Diſcourſe, and free
From Affeētation, with what Graces elſe
Can in the Wife and Daughter of a King
Be wiſh'd, I dare prefer myſelf.

Eub. As I
Bluſh for you, Lady, trumpet your own Praiſes ! 7——

7 *As I*
Bluſh for you, Lady, trumpet your own Praiſes ——

Mr *Dodſley*, in his Colleētion of Old Plays, reads this Paſſage thus :

As I
Bluſh for you, Lady, trumpet not your own Praiſe.

I think that the old Reading ſhould ſtand. He means, that ſhe her-ſelf having loſt all Senſe of Shame, he undertakes to bluſh for her; and therefore ironically bids her proceed.

This

This fpoken by the People, had been heard
With Honour to you ; does the Court afford
No Oil-tongu'd Parafite, that you are forc'd
To be your own grofs Flatterer ?

Ladif. Be dumb,
Thou Spirit of Contradiction.

Hon. The Wolf
But barks againft the Moon, and I contemn it.
The Mafque you promis'd.

A Horn. Enter a Poft.

Ladif. Let 'em enter. How !

Eub. Here's one, I fear, unlook'd for.

Ladif. From the Camp ?

Poft. The General, victorious in your Fortune,
Kiffes your Hand in this, Sir.

Ladif. That great Power,
Who at his Pleafure does difpofe of Battles,
Be ever prais'd for't. Read, Sweet, and partake it :
The *Turk* is vanquifh'd, and with little Lofs
Upon our Part, in which our Joy is doubl'd.

Eub. But let it not exalt you ; bear it, Sir,
With Moderation, and pay what you owe for't.

Ladif. I underftand thee, *Eubulus.* I'll not now
Enquire Particulars. Our Delights deferr'd,
With Rev'rence to the Temples, there we'll tender
Our Soul's Devotions to his dread Might,
Who edg'd our Swords, and taught us how to fight. ⁵

[*Exeunt omnes.*

The End of the Firft Act.

---

⁵ *Who edg'd our Swords, and taught us how to fight.*

Maffinger, as well as *Shakefpear,* has greatly enriched himfelf
from the Holy Scriptures : Thus in the 144th Pfalm, *David* fays,
*Bleffed be the Lord my Strength, which teacheth my Hands to war, and
my Fingers to fight.* And in many other Places we find feveral Paffages fimilar to the above.

ACT

A C T II.   S C E N E I.

Enter Hilario, Corifca.

Hil. YOU like my Speech?
    Corif. Yes, if you give it Action
In the Delivery.
    Hil. If? — I pity you.
I have play'd the Fool before; this is not the firſt Time,
Nor ſhall be, I hope, the laſt.
    Corif. Nay, I think ſo too.
    Hil. And if I put her not out of her Dumps with
        Laughter,
I'll make her howl for Anger.
    Corif. Not too much
Of that, good Fellow *Hilario.* Our ſad Lady
Hath drank too often of that bitter Cup,
A pleaſant one muſt reſtore her. With what Patience
Would ſhe endure to hear of the Death of my Lord;
That merely out of Doubt he may miſcarry,
Afflicts herſelf thus?
    Hil. Um; 'tis a Queſtion
A Widow only can reſolve. There be ſome
That in their Huſband's Sickneſs have wept
Their Pottle of Tears a Day; but being once certain
At Midnight he was dead, have in the Morning
Dry'd up their Handkerchiefs, and thought no more on't.
    Corif. Tuſh, ſhe is none of that Race; if her Sorrow
Be not true and perfect, I againſt my Sex
Will take my Oath, Woman ne'er wept in Earneſt.
She has made herſelf a Priſoner to her Chamber,
Dark as a Dungeon, in which no Beam
Of Comfort enters. She admits no Viſits;
Eats little, and her nightly Muſick is
Of Sighs and Groans, tun'd to ſuch Harmony

VOL. II.　　　　　H　　　　　　　OF

Of feeling Grief, that I, againſt my Nature,
Am made one of the Conſort.   This Hour only
She takes the Air, a Cuſtom every Day
She ſolemnly obſerves, with greedy Hopes,
From ſome that paſs by, to receive Aſſurance
Of the Succeſs and Safety of her Lord.
Now, if that your Device will take ——

  Hil. Ne'er fear it :
I am provided cap-a-peé, and have
My Properties in Readineſs.

  Sophia within. Bring my Veil, there.

  Coriſ. Be gone, I hear her coming.

  Hil. If I do not
Appear, and, what's more, appear perfeft, hiſs me.

[Exit Hilario.

Enter Sophia.

  Soph. I was flatter'd once, I was a Star, but now
Turn'd a prodigious Meteor; and, like one,
Hang in the Air between my Hopes and Fears,
And every Hour (the little Stuff burnt out
That yields a waning Light to dying Comfort)
I do expeft my Fall, and certain Ruin.
In wretched Things more wretched is Delay; [9]
And Hope, a Paraſite to me, being unmaſq'd,
Appears more horrid than Deſpair, and my
Diſtraftion worſe than Madneſs.   E'en my Prayers,
When with moſt Zeal ſent upward, are pull'd down
With ſtrong imaginary Doubts and Fears,
And in their ſudden Precipice o'erwhelm me.
Dreams and fantaſtick Viſions walk the Round [10]

---

  [9] *In wretched Things more wretched is Delay.*
This, I think ſhould be read,
    To *wretched Things,* &c.

  [10] *Dreams and fantaſtick Viſions walk the Round.*
  'Tis thus in the old Copies; but I am inclin'd to think it ſhould be,
    Dreams and fantaſtick Viſions walk their *Round.*

About

About my widow'd Bed, and every Slumber
Broken with loud Alarms : Can thefe be then
But fad Prefages, Girl ?

   Corif. You make 'em fo,
And antedate a Lofs fhall ne'er fall on you.
Such pure Affection, fuch mutual Love,
A Bed, and undefil'd on either Part,
A Houfe without Contention, in two Bodies
One Will and Soul (like to the Rod of Concord)
Kiffing each other, cannot be fhort-liv'd,
Or end in Barrennefs.—If all thefe, dear Madam,
(Sweet in your Sadnefs) fhould produce no Fruit,
Or leave the Age no Models of yourfelves,
To witnefs to Pofterity what you were,
Succeeding Times, frighted with the Example,
But hearing of your Story, would inftruct
Their faireft Iffue to meet fenfually,
Like other Creatures, and forbear to raife
True Love, or *Hymen* Altars.

   Sophia. O *Corifca !*
I know thy Reafons are like to thy Wifhes,
And they are built upon a weak Foundation,
To raife me Comfort. Ten long Days are paft,
Ten long Days, my *Corifca,* fince my Lord
Embark'd himfelf upon a Sea of Danger,
In his dear Care of me. And if his Life
Had not been fhipwreck'd on the Rock of War,
His Tendernefs of me (knowing how much
I languifh for his Abfence) had provided
Some trufty Friend from whom I might receive
Affurance of his Safety.

   Corif. Ill News, Madam,
Are Swallow-wing'd, but what's good walks on Crutches:
With Patience expect it ; and e'er long,
No Doubt, you fhall hear from him.

A Sow-gelder's Horn blown.   A Poſt. [11]

Soph. Ha! What's that?

Coriſ. The Fool has got a Sow-gelder's Horn,
As I take it, Madam.

Soph. It makes this Way ſtill,
Nearer and nearer.

Coriſ. From the Camp, I hope.

Enter Hilario, *with long white Hair and Beard, in an
antick Armour, one with a Horn before him.*

Soph. The Meſſenger appears, and in ſtrange Armour.
Heaven, if it be thy Will!

Hil. It is no Boot
To ſtrive; our Horſes tir'd, let's walk on Foot,
And that the Caſtle which is very near us,
To give us Entertainment, may ſoon hear us,
Blow luſtily, my Lad, and drawing nigh,
Aſk for a Lady which is clep'd *Sophia.*

Coriſ. He names you, Madam.

---

[11] *A Sow-gelder's Horn blown.   A Poſt.*

I have here followed the old Copies, not chuſing to make any abſolute Alteration, though the Paſſage is evidently corrupt: I take it
ſhould be as follows:

A Sow gelder's Horn blown.

Soph. Ha! What's that?
Coriſ. The Fool has got a Sow-gelder's Horn.   [*Aſide.*
      A Poſt, as I take it Madam.
Soph. It makes this Way ſtill,
      Nearer and nearer.
Coriſ. From the Camp, I hope.

If *Coriſca* had told her Miſtreſs, that the Fool had got *a Sow-
gelder's Horn,* ſhe would not ſo readily have believed that he came
from the *Camp:* nor does there ſeem to be any Neceſſity for a *Poſt* to
be mentioned at all, when the Horn is blown. I imagine in the
written Copy there was not Room for the Tranſcriber to write it in
the ſame Line, and therefore he placed it over the Word *Horn,* which
occaſioned this Miſtake in the Printing.

Hil.

Hil. For to her I bring,
Thus clad in Arms, News of a pretty Thing,
By Name *Mathias.*
   Soph. From my Lord ? O Sir !
I am *Sophia,* that *Mathias'* Wife.
So may *Mars* favour you in all your Battles,
As you with Speed unload me of the Burthen
I labour under, till I am confirm'd
Both where and how you left him.
   Hil. If thou art,
As I believe, the Pigſney of his Heart,
Know he's in Health, and what's more, full of Glee;
And ſo much I was will'd to ſay to thee.
   Soph. Have you no Letters from him ?
   Hil. No, meer Words.
In the Camp we uſe no Pens, but write with Swords :
Yet as I am enjoin'd, by Word of Mouth
I will proclaim his Deeds from North to South.
But tremble not while I relate the Wonder,
Though my Eyes like Lightning ſhine, and my Voice
      thunder.
   Soph. This is ſome counterfeit Bragart.
   Corif. Hear him, Madam.
   Hil. The Rear march'd firſt, which follow'd by the Van,
And wing'd with the Battalia, no Man
Durſt ſtay to ſhift a Shirt, or louſe himſelf;
Yet ere the Armies join'd, that hopeful Elf,
Thy Dear, thy dainty Duckling, bold *Mathias,*
Advanc'd, and ſtar'd like *Hercules* or *Golias.*
A hundred thouſand *Turks* (it is no Vaunt)
Aſſail'd him ; every one a Termagant :
But what did he then ? with his keen edge Spear
He cut, and carbonaded 'em : Here and there
Lay Legs and Arms; and, as 'tis ſaid truly
Of *Bevis,* ſome he quarter'd all in three.
   Soph. This is ridiculous.
   Hil. I muſt take Breath :
Then, like a Nightingale, I'll ſing his Death.
   Soph. His Death !

H 3

Hil.

Hil. I am out.

Corif. Recover, Dunder-head.

Hil. How he efcap'd, I fhould have fung, not dy'd;
For, though a Knight, when I faid fo, I ly'd!
Weary he was, and fcarce could ftand upright,
And looking round for fome courageous Knight
To refcue him, as one perplex'd in Woe,
He call'd to me, Help! help, *Hilario!*
My valiant Servant, help.

Corif. He has fpoil'd all.

Soph. Are you the Man of Arms? Then I'll make
        bold
To take of your martial Beard; you had Fool's Hair
Enough without it.   Slave! how durft thou make
Thy Sport of what concerns me more than Life,
In fuch an antick Fafhion? Am I grown
Contemptible to thofe I feed? You, Minion,
Had a Hand in it too, as it appears,
Your Petticoat ferves for Bafes to this Warrior.

Corif. We did it for your Mirth.

Hil. For myfelf, I hope,
I have fpoke like a Soldier.

Soph. Hence, you Rafcal.
I, never but with Reverence name my Lord,
And can I hear it by thy Tongue prophan'd,
And not correct thy Folly? But you are
Transform'd, and turn'd Knight-errant; take your Courfe,
And wander where you pleafe; for here I vow
By my Lord's Life (an Oath I will not break)
'Till his Return, or Certainty of his Safety,
My Doors are fhut againft thee.   [*Exit* Sophia.

Corif. You have made
A fine Piece of Work on't: How do you like the Qua-
You had a foolifh Itch to be an Actor,   [lity?
And may now ftroll where you pleafe.

Hil. Will you buy my Share?

Corif. No, certainly, I fear I have already
Too much of mine own: I'll only as a Damfel

(As

(As the Book fays) thus far help to difarm you ;
And fo, dear Don *Quixote*, taking my Leave,
I leave you to your Fortune.   [*Exit* Corifca.

Hil. Have I fweat
My Brains out for this quaint and rare Invention,
And I am thus rewarded ? I could turn
Tragedian, and roar now, but that I fear
'Twould get me too great a Stomach, having no Meat
To pacify *Colon*, 12 what will become of me ?
I cannot beg in Armour, and fteal I dare not :
My End muft be to ftand in a Corn Field,
And fright away the Crows, for Bread and Cheefe, ·
Or find fome hollow Tree in the Highway,
And there, until my Lord return, fell Switches.
No more *Hilario*, but *Dolorio* now :
I'll weep my Eyes out, and be blind of Purpofe
To move Compaffion; and fo I vanifh.   [*Exit* Hilario.

SCENE II.

Enter Eubulus, Ubaldo, Ricardo, *and others.*

Eub. Are the Gentlemen fent before, as it was order'd
By the King's Direction, to entertain
The General ?

Ric. Long fince ; they by this have met him,
And given him the Beinvenue.

Eub. I hope I need not
Inftruct you in your Parts.

Ubal. How ! us, my Lord ?
Fear not; we know our Diftances and Degrees,
To the very Inch, where we are to falute him.

Ric. The State were miferable, if the Court had none
Of her own Breed, familiar with all Garbs.

---

12 *To pacify* Colon, &c.

In the *Unnatural Combat*, I find this Word, fpelt *Calon*, ufed in
the fame Senfe by *Belgard*, in the Firft Scene, where he fays to
Beaufort, junior,

" But how fhall I do to fatisfy *Calon*, Monfieur ?"

Gracious in *England*, *Italy*, *Spain* or *France*,
With Form and Punctuality to receive
Stranger Embassadors.   For the General,
He's a mere Native, and it matters not
Which Way we do accost him.

   Ubal. 'Tis great Pity
That such as sit at the Helm provide no better
For the training up of the Gentry.   In my Judgment
An Academy erected, with large Pensions
To such as in a Table could set down
The Congees, Cringes, Postures, Methods, Phrase,
Proper to every Nation ——

   Ric. O, it were
An admirable Piece of Work.

   Ubal. And yet rich Fools
Throw away their Charity on Hospitals,
For Beggars and lame Soldiers, and ne'er study
The due Regard to Compliment and Courtship,
Matters of more Import, and are indeed
The Glories of a Monarchy.

   Eub. These, no doubt,
Are State Points, Gallants, I confess ; but sure,
Our Court needs no Aids this Way, since it is
A School of nothing else.   There are some of you,
Whom I forbear to name, whose coining Heads
Are the Mint of all new Fashions, that have done
More Hurt to the Kingdom by superfluous Bravery,
Which the foolish Gentry imitate, than a War,
Or a long Famine; all the Treasure, by
This foul Excess, is got into the Merchants,
Embroiderers, Silkmans, Jewellers, Taylors Hands,
And the third Part of the Land too, the Nobility
Engrossing Titles only.

   Ric. My Lord, you are bitter.

            Enter a Servant.   [*A Trumpet.*

   Serv. The General is alighted, and now enter'd.
   Ric. Were he ten Generals, I am prepar'd,
And know what I will do.   *Eub.*

Eub. Pray you what, *Ricardo?*

Ric. I'll fight at Compliment with him.

Ubal. I'll charge home too.

Eub. And that's a defperate Service, if you come off well.

Enter Ferdinand, Mathias, Baptifta, *two Captains.*

Ferd. Captain, command the Officers to keep .
The Soldier as he march'd in Rank and File,
'Till they hear farther from me.

Eub. Here's one fpeaks
In another Key: This is no canting Language .
Taught in your Academy.

Ferd. Nay, I will prefent you
To the King myfelf.

Math. A Grace beyond my Merit.

Ferd. You undervalue what I cannot fet
Too high a Price on.

Eub. With a Friend's true Heart
I gratulate your Return.

Ferd. Next to the Favour
Of the great King, I am happy in your Friendfhip.

Ubal. By Courtfhip, coarfe on both Sides.

Ferd. Pray you receive
This Stranger to your Knowledge, on my Credit,
At all Parts he deferves it.

Eub. Your Report
Is a ftrong Affurance to me.—Sir, moft welcome.

Math. This faid by you, the Reverence of your Age
Commands me to believe it.

Ric. This was pretty.
But fecond me now.—I cannot ftoop too low
To do your Excellence that due Obfervance
Your Fortune claims.

Eub. He ne'er thinks on his Virtue.

Ric. For being, as you are, the Soul of Soldiers,
And Bulwark of *Bellona.*

Ubal. The Protection

Both

Both of the Court and King.

Ric. And the sole Minion
Of mighty *Mars.*

Ubal. One that with Justice may
Increase the Number of the Worthies.

Eub. Hoy day.

Ric. It being impossible in my Arms to circle
Such Giant Worth,

Ubal. At Distance we presume
To kiss your honour'd Gauntlet.

Eub. What Reply now
Can he make to this Foppery?

Ferd. You have said,
Gallants, so much, and hitherto done so little,
That, 'till I learn to speak, and you to do,
I must take Time to thank you.

Eub. As I live,
Answer'd as I could wish.   How the Fops gape now!

Ric. This was harsh, and scurvy.

Ubal. We will be reveng'd
When he comes to court the Ladies, and laugh at him.

Eub. Nay, do your Offices, Gentlemen, and conduct
The General to the Presence.

Ric. Keep your Order.

Ubal. Make Way for the General.

[*Exeunt all but* Eubulus.

Eub. What wise Man,
That with judicious Eyes looks on a Soldier,
But must confess that Fortune's Swing is more
O'er that Profession, than all Kinds else
Of Life pursu'd by Man? They, in a State,
Are but as *Chirurgeons* to wounded Men; [13]
E'en desp'rate in their Hopes, while Pain and Anguish
Make them blaspheme, and call in vain for Death:
Their Wives and Children kiss the Chirurgeon's Knees;

---

[13] *Are but as Chirurgeons to wounded Men.*

This, I think, would read better thus:

Are but as Chirurgeons *are* to wounded Men:

Promise

Promife him Mountains, if his faving Hand
Reftore the tortur'd Wretch to former Strength.
But when grim Death, by *Æfculapius'* Art,
Is frighted from the Houfe, and Health appears
In fanguine Colours on the fick Man's Face,
All is forgot; and afking his Reward,
He's paid with Curfes, often receives Wounds
From him whofe Wounds he cur'd; fo Soldiers,
Though of more Worth and Ufe, meet the fame Fate,
As it is too apparent. I have obferv'd
In one Hue,
When horrid *Mars*, the Touch of whofe rough Hand
With Palfies fhakes a Kingdom, hath put on
His dreadful Helmet, and with Terror fills
The Place where he, like an unwelcome Gueft,
Refolves to revel; how the Lords of her, like
The Tradefman, Merchant, and litigious Pleader,
(And fuch like *Scarabs* bred i' th' Dung of Peace)
In Hope of their Protection, humbly offer
Their Daughters to their Beds, Heirs to their Service,
And wafh with Tears their Sweat, their Duft, their Scars:
But when thofe Clouds of War that menac'd
A bloody Deluge to th' affrighted State,
Are by their Breath difpers'd, and overblown,
And Famine, Blood, and Death, *Bellona's* Pages,
Whip'd from the quiet Continent to *Thrace* [14]
Soldiers, that like the foolifh Hedge Sparrow
To their own Ruin hatch this Cuckow Peace,
Are ftraight Thought burdenfome, fince want of Means,
Growing from want of Action, breeds Contempt,
And that the worft of Ills fall to their Lot,
Their Service with the Danger's foon forgot.

Enter a Servant.

Serv. The Queen, my Lord, hath made Choice of
this Room,

[14] *Whip'd from the quiet Continent to* Thrace.
Maffinger is here miftaken, for *Thrace* is upon the Continent.

To

To fee the Mafque.

Eub. I'll be Looker on,
My dancing Days are paft.

Loud Mufick as they pafs, a Song in the Praife of War;
  Ubaldo, Ricardo, Ladiflaus, Ferdinand, *and* Honoria, Mathias, Sylva, Acanthe, Baptifta, *and others.*

Ladif. This Courtefy
To a Stranger, my *Honoria*, keeps fair Rank
With all your Rarities.   After your Travel
Look on our Court Delights ; but firft from your
Relation, with erected Ears I'll hear
The Mufick of your War, which muft be fweet,
Ending in Victory.
  Ferd. Not to trouble
Your Majefties with Defcription of a Battle,
Too full of Horror for the Place, and to
Avoid Particulars which I fhould deliver,
I muft trench longer on your Patience then
My Manner will give Way to ; in a Word Sir,
It was well fought on both Sides, and almoft
With equal Fortune, it continuing doubtful
Upon whofe Tents plum'd Victory would take
Her glorious Stand : Impatient of Delay,
With the Flower of our prime Gentlemen, I charg'd
Their main Battalia, and with their Affiftance
Broke in ; but when I was almoft affur'd
That they were routed, by a Stratagem
Of the fubtil *Turk*, who opening his grofs Body,
And rallying up his Troops on either Side,
I found myfelf fo far engag'd (for I
Muft not conceal my Errors) that I knew not
Which Way with Honour to come off.
  Eub. I like
A General that tells his Faults, and is not
Ambitious to ingrofs unto himfelf
All Honour, as fome have, in which with Juftice
They could not claim a Share.

                                            Ferd.

Ferd. Being thus hemm'd in,
Their Scymitars rag'd among us, and my Horfe
Kill'd under me, I every Minute look'd for
An honourable End, and that was all
My Hope cóuld fafhion to me; circl'd thus
With Death and Horror, as one fent from Heaven
This Man of Men, with fome choice Horfe that follow'd
His brave Example, did purfue the Tract
His Sword cut for 'em, and but that I fee him,
Already blufh to hear what he being prefent,
I know would wifh unfpoken, I fhould fay, Sir,
By what he did, we boldly may believe
All that is writ of *Hector.*

   Matb. General,
Pray fpare thefe ftrange Hyperboles.

   Eub. Do not blufh
To hear a Truth; here are a Pair of Monfieurs,
Had they been in your Place, would have run away
And ne'er chang'd Countenance.

   Ubal. We have your good Word ftill.

   Eub. And fhall while you deferve it.

   Ladif. Silence, on.

   Ferd. He, as I faid, like dreadful Lightning thrown
From *Jupiter*'s Shield, difperfed the armed Gire
With which I was environed, Horfe and Man,
Shrunk under his ftrong Arm: More with his Looks
Frighted the valiant fled, with which encourag'd,
My Soldiers (like young Eglets preying under [15]
The Wings of their fierce Dame) as if from him
They took both Spirit and Fire, bravely came on.
By him I was remounted, and infpir'd
With treble Courage; and fuch as fled before,
Boldly made head again; and to confirm 'em,
It fuddenly was apparent, that the Fortune
Of the Day was ours; each Soldier and Commander
Perform'd his Part; but this was the great Wheel
By which the leffer mov'd, and all Rewards

[15] In the *Unnatural Combat Maffinger* has this fame Simile again.
                Act 1. Scene 1.

And

And Signs of Honour, as the *Civic* Garland,
The mural Wreath, the Enemies prime Horfe,
With the Generals Sword, and Armour, (the old Ho-
        nours
With which the *Romans* crown their feveral Leaders)
To him alone are proper.
    Ladif. And they fhall
Defervedly fall on him. Sit, 'tis our Pleafure,
    Ferd. Which I muft ferve, not argue.
    Hon. You are a Stranger,
But in your Service for the King, a Native.
And though a free Queen, I am bound in Duty
To cherifh Virtue wherefoe'er I find it :
This Place is yours.
    Math. It were Prefumption in me
To fit fo near you.
    Hon. Not having our Warrant.
    Ladif. Let the Mafquers enter : By the Preparation
'Tis a *French* Brawl, an apifh Imitation
Of what you really perform in Battle ;
And *Pallas* bound up in a little Volume,
Apollo with his Lute attending on her   [*Song and Dance.*
Serve for the Induction.

Enter the two Boys, one with his Lute, the other like Pallas.
    A Song in the Praife of Soldiers, efpecially being victo-
    rious : The Song ended the King goes on.

Song by *Pallas.*

> *Though we contemplate to exprefs*
>   *The Glory of your Happinefs,*
> *That by your powerful Arm have been*
>   *So true a Victor, that no Sin*
> *Could ever taint you with a Blame*
>   *To leffen your deferved Fame.*
>
> *Or though we contend to fet*
>   *Your Worth in the full Height, or get*
>   *Cæleftial*

Cælestial Singers (crown'd with Bays
    With flourishes to dress your Praise :)
You know your Conquest, but your Story
    Lives in your triumphant Glory.

Ladis. Our Thanks to all.
To the Banquet that's prepar'd to entertain 'em.
What would my best *Honoria ?*

Hon. May it please
My King, that I who by his Suffrage ever
Have had Power to command, may now intreat
An Honour· from him.

Ladis. Why should you desire
What is your own ? What e'er it be, you are
The Mistress of it.

Hon. I am happy in
Your Grant: My Suit, Sir, is, that your Commanders,
Especially this Stranger, may as I
In my Discretion shall think good, receive
What's due to their Deserts.

Ladis. What you determine
Shall know no Alteration.

Eub. The Soldier
Is like to have good Usage when he depends
Upon her Pleasure : Are all the Men so bad,
That to give Satisfaction we must have
A Woman Treasurer. Heaven help all.

Hon. With you, Sir,
I will begin, and as in my Esteem
You are most eminent, expect to have
What's fit for me to give, and you to take ;
The Favour in the quick Dispatch being double.
Go fetch my Casket, and with Speed.

Eub. The Kingdom   [*Exit* Acanthe.
Is very bare of Money, when Rewards
Issue from the Queen's Jewel House, give him Gold
And Store, no Question the Gentleman wants it.
Good Madam, what shall he do with a Hoop Ring,
And a Spark of Diamond in it ? Though you took it,
                                        Enter

Enter Acanthe.

(For the greater Honour) from your Majefty's Finger,
'Twill not increafe the Value.   He muft purchafe
Rich Suits, the gay Caparifon of Courtfhip,
Revel, and Feaft, which, the War ended, is
A Soldier's Glory; and 'tis fit that Way
Your Bounty fhould provide for him.
    Hon. You are rude,
And by your narrow Thoughts proportion mine.
What I will do now, fhall be worth the Envy
Of *Cleopatra,* open it, fee here   [Honoria *defcends,*
The Lapidaries Idol.—Gold is Trafh
And a poor Salary fit for Grooms ; wear thefe
As ftudded Stars in your Armour, and make the Sun
Look dim with Jealoufy of a greater Light
Than his Beams gild the Day with : when it is
Expos'd to View, call it *Honoria's* Gift,
The Queen *Honoria's* Gift, that loves a Soldier;
And to give Ornament and Luftre to him,
Parts freely with her own.   Yet not to take
From the Magnificence of the King, I will
Difpenfe his Bounty too, but as a Page
To wait on mine; for other Loffes take [16]
A hundred thoufand Crowns, your Hand, dear Sir,
And this fhall be thy Warrant.
                    [*Takes off the King's Signet.*
    Eub. I perceive
I was cheated in this Woman : Now fhe is
I' th' giving Vein to Soldiers, let her be proud,
And the King doat, fo fhe go on, I care not.   [*Afide.*
    Hon. This done, our Pleafure is, that all Arrears
Be paid unto the Captains, and their Troops,

---

[16] ———— *For other Loffes take*
          A hundred thoufand Crowns, &c.
This I am apt to think fhould be read thus :
          ———— *For other* Ufes *take*
          A hundred thoufand Crowns, &c.

                                    With

With a large Donative to increaſe their Zeal
For the Service of the Kingdom.

  Eub. Better ſtill;
Let Men of Arms be us'd thus: If they do not
Charge deſperately upon the Cannons Mouth,
Though the Devil roar'd, and fight like Dragons, hang
    me.
(Now they may drink Sack, but ſmall Beer, with a
    Paſſport
To beg with as they Travel, and no Money,
Turns their red Blood to Butter-milk.)

  Hon. Are you pleas'd, Sir,
With what I have done?

  Ladiſ. Yes, and thus confirm it
With this Addition of mine own: You have, Sir,
From our lov'd Queen received ſome Recompence
For your Life hazarded in the late Action;
And that we may follow her great Example [17]
In cheriſhing Valour, without Limit aſk
What you from us can wiſh.

  Matb. If it be true,
Dread Sir, as 'tis affirm'd, that every Soil,
Where he is well, is to a valiant Man
His natural Country; Reaſon may aſſure me
I ſhould fix here, where Bleſſings beyond Hope,
From you, the Spring, like Rivers flow unto me.
If Wealth were my Ambition, by the Queen
I am made rich already, to the Amazement
Of all that ſee, or ſhall hereafter read
The Story of her Bounty; if to ſpend
The Remnant of my Life in Deeds of Arms,
No Region is more fertile of good Knights,
From whom my Knowledge that Way may be better'd;

---

[17] *And that we may follow her great Example*
    In cheriſhing Valour, &c.
This Paſſage Mr. *Dodſley* reads thus:
    And that you may follow, &c.
Which I think muſt be wrong, and that the old Reading is the
right.

Then this your warlike Hungary ; if Favour,
Or Grace in Court could take me, by your Grant,
Far, far beyond my Merit, I may make
In your's a free Election ; but alas ! Sir,
I am not mine own, but by my Deſtiny
(Which I cannot reſiſt) forc'd to prefer
My Country's Smoak before the glorious Fire
With which your Bounties warm me.   All I aſk, Sir,
Though I cannot be ignorant it muſt reliſh
Of foul Ingratitude, is your gracious Licence
For my Departure.
    Ladiſ. Whither ?
    Math. To my own home, Sir, [15]
My own poor home ; which will at my Return
Grow rich by your Magnificence : I am here
But a Body without a Soul, and till I find it
In the Embraces of my conſtant Wife, and to ſet off
            that Conſtancy
In her Beauty and matchleſs Excellencies without a Rival
I am but half myſelf.
    Hon. And is ſhe then
So chaſte and fair as you infer ?
    Math. O, Madam,
Tho' it muſt argue Weakneſs in a rich Man
To ſhow his Gold before an armed Thief,
And I in praiſing of my Wife, but feed
The Fire of Luſt in others to attempt her ;
Such is my full ſail'd Confidence in her Virtue,

---

[15] *To my own home, Sir,*
    My own poor home, &c.

. I have printed this Paſſage after the old Copies, which I always follow ; but in my Opinion it would read much better thus :

Math. To my own home, Sir
        My own poor home : *That* will at my Return
        Grow rich by your Magnificence. I'm here
        A Body without Soul, *which* till I find
        In the Embraces of my conſtant Wife
        (And to ſet off that Conſtancy ; in Beauty
        And matchleſs Excellence without a Rival)
        I am but half myſelf.

                                Though

Though in my Abſence ſhe were now beſieg'd
By a ſtrong Army of laſcivious Wooers,
(And every one more expert in his Art,
Then thoſe that tempted chaſte *Penelope*;)
Though they rais'd Batteries by prodigal Gifts,
By amorous Letters, Vows made for her Service,
With all the Engines wanton Appetite
Could mount to ſhake the Fortreſs of her Honour,
Here, here is my Aſſurance ſhe holds out,

[*Kiſſes the Picture.*]

And is impregnable.

Hon. What's that?

Math. Her fair Figure.

Ladiſ. As I live an excellent Face!

Hon. You have ſeen a better.

Ladiſ. I, ne'er except yours; nay frown not ſweeteſt;
(The *Cyprian* Queen compared to you, in my
Opinion, is a Negro;) as you order'd,
I'll ſee the Soldiers paid, and in my Abſence
Pray you uſe your powerful Arguments to ſtay
This Gentleman in our Service.

Hon. I will do
My Part.

Ladiſ. On to the Camp.

[*Exeunt* Ladiſlaus, Ferdinand, Eubulus, Baptiſta, *Captains.*

Hon. I am full of Thoughts.
And ſomething there is here I muſt give Form to,
Tho' yet an Embrion, you, Signiors,
Have no Buſineſs with the Soldier, as I take it,
You are for other Warfare; quit the Place,
But be within call.

Ric. Employment on my Life, Boy.

Ubal. If it lie in our Road, we are made forever.

[*Exeunt* Ubaldo, Ricardo.

Hon. You may perceive the King is no Way tainted
With the Diſeaſe of Jealouſy, ſince he leaves me
Thus private with you.

Math. It were in him, Madam,

L 2   A

A Sin unpardonable to diftruft fuch Purenefs,
Though I were an *Adonis*.

Hon. I prefume
He neither does, nor dares : And yet the Story
Delivered of you by the General,
With your Heroick Courage (which finks deeply
Into a knowing Woman's Heart) befides
Your promifing Prefence, might beget fome Scruple,
In a meaner Man : But more of this hereafter ;
I'll take another Theme now, and conjure you
By the Honours you have won, and by the Love
Sacred to your dear Wife, to anfwer truly
To what I fhall demand.

Math. You need not ufe
Charms to this Purpofe, Madam.

Hon. Tell me then,
Being yourfelf affur'd 'tis not in Man
To fully with one Spot th' immaculate Whitenefs
Of your Wife's Honour, if you have not fince
The Gordion of your Love was tied by Marriage,
Play'd falfe with her ?

Math. By the Hopes of Mercy, never.

Hon. It may be, not frequenting the Converfe
Of handfome Ladies, you were never tempted,
And fo your Faith's untried yet.

Math. Surely, Madam,
I am no Woman Hater, I have been
Received to the Society of the beft
And faireft of our Climate, and have met with
No common Entertainment, yet ne'er felt
The leaft Heat that Way.

Hon. Strange! and do you think ftill,
The Earth can fhow no Beauty that can drench
In *Lethe* all Remembrance of the Favour
You now bear to your own ?

Math. Nature muft find out
Some other Mould to fafhion a new Creature
Fairer then her *Pandora*, e'er I prove
Guilty or in my Wifhes, or my Thoughts,
To my *Sophia*.

Hon.

Hon. Sir, confider better;
Not one in our whole Sex?

Math. I am conftant to
My Refolution.

Hon. But dare you ftand
The Oppofition, and bind yourfelf
By Oath for the Performance?

Math. My Faith elfe
Had but a weak Foundation.

Hon. I take hold
Upon your Promife, and enjoin your Stay
For one Month here——

Math. I am caught.

Hon. And if I do not
Produce a Lady in that Time that fhall
Make you confefs your Error, I fubmit
Myfelf to any Penalty you fhall pleafe
T' impofe upon me: In the mean Space write
To your chafte Wife, acquaint her with your Fortune;
The Jewels that were mine you may fend to her,
For better Confirmation, I'll provide you
Of' trufty Meffengers: But how far diftant is fhe?

Math. A Day's hard riding.

Hon. There's no retiring,
I'll bind you to your Word.

Math. Well, fince there is
No Way to fhun it, I will ftand the Hazard,
And inftantly make ready my Difpatch:
——'Till theh, I'll leave your Majefty.   [*Exit Mathias.*

Hon. How I burft
With Envy, that there Lives, befides myfelf,
One fair and loyal Woman, 'twas the End
Of my Ambition, to be recorded
The only Wonder of the Age; and fhall I
Give way to a Competitor? Nay more,
To add to my Affliction, the Affurances
That I plac'd in my Beauty have deceiv'd me:
I thought one amorous Glance of mine could bring
All Hearts to my Subjection; but this Stranger,

Unmov'd

Unmov'd as Rocks, contemns me. But I cannot
Sit down fo with my Honour : I will gain
A double Victory, by working him
To my Defire, and taint her in her Honour
Or lofe myfelf. I have read, that fome Time Poifon
Is ufeful ; to fupplant her I'll employ
With any Coft, *Ubaldo* and *Ricardo*,
Two noted Courtiers, of approved Cunning
In all the Windings of Lufts Labyrinth ;
(And in corrupting him I will outgo
Nero's Poppæa : If he fhut his Ears,
Againft my Syren Notes, I'll boldly fwear
Ulyffes lives again ; or that I have found
A frozen Cynic, cold in Spite of all
Allurements ; one, whom Beauty cannot move,
Nor foftest Blandifhments entice to Love.

[Exit Honoria,

The End of the Second Act,

ACT III. SCENE I.

Enter Hilario,

THIN, thin, Provifion ! I am dieted
 Like one fet to watch Hawks ; and to keep me
  waking,
My croaking Guts make a perpetual 'Larum.
Here I ftand Centinel ; and though I fright
Beggars from my Lady's Gate, in Hope to have
A greater Share, I find my Commons mend not.
(I look'd this Morning in my Glafs, the River ;
And there appear'd a Fifh, call'd a poor *John*,
Cut with a lenten Face in my own Likenefs ;
And it feem'd to fpeak, and fay, Goodmorrow Conzen!
No Man comes this Way but has a Fling at me :

A

A Chirurgeon paffing by afk'd, at what Rate
I would fell myfelf? I anfwered, for what Ufe?
To make, faid he, a living Anatomy,
And fet thee up in our Hall, for thou art tranfparent
Without Diffection) and indeed he had Reafon;
For I am fcour'd with this poor Porridge to nothing.
They fay that Hunger dwells in the Camp; but till
My Lord returns, or certain Tidings of him,
He will not part with me.—But Sorrow's dry,
And I muft drink howfover.

Enter Ubaldo, *and* Ricardo, Guide.

Guide. That is her Caftle
Upon my certain Knowledge.
Ubal. Our Horfes held out
To my Defire. I am a Fire to be at it.
Ric. Take the Jades for thy Reward; before I part
  hence,
I hope to be better carried. Give me the Cabinet:
So, leave us now.
Guide. Food Fortune to you Gallants. [*Exit* Guide.
Ubal. Being joint Agents in a Defign, of Truft too,
For the Service of the Queen and our own Pleafure,
Let us proceed with Judgment.
Ric. If I take not
This Fort at the firft Affault, make me an Eunuch,
So I may have Precedence.
Ubal. On no Terms.
We are both to play one Prize; he that works beft
I' the fearching this Mine, fhall carry it
Without Contention.
Ric. Make you your Approaches,
As I directed.
Ubal. I need no Inftruction;
I work not on your Anvil. I'll give Fire
With mine own Linftock; if the Powder be danck,
The Devil rend the Touch-hole. Who have we here?
What Skeleton's this?

Ric.

Ric. A Ghoft; or the Image of Famine.
Where doft thou dwell?

Hilario. Dwell Sir? My Dwelling is
I' th' Highway. That goodly Houfe was once
My Habitation; but I am banifhed,
And cannot be call'd home, 'till News arrive
Of the good Knight *Mathias.*

Ric. If that will
Reftore thee, thou art fafe.

Ubal. We come from him,
With Prefents to his Lady.

Hil. But are you fure
He is in Health?

Ric. Never fo well: Conduct us
To the Lady.

Hil. Though a poor Snake, I will leap
Out of my Skin for Joy. Break, Pitcher, break;
And Wallet, late my Cupboard, I bequeath thee
To the next Beggar; thou red Herring, fwim
To the red Sea again. Methinks I am already
Knuckle Deep in the Flefh-pots; and, though waking,
 dream
Of Wine and Plenty.

Ric. What's the Myftery
Of this ftrange Paffion?

Hil. My Belly, Gentlemen
Will not give me Leave to tell you. When I have
 brought you
To my Ladies Prefence, I am difenchanted.
There you fhall know all. Follow: If I outftrip you,
Know I run for my Belly.

Ubal. A mad Fellow.   [*Exeunt,*

SCENE II.

Enter Sophia, Corifca.

Soph. Do not again delude me.

Corf. If I do, fend me a grazing with my Fellow *Hilario,*

I

I ftood, as you commanded, in the Turret
Obferving all that pafs'd by: And even now
I did difcern a Pair of Cavaliers,
For fuch their Outfide fpoke them, with their Guide
Difmounting from their Horfes; they faid fomething
To our hungry Centinel, that made him caper
And frifk i' th' Air for Joy: And to confirm this,
See, Madam, they're in View.

Enter Hilario, Ubaldo, Ricardo.

Hil. News from my Lord! ·
Tidings of Joy! thefe are no Counterfeits,
But Knights indeed. Dear Madam fign my Pardon,
That I may feed again, and pick up my Crumbs:
I have had a long Faft of it.
 Soph. Eat, I forgive thee.
 Hil. O comfortable Words! Eat, I forgive thee!
And if in this I do not foon obey you,
And ram in to the Purpofe, billet me again
I' th' Highway. Butler and Cook be ready,
For I enter like a Tyrant.   [*Exit* Hilario.
 Ubal. Since mine Eyes
Were never happy in fo fweet an Object,
Without Enquiry I prefume you are
The Lady of the Houfe, and fo falute you.
 Ric. This Letter, with thefe Jewels from your Lord,
Warrant my Boldnefs, Madam.
 Ubal. In being a Servant
To fuch rare Beauty, you muft needs deferve
This Courtefy from a Stranger.   [*To* Corifca,
           - *falutes her.*
 Ric. You are ftill
Before-hand with me. Pretty one, I defcend ·
To take the Height of your Lip; and if I mifs
In the Altitude, hereafter, if you pleafe,
I will make ufe of my *Jacob*'s Staff.
    [Sophia *having in the Interim read the Letter,*
        and open'd the Cafket.
          Corif.

Corif. Thefe Gentlemen
Have certainly had good Breeding, as it appears
By their neat Kiffing, they hit me fo pat on the Lips
At the firft Sight.

Soph. Heaven, in thy Mercy, make me
Thy thankful Handmaid, for this boundlefs Blefling,
In thy Goodnefs fhower'd upon me.

Ubal. I do not like
This fimple Devotion in her ; it is feldom
Practis'd among my Miftreffes.

Ric. Or mine.
Would they kneel to I know not who, for the Poffeffion
Of fuch ineftimable Wealth, before
They thank'd the Bringers of it ? The poor Lady
Does want Inftruction ; but I'll be her Tutor,
And read her another Leffon.

Soph. If I have
Shown Want of Manners, Gentlemen, in my Slownefs
To pay the Thanks I owe you for your Travel,
To do my Lord and me (howe'er unworthy
Of fuch a Benefit) this noble Favour :
Impute it, in your Clemency, to the Excefs
Of Joy that overwhelm'd me.——

Ric. She fpeaks well.

Ubal. Polite and courtly.

Soph. And howe'er it may
Increafe th' Offence, to trouble you with more
Demands touching my Lord, before I have
Invited you to tafte fuch as the Coarfenefs
Of my poor Houfe can offer ; pray you convine
On my weak Tendernefs, though I intreat
To learn from you fomething he hath, it may be,
In his Letter left unmention'd.

Ric. I can only
Give you Affurance that he is in Health,
Grac'd by the King and Queen.

Ubal. And in the Court
With Admiration look'd on.

Ric. You muft therefore

Put

Put off thefe Widow's Garments, and appear
Like to yourfelf.

   Ubal. And entertain all Pleafures
Your Fortune marks out for you.

   Ric. There are other
Particular Privacies, which on Occafion
I will deliver to you.

   Soph. You oblige me
To your Service ever.

   Ric. Good! your Service; 'mark that.

   Soph. In the mean Time, by your Acceptance make
My ruftick Entertainment relifh of
The Curioufnefs of the Court.

   Ubal. Your Looks, fweet Madam,
Cannot but make each Difh a Feaft.

   Soph. It fhall be
Such; in the Freedom of my Will to pleafe you.
I'll fhew the Way: This is too great an Honour
From fuch brave Guefts, to me fo mean an Hoftefs.
                            [Exeunt.

SCENE III.

Enter Acanthe *to four or five with Vizards.*

   Acan. You know your Charge; give it Action, and
           expect
Rewards beyond your Hopes.

   1 *Viz.* If we but eye 'em,
They are ours, I warrant you.

   2 *Viz.* May we not afk why
We are put upon this?

   Acan. Let that ftop your Mouth,
And learn more Manners, Groom. 'Tis upon the Hour
In which they ufe to walk here: When you have 'em
In your Power, with Violence carry them to the Place
Where I appointed: There I will expect you.
Be bold, and careful.   *[Exit* Acanthe.

                                 Enter

Enter Mathias *and* Baptifta.

1 *Viz.* Thefe are they.

2 *Viz.* Are you fure?

1 *Viz.* Am I fure I am myfelf?

2 *Viz.* Seize on him ftrongly; if he have but Means
To draw his Sword, 'tis ten to one we fmart for't.
Take all Advantages.

Math. I cannot guefs
What her Intents are; but her Carriage was
As I but now related.

Bapt. Your Affurance
In the Conftancy of your Lady, is the Armour
That muft defend you. Where's the Picture?

Math. Here,
And no Way alter'd.

Bapt. If fhe be not perfect,
There is no Truth in Art.

Math. By this, I hope,
She hath receiv'd my Letters.

Bapt. Without Queftion.
Thefe Courtiers are rank Riders, when they are
To vifit a handfome Lady.

Math. Lend me your Ear.
One Piece of her Entertainment will require
Your deareft Privacy.

1 *Viz.* Now they ftand fair,
Upon 'em.

Math. Villains!

1 *Viz.* Stop their Mouths. We come not
To try your Valours. Kill him, if he offer
To open his Mouth.—We have you.—'Tis in vain
To make Refiftance.—Mount 'em, and away.

[*Exeunt.*

SCENE

SCENE IV.

Enter Servants with Lights, Ladiſlaus, Ferdinand, Eubulus.

Ladiſ. 'Tis late. Go to your Reſt; But do not envy
The Happineſs I draw near to.
    Eub. If you enjoy it
The moderate Way, the Sport yields, I confeſs,
A pretty Titilation; but too much of't
Will bring you on your Knees. In my younger Days
I was myſelf a Gameſter; and I found
By ſad Experience, there is no ſuch Soker
As a young ſpongy Wife; ſhe keeps a thouſand
Horſe Leeches in her Box, and the Thieves will ſuck
    out
Both Blood and Marrow! I feel a Kind of Cramp
In my Joints when I think on't. But it may be Queen,
And ſuch a Queen as yours is, has the Art ——
    Ferd. You take Leave
To talk, my Lord.
    Ladiſ. He may, ſince he can do nothing.
    Eub. If you ſpend this way too much of your royal
E'er long we may be Puefellows.   [Stock,
    Ladiſ. The Door ſhut!
Knock gently; harder. So, here comes her Woman.
Take off my Gown.

Enter Acanthe.

    Acan. My Lord, the Queen by me
This Night deſires your Pardon.
    Ladiſ. How, *Acanthe!*
I come by her Appointment; 'twas her Grant;
The Motion was her own.
    Acan. It may be, Sir;
But by her Doctors ſhe is ſince advis'd,
For her Health ſake, to forbear.

                            Eub.

Eub. I do not like
This phyſical Letchery; the old downright Way
Is worth a thouſand of 't.

Ladiſ. Prythee, *Acanthe*,
Mediate for me.

Eub. O the Fiends of Hell!
Would any Man bribe his Servant, to make way
To his own Wife? If this be the Court State,
Shame fall on ſuch as uſe it.

Acan. By this Jewel,
This Night I dare not move her; but to-morrow
I will watch all Occaſion.

Ladiſ. Take this
To be mindful of me.   [*Exit* Acanthe.

Eub. 'Slight, I thought a King
Might have taken up any Woman at the King's Price:
And muſt he buy his own, at a dearer Rate
Than a Stranger in a Brothel?

Ladiſ. What is that
You mutter, Sir?

Eub. No Treaſon to your Honour:
I'll ſpeak it out, though it anger you: If you pay for
Your lawful Pleaſure, in ſome Kind, great Sir,
What do you make the Queen? Cannot you clicket
Without a Fee? or when ſhe has a Suit for you to grant?

Ferd. O hold, Sir! [19]

Ladiſ. Off with his Head.

Eub. Do when you pleaſe; you but blow out a Taper
That would light your Underſtanding, and in Care of 't
Is burnt down to the Socket. Be as you are, Sir,

---

[19] *Ferd. O bold, Sir,* &c.

This, I think, ſhould be read thus:

 Ferd. O hold, Sir!
 Ladiſ. Off with 's Head.
 Eub. Do when you pleaſe;
   You but blow out a Taper that would light
   Your Underſtanding, and is in Care of 't
   Burnt down to th' Socket. Be as you are, Sir,
   An abſolute, &c.

An

An abfolute Monarch: It did fhew more King-like
In thofe libidinous *Cæfars*, that compell'd
Matrons and Virgins of all Ranks to bow
Unto their rav'nous Lufts ; and did admit
Of more Excufe than I can urge for you,
That flave yourfelf to th' imperious Humour
Of a proud Beauty.

    Ladif. Out of my Sight.

    Eub. I will, Sir,
Give Way to your furious Paffion : But when Reafon
Hath got the better of it, I much hope
The Counfel that offends now, will deferve
Your royal Thanks. Tranquillity of Mind
Stay with you, Sir.—I do begin to doubt
There's fomething more in the Queen's Strangenefs than
Is yet difclos'd ; and I'll find it out,
Or lofe myfelf in the Search.   [*Exit* Eubulus.

    Ferd. Sure he is honeft,
And from your Infancy hath truly ferv'd you :
Let that plead for him, and impute this Harfhnefs
To the Frowardnefs of his Age.

    Ladif. I am much troubled,
And do begin to ftagger. *Ferdinand*, good Night!
To-morrow vifit us. Back to our own Lodgings.
                        [*Exeunt.*

SCENE V.

Enter Acanthe, *the Vizarded Servants*, Mathias, Baptifta.

    Acan. You have done bravely. Lock this in that
        Room,   [*They carry off* Baptifta.
There let him ruminate ; I'll anon unhood him :
The other muft ftay here. As foon as I
Have quit the Place, give him the Liberty
And Ufe of his Eyes ; that done, difperfe yourfelves
As privately as you can : But, on your Lives,
No Word of what hath pafs'd.   [*Exit* Acanthe.

    1 *Viz.* If I do, fell
My Tongue to a Tripe-Wife.—Come, unbind his Arms;
                              You

You are now at your own Difpofure, and however
We us'd you roughly, I hope you will find here
Such Entertainment as will give you Caufe
To thank us for the Service : and fo we leave you.

[*Exeunt Servants.*

Math. If I am in a Prifon, 'tis a neat one.
What *Œdipus* can refolve this Riddle? Ha!
I never gave juft Caufe to any Man
Bafely to plot againft my Life.—But what is
Become of my true Friend? for him I fuffer
More than myfelf.

Acan. Remove that idle Fear;   [*From behind.*
He's fafe as you are.

Math. Whofoe'er thou art,
For him I thank thee. I cannot imagine
Where I fhould be: Though I have read the Table
Of Errant-knighthood, ftuff'd with the Relations
Of magical Enchantments; yet I am not
So fottifhly credulous to believe the Devil
Hath that Way Power. Ha! Mufick!

Mufick above, a Song of Pleafure.

The blufhing Rofe and purple Flower,
    Let grow too long, are foonest blasted.
Dainty Fruits, though fweet, will four,
    And rot in Ripenefs, left untasted.
Yet here is one more fweet than thefe;
The more you tafte, the more fhe'll pleafe.

Beauty, tho' inclos'd with Ice,
    Is a Shadow chafte as rare:
Then how much thofe Sweets intice,
    That have Iffue full as fair!
Earth cannot yield from all her Powers,
One equal for Dame Venus' *Bowers.*

A Song too! Certainly, be it he or fhe
That owns this Voice, it hath not been acquainted

With

With much Affliction. Whofoe'er you are
That do inhabit here, if you have Bodies,
And are not mere aërial Forms, appear,

Enter Honoria *mafk'd.*

And make me know your End with me. Moft ftrange!
What have I conjur'd up ? · Sure, if this be
A Spirit, 'tis no damn'd one. What a Shape's here!
Then with what Majefty it moves. If *Juno*
Were now to keep her State among the Gods,
And *Hercules* to be made again her Gueft,
She could not put on a more glorious Habit,
Though her Handmaid, *Iris*, lent her various Colours,
Or could *Oceanus* ravifh'd from the deep,
All Jewels fhipwreck'd in it. As you have
Thus far made known yourfelf, if that your Face
Have not too much Divinity about it
For mortal Eyes to gaze on, perfect what
You have begun, with Wonder and Amazement
To my aftonifh'd Senfes. How! the Queen! [*Kneels.*
                            [*She pulls off her Mafk.*
   Hon. Rife, Sir, and hear my Reafons in Defence
Of the Rape (for fo you may conceive) which I
By my Inftruments made upon you. You, perhaps,
May think what you have fuffer'd for my Luft
Is a common Practice with me; but I call
Thofe ever fhining Lamps, and their great Maker,
As Witneffes of my Innocence : I ne'er look'd on
A Man but your beft felf, on whom I ever
(Except the King) vouchfaf'd an Eye of Favour.
   Matb. The King, indeed, and only fuch a King,
Deferves your Rarities, Madam ; and, but he,
'Twere giant-like Ambition in any
In his Wifhes only to prefume to tafte
The Nectar of your Kiffes ; or to feed
His Appetite with that Ambrofia, due
And proper to a Prince ; and what binds more,
A lawful Hufband. For myfelf, great Queen,

I am

I am a Thing obfcure, disfurnifh'd of
All Merit that can raife me higher than
In my moft humble Thankfulnefs for your Bounty,
To hazard my Life for you, and that Way
I am moft ambitious.

   Hon. I defire no more
Than what you promife.   If you dare expofe,
Your Life, as you profefs, to do me Service,
How can it better be employ'd, than in
Preferving mine ? which only you can do,
And muft do with the Danger of your own.
A defperate Danger too ! If private Men
Can brook no Rivals in what they affect,
But to the Death purfue fuch as invade
What Law makes their Inheritance; the King,
To whom you know I am dearer than his Crown,
His Health, his Eyes, his After-hopes, with all
His prefent Bleffings, muft fall on that Man
Like dreadful Lightning, that is won by Prayers,
Threats, or Rewards, to ftain his Bed, or make
His hop'd-for Iffue doubtful.

   Math. If you aim
At what I more than fear you do, the Reafons
Which you deliver fhould in Judgment rather
Deter me, than invite a Grant, with my
Affured Ruin.

   Hon. True, if that you were
Of a cold Temper, one whom Doubt, or Fear,
In the moft horrid Forms they could put on,
Might teach to be ingrateful.   Your Denial
To me that have deferv'd fo much, is more,
If it can have Addition.

   Math. I know not
What your Commands are.

   Hon. Have you fought fo well
Among arm'd Men, yet cannot guefs what Lifts
You are to enter, when you are in private
With a willing Lady ? One, that to enjoy
Your Company, this Night deny'd the King

Accefs

Accefs to what's his own. If you will prefs me
To fpeak in plainer Language——
　Math. Pray you forbear;
I would I did not underftand too much
Already. By your Words I am inftructed
To credit that, which, not confirm'd by you,
Had bred Sufpicion in me of Untruth,
Though an Angel had affirm'd it. But fuppofe
That, cloy'd with Happinefs (which is ever built
On virtuous Chaftity) in the Wantonnefs
Of Appetite you defire to make Trial
Of the falfe Delights propos'd by vicious Luft;
Among ten thoufand, every way more able
And apter to be wrought on, fuch as owe you
Obedience, being your Subjects, why fhould you
Make Choice of me, a Stranger?
　Hon. Though yet Reafon
Was ne'er admitted in the Court of Love,
I'll yield you one unanfwerable. As I urg'd
In our laft private Conference, you have
A pretty promifing Prefence; but there are
Many in Limbs and Feature who may take
That Way the Right-hand File of you: Befides,
Your *May* of Youth is paft, and the Blood fpent
By Wounds (though bravely taken) render you
Difabled for Love's Service; and that Valour
Set off with better Fortune, which it may be
Swells you above your Bounds, is not the Hook
That hath caught me, good Sir: I need no Champion
With his Sword to guard my Honour or my Beauty;
In both I can defend myfelf, and live
My own Protection.
　Math. If thefe Advocates,
The beft that can plead for me, have no Power;
What elfe can you find in me, that may tempt you
With irrecoverable Lofs unto yourfelf
To be a Gainer from me?
　Hon. You have, Sir,
A Jewel of fuch matchlefs Worth and Luftre,

As does difdain Comparifon, and darkens
All that is rare in other Men ; and that
I muft, or win, or leffen.

Math. You heap more
Amazement on me ! What am I poffefs'd of
That you can covet ? Make me underftand it,
If it have a Name ?

Hon. Yes, an imagin'd one ;
But is in Subftance nothing, being a Garment
Worn out of Fafhion, and long fince given o'er
By the Court and Country ; 'tis your Loyalty,
And Conftancy to your Wife ; 'tis that I dote on,
And does deferve my Envy ; and that Jewel,
Or by fair Play, or foul, I muft win from you.

Math. Thefe are mere Contraries. If you love me,
   Madam,
For my Conftancy, why feek you to deftroy it ?
In my keeping, it preferves me worth your Favour !
Or if it be a Jewel of that Value,
As you with labour'd Rhetorick would perfuade me,
What can you ftake againft it ?

Hon. A Queen's Fame,
And equal Honour.

Math. So, whoever wins,
Both fhall be Lofers.

Hon. That is what I aim at.
Yet on the Dye I lay my Youth, my Beauty,
This moift Palm, this foft Lip, and thofe Delights
Darknefs fhould only judge of ! Do you find 'em
Infectious in the Trial, that you ftart
As frighted with their Touch ?

Math. Is it in Man
To refift fuch ftrong Temptations ?

Hon. He begins
To waver.   [*Afide.*

Math. Madam, as you are gracious,
Grant this fhort Night's Deliberation to me,
And with the rifing Sun from me you fhall
Receive full Satisfaction.

                                             Hon.

Hon. Though Extreams
Hate all Delay, I will deny you nothing,
This Key will bring you to your Friend; you are both
    fafe:
And all Things ufeful that could be prepar'd
For one I love and honour, wait upon you.
Take Counfel of your Pillow, fuch a Fortune
As with Affection's fwifteft Wings flies to you,
Will not be often tendred.   [*Exit* Honoria.

Math How my Blood
Rebels! I now could call her back—and yet
There's fomething ftays me: If the King had tender'd
Such Favours to my Wife, 'tis to be doubted
They had not been refus'd: But, being a Man,
I fhould not yield firft, or prove an Example
For her Defence of Frailty. By this, *fans* Queftion,
She's tempted too; and here I may examine
                    [*Look on the Picture.*
How fhe holds out. She's ftill the fame, the fame
Pure Chryftal Rock of Chaftity! Perifh all
Allurements that may alter me! The Snow
Of her fweet Coldnefs, hath extinguifhed quite
The Fire that but even now began to flame:
And I by her confirm'd, Rewards, nor Titles,
Nor certain Death from the refufed Queen,
Shall fhake my Faith; fince I refolve to be
Loyal to her, as fhe is true to me.   [*Exit* Mathias.

SCENE VI.

Enter Ubaldo, Ricardo.

Ubal. What we fpake on the Volley begins to work,
We have laid a good Foundation
    Ric. Build it up,
Or elfe 'tis nothing: You have by Lot the Honour
Of the firft Affault; but, as it is condition'd,
Obferve the Time proportion'd; I'll not part with
My

My Share in the Atchievement; when I whiftle,
Or hem, fall off.

Enter Sophia.

Ubal. She comes.   Stand by, I'll watch
My Opportunity.
   Soph. I find myfelf
Strangely diftracted with the various Stories,
Now well, now ill, then doubtfully, by my Guefts
Deliver'd of my Lord : And like poor Beggars
That in their Dreams find Treafure, by Reflection
Of a wounded Fancy make it queftionable
Whither they fleep, or not; yet tickl'd with
Such a phantaftick Hope of Happinefs,
Wifh they may never wake : In fome fuch Meafure,
Incredulous of what I fee, and touch,
As 'twere a fading Apparition, I
Am ftill perplex'd, and troubled ; and when moft
Confirm'd 'tis true, a curious Jealoufy
To be affur'd, by what Means, and from whom,
Such a Mafs of Wealth was firft deferv'd, then gotten,
Cunningly fteals into me.   I have practis'd,
For my certain Refolution, with thefe Courtiers ;
Promifing private Conference to either.
And at this Hour, if in Search of the Truth,
I hear, or fay, more than becomes my Virtue,
Forgive me my *Mathias*.
   Ubal. Now I make in.
Madam, as you commanded, I attend
Your Pleafure.
   Soph. I muft thank you for the Favour.
   Ubal. I am no ghoftly Father ; yet if you have
Some Scruples, touching your Lord, you would be re-
     folv'd of,
I am prepar'd.
   Soph. But will you take your Oath,
To anfwer truly ?
   Ubal. (On the Hem of your Smock if you pleafe,

A

A Vow I dare not break, it being a Book
I would gladly fwear on.)

Soph. To fpare, Sir, that Trouble,
I'll take your Word, which in a Gentleman
Should be of equal Value. Is my Lôrd, then,
In fuch Grace with the Queen?

Ubal. You fhould beft know
By what you have found from him, whether he can
Deferve Grace or no.

Soph. What Grace do you mean?

Ubal. That fpecial Grace (if you'll have It)
He laboured fo hard for between a Pair of Sheets
On your wedding Night, when your Ladyfhip
Loft you know what.

Soph. Fie, be more modeft,
Or I muft leave you.

Ubal. I would tell a Truth
As cleanly as I could, and yet the Subject
Makes me run out a little.

Soph. You would put now
A foolifh Jealoufy in my Head, my Lord
Hath gotten a new Miftrefs.

Ubal. One! a hundred:
But under Seal I fpeak it; I prefume
Upon your Silence, it being for your Profit,
(They talk of *Hercules'* Back for fifty in a Night; ²⁰
'Twas weil; but yet to yours he was a Pidler:
Such a Soldier, and Courtier never came
To *Alba regalis*, the Ladies run mad for him,
And there is fuch Contention among 'em

²⁰ *Thy Talk of* Hercules' *Back for fifty in a Night,*
 'Twas well, &c.

This Freedom of Language, I am afraid, will be apt to difpleafe many of *Maffinger's* Readers; who, perhaps, will think that fuch Scenes had better have been quite omitted: But as that would not be confiftent with my Plan, I fhall urge in Defence, that it was the Vice of the Age he lived in; and that *Maffinger* was perhaps, obliged more from Neceffity than Inclination to comply with the Tafte of his Au-dience, in order to fecure his Pieces a favourable Reception.

K 4

Who

Who fhall ingrofs him wholly, that the like
Was never heard of.)

Soph. Are they handfome Women?

Ubal. Fie, no, courfe Mammets, and what's worfe
    they are old too
Some fifty, fome threefcore, and they pay dear for't,
Believing, that he carries a Powder in his Breeches
Will make 'em young again, and thefe fuck fhrewdly,

Ric. Sir I muft fetch you off.   [*Whiftles.*

Ubal. I could tell you Wonders
Of the Cures he has done, but a Bufinefs of Import
Calls me away; but that difpatch'd I will
Be with you prefently.   [*He fteps afide.*

Soph. There is fomething more
In this then bare Sufpicion,

Ric. Save you, Lady:
Now you look like yourfelf! I have not look'd on
A Lady more compleat, yet have feen a Madam
Wear a Garment of this Fafhion, of the fame Stuff too,
One juft of your Dimenfions; fat the Wind there Boy?

Soph. What Lady, Sir?

Ric. Nay, nothing; and methinks
I fhould know this Ruby: Very good; 'tis the fame.
This Chain of orient Pearl, and this Diamond too,
Have been worn before; but much Good may they do
    you;
(Strength to the Gentleman's Back, he toil'd hard for
    'em,)
Before he got 'em.

Soph. Why? How were they gotten? [Ubaldo *hems.*

Ric. Not in the Field with his Sword, upon my Life,
He may thank his clofe Stillet too. Plague upon it;
Run the Minutes fo faft? Pray excufe my Manners
I left a Letter in my Chamber Window,
Which I would not have feen on any Terms; Fie on it,
Forgetful as I am; but I'll ftrait attend you.

        [Ricardo *fteps afide.*

Soph. This is ftrange; his Letters faid thefe Jewels
    were

                Prefented

Prefented him by the Queen, as a Reward
For his good Service, and the Trunks of Clothes
That followed them this laft Night, with Hafte made up
By his Direction.

Enter Ubaldo.

Ubal. I was telling you
Of Wonders, Madam.
Soph. If you are fo fkilful,
Without Premeditation anfwer me,
Know you this Gown, and thefe rich Jewels?
Ubal. Heaven!
How Things will come out! but that I fhould offend
    you,
And wrong my more then noble Friend
Your Hufband (for we are fworn Brothers) in the Dif-
    covery
Of his neareft Secrets, I could——
Soph. By the Hope of Favour
That you have from me, out with it.
Ubal. 'Tis a potent Spell,
I cannot refift; why I will tell you, Madam,
And to how many feveral Women you are
Beholding for your Bravery,—this was
The wedding Gown of *Paulina*, a rich Strumpet,
Worn but a Day, when fhe married old *Gonzage*,
And left off trading.
Soph. O my Heart!
Ubal. This Chain
Of Pearl was a great Widow's that invited
Your Lord to a Mafque, and the Weather proving foul,
He lodg'd in her Houfe all Night, and merry they were;
But how he came by it I know not.
Soph, Perjur'd Man!
Ubal, This Ring was *Julietta*'s; a fine Piece,
But very good at the Sport. This Diamond
Was Madam *Acanthe*'s, given him for a Song
Prick'd in a private Arbour, as fhe faid,

(When

(When the Queen afk'd for it,) and fhe heard him fing
    too,
And danc'd to his Hornpipe, or there are Liars abroad.
There are other Toys about you
The fame Way purchas'd, but parallel'd
With thefe not worth the Relation.
You are happy in a Hufband; never Man
Made better Ufe of his Strength, would you have him
    wafte,
His Body away for nothing? If he holds out,
There's not an embroider'd Petticoat in the Court
But fhall be at your Service.

    Soph. I commend him:
It is a thriving Trade; but pray you leave me
A little to myfelf.

    Ubal. You may command
Your Servant, Madam, fhe's ftung unto the quick, Lad.

    Ric. I did my Part; if this work not, hang me;
Let her fleep as well as fhe can to Night, To-morrow
We'll mount new Batteries.

    Ubal. And till then leave her.

                        [*Exit* Ubaldo, Ricardo.

    Soph. You Powers, that take into your Care the Guard
Of Innocence, aid me; for I am Creature,
So forfeited to Defpair, Hope cannot fancy
A Ranfom to redeem me, I begin
To waver in my Faith, and make it doubtful,
Whither the Saints that were canoniz'd for
Their Holinefs of Life, finn'd not in Secret,
Since my *Mathias* is fall'n from his Virtue
In fuch an open Fafhion. Could it be elfe,
That fuch a Hufband, fo devoted to me,
So vow'd to Temperance; for lafcivious Hire,
Should proftitute himfelf to common Harlots,
Old and deform'd too, waft for this he left me?
And on a feign'd Pretence for want of Means
To give me Ornament? Or to bring home
Difeafes to me? Suppofe thefe are falfe,
And luftful Goats, if he were true and right

                                      Why

Why ſtays he ſo long from 'me, being made rich
And that the only Reaſon why he left me?
No, he is loſt; and I ſhall wear the Spoils,
And Salaries of Luſt? They cleave unto me
Like *Neſſus'* poiſon'd Shirt. No, in my Rage
I'll tear 'em off, and from my Body waſh
The Venom with my Tears. Have I no Spleen
Nor Anger of a Woman? Shall he build
Upon my Ruins, and I, unreveng'd,
Deplore his Falſhood? No, with the ſame Traſh
For which he had diſhonour'd me, I'll purchaſe
A juſt Revenge. I am not yet ſo much
In Debt to Years, nor ſo miſhap'd, that all
Should fly from my Embraces. Chaſtity,
Thou only art a Name, and I renounce thee,
I am now a Servant to Voluptuouſneſs;
Wantons of all Degrees and Faſhions, welcome;
You ſhall be entertain'd, and if I ſtray
Let him condemn himſelf, that led the Way.　[*Exit.*

The End of the Third Act.

ACT IV.　SCENE I.

Enter Mathias *and* Baptiſta.

Bapt. WE are in a deſperate Straight; there's no
　　　Evaſion
Nor Hope left to come of, but by your yielding
To the Neceſſity; you muſt feign a Grant
To her violent Paſſion, or
　Math. What, my *Baptiſta?*
　Bapt. We are but dead elſe.
　Math. Were the Sword now heav'd up,
And my Neck upon the Block, I would not buy
An Hour's Reprieve with the Loſs of Faith and Virtue
　　　　　　　　　　　　　　　　　　To

To be made immortal here.   Art thou a Scholar,
Nay, almoſt without a Parallel, and yet fear
To die, which is inevitable? You may urge
The many Years that by the Courſe of Nature
We may travel in this tedious Pilgrimage,
And hold it as a Bleſſing, as it is,
When Innocence is our Guide; yet know, *Baptiſta*,
Our Virtues are preferr'd before our Years,
By the great Judge.   To die untainted in
Our Fame and Reputation is the greateſt;
And to loſe that, can we deſire to live?
Or ſhall I, for a momentary Pleaſure,
Which ſoon comes to a Period, to all Times
Have Breach of Faith and Perjury remembred
In a ſtill living Epitaph? No, *Baptiſta*,
Since my *Sophia* will go to her Grave
Unſpotted in her Faith, I'll follow her
With equal Loyalty; but look on this,
Your own great Work, your Maſter-piece, and then
She being ſtill the ſame, teach me to alter.
Ha! ſure I do not ſleep! or, if I dream,

                         [*The Picture altered.*

This is a terrible Viſion! I will clear
My Eyeſight, perhaps melancholly makes me
See that which is not.

    Bapt. It is too apparent.
I grieve to look upon't; beſides the yellow,
That does aſſure ſhe's tempted, there are Lines
Of a dark Colour, that diſperſe themſelves
O'er every Miniature of her Face, and thoſe
Confirm.——

    Math. She is turn'd Whore.

    Bapt. I muſt not ſay ſo.
Yet as a Friend to Truth, if you will have me
Interpret it, in her Conſent, and Wiſhes
She's falſe, but not in fact yet.

    Math. Fact! *Baptiſta?*
Make not yourſelf a Pandar to her Looſeneſs,
In labouring to palliate what a Vizard

                                           Of

Of Impudence cannot cover. Did e'er Woman
In her Will decline from Chaſtity, but found Means
To give her hot Luſt full Scope? It is more
Impoſſible in Nature for groſs Bodies
Deſcending of themſelves, to hang in the Air,
Or with my ſingle Arm to underprop
A falling Tower; nay, in its violent Courſe
To ſtop the Light'ning, then to ſtay a Woman
Hurried by two Furies, Luſt and Falſhood,
In her full Career to Wickedneſs.

Bapt. Pray you temper
The Violence of your Paſſion.

Math. In Extreams
Of this Condition, can it be in Man
To uſe a Moderation? I am thrown
From a ſteep Rock headlong into a Gulph
Of Miſery, and find myſelf paſt Hope,
In the ſame Moment that I apprehend
That I am falling, and this, the Figure of
My Idol, few Hours ſince, while ſhe continued
In her Perfection, that was late a Mirror,
In which I ſaw miraculous Shapes of Duty,
Staid Manners, with all Excellency a Huſband
Could wiſh in a chaſte Wife, is on the ſudden
Turn'd to a magical Glaſs, and does preſent
Nothing but Horns and Horror.

Bapt. You may yet
(And 'tis the beſt Foundation) build up Comfort
On your own Goodneſs.

Math. No, that hath undone me,
For now I hold my Temperance a Sin
Worſe then Exceſs, and what was Vice a Virtue.
Have I refus'd a Queen, and ſuch a Queen
(Whoſe raviſhing Beauties at the firſt Sight had tempted
A Hermit from his Beads, and chang'd his Prayers
To amorous Sonnets,) to preſerve my Faith
Inviolate to thee, with the Hazard of
My Death with Torture, ſince ſhe could inflict
No leſs for my Contempt, and have I met
Such a Return from thee? I will not curſe thee,

Nor

Nor for thy Falfhood rail againft the Sex;
'Tis poor, and common; I'll only with wife Men
Whifper unto myfelf, howe'er they feem;
Nor prefent, nor paft Times, nor the Age to come
Hath heretofore, can now, or ever fhall
Produce one conftant Woman.

    Bapt. This is more
Then the Satyrifts wrote againft 'em.

    Math. There's no Language
That can exprefs the Poifon of thefe Afpicks,
Thefe weeping Crocodiles, and all too little
That hath been faid againft 'em. But I'll mould
My Thoughts into another Form, and if
She can outlive the Report of what I have done,
This Hand, when next fhe comes within my Reach,
Shall be her Executioner.

Enter Honoria.

    Bapt. The Queen, Sir.

    Hon. Wait our Command at Diftance; Sir, you too
      have
Free Liberty to depart.

    Bapt. I know no Manners,
And thank you for the Favour.   [*Exit* Baptifta.

    Hon. Have you taken
Good Reft in your new Lodgings? I expect now
Your refolute Anfwer; but advife maturely
Before I hear it,

    Math. Let my Actions, Madam,
For no Words can dilate my Joy, in all
You can command with Chearfulnefs to ferve you,
Affure your Highnefs; and in Sign of my
Submiffion, and Contrition for my Error,
My Lips, that but the laft Night fhun'd the Touch
Of your's as Poifon, taught Humility now,
Thus on your Foot, and that too great an Honour
For fuch an Undeferver, feals my Duty.
A cloudy Mift of Ignorance, equal to

Cim-

Cimmerian Darkneſs, would not let me ſee then,
What now with Adoration and Wonder,
With Reverence I look up to : But thoſe Fogs
Diſpers'd and ſcatter'd by the powerful Beams
With which yourſelf the Sun of all Perfection,
Vouchſafe to cure my Blindneſs, like a Suppliant
As low as I can kneel, I humbly beg
What you once pleaſed to tender.

   Hon. This is more
Then I could hope; what find you ſo attractive
Upon my Face in ſo ſhort Time to make
This ſudden Metamorphoſis? Pray you riſe;
I for your late Neglect thus ſign your Pardon.
Aye now you kiſs like a Lover, and not as Brothers
Coldly ſalute their Siſters.

   Math. I am turn'd
All Spirit and Fire.

   Hon. Yet to give ſome Allay
To this hot Fervour, 'twere good to remember
The King, whoſe Eyes and Ears are every where,
With the Danger too that follows, this diſcover'd.

   Math. Danger? A Bugbear Madam, let me ride once
Like *Phaeton* in the Chariot of your Favour,
And I contemn *Jove*'s Thunder: Though the King
In our Embraces ſtood a Looker on,
His Hangmen too, with ſtudied Cruelty ready
To drag me from your Arms, it ſhould not fright me
From the enjoying that, a ſingle Life is
Too poor a Price for: (O, that now all Vigour
Of my Youth were recollected for an Hour,
That my Deſire might meet with your's, and draw
The Envy of all Men in the Encounter
Upon my Head,) I ſhould—but we loſe Time,
Be gracious, mighty Queen.

   Hon. Pauſe yet a little :
The Bounties of the King, and what weighs more,
Your boaſted Conſtancy to your matchleſs Wife,
Should not ſoon be ſhaken.

                              Math.

Math. The whole Fabrick,
When I but look on you, is in a Moment
O'erturn'd and ruin'd, and as Rivers loofe
Their Names, when they are fwallow'd by the Ocean,
In you alone all Faculties of my Soul
Are wholly taken up, my Wife, and King
At the beft as Things forgotten.

   Hon. Can this be?
❡ have gain'd my End now.   *[Afide.*

   Math. Wherefore ftay you, Madam?

   Hon. In my Confideration what a Nothing
Man's Conftancy is.

   Math. Your Beauties make it fo,
In me, fweet Lady.

   Hon. And it is my Glory:
I could be coy now as you were, but I
Am of a gentler Temper; howfoever,
And in a juft Return of what I have fuffer'd
In your Difdain, with the fame Meafure grant me
Equal Deliberation: I e'er long
Will vifit you again, and when I next
Appear, as conquer'd by it, Slave-like wait
On my triumphant Beauty.   *[Exit* Honoria.

   Math. What a Change
Is here beyond my Fear! but by thy Falfhood,
Sophia, not her Beauty, is it deny'd me
To fin but in my Wifhes.   What a Frown
In Scorn, at her Departure, fhe threw on me?
I am both Ways loft; Storms of Contempt, and Scorn
Are ready to break on me, and all Hope
Of Shelter doubtful: I can neither be
Difloyal, nor yet honeft; I ftand guilty
On either Part; at the worft Death will end all,
And he muft be my Judge to write my Wrong,
Since I have lov'd too much and liv'd too long.
                         [Exit Mathias.

                                    S C E N E

SCENE II.

Enter Sophia *sola, with a Book and a Note.*

Soph. Nor Cuſtom nor Example, nor vaſt Numbers
Of ſuch as do offend, make leſs the Sin.
For each particular Crime a ſtrict Accompt
Will be exacted ; and that Comfort which
The Damn'd pretend (Fellows in Miſery)
Takes nothing from their Torments ; every one
Muſt ſuffer in himſelf the Meaſure of
His Wickedneſs. If ſo, as I muſt grant,
It being unrefutable in Reaſon,
Howe'er my Lord offend, it is no Warrant
For me to walk in his forbidden Paths :
What Penance then can expiate my Guilt
For my Conſent (tranſported then with Paſſion)
To Wantonneſs ? The Wounds I give my Fame
Cannot recover his ; and though I have fed
Theſe Courtiers with Promiſes and Hopes,
I am yet in Fact untainted ; and I truſt
My Sorrow for it, with my Purity
And Love to Goodneſs for itſelf, made powerful,
Though all they have alledg'd prove true or falſe,
Will be ſuch Exorciſms as ſhall command
This Fury Jealouſy from me.   What I have
Determin'd touching them, I am reſolv'd
To put in Execution.   Within there !
Where are my noble Gueſts ?

Enter Hilario, Coriſco, *with other Servants.*

Hil. The elder, Madam,
Is drinking by himſelf to your Ladyſhip's Health
In Muſkadine and Eggs ; and for a Raſher
To draw his Liquor down, he hath got a Pye
Of Marrow-bones, Potatoes and Eringo's,
With many ſuch Ingredients, and 'tis ſaid
He hath ſent his Man in Poſt to the next Town,

For a Pound of Ambergrife, and half a Peck
Of Fifhes call'd Cantharides.

Corif. The younger
Prunes up himfelf, as if this Night he were
To act a Bridegroom's Part; but to what Purpofe
I am Ignorance itfelf.

Soph. Continue fo.   [*Gives a Paper.*
Let thofe Lodgings be prepar'd as this directs you,
And fail not in a Circumftance, as you
Refpect my Favour.

1 *Serv.* We have our Inftructions.

2 *Serv.* And punctually will follow 'em.

[*Exeunt Servants.*

Enter Ubaldo.

Hil. Madam, here comes
The Lord *Ubaldo.*

Ubal. Pretty one, there's Gold
To buy thee a new Gown; and there's for thee:
Grow fat, and fit for Service. I am now
As I fhould be, at the Height, and able to
Beget a Giant. O my better Angel,
In this you fhew your Wifdom, when you pay
The Letcher in his own Coin; fhall you fit puling,
Like a patient *Grizzle,* and be laugh'd at? No,
This is a fair Revenge, fhall we to it?

Soph. To what, Sir?

Ubal. The Sport you promis'd.

Soph. Could it be done with Safety?

Ubal. I warrant you! I am found as a Bell, a tough
Old Blade, and Steel to the Back, as you fhall find me
In the Trial on your Anvil.

Soph. So; but how, Sir,
Shall I fatisfy your Friend, to whom, by Promife,
I am equally engag'd?

Ubal. I muft confefs
The more the merrier; but of all Men living
Take heed of him; you may fafer run upon

The

The Mouth of a Cannon when it is unlading,
And come off colder.

Soph. How! is he not wholesome?

Ubal. Wholesome! I'll tell you for your Good; he is
A Spital of Diseases, and indeed
More loathsome and infectious; the Tub is
His weekly Bath: He hath not drank this seven Years,
Before he came to your House, but Compositions
Of Saffafras and Guaicum, and dry Mutton's
His daily Portion; name what Scratch soever
Can be got by Women, and the Surgeons will resolve
At this Time or at that, *Ricardo* had it. [you,

Soph. Bless me from him.

Ubal. 'Tis a good Prayer, Lady,
It being a Degree unto the Pox
Only to mention him; if my Tongue burn not, hang
When I but name *Ricardo*. [me,

Soph. Sir, this Caution
Must be rewarded.

Ubal. I hope I have marr'd his Market.
But when?

Soph. Why presently; follow my Woman,
She knows where to conduct you, and will serve
To Night for a Page. Let the Waistcoat I appointed,
With the Cambrick Shirt perfum'd, and the rich Cap,
Be brought into his Chamber.

Ubal. Excellent Lady!
And a Caudle too in the Morning.

Corif. I will fit you. [*Exeunt* Ubaldo *and* Corifca.

Enter Ricardo.

Soph. So hot on the Scent! Here comes the other
    Beagle.

Ric. Take Purse and all.

Hil. If this Company would come often,
I should make a pretty Term on't.

Soph. For your Sake
I have put him off; he only begg'd a Kiss;

I gave

I gave it, and so parted.

 Ric. I hope better,
He did not touch your Lip?

 Soph. Yes, I assure you.
There was no Danger in it?

 Ric. No! eat presently
These Lozenges, of forty Crowns an Ounce,
Or you are undone.

 Soph. What is the Virtue of 'em?

 Ric. They are Preservatives against stinking Breath,
Rising from rotten Lungs.

 Soph. If so, your Carriage
Of such dear Antidotes, in my Opinion,
May render your's suspected.

 Ric. Fie, no, I use 'em
When I talk with him, I should be poison'd else.
But I'll be free with you.   He was once a Creature
It may be of God's making, but long since
He is turn'd to a Druggist's Shop; the Spring and Fall
Hold all the Year with him; that he lives, he owes
To Art, not Nature; she has giv'n him o'er.
He moves, like the Fairy King, on Screws and Wheels
Made by his Doctor's Recipes, and yet still
They are out of joint, and every Day repairing:
He has a Regiment of Whores he keeps
At his own Charge in a Lazar-house: But the best is,
There's not a Nose among 'em.   He's acquainted
With the Green Water, and the Spitting Pill's
Familiar to him.   In a frosty Morning
You may thrust him in a Pottle-pot, his Bones
Rattle in his Skin, like Beans tofs'd in a Bladder.
If he but hear a Coach, the Fomentation,
The Friction with Fumigation cannot save him
From the Chin-Evil.   In a Word, he is
Not one Disease, but all: Yet, being my Friend,
I will forbear his Character; for I would not
Wrong him in your Opinion.

 Soph. The best is,
The Virtues you bestow on him, to me,

Are Myfteries I know not : But, however,
I am at your Service. Sirrah, let it be your Care
T' uncloath the Gentleman, and with Speed : Delay
Takes from Delight.

Ric. Good, there's my Hat, Sword, Cloak——
A Vengeance on thefe Buttons ; off with my Doublet,
I dare fhow my Skin, in the Touch you will like it
    better ;
Prythee cut my Códpiece-point, and for this Service,
When I leave them off they are thine.

Hil. I take your Word, Sir.

Ric. Dear Lady, ftay not long.

Soph. I may come too foon, Sir.

Ric. No, no, I am ready now.

Hil. This is the Way, Sir.

                [*Exeunt* Hilario *and* Ricardo.

Soph. I was much to blame to credit their Reports
Touching my Lord, that fo traduce each other,
And with fuch virulent Malice, though I prefume
They are bad enough ; but I have ftudied for 'em
A Way for their Recovery.

        [*The Noife of clapping a Door*, Ubaldo *above*
                         in his Shirt.

Ubal. What doft thou mean, Wench ?
Why doft thou fhut the Door upon me ? Ha ?
My Cloaths are ta'en away too ! fhall I ftarve here ?
Is this my Lodging ? I am fure the Lady talk'd of
A rich Cap, a perfum'd Shirt, and a Waiftcoat ;
But here is nothing but a little frefh Straw,
A Petticoat for a Coverlet, and that torn too ;
And an old Woman's Biggen for a Night-cap.

        Enter Corifca *to* Sophia.

'Slight, 'tis a Prifon, or a Pig-fty. Ha !
The Windows grated with Iron, I cannot force 'em,
And if I leap down, here, I break my Neck ;
I am betray'd. Rogues ! Villains ! let me out ;
I am a Lord, and that's no common Title,

            L 3   And

And fhall I be us'd thus?

Soph. Let him rave, he's faft;
I'll parley with him at Leifure.

Ricardo *entering with a great Noife below, as fallen.*

Ric. Zoons, have you Trap-doors?
Soph. The other Bird's i' th' Cage too, let him flutter.
Ric. Whither am I fall'n, into Hell?
Ubal. Who makes that Noife there?
Help me, if thou art a Friend.
Ric. A Friend? I am where
I cannot help myfelf; let me fee thy Face.
Ubal. How, *Ricardo!* prythee throw me
Thy Cloak, if thou canft, to cover me, I am almoft
Frozen to Death.
Ric. My Cloak! I have no Breeches;
I am in my Shirt, as thou art; and here's nothing
For myfelf but a Clown's caft-off Suit.
Ubal. We are both undone.
Pr'ythee roar a little.—Madam!

Enter Hilario *in* Ricardo's *Suit.*

Ric. Lady of the Houfe!
Ubal. Grooms of the Chamber!
Ric. Gentlewomen! Milkmaids!
Ubal. Shall we be murther'd?
Soph. No, but foundly punifh'd,
To your Deferts.
Ric. You are not in Earneft, Madam?
Soph. Judge as you find, and feel it; and now hear
What I irrevocably purpofe to you.
Being receiv'd as Guefts into my Houfe,
And with all it afforded entertain'd,
You have forgot all hofpitable Duties,
And with the Defamation of my Lord,
Wrought on my Woman Weaknefs, in Revenge
Of his Injuries, as you fafhion'd 'em to me,

To

To yield my Honour to your lawlefs Luſt.

Hil. Mark that, poor Fellows.

Soph. And ſo far you have
Tranſgreſs'd againſt the Dignity of Men,
(Who ſhould, bound to it by Virtue, ſtill defend
Chaſte Ladies Honours) that it was your Trade
To make 'em infamous : But you are caught
In your own Toils, like luſtful Beaſts, and therefore
Hope not to find the Uſage of Men from me ;
Such Mercy you have forfeited, and ſhall ſuffer
Like the moſt ſlaviſh Women.

Ubal. How will you uſe us ?

Soph. Eaſe and Exceſs in Feeding made you wanton ;
A Plurify of ill Blood you muſt let out.
By Labour, and ſpare Diet, that Way got too,
Or periſh with Hunger.—Reach him up that Diſtaff
With the Flax upon it, though no Omphale,
Nor you a ſecond *Hercules*, as I take it ;
As you ſpin well at my Command, and pleaſe me,
Your Wages, in the coarſeſt Bread and Water,
Shall be proportionable.

Ubal. I will ſtarve firſt.

Soph. That's as you pleaſe.

Ric. What will become of me now ?

Soph. You ſhall have gentler Work ; I have oft ob-
ſerv'd
You were proud to ſhew the Fineneſs of your Hands,
And Softneſs of your Fingers ; you ſhould reel well
What he ſpins, if you give your Mind to it, as I'll
force you.
Deliver him his Materials. Now you know
Your Penance, fall to work, Hunger will teach you ;
And ſo, as Slaves to your Luſt, not me, I leave you.

[*Exit* Sophia *and Servants.*

Ubal. I ſhall ſpin a fine Thread out now.

Ric. I cannot look
On theſe Devices, but they put me in Mind
Of Rope-makers.

Hil. Fellow, think of thy Taſk,

Forget

Forget such Vanities, my Livery there
Will serve thee to work in.

 Ric. Let me have my Cloaths, yet
I was bountiful to thee.

 Hil. They are past your Wearing,
And mine by Promise, as all these can witness;
You have no Holydays coming, nor will I work
While these and this lasts; and so when you please
You may shut up your Shop-windows.

[Exit Hilario,

 Ubal. I am faint,
And must lie down.

 Ric. I am hungry too, and cold.——
O cursed Women.——

 Ubal. This comes of our Whoring.
But let us rest as well as we can to-night,
But not o'ersleep ourselves, lest we fast to-morrow.

[They draw the Curtains.

SCENE III.

Enter Ladislaus, Honoria, Eubulus, Ferdinand, Acanthe, *Attendants.*

 Hon. Now you know all, Sir, with the Motives why
I forc'd him to my Lodging.

 Ladif. I desire
No more such Trials, Lady.

 Hon. I presume, Sir,
You do not doubt my Chastity.

 Ladif. I would not;
But these are strange Inducements.

 Eub. By no Means, Sir.
Why, though he were with Violence seiz'd upon,
And still detain'd, the Man, Sir, being no Soldier,
Nor us'd to charge his Pike, when the Breach is open,
There was no Danger in't: You must conceive, Sir,
Being religious, she chose him for a Chaplain
To read old Homilies to her in the Dark;
She's bound to it by her Canons.

Ladif.

Ladif. Still tormented
With thy Impertinence?
Hon, By yourſelf, dear Sir,
I was ambitious only to overthrow
His boaſted Conſtancy in his Conſent,
But for Fact I contemn him; I was never
Unchaſte in Thought, I laboured to give Proof
What Power dwells in this Beauty you admire ſo,
And when you ſee how ſoon it hath transform'd him,
And with what ſuperſtition he adores it,
Determine as you pleaſe.
Ladif. I will look on
This Pageant; but ——
Hon. When you have ſeen and heard, Sir,
The Paſſages which I myſelf diſcover'd,
And could have kept conceal'd, had I meant baſely,
Judge as you pleaſe.
Ladif. Well, I'll obſerve the Iſſue.
Eub. How had you took this, General, in your
          Wife?
Ferd. As a ſtrange Curioſity; but Queens
Are priviledg'd above Subjects, and 'tis fit, Sir.
                              [*Exeunt.*

S C E N E IV.

Enter Mathias, Baptiſta.

Bapt. You are much alter'd, Sir, ſince the laſt Night
When the Queen left you, and look chearfully,
Your Dulneſs quite blown over.
Math. I have ſeen a Viſion,
This Morning makes it good, and never was
In ſuch Security as at this Inſtant:
Fall what can fall, and when the Queen appears,
Whoſe ſhorteſt Abſence now is tedious to me,
Obſerve th' Encounter.

                                        Enter

Enter Honoria *to* Mathias. (Ladiſlaus, Eubulus, Ferdinand, Acanthe, *with others enter above.*)

Bapt. She already is
Enter'd the Liſts.
Math. And I prepar'd to meet her.
Bapt. I know my Duty.
Hon. Not ſo, you may ſtay now
As a Witneſs of our Contract.
Bapt. I obey
In all Things, Madam.
Hon. Where's that Reverence,
Or rather ſuperſtitious Adoration,
Which, Captive-like, to my triumphant Beauty
You paid laſt Night ? No humble Knee ? nor Sign
Of vaſſal Duty ? Sure this is the Foot
To whoſe proud Cover, and then happy in it,
Your Lips were glew'd ; and that the Neck then offer'd
To witneſs your Subjection to be trod on :
Your certain Loſs of Life in the King's Anger,
Was then too mean a Price to buy my Favour ;
And that falſe Glow-Worm Fire, of Conſtancy
To your Wife, extinguiſh'd by a greater Light
Shot from our Eyes ; and that, it may be (being
Too glorious to be look'd on) hath depriv'd you
Of Speech, and Motion : But I will take off
A little from the Splendor, and deſcend
From my own Height, and in your Lowneſs hear you
Plead as a Suppliant.
Math. I do remember
I once ſaw ſuch a Woman.
Hon. How !
Math. And then
She did appear a moſt magnificent Queen ;
And what's more, virtuous, tho' ſomewhat darken'd
With Pride and Self-Opinion.
Eub. Call you this Courtſhip ?
Math. And ſhe was happy in a Royal Huſband,

Whom

Whom Envy could not tax, unlefs it were
For his too much Indulgence to her Humours.
   Eub. Pray you, Sir, obferve that Touch, 'tis to the
      Purpofe;
I like the Play the better for't.
   Math. And fhe liv'd
Worthy her Birth and Fortune; you retain yet
Some Part of her angelical Form; but when
Envy to the Beauty of another Woman
Inferior to her's, (one fhe never
Had feen, but in her Picture) had difpers'd
Infection through her Veins, and Loyalty
(Which a great Queen as fhe was, fhould have nourifh'd)
Grew odious to her——
   Hon. I am Thunderftruck.
   Math. And Luft, in all the Bravery it could borrow
From Majefty, howe'er difguis'd, had took
Sure Footing in the Kingdom of her Heart,
(Once the Throne of Chaftity,) how in a Moment
All that was gracious, great, and glorious in her,
And won upon all Hearts; like feeming Shadows,
Wanting true Subftance, vanifh'd.
   Hon. How his Reafons
Work on my Soul!
   Math. Retire into yourfelf.
Your own Strength's, Madam, ftrongly man'd with
      Virtue,
And be but as you were, and there's no Office
So bafe, beneath the Slavery that Men
Impofe on Beafts, but I will gladly bow to.
But as you play and juggle with a Stranger,
Varying your Shapes like *Thetis*, though the Beauties
Of all that are by Poets Raptures painted,
Were now in you united, you fhould pafs
Pitied by me perhaps, but not regarded.
   Eub. If this take not, I am cheated.
   Math. To flip once
Is incident, and excus'd by human Frailty;
But to fall ever, damnable. We were both

Guilty,

Guilty, I grant, in tendering our Affection,
But, as I hope you will do, I repented.
When we are grown up to Ripenefs, our Life is
Like to this Picture. While we run
A conftant Race in Goodnefs, it retains
The juft Proportion. But the Journey being
Tedious, and fweet Temptations in the Way,
That may in fome Degree divert us from
The Road that we put forth in, e'er we end
Our Pilgrimage, it may, like this, turn Yellow,
Or be with Blacknefs clouded. But when we
Find we have gone aftray, and labour to
Return unto our never-failing Guide
Virtue, Contrition (with unfeigned Tears,
The Spots of Vice wafh'd off) will foon reftore it
To the firft Purenefs.

    Hon. I am difenchanted:
Mercy, O Mercy, Heavens?   [*Kneels.*
    Ladif. I am ravifh'd with
What I have feen and heard.
    Ferd. Let us defcend, and hear
The reft below.
    Eub. This hath fall'n out beyond
My Expectation.   [*They defcend.*
    Hon. How have I wander'd
Out of the Tract of Piety! and mifled
By overweening Pride, and Flattery
Of fawning Sycophants, (the Bane of Greatnefs)
Could never meet till now a Paffenger,
That in his Charity would fet me right,
Or ftay me in my Precipice to Ruin!
How ill have I return'd your Goodnefs to me?

Enter the King and others.

The Horror in my Thought of't turns me Marble.
But if it may be yet prevented, O Sir,
What can I do to fhew my Sorrow, or

                                        With

With what Brow afk your Pardon ?

Ladif. Pray you rife.

Hon. Never, till you forgive me, and receive
Unto your Love and Favour, a chang'd Woman.
My State and Pride turn'd to Humility, henceforth
Shall wait on your Commands, and my Obedience
Steer'd only by your Will.

Ladif. And that will prove
A fecond and a better Marriage to me; all is forgot—

Hon. Sir, I muft not rife yet,
Till with a free Confeffion of a Crime,
Unknown to you yet, and a following Suit,
Which thus I beg, be granted.

Ladif. I melt with you.
'Tis pardon'd, and confirm'd thus.

Hon. Know then, Sir.
In Malice to this good Knight's Wife, I practis'd
Ubaldo, and *Ricardo,* to corrupt her.

Bapt. Thence grew the Change of the Picture.

Hon. And how far
They have prevail'd, I am ignorant. Now, if you, Sir,
For the Honour of this good Man, may be intreated
To travel thither, it being but a Day's Journey,
To fetch 'em off—

Ladif. We will put on to Night.

Bapt. I, if you pleafe, your Harbinger.

Ladif. I thank you.
Let me embrace you in my Arms, your Service
Done on the *Turk,* compared with this, weighs nothing.

Matb. I am ftill your humble Creature.

Ladif. My true Friend.

Ferd. And fo you are bound to hold him.

Eub. Such a Plant
Imported to your Kingdom, and here grafted,
Would yield more Fruit, than all the idle Weeds
That fuck up your Reign of Favour.

Ladif. In my Will
I'll not be wanting, prepare for our Journey.

In

In Act be my *Honoria* now, not Name,
And to all after Times preserve thy Fame.   [*Exeunt.*

The End of the Fourth Act.

ACT V.   SCENE I.

Sophia,. Corisca, Hilario.

Soph. ARE they then so humble?
Hil.   Hunger and hard Labour
Have tam'd 'em, Madam; at first they bellow'd
Like Stags ta'en in a Toil, and would not work
For Sullenness, but when they found without it
There was no Eating, and that to starve to Death
Was much against their Stomachs, by Degrees
Against their Wills, they fell to it.
  Coris. And now feed on
The little Pittance you allow, with Gladness.
  Hil. I do remember that they stop'd their Noses
At the Sight of Beef and Mutton as course Feeding
For their fine Palates; but now their Work being ended,
They leap at a Barley Crust, and hold Cheese-parings,
With a Spoonful of pall'd Wine pour'd in their Water,
For festival Exceedings. [21]
  Coris. When I examine
My Spinster's Work, he trembles like a 'Prentice,
And takes a Box on the Ear when I spy Faults
And Botches in his Labour, as a Favour
From a curst Mistress.
  Hil. The other too reels well
For his Time; and if your Ladyship would please
To see 'em for your Sport, since they want airing,

---

[21] *For Festival Exceedings.*

Thus we read in all the old Copies, and it is thus in the *City Madam*; but I think that *exceeding Festivals* is better, though indeed as the Sense is the same, it is of little or no Consequence.

It

It would do well in my Judgment, you fhall hear
Such a hungry Dialogue from 'em.

Soph. But fuppofe .
When they are out of Prifon they fhould grow
Rebellious ?

Hil. Never fear't; I'll undertake
To lead 'em out by the Nofe with a coarfe Thread,
Of the one's Spinning, and make the other reel after,
And without grumbling; and when you are weary of
Their Company, as eafily return 'em.

Corif. Dear Madam, it will help to drive away
Your Melancholy.

Soph. Well, on this Affurance
I am content, bring 'em hither.

Hil. I will do it
In ftately Equipage.   [*Exit* Hilario.

Soph. They have confeffed then
They were fet on by the Queen to taint me in
My Loyalty to my Lord ?

Corif. 'Twas the main Caufe,
That brought 'em hither.

Soph. I am glad I know it;
And as I have begun, before I end,
I'll at the Height revenge it; let us ftep afide;
They come, the Objects fo ridiculous,
In Spight of my fad Thoughts I cannot but
Lend a forc'd Smile to grace it.

Enter Hilario, Ubaldo *fpinning*, Ricardo *reeling*.

Hil. Come away,
Work as you go, and lofe no Time, 'tis precious,
You'll find it in your Commons.

Ric. Commons, call you it!
The Word is proper; I have graz'd fo long
Upon your Commons, I am almoft ftarv'd here.

Hil. Work harder, and they fhall be better'd.

Ubal. Better'd ?
Worfer they cannot be : Would I might lie

                         Like

Like a Dog under her Table and ferve for a Footftool,
So I might have my Belly full of that
Her Ifland Cur refufes.

    Hil. How do you like
Your airing? Is it not a Favour?

    Ric. Yes;
Juft fuch a one as you.ufe to a Brace of Greyhounds
When they are led out of their Kennels to fcumber;
But our Cafe is ten Times harder, we have nothing
In our Bellies to be vented: If you will be
An honeft Yeoman Phenterer, feed us firft,
And walk us after?

    Hil. Yeoman Phenterer!
Such another Word to your Governor, and you go
Supperlefs to Bed for't.

    Ubal. Nay, even as you pleafe.
(The comfortable Names of Breakfaft, Dinner,
Collations, Supper, Beverage, are Words,
Worn out of our Remembrance.)

    (Ric. O for the Steam
Of Meat in a Cook's Shop?)

    Ubal. I am fo dry,
I have not Spittle enough to wet my Fingers
When I draw my Flax from my Diftaff.

    Ric. Nor I Strength
To raife my Hand to the Top of my Reeler. Oh!
I have the Cramp all over me.

    Hil. What do you think
Were beft to apply to it? A Cramp-ftone, as I take it,
Were very ufeful.

    Ric. Oh! no more of Stones,
We have been us'd too long like Hawks already.

    Ubal. We are not fo high in our Flefh now to need
      cafting,
We will come to an empty Fift.

    Hil. Nay, that you fhall not.
So ho, Birds, how the Eye-affes fcratch, and fcramble!
Take Heed of a Surfeit: Do not caft your Gorges,
This is more then I have Commiffion for; be thankful.

                       Soph.

Soph. Were all that ſtudy the Abuſe of Women
Us'd thus, the City would not ſwarm with Cuckolds,
Nor ſo many Tradeſmen break.

Coriſ. Pray you appear now,
And mark the Alteration.

Hil. To your Work,
My Lady is in Preſence ; ſhew your Duties
Exceeding well.

Soph. How do your Scholars profit ?

Hil. Hold up your Heads demurely.   Prettily
For young Beginners.

Coriſ. And will do well in Time
If they be kept in Awe.

Ric. In Awe! I am ſure
I quake like an Aſpen Leaf.

Ubal. No Mercy, Lady ?

Ric. Nor Intermiſſion ?

Soph. Let me ſee your Work.
Fie upon't, what a Thread's here! a poor Cobler's Wife
Would make a finer to ſow a Clown's Rent ſtart up ;
And here you reel as you were drunk.

Ric. I am ſure it is not with Wine

Soph. O, take heed of Wine ;
Cold Water is far better for your Healths,
Of which I am very tender ; you had foul Bodies,
And muſt continue in this phyſical Diet,
Till the Cauſe of your Diſeaſe be ta'en away
For fear of a Relapſe, and that is dangerous ;
Yet I hope already that you are in ſome
Degree recovered, and that Way to reſolve me
Anſwer me truly ; nay, what I propound
Concerns both, nearer ; what would you now give,
If your Means were in your Hands, to lie all Night
With a freſh and handſome Lady ?

Ubal. How! a Lady ?
O! I am paſs'd it, (Hunger with her Razor
Hath made me an Eunuch.)

Ric. For a Meſs of Porridge,
Well ſopp'd with a Bunch of Raddiſh and a Carrot,

I would fell my Barony; but for Women, oh!
No more of Women, (not a Dite for a Doxy)
After this hungry Voyage.

Soph. Thefe are truly
Good Symptoms; let them not venture too much in the
 Air
Till they are weaker.

Ric. This is Tyranny.

Ubal. Scorn upon Scorn.

Soph. You were fo
In your malicious Intents to me,

Enter a Servant.

And therefore 'tis but Juftice—What's the Bufinefs?

 Serv. My Lord's great Friend, Signior *Baptifta*,
  Madam,
Is newly lighted from his Horfe, with certain
Affurance of my Lord's Arrival.

 Soph. How!
And ftand I trifling here? Hence with the Mungrels
To there feveral Kennels, there let them howl in private,
I'll be no farther troubled. [*Exeunt* Sophia *and Servant.*

 Ubal. O that ever
I faw this Fury!

 Ric. Or look'd on a Woman
But as a Prodigy in Nature!

 Hil. Silence,
No more of this.

 Corif. Methinks you have no Caufe
To repent your being here.

 Hil. Have you not learnt,
When your 'States are fpent, your feveral Trades to live
 by,
And never charge the Hofpital?

 Corif. Work but tightly,
And we will not ufe a Difh-clout in the Houfe
But of your Spinning.

          Ubal.

Ubal. O! I would this Hemp
Were turn'd to a Halter.

Hil. Will you march?

Ric. A foft one,
Good General, I befeech you;

Ubal. I can hardly
Draw my Legs after me.

Hil. For a Crutch you may ufe
Your Diftaff, a good Wit makes Ufe of all Things. [**22**]

[*Exeunt.*

SCENE II.

Enter Sophia, Baptifta.

Soph. Was he jealous of me?

Bapt. There's no perfect Love
Without fome Touch of't, Madam.

Soph. And my Picture
Made by your divelifh Art, a Spy upon
My Actions? I never fat to be drawn,
Nor had you, Sir, Commiffion for't.

Bapt. Excufe me;
At his earneft Suit I did it.

Soph. Very good:
Was I grown fo cheap in his Opinion of me?

Bapt. The profperous Events that crown'd his Fortunes
May qualify the Offence.

Soph. Rood the Events [**23**]

[**22**] ————— *A good Wit makes Ufe of all Things.*

I would not interrupt the Reader in the foregoing Scene, but I fhall now obferve that the Device practifed on the two wanton Gentlemen, in Revenge for their Falfhood and their Attempts on *Sophia*, is very mean, conduces but little to the Plot, and on the whole, is far inferior to the other Parts of this excellent Play, but *great Beauties are always in the Confines of great Faults.*

[**23**] Sophia. *Rood the Events.*

This is the Reading of all the old Editions, and is followed by Mr. *Dodfley*; but I think we ought to read

Soph. Good *the Events,* &c.

M 2

. The

The Sanctuary Fools and Madmen fly to,
When their rash and desperate Undertakings thrive
    well;
But good and wise Men are directed by
Grave Counsels, and with such Deliberation
Proceed in their Affairs, that Chance has nothing
To do with 'em. Howsoe'er, take the Pains, Sir,
To meet the Honour in the King and Queen's
Approaches to my House, that breaks upon me,
I will expect them with my best of Care.
    Bapt. To entertain such royal Guests.
    Soph. I know it.   [*Exit* Baptista.
Leave that to me, Sir, what should move the Queen,
So given to Ease and Pleasure, as Fame speaks her,
To such a Journey? Or work on my Lord
To doubt my Loyalty? Nay, more, to take
For the Resolution of his Fears, a Course
That is by holy Writ deny'd a Christian?
'Twas impious in him, and perhaps the Welcome
He hopes in my Embraces may deceive
His Expectation. The Trumpets speak
The King's Arrival. Help a Woman's Wit now,
To make him know his Fault and my just Anger.
                        [*Exit* Sophia.

SCENE *the last.*

Loud Musick. Enter Ladislaus, Mathias, Eubulus, Honoria, Ferdinand, Baptista, Acanthe, *with Attendants.*

    Eub. Your Majesty must be weary.
    Hon. No, my Lord,
A willing Mind makes a hard Journey easy.
    Math. Not *Jove,* attended on by *Hermes,* was
More welcome to the Cottage of *Philemon,*
And his poor *Baucis,* then your gracious self,
Your matchless Queen, and all your royal Train
Are to your Servant and his Wife.
    Ladis. Where is she?

                               Hon,

Hon. I long to fee her as my now loud Rival.

Eub. And I to have a Smack at her; ('tis a Cordial
To an old Man, better then Sack and a Toaſt
Before he goes to Supper.)

Math. Ha! is my Houſe turn'd
To a Wilderneſs? Nor Wife nor Servants ready
With all Rites due to Majeſty, to receive
Such unexpected Bleſſings, you aſſur'd me
Of better Preparation, hath not
Th' Exceſs of Joy tranſported her beyond
Her Underſtanding?

Bapt. I now parted from her,
And gave her your Directions.

Math. How ſhall I beg
Your Majeſty's Patience? Sure my Family's drunk,
Or by ſome Witch, in Envy of my Glory,
A dead Sleep thrown upon 'em.

Enter Hilario, *and Servants.*

1 *Serv.* Sir.

Math. But that
The ſacred Preſence of the King forbids it,
My Sword ſhould make a Maſſacre among you.
Where is your Miſtreſs?

Hil. Firſt, you are welcome home, Sir,
Then know, ſhe ſays ſhe's ſick, Sir, there's no Notice
Taken of my Bravery.

Math. Sick at ſuch a Time!
It cannot be though ſhe were on her Death-bed,
And her Spirit even now departed, here ſtand they
Could call it back again, and in this Honour
Give her a ſecond Being, bring me to her;
I know not what to urge, or how to redeem
This Mortgage of her Manners.

[*Exit* Mathias *and* Hilario.

Eub. There's no Climate
In the World, I think, where one Jade's Trick or other
Reigns not in Women.

Ferd.

Ferd. You were ever bitter
Againſt the Sex.

Ladiſ. This is very ſtrange,

Hon. Mean Women
Have their Faults as well as Queens.

Ladiſ. O ſhe appears now.

Enter Mathias, Sophia.

Math. The Injury that you conceive I have done yoʊ
Diſpute hereafter, and in your Perverſeneſs
Wrong not yourſelf, and me.

Soph. I am paſs'd my Childhood,
And need no Tutor.

Math, This is the great King,
To whom I am engag'd till Death, for all
I ſtand poſſeſs'd of.

Soph. My humble Roof is proud, Sir,
To be the Canopy of ſo much Greatneſs,
Set off with Goodneſs.

Ladiſ, My own Praiſes flying
In ſuch pure Air, as your ſweet Breath, fair Lady,
Cannot but pleaſe me,

Math. This is the Queen of Queens,
In her Magnificence to me.

Soph. In my Duty
I kiſs her Highneſs Robe,

Hon. You ſtoop to low
To her whoſe Lips would meet with yours,

Soph. Howe'er,
It may appear prepoſt'rous in Women
So to encounter, 'tis your Pleaſure, Madam,
And not my proud Ambition—do you hear, Sir ?
Without a magical Picture, in the Touch
I find your Print of cloſe and wanton Kiſſes
On the Queen's Lips.

Math. Upon your Life be ſilent.
And now ſalute theſe Lords.

Soph. Since you'll have me,

You

You fhall fee I am experienc'd at the Game,
And can play it tightly.—You are a brave Man, Sir,
And do deferve a free and hearty Welcome.
Be this the Prologue to it.

Eub. An old Man's Turn
Is ever laft in Kiffing. I have Lips too,
Howe'er, cold ones, Madam.

Soph. I will warm 'em
With the Fire of mine.

Eub. And fo fhe has, I thank you;
I fhall fleep the better all Night for't.

Math. You exprefs
The Boldnefs of a wanton Courtezan,
And not a Matron's Modefty ; take up,
Or you are difgrac'd for ever.

Soph. How ? with kiffing
Feelingly, as you taught me ? Would you have me
Turn my Cheek to 'em, as proud Ladies ufe
To their Inferiors, as if they intended
Some Bufinefs fhould be whifper'd in their Ear,
And not a Salutation ? What I do,
I will do freely ; now I am in the Humour
I'll fly at all, are there any more ?

Math. Forbear,
Or you will raife my Anger to a Height
That will defcend in Fury.

Soph. Why ? you know
How to refolve yourfelf what my Intents are,
By the Help of Mephoftophilos, and your Picture.
Pray you look upon't again. I humbly thank
The Queen's great Care of me, while you were abfent.
She knew how tedious 'twas for a young Wife,
And being for that Time a Kind of Widow,
To pafs away her melancholy Hours
Without good Company, and in Charity therefore
Provided for me ; out of her own Store
She cull'd the Lords *Ubaldo* and *Ricardo*,
Two principal Courtiers for Ladies Service,
To do me all good Offices ; and as fuch

Employ'd

Employ'd by her, I hope I have receiv'd,
And entertain'd 'em; nor shall they depart
Without the Effect arising from the Cause
That brought 'em hither.

    Math. Thou dost belye thyself:
I know that in my Absence thou wer't honest,
However now turn'd Monster.

    Soph. The Truth is,
We did not deal like you, in Speculations
On cheating Pictures; we knew Shadows were
No Substances, and actual Performance
The best Assurance. I will bring 'em hither
To make good in this Presence so much for me.
Some Minutes Space I beg your Majesty's Pardon ——
You are mov'd; now champ upon this Bit a little,
Anon you shall have another. Wait me, *Hilario.*

                [*Exeunt* Sophia *and* Hilario.

    Ladis. How now? turn'd Statue, Sir?

    Math. Fly, and fly quickly
From this cursed Habitation, or this Gorgon
Will make you all as I am. In her Tongue
Millions of Adders hiss, and every Hair
Upon her wicked Head, a Snake more dreadful
Than that *Tisiphon* threw on *Athamas,*
Which in his Madness forc'd him to dismember
His proper Issue. O that ever I
Repos'd my Trust in Magick, or believ'd
Impossibilities! or that Charms had Power
To sink and search into the bottomless Hell,
For a false Woman's Heart.

    Eub. These are the Fruits
Of Marriage; and old Batchelor, as I am,
And what's more, will continue so, is not troubled
With these fine Fagaries.

    Ferd. 'Till you are resolv'd, Sir,
Forsake not Hope.

    Bapt. Upon my Life, this is
Dissimulation.

    Ladis. And it suits not with

                         Your

Your Fortitude and Wifdom, to be thus
Tranfported with your Paffion.

Hon. You were once
Deceiv'd in me, Sir, as I was in you;
Yet thé Deceit pleas'd both.

Math. She hath confefs'd all,
What further Proof fhould I afk?

Hon. Yet remember
The Diftance that is interpos'd between
A Woman's Tongue and her Heart, and you muft grant
You build upon no Certainties.

Enter Sophia, Corifca, Hilario, Ubaldo, *and* Ricardo,
as before.

Eub. What have we here?
Soph. You muft come on, and fhew yourfelves.
Ubal. The King!
Ric. And Queen too! Would I were as far under the
As I am above it.   [Earth

Ubal. Some Poet will
From this Relation, or in Verfe, or Profe,
Or both together blended, render us
Ridiculous to all Ages.

Ladif. I remember
This Face when it was in a better Plight:
Are not you *Ricardo?*

Hon. And this Thing, I take it,
Was once *Ubaldo.*

Ubal. I am now I know not what.
Ric. We thank your Majefty for employing us
To this fubtle Circe.

Eub. How, my Lord, turn'd Spinfter!
Do you work by the Day, or by the Great?

Ferd. Is your Theorbo
Turn'd to a Diftaff, Signior? and your Voice,
With which you chanted Room for a lufty Gallant,
Turn'd to the Note of Lacrymæ?

Eub. Pr'ythee tell me,

For

For I know thou art free, how often, and to the Purpoſe,
Have you been merry with this Lady?

 Ric. Never, never.

 Ladiſ. Howſoever you ſhould ſay ſo, for your Credit,
Being the only Court Bull.

 Ubal. O that ever
I ſaw this kicking Heifer!

 Soph. You ſee, Madam,
How I have cur'd your Servants, and what Favours
They with their rampant Valour have won from me.
You may, as they are phyſick'd, I preſume,
Truſt a fair Virgin with 'em; they have learn'd
Their ſeveral Trades to live by, and paid nothing
But Cold and Hunger for 'em, and may now
Set up for themſelves, for here I give 'em over.
And now to you, Sir, why do you not again
Peruſe your Picture, and take the Advice
Of your learned Conſort? Theſe are the Men, or none,
That made you, as the *Italian* ſays, a *Beco*.

 Math. I know not which Way to entreat your Pardon;
Nor am I worthy of it, my *Sophia*,
My beſt *Sophia*, here before the King,
The Queen, theſe Lords, and all the Lookers on,
I do renounce my Error, and embrace you,
As the great Example to all After-times
For ſuch as would die chaſte and noble Wives,
With Reverence to imitate.

 Soph. Not ſo, Sir.
I yet hold off. However I have purg'd
My doubted Innocence, the foul Aſperſions,
In your unmanly Doubts caſt on my Honour,
Cannot ſo ſoon be waſh'd off.

 Eub. Shall we have
More Jiggobobs yet?

 Soph. When you went to the Wars,
I ſet no Spy upon you, to obſerve
Which Way you wander'd, though our Sex by Nature
Is ſubject to Suſpicions and Fears;
My Confidence in your Loyalty freed me from 'em.

But

But to deal as you did 'gainſt your Religion,
With this Enchanter to ſurvey my Actions,
Was more than Woman's Weakneſs; therefore know,
And 'tis my Boon unto the King, I do
Deſire a Separation from your Bed;
For I will ſpend the Remnant of my Life
In Prayer and Meditation.

 Math. O take Pity
Upon my Weak Condition, or I am
More wretched in your Innocence, than if
I had found you guilty.   Have you ſhewn a Jewel
Out of the Cabinet of your rich Mind
To lock it up again ? — She turns away.
Will none ſpeak for me ?   Shame and Sin hath robb'd
Of the Uſe of my Tongue.   [me

 Ladiſ. Since you have conquer'd, Madam,
You wrong the Glory of your Victory,
If you uſe it not with Mercy.

 Ferd. Any Penance
You pleaſe to impoſe upon him, I dare warrant
He will gladly ſuffer.

 Eub. Have I liv'd to ſee
But one good Woman, and ſhall we for a Trifle
Have her turn Nun ? I will firſt pull down the Cloyſter.
To the old Sport again, with a good Luck to you :
'Tis not alone enough that you are good,
We muſt have ſome of the Breed of you : Will you
  deſtroy
The Kind, and Race of Goodneſs ? I am converted,
and aſk your Pardon, Madam, for my ill Opinion
Againſt the Sex, and ſhew me but two ſuch more,
I'll marry yet, and love 'em.

 Hon. She that yet
Ne'er knew what 'twas to bend but to the King,
Thus begs Remiſſion for him.

 Soph. O dear, Madam,
Wrong not your Greatneſs ſo.

 Omnes. We all are Suitors.

 Ubal. I do deſerve to be heard among the reſt.

              Ric.

Ric. And we have suffer'd for it.

Soph. I perceive
There's no Resistance: But suppose I pardon
What's past, who can secure me he'll be free
From Jealousy hereafter?

Math. I will be
My own Security: Go ride where you please;
Feast, revel, banquet, and make Choice with whom,
I'll set no Watch upon you; and for Proof of't
This cursed Picture I surrender up
To the consuming Fire.

Bapt. As I abjure
The Practice of my Art.

Soph. Upon these Terms
I am reconcil'd; and for these that have paid
The Price of their Folly, I desire your Mercy.

Ladis. At your Request they have it.

Ubal. Hang all Trades now.

Ric. I will find a new one, and that is to live honest.

Hil. These are my Fees.

Ubal. Pray you take 'em with a Mischief.

Ladis. So, all ends in Peace now.
And to all married Men be this a Caution,
Which they should duly tender as their Life,
Neither to doat too much, nor doubt a Wife.

           [*Exeunt omnes.*

F I N I S.

THE
FATAL DOWRY.

A
TRAGEDY.

As it hath been often acted at the Private House in
Black-Fryers, by his Majesty's Servants. 1632.

WRITTEN

By PHILIP MASSINGER,

AND

NATHANIEL FIELD.

Dramatis Personæ.

CHARALOIS.	FLORIMEL. ⎫
ROMONT.	BELLAPERT. ⎬
CHARMI.	AYMER.
NOVALL, Sen.	NOVALL, Jun.
LILADAM.	Advocates.
DU CROY.	Three Creditors.
ROCHFORT.	Officers.
BEAUMONT.	Priest.
PONTALIER.	Taylor.
MALOTIN.	Barber.
BEAUMELLE.	Perfumer.

The Scene, Dijon *in* Burgundy.

THE

THE

FATAL DOWRY.*

ACT I.   SCENE I.

Enter Charalois, *with a Paper*, Romont, Charmi.

Charmi.

⁜ S ⁜ IR, I may move the Court to ferve your
Will;
But therein fhall both wrong you and myfelf.
  Rom. Why think you fo, Sir?
 Charmi. 'Caufe I am familiar
With what will be their Anfwer: They will fay,
'Tis againft Law, and argue me of Ignorance,
For off'ring them the Motion.
 Rom. You know not, Sir,
How, in this Caufe, they may difpenfe with Law,
And therefore frame not you their Anfwer for them,
But do your Parts.
 Charmi. I love the Caufe fo well,
That I could run the Hazard of a Check for't.
 Rom. From whom?
 Charmi. Some of the Bench, that watch to give it,
More than to do the Office that they fit for:
But give me, Sir, my Fee.
 Rom. Now you are noble.

* *Maffinger* was affifted in writing this Tragedy by Mr. *Nathaniel Field*, the Author of two Comedies befide; and, as a Poet, very much efteemed by the Cotemporaries of the Age in which he lived.

            Charmi.

Charmi. I shall deserve this better yet, in giving
My Lord some Counsel (if he please to hear it)
Than I shall do with Pleading.

Rom. What may it be, Sir?

Charmi. That it would please his Lordship, as the
   Presidents
And Counsellors of Court come by, to stand
Here, and but shew yourself, and to some one
Or two, make his Request: There is a Minute,'
When a Man's Presence speaks in his own Cause,
More than the Tongues of twenty Advocates.

Rom. I have urg'd that.

Enter Rochfort, Du Croy.

Charmi. Their Lordships here are coming,
I must go get me a Place.—You'll find me in Court,
And at your Service.   [*Exit* Charmi.

Rom. Now, put on your Spirits!

DuCroy. The Ease that you prepare yourself, my Lord,
In giving up the Place you hold in Court,
Will prove, I fear, a Trouble in the State;
And that no slight one.

Roch. Pray you, Sir, no more.

Rom. Now, Sir, lose not this offer'd Means: Their
   Looks,
Fix'd on you with a pitying Earnestness,
Invite you to demand their Furtherance
To your good Purpose.—This such a Dulness,
So foolish, and untimely, as ———

Du Croy. You know him?

' ——— *There is a Minute*
 When a Man's Presence speaks, &c.

So *Shakespear*, in *Julius Cæsar*, says,

 There is a Tide in the Affairs of Men,
 Which, taken at the Flood, leads on to Fortune;
 Omitted, all the Voyage of their Life
 Is bound in Shallows, and in Misery.

      Act IV. Scene V.
       Roch.

Roch. I do; and much lament the fudden Fall
Of his brave Houfe.   It is young *Charalois*,
Son to the Marfhal, from whom he inherits
His Fame and Vertues only.

Rom. Ha! they name you.

Du Croy. His Father died in Prifon two Days fince.

Roch. Yes, to the Shame of this ungrateful State;
That fuch a Mafter in the Art of War,
So noble, and fo highly meriting
From this forgetful Country, fhould, for Want
Of Means to fatisfy his Creditors
The Sum he took up for the general Good,
Meet with an End fo infamous.

Rom. Dare you ever hope for like Opportunity?

Du Croy. My good Lord!

Roch. My Wifh bring Comfort to you.

Du Croy. The Time calls us.

Roch. Good morrow, Colonel!

[*Exeunt* Rochfort, Du Croy.

Rom. This obftinate Spleen,
You think becomes your Sorrow, and forts well
With your black Suits: But, grant me Wit, or Judg-
    ment,
And, by the Freedom of an honeft Man,
And a true Friend to boot, I fwear, 'tis fhameful:
And therefore, flatter not yourfelf with Hope,
Your fable Habit, with the Hat and Cloak,
No, though the Ribbons help, have Power to work 'em
To what you would: For thofe, that had no Eyes
To fee the great Acts of your Father, will not,
From any Fafhion Sorrow can put on,
Be taught to know their Duties.

Char. If they will not,
They are too old to learn, and I too young
To give them Counfel; fince, if they partake
The Underftanding, and the Hearts of Men,
They will prevent my Words and Tears: If not,
What can Perfuafion, though made eloquent

With

With Grief, work upon such as have chang'd Natures
In the most savage Beast? Blest, blest be ever
. Memory of that happy Age, when Justice
no Guards to keep off wrong'd Innocence
flying to her Succours, and, in that,
ence of Redress: Whereas now, *Romont*,
he Damn'd, with more Ease may ascend from Hell,
Then we arrive at her. One *Cerberus*, there,
Forbids the Passage; in our Courts, a thousand,
As loud and fertile-headed; and the Client,
That wants the Sops, to fill their rav'nous Throats,
Must hope for no Access. Why should I, then,
Attempt Impossibilities, you, Friend, being
Too well acquainted with my Dearth of Means
To make my Entrance that Way?

   Rom. Would I were not.
But, Sir! you have a Cause, a Cause so just,
Of such Necessity, not to be deferr'd,
As would compel a Maid, whose Foot was never
Set o'er her Father's Threshold, nor within
The House where she was born, ever spake Word
Which was not usher'd with pure Virgin Blushes,
To drown the Tempest of a Pleader's Tongue,
And force Corruption to give back the Hire
It took against her:—Let Examples move you.
You see Men great in Birth, Esteem and Fortune,
Rather than lose a Scruple of their Right,
Fawn basely upon such, whose Gowns put off,
They would disdain for Servants.

   Char. And to these can I become a Suitor?

   Rom. Without Loss;
Would you consider, that, to gain their Favours,
Our chastest Dames put off their Modesties,
Soldiers forget their Honours, Usurers
Make Sacrifice of Gold, Poets of Wit,
And Men religious part with Fame, and Goodness.
Be therefore won to use the Means that may
Advance your pious Ends.

                             Char.

Char. You ſhall o'ercome.

Rom. And you receive the Glory. Pray you, now,
      practiſe.
'Tis well.

Enter Old Noval, Liladam, *and three Creditors.*

Char. Not look on me !

Rom. You muſt have Patience——Offer't again.

Char. And be again contemn'd !

Nov. I know what's to be done.——

1 *Cred.* And, that your Lordſhip
Will pleaſe to do your Knowledge, we offer, firſt
Our thankful Hearts here, as a bounteous Earneſt
To what we will add.——

Nov. One Word more of this,
I am your Enemy.   Am I a Man,
Your Bribes can work on ? Ha?

Lilad. Friends! you miſtake
The Way to win my Lord ;—he muſt not hear this,
But I, as one in Favour, in his Sight,
May hearken to you for my Profit.   Sir !
—I pray hear 'em.

Nov. 'Tis well.

Lilad. Obſerve him, now.

Nov. Your Cauſe being good, and your Proceedings
      ſo,
Without Corruption ;—I am your Friend,
Speak your Deſires.

2 *Cred.* Oh, they are charitable ;
The Marſhal ſtood engag'd, unto us three
Two hundred thouſand Crowns, which by his Death
We are defeated of.   For which great Loſs
We aim at nothing but his rotten Fleſh ;
Nor is that Cruelty.

1 *Cred.* I have a Son
That talks of nothing but of Guns and Armour,
And ſwears he'll be a Soldier ; 'tis an Humour

I would divert him from; and I am told,
That if I minifter to him, in his Drink,
Powder, made of this Bankrupt Marfhal's Bones,
Provided that the Carcafe rot above Ground,
'Twill cure his foolifh Frenzy.

Nov. You fhew in it
A Father's Care.   I have a Son myfelf,
A fafhionable Gentleman, and a peaceful:
And, but I am affur'd he's not fo given,
He fhould take of it too.—Sir! what are you?

Char. A Gentleman.

Nov. So are many that rake Dunghills.
If you have any Suit, move it in Court:
I take no Papers in Corners.

Rom. Yes, as the Matter may be carried, and hereby
To manage the Conveyance——Follow him.

Lilad. You're rude: I fay, he fhall not pafs.

        [*Exeunt* Novall, Charalois, *and Advocates.*

Rom. You fay fo? On what Affurance?
For the well-cutting of his Lordfhip's Corns,
Picking his Toes, or any Office elfe
Nearer to Bafenefs?

Lilad. Look upon me better;
Are thefe the Enfigns of fo coarfe a Fellow?
Be well advis'd.

Rom. Out, Rogue! do not I know   [*Kicks him.*
Thefe glorious Weeds fpring from the fordid Dunghill
Of thy officious Bafenefs? Wert thou worthy
Of any Thing from me, but my Contempt,
I would do more then this,—more, you Court-Spider!

Lilad. But that this Man is lawlefs; he fhould find
That I am valiant.

  1 *Cred.* If your Ears are faft,
'Tis nothing.   What's a Blow or two? As much—

  2 *Cred.* Thefe Chaftifements, as ufeful are as fre-
    quent
To fuch as would grow rich.

                                Rom.

Rom. Are they fo, Rafcals? I will befriend you then——
                                                    [*Kicks them.*

1 *Cred.* Bear Witnefs, Sirs!

Lilad. Truth, I have born my Part already, Friends!
In the Court you fhall hear more.   [*Exit.*

Rom. I know you for
The worft of Spirits, that ftrive to rob the Tombs
Of what is their Inheritance, the Dead :
For Ufurers, bred by a riotous Peace ;
That hold the Charter of your Wealth and Freedom,
By being Knaves and Cuckolds, that ne'er pray'd,
But when you fear the rich Heirs will grow wife,
To keep their Lands out of your Parchment Toils;
And then, the Devil your Father's call'd upon,
T' invent fome Ways of Luxury ne'er thought on.
Be gone, and quickly, or I'll leave no Room
Upon your Foreheads for your Horns to fprout on,
Without a Murmur, or I will undo you; .
For I will beat you honeft.

1 *Cred.* Thrift forbid !
We will bear this, rather then hazard that.
                                          [*Exit Creditor.*

Enter Charalois.

Rom. I am fomewhat eas'd in this yet.——

Char. Only Friend!
To what vain Purpofe do I make my Sorrow
Wait on the Triumph of their Cruelty ?
Or teach their Pride from my Humility,
To think it has o'ercome ? They are determin'd
What they will do; and it may well become me,
To rob them of the Glory they expect
From my fubmifs Intreaties.

Rom. Think not fo, Sir !
The Difficulties that you encounter with,
Will crown the Undertaking——Heaven! you weep
And I could do fo too; but that I know,
There's more expected, from the Son and Friend

Of

Of him whose fatal Loss now shakes our Natures,
Than Sighs, or Tears, in which a Village-Nurse,
Or cunning Strumpet, when her Knave is hang'd,
May overcome us. We are Men, young Lord,
Let us not do like Women.—To the Court,
And there speak like your Birth: Wake sleeping Justice,
Or dare the Axe. This is a Way will sort
With what you are: I call you not to that
I will shrink from myself, I will deserve
Your Thanks, or suffer with you—O how bravely
That sudden Fire of Anger shews in you!
Give Fuel to it, since you're on a Shelf,
Of extreme Danger, suffer like yourself.   [*Exeunt.*

SCENE II.

Enter Rochfort, Novall, *sen.* Charmi, Du Croy, *Advocates,* Beaumont, *and Officers, and three Presidents.*

  Du Croy. Your Lordship's seated. May this Meeting prove
Prosperous to us, and to the general Good of *Burgundy.*
  Nov. sen. Speak to the Point!
  Du Croy. Which is
With Honour to dispose the Place and Power
Of Primier President, which this reverend Man,
Grave *Rochfort,* (whom for Honour's Sake I name)
Is purpos'd to resign a Place, my Lords,
In which he hath, with such Integrity,
Perform'd the first and best Parts of a Judge;
That, as his Life transcends all fair Examples
Of such as were before him in *Dijon,*
So it remains to those that shall succeed him,
A Precedent that they may imitate, but not equal.
  Roch. I may not fit to hear this.
  Du Croy. Let the Love,
And Thankfulness we're bound to pay to Goodness,
In this o'ercome your Modesty.
  Roch. My Thanks

                                        For

For this great Favour ſhall prevent your Trouble.
The honourable Truſt, that was impos'd
Upon my Weakneſs, ſince you witneſs for me,
It was not ill diſcharg'd, I will not mention ;
Nor now, if Age had not depriv'd me of
The little Strength I had to govern well
The Province that I undertook, forſake it.

   Nov. ſen. That we could lend you of our Years.
   Du Croy. Or Strength !
   Nov. ſen. Or, as you are, perſuade you to continue
The noble Exerciſe of your knowing Judgment !
   Rocb. That may not be ; nor can your Lordſhip's
      Goodneſs,
Since your-Employments have conferr'd upon me
Sufficient Wealth, deny the Uſe of it ;
And, though old Age, when one Foot's in the Grave,
In many, when all Humours elſe are ſpent
Feeds no Affection in them, but Deſire
To add Height to the Mountain of their Riches :
In me it is not ſo : I reſt content
With th' Honours, and Eſtate I now poſſeſs,
And, that I may have Liberty to uſe,
What Heav'n, ſtill bleſſing my poor Induſtry,
Hath made me Maſter of, I pray the Court
To eaſe me of my Burthen ; that I may
Employ the ſmall Remainder of my Life,
In living well, and learning how to die ſo.

       Enter Romont, *and* Charalois

   Rom. See Sir, our Advocate.
   Du Croy. The Court intreats
Your Lordſhip will be pleas'd to name t.
Which you would have your Succeſſor,   r a
All promiſe to confirm it.
   Rocb. I embrace it
As an Aſſurance of their Favour to me
And name my Lord *Novel.*
   Du Croy. The Court allows it.

Roch. But there are Suiters wait here, and their Caufes
May be of more Neceffity to be heard,
And therefore wifh that mine may be deferr'd,
And theirs have Hearing.

Du Croy. If your Lordfhip pleafe
To take the Place, we will proceed.

Charmi. The Caufe
We come to offer to your Lordfhip's Cenfure,
Is in itfelf fo noble, that it needs not
Or Rhetorick in me that plead, or Favour
From your grave Lordfhips, to determine of it.
Since, to the Praife of your impartial Juftice
(Which guilty, nay, condemn'd Men, dare not fcandal)
It will erect a Trophy of your Mercy
Which marry'd to that Juftice.——

Nov. fen. Speak to the Caufe.

Charmi. I will, my Lord! to fay, the late dead Mar-
fhal,
The Father of this young Lord here, my Client,
Hath done his Country great and faithful Service,
Might tafk me of Impertinence, to repeat
What your grave Lordfhips cannot but remember,
He, in his Life, become indebted to
Thefe thrifty Men, (I will not wrong their Credits,
By giving them the Attributes they now merit)
And failing, by the Fortune of the Wars,
Of Means to free himfelf from his Engagements,
He was arrefted, and for Want of Bail,
Imprifon'd at their Suit: And not long after
With Lofs of Liberty ended his Life.
And, though it be a Maxim in our Laws,
All Suits die with the Perfon, thefe Men's Malice
In Death find Matter for their Hate to work on,
Denying him the decent Rites of Burial,
Which the fworn Enemies of the Chriftian Faith
Grant freely to their Slaves : May it, therefore, pleafe
Your Lordfhips, fo to fafhion your Decree,
That, what their Cruelty doth forbid, your Pity
May give Allowance to.

Nov.

Nov. fen. How long have you, Sir, practis'd in Court?

Charmi. Some twenty Years, my Lord.

Nov. fen. By your grofs Ignorance, it fhould appear,
Not twenty Days.

Charmi. I hope I have giv'n no Caufe in this, my
·Lord——

Nov. fen. How dare you move the Court ·
To the difpenfing with an Act confirm'd
By Parliament, to the Terror of all Bankrupts?
Go home! and with more Care perufe the Statutes;
Or the next Motion, favouring of this Boldnefs,
May force you to leap (againft your Will)
. Over the Place you plead at.

Charmi. I forefaw this.

Rom. Why, does your Lordfhip think, the moving of
A Caufe, more honeft than this Court had ever
The Honour to determine, can deferve
A Check like this?

Nov. fen. Strange Boldnefs!

Rom. 'Tis fit Freedom :
Or, do you conclude, an Advocate cannot hold
His Credit with the Judge, unlefs he ftudy
His Face more than the Caufe for which he pleads?

Charmi. Forbear!

Rom. Or, cannot you, that have the Power
To qualify the Rigour of the Laws
When you are pleafed, take a little from
The Strictnefs of your four Decrees, enacted
In Favour of the greedy Creditors
Againft the o'erthrown Debtor?

Nov. fen. Sirrah! you that prate
Thus faucily, what are you?

Rom. Why, I'll tell you,
Thou Purple-colour'd Man! I'm one to whom
Thou ow'ft the Means thou haft of fitting there
A corrupt Elder.

Charmi. Forbear!

Rom. The Nofe thou wear'ft, is my Gift, and thofe
Eyes,

That

That meet no Object so base as their Master,
Had been long since, torn from that guilty Head,
And thou thyself Slave to some needy *Swifs*,
Had I not worn a Sword, and us'd it better
Than in thy Prayers thou ever didst thy Tongue.

  Nov. sen. Shall such an Insolence pass unpunish'd?
  Charmi. Hear me!

  Rom. Yet I, that, in my Service done my Country,
Disdain to be put in the Scale with thee,
Confess myself unworthy to be valu'd
With the least Part, nay, Hair of the dead Marshal,
Of whose so many glorious Undertakings,
Make Choice of any one, and that the meanest,
Perform'd against the subtle Fox of *France*,
The politick *Lewis*, or the more desperate *Swifs*,
And 'twill outweigh all the good Purpose,
Though put in Act, that ever Gownman practis'd.

  Nov. sen. Away with him to Prison!

  Rom. If that Curses,
Urg'd justly, and breath'd forth so, ever fell
On those that did deserve them; let not mine
Be spent in vain now, that thou from this Instant
May'st, in thy Fear that they will fall upon thee,
Be sensible of the Plagues they shall bring with them,
And for denying of a little Earth,
To cover what remains of our great Soldier:
May all your Wives prove Whores, your Factors Thieves,
And, while you live, your riotous Heirs undo you.
And thou, the Patron of their Cruelty,
Of all thy Lordships live not to be Owner
Of so much Dung as will conceal a Dog,
Or, what is worse, thyself in.   And thy Years,
To th' End thou mayst be wretched, I wish many;
And, as thou hast deny'd the Dead a Grave,
May Misery in thy Life make thee desire one,
Which Men and all the Elements keep from thee:
I have begun well, imitate, exceed.

  Roch. Good Counsel, were it a Praise-worthy Deed.
                    [*Exit Officers with* Romont.
                              Du Croye.

Du Croye. Remember what we are.

Char. Thus low my Duty
Anfwers your Lordſhip's Counſel. I will uſe
In the few Words, with which I am to trouble
Your Lordſhip's Ears the Temper that you wiſh me;
Not that I fear to ſpeak my Thoughts as loud,
And with a Liberty beyond *Romont ;*
But that I know, for me, that am made up
Of all that's wretched, ſo to haſte my End,
Would ſeem to moſt, rather a Willingneſs
To quit the Burthen of a hopeleſs Life,
Than Scorn of Death, or Duty to the Dead.
I, therefore, bring the Tribute of my Praiſe
To your Severity, and commend the Juſtice
That will not, for the many Services
That any Man hath done the Common-wealth,
Wink at his leaſt of Ills : What, though my Father
Writ Man before he was ſo, and confirm'd it,
By numbring that Day, no Part of his Life,
In which he did not Service to his Country ;
Was he to be free, therefore, from the Laws,
And ceremonious Form in your Decrees ?
Or elſe, becauſe he did as much as Man
In thoſe three memorable Overthrows
At *Granfon, Morat, Nancy,* where his Maſter,
The warlike *Charalois* (with whoſe Misfortunes
I bear his Name) loſt Treaſure, Men and Life,
To be excus'd from Payment of thoſe Sums
Which (his own Patrimony ſpent) his Zeal,
To ſerve his Country, forc'd him to take up ?

Nov. ſen. The Precedent were ill.

Char. And yet, my Lord, thus much
I know you'll grant; after thoſe great Defeatures,
Which in their dreadful Ruins buried quick

Enter Officers.

Courage and Hope, in all Men but himſelf,
He forc'd the proud Foe, in his Height of Conqueſt,

To

To yield unto an honourable Peace,
And in it fav'd an hundred thoufand Lives,
To end his own, that was fure Proof againſt
The fcalding Summer's Heat, and Winter's Froſt,
Ill Airs, the Cannon, and the Enemy's Sword,
In a moſt loathfome Prifon.

   Du Croy. 'Twas his Fault
To be fo prodigal.

   Nov. fen. He had from the State
Sufficient Entertainment for the Army.

   Char. Sufficient, my Lord ? You fit at Home,
And, though your Fees are boundleſs at the Bar,
Are thrifty in the Charges of the War,
But your Wills be obey'd.   To thefe I turn,
To thefe foft-hearted Men, that wifely know
They're only good Men, that pay what they owe.

   2 *Cred.* And fo they are.

   1 *Cred.* 'Tis the City-Doctrine ;
We ſtand bound to maintain it.

   Char. Be conſtant in it ;
And, fince you are as mercileſs in your Natures,
As bafe and mercenary in your Means
By which you get your Wealth, I will not urge
The Court to take away one Scruple from
The Right of their Laws, or one good Thought
In you to mend your Difpofition with.
I know there is no Mufick to your Ears
So pleafing as the Groans of Men in Prifon,
And that the Tears of Widows, and the Cries
Of famifh'd Orphans, are the Feaſts that take you.
That to be in your Danger, with more Care
Should be avoided, than infectious Air,
The loath'd Embraces of difeafed Women,
A Flatterer's Poifon, or the Lofs of Honour.
Yet, rather than my Father's reverend Duſt
Shall want a Place in that fair Monument,
In which our noble Anceſtors lie intomb'd,
Before the Court I offer up myfelf
A Prifoner for it : Load me with thofe Irons

                                That

That have worn out his Life; in my beſt Strength
I'll run to the Encounter of cold Hunger,
And chooſe my Dwelling where no Sun dares enter,
So he may be releas'd.

    1 *Cred.* What mean you, Sir?

    2 *Advo.* Only your Fee again: There's ſo much ſaid
Already in this Cauſe, and ſaid ſo well,   ·
That, ſhould I only offer to ſpeak in it,
I ſhould not be heard, or laugh'd at for it.

    1 *Cred.* 'Tis the firſt Money Advocate e'er gave back,
'Though he ſaid nothing.

    Roch. Be advis'd, young Lord,
And well conſiderate; you throw away
Your Liberty, and Joys of Life together:
Your Bounty is employ'd upon a Subject
That is not ſenſible of it, with which wiſe Man
Never abus'd his Goodneſs; the great Virtues
Of your dead Father vindicate themſelves
From theſe Mens Malice, and break ope the Priſon,
Though it contain his Body.

    Nov. ſen. Let him alone:
If he love Cords, a God's Name, let him wear 'em,
Provided theſe conſent.

    Char. I hope they are not
So ignorant in any Way of Profit,
As to neglect a Poſſibility
To get their own, by ſeeking it from that
Which can return them nothing, but ill Fame,
And Curſes for their barbarous Cruelties.

    3 *Cred.* What think you of the Offer?

    2 *Cred.* Very well.

    1 *Cred.* Accept it by all Means: Let's ſhut him up,
He is well-ſhap'd, and has a villainous Tongue,
And ſhould he ſtudy that Way of Revenge,
As I dare almoſt ſwear he loves a Wench,
We have no Wives, nor ever ſhall get Daughters
That will hold out againſt him.

    Du Croy. What's your Anſwer?

    2 *Cred.* Speak you for all.

                               1 *Cred.*

1 *Cred.* Why, let our Executions
That lie upon the Father, be return'd
Upon the Son, and we releafe the Body.
    Nov. fen. The Court muft grant you that.
    Char. I thank your Lordfhips,
They have in it confirm'd on me fuch Glory,
As no Time can take from me : I am ready,
Come lead me where you pleafe : Captivity,
That comes with Honour, is true Liberty.
        [*Exit* Charalois, *Creditors and Officers.*
    Nov. fen. Strange Rafhnefs.
    Roch. A brave Refolution rather,
Worthy a better Fortune ; but, however,
It is not now to be difputed, therefore
To my own Caufe.   Already I have found
Your Lordfhips bountiful in your Favours to me ;
And that fhould teach my Modefty to end here,
And prefs your Loves no farther.
    Du Croy. There is nothing
The Court can grant, but with Affurance you
May afk it, and obtain it.
    Roch. You encourage a bold Petitioner, and 'tis not
Your Favours fhould be loft.   Befides, 'thas been   [fit
A Cuftom many Years, at the furrend'ring
The Place I now give up, to grant the Prefident
One Boon, that parted with it.   And, to confirm
Your Grace towards me, againft all fuch as may
Detract my Actions, and Life hereafter,
I now prefer it to you.
    Du Croy. Speak it freely.
    Roch. I then defire the Liberty of *Romont*,
And that my Lord *Noval*, whofe private Wrong
Was equal to the Injury that was done
To the Dignity of the Court, will pardon it,
And now fign his Enlargement.
    Nov. fen. Pray you demand
The Moiety of my Eftate, or any Thing
Within my Power, but this.
    Roch. Am I deny'd then—my firft and laft Requeft ?
                                Du Croy.

Du Croy. It muſt not be.

2 *Pre.* I have a Voice to give in it.

3 *Pre.* And I.
And, if Perſuaſion will not work him to it,
We will make known our Power.

Nov. ſen. You are too violent;
You ſhall have my Conſent.—But would you had
Made Trial of my Love in any thing
But this, you ſhould have found then—But it ſkills not.
You have what you deſire.

Roch. I thank your Lordſhips.

Du Croy. The Court is up — Make Way.

[*Exeunt all but* Rochfort *and* Beaumont.

Roch. I follow you — Beaumont!

Beaum. My Lord.

Roch. You are a Scholar, *Beaumont!*
And can ſearch deeper into th' Intents of Men,
Than thoſe that are leſs knowing.—How appear'd
The Piety and brave Behaviour of
Young *Charalois* to you?

Beaum. It is my Wonder,
Since I want Language to expreſs it fully;
And ſure the Colonel ——

Roch. Fie! he was faulty.— What preſent Money
        have I?

Beaum. There is no Want
Of any Sum a private Man has Uſe for.

Roch. 'Tis well:
I am ſtrangely taken with this *Charalois*;
Methinks, from his Example, the whole Age
Should learn to be good, and continue ſo.
Virtue works ſtrangely with us; and his Goodneſs
Riſing above his Fortune, ſeems to me,
Prince-like, to will, not aſk a Courteſy.   [*Exeunt.*

The End of the Firſt Act.

ACT

✖:✖✖✖✖✖✖✖✖✖✖✖✖✖✖✖✖✖✖✖:✖

ACT II.   SCENE I.

Enter Pontalier, Malotin, Beaumont.

Malot. 'TIS ſtrange.
  Beaum. Methinks ſo.
 Pont. In a Man, but young,
Yet old in Judgment, theorick and practick,
In all Humanity, and (to increaſe the Wonder)
Religious, yet a Soldier, that he ſhould
Yield his free-living Youth a Captive, for
The Freedom of his aged Father's Corps,
And rather chooſe to want Life's Neceſſaries,
Liberty, Hope of Fortune, than it ſhould
In Death be kept from Chriſtian Ceremony.
 Malot. Come, 'tis a golden Precedent in a Son
To let ſtrong Nature have the better Hand,
(In ſuch a Caſe) of all affected Reaſon.
What Years ſit on this *Charalois ?*
 Beaum. Twenty-eight ;
For ſince the Clock did ſtrike him ſeventeen old,
Under his Father's Wing, this Son hath fought,
Serv'd and commanded, and ſo aptly both,
That ſometimes he appear'd his Father's Father,
And never leſs than's Son ; the old Man's Virtues
So recent in him, as the World may ſwear,
Nought but a fair Tree could ſuch fair Fruit bear.
 Pont. But wherefore lets he ſuch a barb'rous Law,
And Men more barbarous to execute it,
Prevail on his ſoft Diſpoſition,
That he had rather die alive for Debt
Of the old Man in Priſon, than they ſhould
Rob him of Sepulture, conſidering
Theſe Monies borrow'd bought the Lenders Peace,
And all their Means they enjoy, nor was diffus'd
In any impious or licentious Path ?

        Beaum.

Beaum. True! for my Part, were it my Father's Trunk,
The tyrannous Ram-heads, with their Horns fhould
  gore it,
Or caft it to their Curs, than they lefs currifh,
E'er prey on me fo, with their Lion-Law,
Being in my Free Will (as in his) to fhun it,
 Pont. Alas! he knows himfelf in Poverty loft:
For in this partial avaricious Age
What Price bears Honour ²? Virtue? Long ago
It was but prais'd, and freez'd, but now-a-days
'Tis colder far, and has, nor Love, nor Praife;
Very Praife now freezeth too: For Nature
Did make the Heathen far more Chriftian then,
Than Knowledge us (lefs heathenifh) Chriftian.
 Malo. This Morning is the Funeral.
 Pont. Certainly!
And from this Prifon 'twas the Son's Requeft
That his dear Father might Interment have.
        [Recorders Mufick.
See the young Son interr'd a lively Grave.
 Beaum. They come — Obferve their Order.

*Enter Funeral. The Body borne by four. Captains and
 Soldiers, Mourners, 'Scutcheons, &c. in very good Or-
 der. Charalois and* Romont *meet it.* Charalois *fpeaks.*
 Romont *weeping. Solemn Mufick. Three Creditors.*

 Char. How like a filent Stream fhaded with Night,
And gliding foftly with our windy Sighs,
Moves the whole Frame of this Solemnity!
Tears, Sighs and Blacks filling the Simile!
Whilft I, the only Murmur in this Grove
Of Death, thus hollowly break forth!—Vouchfafe

---

  ² ———— *In this partial avaricious Age
  What Price bears Honour,* &c.

 This beautiful and juft Reflection holds no lefs true in thefe Days,
than it did in thofe of Old.

To ſtay awhile.—Reſt, reſt in Peace, dear Earth !
Thou, that brought'ſt Reſt to their unthankful Lives,
Whoſe Cruelty deny'd thee Reſt in Death !
Here ſtands thy poor Executor, thy Son,
That makes his Life Priſoner, to bail thy Death :
Who gladlier puts on this Captivity,
Than Virgins, long in Love, their Wedding Weeds :
Of all that ever thou haſt done Good to,
Theſe only have good Memories ; for they
Remember beſt, forget not Gratitude.
I thank you for this laſt and friendly Love.
And, though this Country, like a vip'rous Mother,
Not only hath eat up ungratefully
All Means of thee her Son, but laſt thyſelf,
Leaving thy Heir ſo bare and indigent,
He cannot raiſe thee a poor Monument,
Such as a Flatterer, or an Uſurer hath.
Thy Worth, in every honeſt Breaſt, builds one,
Making their friendly Hearts thy Funeral Stone.

 Pont. Sir !
 Char. Peace! O Peace! This Scene is wholly mine.
What! Weep ye, Soldiers ? — Blanch not. — *Romont*
  weeps.
Ha ! let me ſee ! my Miracle is eas'd :
The Jailors and the Creditors do weep :
E'en they that make us weep, do weep themſelves.
Be theſe thy Body's Balm : Theſe and thy Virtue
Keep thy Fame ever odoriferous,
Whilſt the great, proud, rich, undeſerving Man,
Alive ſtinks in his Vices, and being vaniſh'd,
The golden Calf that was an Idol, deck'd
With Marble Pillars, Jet, and Porphyry,
Shall quickly both in Bone and Name conſume,
Though wrapt in Lead, Spice, Searcloth, and Perfume.

 1 *Cred.* Sir !
 Char. What ! — Away, for Shame ! you prophane
  Rogues
Muſt not be mingled with theſe holy Reliques :
This is a Sacrifice — Our Show'r ſhall crown

            His

His Sepulchre with Olive, Myrrh, and Bays,
The Plants of Peace, of Sorrow, Victory;
Your Tears would spring but Weeds.

1 *Cred.* Would they so?
We'll keep them to stop Bottles then.

Rom. No, keep 'em for your own Sins, you Rogues,
'Till you repent; you'll die else, and be damn'd.

2 *Cred.* Damn'd, ha! ha! ha!

Rom. Laugh ye?

3 *Cred.* Yes faith, Sir; we'ld be very glad
To please you either Way.

1 *Cred.* Ye're ne'er content,
Crying nor laughing.

Rom. Both with a Birth she rogues.

2 *Cred.* Our Wives, Sir, taught us.

Rom. Look, look, you Slaves! your thankless Cru-
And savage Manners of unkind *Dijon*, [elty,
Exhauft these Floods, and not his Father's Death.

1 *Cred.* 'Slid, Sir! what would you, you're so cholerick?

1 *Cred.* Most Soldiers are so i' faith.—Let him alone,
They've little else to live on; we've not had
A Penny of him, have we?

3 *Cred.* 'Slight, would you have our Hearts?

1 *Cred.* We've nothing but his Body here in Durance
For all our Money.

Prieft. On.

Char. One Moment more,
But to bestow a few poor Legacies,
All I have left in my dead Father's Rights,
And I have done. Captain, wear thou these Spurs,
That yet ne'er made his Horse run from a Foe.
Lieutenant, thou this Scarf; and may it tie
Thy Valour and thy Honesty together:
For so it did in him. Ensign, this Cuirass,
Your General's Necklace, once. You gentle Bearers,
Divide this Purse of Gold: This other, strew
Among the Poor.—'Tis all I have. *Romont*,
Wear thou this Medal of himself, that, like

A

A hearty Oak, grew'ft clofe to this tall Pine,
E'en in the wildeft Wildernefs of War,
Whereon Foes broke their Swords, and tir'd themfelves;
Wounded and hack'd ye were, but never fell'd.
For me, my Portion provide in Heaven :
My Root is earth'd, and I, a defolate Branch,
Left fcatter'd in the Highway of the World ;
Trod under Foot, that might have been a Column
Mainly fupporting our demolifh'd Houfe,
This would I wear as my Inheritance.
And what Hope can arife to me from it,
When I and it are both here Prifoners ?
Only may this, if ever we be free,
Keep, or redeem me from all Infamy.

S O N G.

> Fie ! ceafe to wonder !
> *Though you hear* Orpheus, *with his Ivory Lute,*
>   *Move Trees and Rocks,*
> *Charm Bulls, Bears, and Men more favage, to be mute,*
>   *Weak foolifh Singer, here is one*
>   *Would have transform'd thyfelf, to Stone.*

   1 *Cred.* No farther ! look to 'em at your own Peril.
   2 *Cred.* No, as they pleafe :—Their Mafter's a good
I would they were at the *Bermudas.*   [Man.
   Jailor. You muft no farther.——
The Prifon limits you, and the Creditors
Exact the Strictnefs.
   Rom. Out, you wolfifh Mongrels !
Whofe Brains fhould be knock'd out, like Dogs in *July,*
Left your Infection poifon a whole Town.
   Char. They grudge our Sorrow. — Your ill Wills,
     perforce,
Turn now to Charity : They would not have us
Walk too far mourning, Ufurer's Relief
Grieves, if the Debtors have to much of Grief.
                 [*Exeunt.*
            S C E N E

S C E N E II.

Enter Beaumelle, Florimel, Bellapert.

Beaumel. I pr'ythee tell me, *Florimel,* why do Women marry?

Flor. Why truly, Madam, I think, to lie with their Hufbands.

Bellap. You are a Fool. She lies, Madam; Women marry Hufbands,
To lie with other Men.

Flor. 'Faith, e'en fuch a Woman wilt thou make. By this Light, Madam, this Wagtail will fpoil you, if you take Delight in her Licence.

Beaumel. 'Tis true, *Florimel,* and thou wilt make me too good for a young Lady. What an Electuary found my Father out for his Daughter, when he compounded you two my Women? for thou, *Florimel,* art e'en a Grain too heavy—fimply for a Waiting-Gentlewoman.

Flor. And thou, *Bellapert,* a Grain too light.

Bellap. Well, go thy Ways, goodly Wifdom, whom no-body regards. I wonder, whether be elder, thou or thy Hood: You think, becaufe you ferve my Lady's Mother, are thirty-two Years old, which is a Peep-out, you know.

Flor. Well faid, Whirligig.

Bellap. You are deceiv'd: I want a Peg i' th' Middle, Out of thefe Prerogatives! you think to be Mother of the Maids here, and mortify 'em with Proverbs: Go, go, govern the Sweet-meats, and weigh the Sugar, that the Wenches fteal none: Say your Prayers twice a Day, and, as I take it, you have performed your Function.

Flor. I may be even with you.

Bellap. Hark! the Court's broke up. Go, help my old Lord out of his Caroch, and fcratch his Head till Dinner-time.

Flor. Well. [*Exit.*

Bellap. Fie, Madam! how you walk! By my Maiden-

head,

head, you look feven Years older than you did this
Morning: Why, there can be nothing under the Sun
valuable, to make you thus a Minute.

Beaumel. Ah, my fweet *Bellapert!* thou Cabinet
To all my Counfels, thou doft know the Caufe
That makes thy Lady wither thus in Youth.

Bellap. Uds-light, enjoy your Wifhes: Whilft I live,
One Way or other you fhall crown your Will.
Would you have him your Hufband that you love,
And can't not be? He is your Servant, though,
And may perform the Office of a Hufband.

Beaumel. But there is Honour, Wench.

Bellap. Such a Difeafe
There is indeed, for which ere I would die ——

Beaumel. Pr'ythee, diftinguifh me a Maid and Wife.

Bellap. 'Faith, Madam, one may bear any Man's
Children,
T'other muft bear no Man's.

Beaumel. What is a Hufband?

Bellap. Phyfick, that, tumbling in your Belly, will
make you fick i' th' Stomach. The only Diftinction betwixt a Hufband and a Servant is, the firft will lie with
you, when he pleafes; the laft fhall lie with you, when
you pleafe. Pray tell me, Lady, do you love, to marry
after; or would you marry, to love after?

Beaumel. I would meet Love and Marriage both at
once.

Bellap. Why then you are out of the Fafhion, and
will be contemn'd: For, I'll affure you, there are few
Women in the World, but either they have married
firft, and love after; or love firft, and married after.
You muft do as you may, not as you would: Your
Father's Will is the Goal you muft fly to. If a Hufband approach you, you would have farther off, is he
your Love? the lefs near you. A Hufband in thefe
Days is but a Cloak to be oftener laid upon your Bed,
than in your Bed.

Beaumel. Hum!

Bellap. Sometimes you may wear him on your Shoulder;

der; and now and then under your Arm; but seldom or never let him cover you; for 'tis not the Fashion.

Enter Novall, *jun.* Pontalier, Malotin, Liladam, Aymer.

Nov. jun. Best Day to Nature's Curiosity,
Star of *Dijon,* the Lustre of all *France!*
Perpetual Spring dwell on thy rosy Cheeks,
Whose Breath is Perfume to our Continent,
See *Flora* turn'd in her Varieties. [1]

Bellap. Oh divine Lord!

Nov. jun. No Autumn, nor no Age ever approach
This heavenly Piece, which Nature having wrought,
She lost her Needle, and did then despair
Ever to work so lively and so fair.

Lilad. Uds-light, my Lord, one of the Purls of your Band
Is, without all Discipline, fall'n out of his Rank.

Nov. jun. How? I would not for a thousand Crowns she had seen't. Dear *Liladam,* reform it.

Bellap. Oh Lord! *Per se,* Lord! Quintessence of Honour! she walks not under a Weed that could deny thee any Thing.

Beaumel. Pr'ythee Peace, Wench! thou dost but blow the Fire, that flames too much already.

[Liladam *and* Aymer *trim* Novall, *whilst* Bellapert *her Lady.*

Aymer. By Gad, my Lord, you have the divinest Taylor in *Christendom;* he hath made you look like an Angel in your Cloth of Tissue Doublet.

Pont. This is a three legg'd Lord: There's a fresh Assault. Oh! that Men should spend Time thus! —

---

[1] *See* Flora *turn'd in her Varieties.*

Thus it stands in the old Copies; but certainly false: We ought to read

See Flora *trim'd in her Varieties.*

See, fee how her Blood drives to her Heart, and ftrait
vaults to her Cheeks again.

Malot. What are thefe?

Pont. One of 'em there, the lower, is a good, foolifh, knavifh, fociable Gallimaufry of a Man, and has
much taught my Lord with Singing; he is Mafter of a
Mufick Houfe. The other is his Dreffing-Block, upon
whom my Lord lays all his Cloaths, and Fafhions, ere
he vouchfafes 'em his own Perfon; you fhall fee him
i' th' Morning in the Galley-foift, at Noon in the Bul-
lion, i' th' Evening in Quirpo, and all Night in —.

Malat. A Baudy-houfe.

Pont. If my Lord deny, they deny; if he affirm,
they affirm: They fkip into my Lord's caft Skins
fome twice a Year; and thus they live to eat, eat to
live, and live to praife my Lord.

Malot. Good Sir, tell me one Thing.

Pont. What's that?

Malot. Dare thefe Men ever fight, on any Caufe?

Pont. Oh, no, 'twould fpoil their Cloaths, and put
their Bands out of Order.

Nov. jun. Muft you hear the News: Your Father has
refign'd his Prefidentfhip to my Lord my Father.

Malot. And Lord *Charalois* undone for ever.

Pont. Troth, 'tis Pity, Sir!
A braver Hope of fo affur'd a Father
Did never comfort *France,*

Lilad. A good dumb Mourner.

Aymer. A filent Black.

Nov. jun. Oh, fie upon him, how he wears his Cloaths!
As if he had come this *Chriftmas* from *St. Omers,*
To fee his Friends, and return'd after Twelf-tide.

Lilad. His Colonel looks finely like a Drover.——

Nov. jun. That had a Winter lain perdieu i' th' Rain,

Aymer. What, he that wears a Clout about his Neck?
His Cuffs in's Pocket, and his Heart in's Mouth?

Nov. jun. Now, out upon him!

Beaumel. Servant, tie my Hand.

How

How your Lips blufh, in Scorn that they fhould pay
Tribute to Hands, when Lips are in the Way!
    Nov. jun. I thus recant; yet now your Hand looks
      white,
Becaufe your Lips rob'd it of fuch a Right.
Monfieur Aymer, I prythee fing the Song
Devoted to my Miftrefs,   *[Mufick.*

SONG.

A Dialogue between a Man and a Woman.

Man. *Set* Phœbus! *fet; a fairer Sun doth rife*
    From the bright Radiance of my Miftrefs' Eyes
    Than ever thou begat'ft : I dare not look;
    Each Hair a golden Line, each Word a Hook
    The more I ftrive, the more ftill I am took.
Wom. *Fair Servant! come; the Day thefe Eyes do lend*
    To warm thy Blood, thou doft fo vainly fpend,
    Come ftrangled Breath.
Man. *What Note fo fweet as this*
    That calls the Spirits to a further Blifs ?
Wom. *Yet this out-favours Wine, and this Perfume.*
Man. *Let's die, I languifh, I confume.*

After the Song, enter Rochfort *and* Beaumont.

Beaum. *Remont* will come, Sir, ftraight.
Roch. 'Tis well.
Beaumel. My Father,
Nov. jun, My honourable Lord.
Roch. My Lord *Novall !* this is a Virtue in you,
So early up and ready before Noon ;
That are the Map of Dreffing through all *France*.
    Nov. jun, I rife to fay my Prayers, Sir, here's my Saint.
    Roch. 'Tis well and courtly;—you muft give me
      Leave,
I have fome private Conference with my Daughter,
Pray ufe my Garden, you fhall dine with me.
    Lilad. We'll wait on you.   *Nov.*

Nov. jun. Good morn unto your Lordſhip,
Remember what you have vow'd—   [*To* Beaumelle.
            [*Exeunt all but* Rochfort *and* Beaumelle.
Beau. Perform I muſt.
Roch. Why how now, *Beaumelle*, thou look'ſt not well.
Th'art ſad of late,—come cheer thee ; I have found
A wholeſome Remedy for theſe maiden Fits,
A goodly Oak whereon to twiſt my Vine,
Till her fair Branches grow up to the Stars.
Be near at Hand, Succeſs crown my Intent,
My Buſineſs fills my little Time ſo full,
I cannot ſtand to talk : I know, thy Duty
Is Handmaid to my Will, eſpecially
When it preſents nothing but good and fit.
    Beaum. Sir, I am yours.—Oh ! if my Tears prove
        true,
Fate hath wrong'd Love, and will deſtroy me too.
                            [*Exit* Beaumelle.

            Enter Romont, *Keeper.*
    Rom. Sent you for me, Sir ?
    Roch. Yes.
    Rom. Your Lordſhip's Pleaſure ?
    Roch. Keeper, this Priſoner I will ſee forth coming.
Upon my Word—Sit down, good Colonel.
                            [*Exit Keeper.*
Why I did wiſh you hither, noble Sir,
Is, to adviſe you from this Iron Carriage,
Which, ſo affected, *Romont*, you will wear,
To pity, and to Counſel you ſubmit
With Expedition to the great *Novall :*
Recant your ſtern Contempt, and ſlight Neglect
Of the whole Court, and him, and Opportunity ;
Or you will undergo a heavy Cenſure
In public very ſhortly.
    Rom. Reverend Sir,
I have obſerv'd you, and do know you well ;
And am now more afraid you know not me,
By wiſhing my Submiſſion to *Novall,*
                                    Then

Then I can be of all the bellowing Mouths
That wait upon him to pronounce the Cenfure,
Could it determine me to Torments, and Shame.
Submit, and crave Forgivenefs of a Beaft?
'Tis true, this Boil of State wears purple Tiffue,
Is high fed, proud:—So is his Lordfhip's Horfe,
And bears as rich Caparifons. I know,
This Elephant carries on his Back not only
Tow'rs, Caftles, but the ponderous Republick,
And never ftoops for't, with his ftrong Breath Trunk
Snuffs other Titles, Lordfhips, Offices,
Wealth, Bribes, and Lives, under his ravenous Jaws:
What's this unto my Freedom? I dare die;
And therefore afk this Camel, if thefe Bleffings
(For fo they would be underftood by a Man)
But mollify one Rudenefs in his Nature,
Sweeten the eager Relifh of the Law,
At whofe great Helm he fits. Helps he the poor
In a juft Bufinefs? Nay, does he not crofs
Every deferved Soldier and Scholar,
As if, when Nature made him, fhe had made
The general Antipathy of all Virtue?
How favagely, and blafphemoufly he fpake
Touching the General, the grave General dead!
I muft weep, when I think on't.

   Roch. Sir.

   Rom. My Lord, I am not ftubborn: I can melt, you
      fee,
And prize a Virtue better then my Life:
For though I be not learn'd, I ever lov'd
That holy Mother of all Iffues, good,
Whofe white Hand for a Scepter holds a File,
To polifh rougheft Cuftoms, and in you
She has her Right: See! I am calm as Sleep,
But, when I think of the grofs Injuries,
The godlefs Wrong done to my General dead,
I rave indeed, and could eat this *Novall*
A Soul-lefs Dromedary.

   Roch. Oh! be temperate,

Sir,

Sir, though I would perfuade, I'll not conftrain;
Each Man's Opinion freely is his own,
Concerning any Thing, or any Body,
Be it right or wrong, 'tis at the Judges Peril.

Enter Beaumont.

Beaum. Thefe Men, Sir! wait without; my Lord is
    come too.

Roch. Pay 'em thofe Sums upon the Table; take
Their full Releafes :—Stay—I want a Witnefs :
Let me intreat you, Colonel, to walk in,
And ftand but by, to fee this Money paid,
It does concern you and your Friends; it was
The better Caufe you were fent for, though faid other-
    wife.
The Deed fhall make this my Requeft more plain.

Rom. I fhall obey your Pleafure, Sir, though ignorant
To what it tends?   [*Exit* Romont, *Servant,*

Enter Charalois.

Roch. Worthieft Sir,
You are moft welcome: Fie, no more of this:
You have out-wept a Woman, noble *Charalois!*
No Man but has, or muft bury a Father.

Char. Grave Sir! I buried Sorrow, for his Death,
In the Grave with him. I did never think
He was immortal—though I vow I grieve,
And fee no Reafon why the vicious,
Virtuous, valiant, and unworthy Men,
Should die alike.

Roch. They do not.

Char. In the Manner,
Of dying Sir, they do not, but all die,
And therein differ not :—But I have done.
I fpy'd the lively Picture of my Father,
Paffing your Gallery, and that caft this Water
Into mine Eyes: See,—foolifh that I am,
To let it do fo.

                                  Roch.

Roch. Sweet and gentle Nature!
How filken is this well comparatively
To other Men! I have a Suit to you Sir.

Char. Take it; 'tis granted.

Roch. What?

Char. Nothing, my Lord.

Roch. Nothing is quickly granted.

Char. Faith, my Lord!
That nothing granted, is even all I have,
For, all know, I have nothing left to grant.

Roch. Sir, have you any Suit to me? I'll grant
You fome Thing, any Thing.

Char. Nay, furely, I, that can
Give nothing, will but fue for that again.
No Man will grant me any Thing I fue for.
But begging nothing, every Man will give't.

Roch. Sir! the Love I bore your Father, and the
        Worth
I fee in you, fo much refembling his,
Made me thus fend for you. And tender here
                    [*Draws a Curtain.*
Whatever you will take, Gold, Jewels, both,
All, to fupply your Wants, and free yourfelf.
Where heavenly Virtue in high-blooded Veins
Is lodg'd, and can agree, Men fhould kneel down,
Adore, and facrifice all that they have;
And well they may, it is fo feldom feen.
Put off your Wonder, and here freely take
Or fend your Servants: Nor, Sir, fhall you ufe
In aught of this, a poor Man's Fee, or Bribe,
Unjuftly taken of the Rich, but what's
Directly gotten, and yet by the Law.

Char. How ill, Sir, it becomes thofe Hairs to mock!

Roch. Mock? Thunder ftrike me then.

Char. You do amaze me.
But you fhall wonder too; I will not take
One fingle Piece of this great Heap. Why fhould I
Borrow, that have not Means to pay; nay, am
A very Bankrupt, even in flatt'ring Hope

Of

Of ever raifing any.   All my begging,
Is *Romont*'s Liberty.

Enter Romont, *Creditors loaden with Money*. Beaumont.

Roch. Here is your Friend,
Enfranchife e'er you fpake.   I give him you:
And, *Charalois*, I give you to your Friend,
As free a Man as he: Your Father's Debts
Are taken off.
 Char. How?
 Rom. Sir, it is moft true.
I am the Witnefs.
  1 *Cred.* Yes, faith, we are paid.
  2 *Cred.* Heaven blefs his Lordfhip—I did think him
   wifer.
  3 *Cred.* He a Statefman? He an Afs—Pay other
   Men's Debts?
  1 *Cred.* That he was never bound for.
 Rom. One more fuch
Would fave the reft of Pleaders.
 Char. Honour'd *Rochfort*.
Lie ftill my Tongue, and Blufhes, fcal'd my Cheeks,
That offer Thanks in Words, for fuch great Deeds.
 Roch. Call in my Daughter:—Still I have a Suit to
  you.   [*Exit* Beaumont.
Would you requite me.
 Rom. With his Life, I affure you.
 Roch. Nay, would you make me now your Debtor,
  Sir!

Enter Beaumelle.

This is my only Child: What fhe appears,
Your Lordfhip well may fee her Education, *Beaumelle*
Follows not any: For her Mind, I know it
To be far fairer than her Shape, and hope
It will continue fo: If now her Birth
Be not too mean for *Charalois*, take her

           This

This Virgin by the Hand, and call her Wife,
Indow'd with all my Fortunes: Blefs me fo,
Requite me thus, and make me happier,
In joining my poor empty Name to yours,
Then if my 'State were multiplied tenfold.
  Char. Is this the Payment, Sir, that you expect?
Why, you precipitate me more in Debt,
That nothing but my Life can ever pay.
This Beauty being your Daughter (in which yours)
I muft conceive Neceffity of her Virtue
Without all Dowry is a Prince's Aim.
Then, as fhe is, for poor and worthlefs me
How much too worthy!—Waken me, *Romont*,
That I may know I dream'd, and find this vanifh'd.
  Rom. Sure, I fleep not.
  Roch. Your Sentence—Life or Death.
  Charmi. Fair *Beaumelle*, can you love me?
  Beaum. Yes, my Lord.

Enter Noval, *jun.* Ponta, Malotin, Liladam, Aymer.
              All falute.

  Char. You need not queftion me, if I can you.
You are the faireft Virgin in *Dijon*,
And *Rochfort* is your Father.
  Nov. jun. What's this Change?
  Roch. You met my Wifhes, Gentlemen.
  Rom. What make
Thefe Dogs in Doublets here?
  Beaum. A Vifitation, Sir.
  Char. Then thus, fair *Beaumelle!* I write my Faith,
Thus feal it in the Sight of Heaven and Men.
Your Fingers tie my Heart-ftrings with this Touch,
In true-love Knots, which nought but Death fhall loofe.
And yet thefe Tears (an Emblem of our Loves)
Like Cryftal Rivers individually
Flow into one another, make one Source,
Which never Man diftinguifh, lefs divide:
Breath, marry, Breath, and Kiffes, mingle Souls.

                                    Two

Two Hearts, and Bodies, here incorporate :
And, though with little wooing I have won,
My future Life fhall be, a wooing Time.
And every Day new as the Bridal one.
Oh, Sir! I groan under your Courtefies,
More then my Father's Bones under his Wrongs,
You, *Curtius*-like, have thrown into the Gulf,
Of this his Country's foul Ingratitude,
Your Life and Fortunes, to redeem their Shames.

   Roch. No more, my Glory! come, let's in, and haften
This Celebration.

Romont, Malotin, Pontalier, Beaumont.

All fair Blifs upon it.
        [*Exeunt* Rochfort, Charalois, Romont, Beau-
        mont, Malotin.
   Nov. jun. Miftrefs!
   Beaum. Oh Servant, Virtue ftrengthen me!
Thy Prefence blows round my Affection's Vane :
You will undo me, if you fpeak again.
                  [*Exit* Beaumelle.
   Lilad. Aym. Here will be Sport for you. This works.
             [*Exeunt* Liladam, *Aymer.*
   Nov. jun. Peace! Peace!
   Pont. One Word, my Lord *Novall!*
   Nov. jun. What, thou would'ft Money—there.
   Pont. No, I'll none, I'll not be bought a Slave,
A Pander, or a Parafite, for all
Your Father's Worth ; though you have fav'd my Life,
Refcu'd me often from my Wants, I muft not
Wink at your Follies ; that will ruin you.
You know my blunt Way, and my Love to Truth :
Forfake the Purfuit of this Lady's Honour,
Now do you fee her made another Man's,
And fuch a Man's fo good, fo popular,
Or you will pluck a thoufand Mifchiefs on you.
The Benefits you've done me, are not loft,
Nor caft away, they are purs'd here in my Heart,

But

But let me pay you, Sir, a fairer Way
Than to defend your Vices, or to footh 'em.
Nov. jun. Ha, ha, ha! what are my Courses unto
    thee?
Good Coufin *Pontalier*, meddle with that
That fhall concern thyfelf.   [*Exit* Novall.
  Pont. No more but Scorn?
Move on then, Stars! work your pernicious Will!
Only the wife Rule, and prevent your Ill.   [*Exit.*

        H A U T B O Y S.

Here a Paffage over the Stage, while the Act is playing for
  the Marriage of Charalois *with* Beaumelle, *&c.*

A C T III.   S C E N E I.

Enter Novall *jun.* Bellapert.

Nov. jun. FLY not to thefe Excufes: Thou haft been
    Falfe in thy Promife—and, when I have
    faid
Ungrateful, all is fpoke.
  Bellap. Good my Lord! but hear me only.
  Nov. jun. To what Purpofe, Trifler?
Can any Thing that thou canft fay, make void
The Marriage? Or thofe Pleafures but a Dream,
Which *Charalois* (oh *Venus!*) hath enjoy'd?
  Bellap. I yet could fay, that you receive Advantage
In what you think a Lofs, would you vouchfafe me;
That you were never in the Way till now
With Safety to arrive at your Defires;
That Pleafure makes Love to you, unattended
By Danger or Repentance?
  Nov. jun. That I could
But apprehend one Reafon how this might be,
Hope would not then forfake me.
  Bellap. The enjoying
Of what you moft defire; I fay th' enjoying

Shall, in the full Poſſeſſion of your Wiſhes,
Confirm that I am faithful.

 Nov. jun. Give ſome Reliſh
How this may appear poſſible.

 Bellap. I will.

Reliſh, and taſte, and make the Banquet eaſy .
You ſay my Lady's married—I confeſs it :
That *Charalois* hath enjoyed her—'tis moſt true:
That with her, he's already Maſter of
The beſt Part of my old Lord's 'State. Still better :
·But, that the firſt, or laſt, ſhould be your Hindrance,
I utterly deny : For, but obſerve me,
While ſhe went for, and was, I ſwear, a Virgin,
What Courteſy could ſhe with her Honour give,
Or you receive with Safety—take me with you ;
When I ſay Courteſy, do not think I mean
A Kiſs; the tying of her Shoe or Garter ;
An Hour of private Conference : Thoſe are Trifles.
In this Word Courteſy, we, that are Gameſters, point at
'The Sport direct, where not alone the Lover
Brings his Artillery, but uſes it :
Which Word expounded to you, ſuch a Courteſy
Do you expect, and ſudden.

 Nov. jun. But he taſted the firſt Sweets, *Bellapert !*

 Bellap. He wrong'd you ſhrewdly ;
He toil'd to climb up to the *Phœnix'* Neſt,
And in his Prints leaves your Aſcent more eaſy.
I do not know, you, that are perfect Criticks
In Women's Books, may talk of Maidenheads.

 Nov. jun. But for her Marriage.——

 Bellap. 'Tis a fair Protection
'Gainſt all Arreſts of Fear, or Shame for ever.
Such as are fair, and yet not fooliſh, ſtudy
To have one at thirteen ; but they are mad
That ſtay till twenty. Then, Sir ! for the Pleaſure ;
To ſay Adultery's ſweeter, that is ſtale.
This only—Is not the Contentment more,
To ſay, this is my Cuckold, than my Rival.
More I could ſay—but, briefly, ſhe doats on you,

             If

If it prove otherwife, fpare not, poifon me
With the next Gold you give me.

Enter Beaumelle.

Beaumel. How's this, Servant? Courting my Woman?
Bellap. As an Entrance to
The Favour of the Miftrefs: You are together
And I am perfect in my Cue.   *[Going.*
Beaumel. Stay *Bellapert.*
Bellap. In this, I muft not, with your Leave, obey you.
Your Taylor and your Tire-woman wait without
And ftay my Counfel, and Direction for
Your next Day's Dreffing. I have much to do,
Nor will your Ladyfhip, now, Time is precious,
Continue idle; this Choice Lord will find
So fit Employment for you.   *[Exit* Bellapert.
Beaumel. I fhall grow angry.
Nov. jun. Not fo; you have a Jewel in her, Madam!

Enter Bellapert.

Bellap. I had forgot to tell your Ladyfhip
The Clofet is private and your Couch ready;
And, if you pleafe that I fhall lofe the Key,
But fay fo, and 'tis done.   *[Exit* Bellapert.
Beaumel. You come to chide me, Servant! and bring
    with you
Sufficient Warrant. You will fay, and truly,
My Father found too much Obedience in me,
By being won too foon: Yet, if you pleafe
But to remember, all my Hopes and Fortunes
Had Reverence to this Likening you will grant,
That, though I did not well towards you, I yet
Did wifely for myfelf.
Nov. jun. With too much Fervor
I have fo long lov'd and ftill love you, Miftrefs;
To efteem that an Injury to me
Which was to you convenient;—that is paft

My

My Help, is paſt my Cure.   You yet may, Lady,
In Recompence of all my duteous Service,
(Provided that your Will anſwer your Power)
Become my Creditreſs.

Beaumel. I underſtand you;
And for Aſſurance, the Requeſt you make
Shall not be long unanſwered, pray you ſit,
And by what you ſhall hear, you'll eaſily find,
My Paſſions are much fitter to deſire,
Than to be ſued to.

Enter Romont *and* Florimel.

Flor. Sir, 'tis not Envy
At the Start my Fellow has got of me in
My Ladies good Opinion, that's the Motive
Of this Diſcovery; but due Payment
Of what I owe her Honour.

Rom. So I conceive it.

Flor. I have obſerv'd too much, nor ſhall my Silence
Prevent the Remedy——yonder they are,
I dare not be ſeen with you.   You may do
What you think 'fit, which will be, I preſume,
The Office of a faithful and try'd Friend
To my young Lord.   [*Exit* Florimel.

Rom. This is no Viſion: Ha!

Nov. jun. With the next Opportunity.

Beaumel. By this Kiſs, and this, and this.

Nov. jun. That you would ever ſwear thus.

Rom. If I ſeem rude, your Pardon, Lady! yours.
I do not aſk: Come, do not dare to ſhew me
A Face of Anger, or the leaſt Diſlike,
Put on, and ſuddenly, a milder Look;
I ſhall grow rough, elſe.

Nov. jun. What have I done, Sir!
To draw this harſh unſavory Language from you?

Rom. Done, Popinjay? Why, doſt thou think that, if
I e'er had dreamt that thou hadſt done me Wrong,
Thou ſhouſdſt outlive it?

Beau-

Beaumel. This is fomething more
Than my Lord's Friendfhip gives Commiffion for.

   Nov. jun. Your Prefence and the Place, makes him
     prefume
Upon my Patience.

   Rom. As if thou e'er wer't angry
But with thy Taylor, and yet that poor Shred
Can bring more to the making up of a Man,
Than can be hop'd from thee: Thou art his Creature,
And, did he not each Morning new create thee
Thou'dft ftink and be forgotten. I'll not change
One Syllable more with thee, until thou bring
Some Teftimony, under good Mens Hands,
Thou art a Chriftian. I fufpect thee ftrongly,
And will be fatisfied: 'Till which Time, keep from me.
The Entertainment of your Vifitation
Has made what I intended on a Bufinefs.

   Nov. jun. So we fhall meet—Madam!

   Rom. Ufe that Leg again, and I'll cut off the other.

   Nov. jun. Very good.   *{Exit Novall.*

   Rom. What a Perfume the Mufk-cat leaves behind
     him!
Do you admit him for a Property,
To fave you Charges Lady?

   Beaumel. 'Tis not ufelefs,
Now you are to fucceed him.

   Rom. So I refpect you,
Not for yourfelf, but in Remembrance of
Who is your Father, and whofe Wife you now are,
That I choofe rather not to underftand
Your nafty Scoff than,——

   Beaumel. What, you will not beat me,
If I expound it to you. Here's a Tyrant
Spares neither Man nor Woman.

   Rom. My Intents,
Madam, deferve not this ; nor do I ftay
To be the Whetftone of your Wit: Preferve it
To fpend on fuch, as know how to admire
Such colour'd Stuff. In me there is, now fpeaks to you

As true a Friend and Servant to your Honour,
And one that will with as much Hazard guard it,
As ever Man did Goodnefs.——But then Lady!
You muft endeavour, not alone to be,
But to appear, worthy fuch Love and Service.

   Beaumel. To what tends this?

   Rom. Why, to this Purpofe, Lady!
I do defire you fhould prove fuch a Wife
To *Charalois* (and fuch a one he Merits)
As *Cæfar*, did he live, could not except at,
Not only innocent from Crime, but free
From all Taint and Sufpicion.

   Beaumel. They are bafe that judge me otherwife,

   Rom. But yet, be careful!
Detraction's a bold Monfter, and fears not
To wound the Fame of Princes, if it find
But any Blemifh in their Lives to work on:
But I'll be plainer with you: Had the People
Been learn'd to fpeak, but what even now I faw,
Their Malice out of that would raife an Engine
To overthrow your Honour. In my Sight,
With yonder painted Fool I frighted from you,
You us'd Familiarity beyond
A modeft Entertainment: You embrac'd him
With too much Ardour for a Stranger, and
Met him with Kiffes neither chafte nor comely:
But learn you to forget him, as I will
Your Bounties to him; you will find it fafer
Rather to be uncourtly, then immodeft.

   Beaumel. This pretty Rag about your Neck fhews well,
And, being coarfe and little Worth, it fpeaks you
As terrible as thrifty.

   Rom. Madam!

   Beaumel. Yes.
And this ftrong Belt in which you hang your Honour
Will out-laft twenty Scarfs.

   Rom. What mean you, Lady?

   Beaumel. And all elfe about you Cap-a-pe,
So uniform in Spite of Handfomenefs,

Shews

Shews such a bold Contempt of Comeliness,
That 'tis not strange your Laundress in the League,
Grew mad with Love of you.

Rom. Is my free Counsel
Answer'd with this ridiculous Scorn?

Beaumel. These Objects
Stole very much of my Attention from me;
Yet something I remember, to speak Truth,
Deliver'd gravely, but to little Purpose,
That almost would have made me swear some Curate
Had stol'n into the Person of *Romont*,
And, in the Praise of Good-wife Honesty,
Had read an Homily.

Rom. By this Hand.——

Beaumel. And Sword;
I will make up your Oath, 'twill want Weight else.
You're angry with me, and poor I laugh at it.
Do you come from the Camp, which affords only
The Conversation of cast Suburb Whores,
To set down to a Lady of my Rank,
Limits of Entertainment?

Rom. Sure a Legion has possest this Woman.

Beaumel. One Stamp more would do well: Yet I de-
sire not
You should grow Horn-mad, till you have a Wife.
You are come to warm Meat, and perhaps clean Linen:
Feed, wear it, and be thankful. For me, know,
That, though a thousand Watches were set on me,
And you the Master-spy, I yet would use
The Liberty that best likes me. I will revel,
Feast, kiss, embrace. Perhaps, grant larger Favours.
Yet such as live upon my Means, shall know
They must not murmur at it. If my Lord
Be now grown yellow, and has chose out you
To serve his Jealousy that Way, tell him this,—
You've something to inform him.   [*Exit* Beaumelle.

Rom. And I will.
Believe it, wicked one, I will. Hear, Heaven!
But, hearing, pardon me: If these Fruits grow,
Upon the Tree of Marriage, let me shun it,

As

As a forbidden Sweet.   An Heir and rich,
Young, beautiful—yet add to this—a Wife,
And I will rather choose a Spital Sinner
Carted an Age before, though three Parts rotten,
And take it for a Blessing, rather than
Be fetter'd to the hellish Slavery [4]
Of such an Impudence.

Enter Beaumont *with Writings.*

Beaum. Colonel! good Fortune
To meet you thus: You look sad, but I'll tell you
Something that shall remove it.   Oh, how happy
Is my Lord *Chalarois* in his fair Bride!

Rom. A happy Man, indeed!—pray you in what?

Beaum. I dare swear, you would think so good a Lady,
A Dower sufficient.

Rom. No doubt.—But on.

Beaum. So fair, so chaste, so virtuous;—Indeed
All that is excellent.

Rom. Women have no Cunning to gull the World.

Beaum. Yet, to all these, my Lord,
Her Father gives the full Addition of
All he does now possess in *Burgundy:*
These Writings to confirm it, are new seal'd,
And I most fortunate to present him with them,
I must go seek him out, can you direct me?

Rom. You'll find him breaking a young Horse.

Beaum. I thank you.   [*Exit* Beaumont.

4 In an Advertisement prefixed to the *Bond-man*, which was revived
in 1710, we are told that Mr. *Rowe* had revis'd the Works of *Maf-
singer*, and did intend to publish them; I am apt to think this Asser-
tion true, and that Mr. *Rowe* was a great Admirer of our Author, his
excellent Play of the *Fair Penitent* being founded on the Tragedy now
before us.   The beautiful Scene between *Horatia* and *Califta* is evidently copied from the foregoing, as is that between *Altamont* and *Horatia* in the third Act where they quarrel, from the last Scene of this;
The curious Reader may not be disagreeably amused in comparing
many other similar Parts of these excellent Tragedies together.

Rom.

Rom. I muſt do ſomething worthy *Charalois* Friend-
ſhip.
If ſhe were well inclin'd, to keep her ſo
Deſerv'd not Thanks : And yet, to ſtay a Woman ⁵
Spur'd headlong by hot Luſt to her own Ruin
Is harder than to prop a falling Tower
With a deceiving Reed.

Enter Rochfort.

Roch. Some one ſeek for me,
As ſoon as he returns.
Rom. Her Father ? ha !——
How if I break this to him ? Sure it cannot
Meet with an ill Conſtruction.   His Wiſdom,
Made powerful by th' Authority of a Father,
Will warrant and give Privilege to his Counſels.
It ſhall be ſo—My Lord!
Roch. Your Friend, *Romont :*
Would you aught with me ?
Rom. I ſtand ſo engag'd
To your ſo many Favours, that I hold it
A Breach in Thankfulneſs, ſhould I not diſcover,
Though with ſome Imputation to myſelf,
All Doubts that may concern you.
Roch. The Performance
Will make this Proteſtation worth my Thanks.

⁵ *To ſtay a Woman
Spur'd Headlong, by hot Luſt,* &c.
Thus in the *Picture.*

—————— It is more
Impoſſible in Nature for groſs Bodies
Deſcending of themſelves, to hang in the Air,
Or with my ſingle Arm to underprop
A falling Tower ; nay, in its violent Courſe
To ſtop the Lightning, than to ſtay a Woman,
Hurried by two Furies, Luſt and Falſhood,
In her full Career to Wickedneſs,

Act 4. Scene 1.

Rom.

Rom. Then, with your Patience, lend me your Attention :
For what I muſt deliver, whiſper'd only,
You will with too much Grief receive.

Enter Beaumelle, Bellapert.

Beaumel. See, Wench!
Upon my Life as I foreſpake, he's now
Preferring his Complaint : But be thou perfect,
And we will fit him.

Bellap. Fear not me, pox on him !
A Captain turn Informer againſt kiſſing?
Would he were hang'd up in his ruſty Armour!
But, if our freſh Wits cannot turn the Plots
Of ſuch a mouldy Murrion on itſelf;
Rich Cloaths, choice Fare, and a true Friend at a Call,
With all the Pleaſures the Night yields, forſake us.

Roch. This in my Daughter? Do not wrong her.

Bellap. Now begin.
The Games a-foot, and we in Diſtance.

Beaumel. 'Tis thy Fault, fooliſh Girl! pin on my Veil,
I will not wear thoſe Jewels.   Am I not
Already match'd beyond my Hopes ? Yet ſtill
You prune and ſet me forth, as if I were.
Again to pleaſe a Suiter.

Bellap. 'Tis the Courſe
That our great Ladies take.

Rom. A weak Excuſe !

Beaumel. Thoſe that are better ſeen, in what concerns
A Lady's Honour and fair Fame, condemn it.
You wait well : in your Abſence, my Lord's Friend,
The underſtanding, grave, and wiſe *Romont*.———

Rom. Muſt I be ſtill her Sport ?   [*Aſide.*

Beaumel. Reprove me for it.
And he has travell'd to bring home a Judgment
Not to be contradicted.   You will ſay
My Father, that owes more to Years than he,
Has brought me up to Muſick, Language, Courtſhip,
And I muſt uſe them.   True, but not t' offend,
Or render me ſuſpected.   *Roch.*

Roch. Does your fine Story begin from this?

Beaumel. I thought a parting Kiſs
From young *Novall* would have diſpleas'd no more
Than heretofore it hath done; but I find
I muſt reſtrain ſuch Favours now; look therefore,
As you are careful to continue mine,
That I no more be viſited. I'll endure
The ſtricteſt Courſe of Life that Jealouſy
Can think ſecure enough, ere my Behaviour
Shall call my Fame in Queſtion.

Rom. Ten Diſſemblers
Are in this ſubtle Devil. You believe this?

Roch. So far, that if you trouble me again
With a Report like this, I ſhall not only
Judge you malicious in your Diſpoſition,
But ſtudy to repent what I have done
To ſuch a Nature.

Rom. Why, 'tis exceeding well.

Roch. And for you, Daughter, off with this; off
with it:
I have that Confidence in your Goodneſs, I,
That I will not conſent to have you live
Like to a Recluſe in a Cloyſter: Go,
Call in the Gallants, let them make you merry,
Uſe all fit Liberty.

Bellap. Bleſſing on you.
If this new Preacher with the Sword and Feather
Could prove his Doctrine for Canonical,
We ſhould have a fine World.   [*Exit* Bellapert.

Roch. Sir, if you pleaſe
To bear yourſelf as fits a Gentleman,
The Houſe is at your Service; but, if not,
Though you ſeek Company elſewhere, your Abſence
Will not be much lamented ——   [*Exit* Rochfort.

Rom. If this be
The Recompence of ſtriving to preſerve
A wanton Gigglet honeſt, very ſhortly
'Twill make all Mankind Panders.—Do you ſmile,
Good Lady *Looſeneſs?* Your whole Sex is like you,
                                        And

And that Man's mad that feeks to better any:
What new Change have you next?

Beaumel. Oh, fear not you, Sir!
I'll fhift into a Thoufand, but I will
Convert your Herefy.

Rom. What Herefy? fpeak!

Beaumel. Of keeping a Lady that is married,
From entertaining Servants.———

Enter Novall, *jun.* Malotin, Liladam, Aymer, Pontalier.

O, you're welcome.
Ufe any Means to vex him,
And then with Welcome follow me, 　　[*Exit* Beaumel.

Nov. jun. You are tir'd
With your grave Exhortations, Colonel!

Lilad. How is it? Faith, your Lordfhip may do well
To help him to fome Church-Preferment: 'Tis
Now the Fafhion, for Men of all Conditions,
However they have liv'd, to end that Way.

Aymer. That Face would do well in a Surplice.

Rom. Rogues, be filent — or —

Pont. S'Death! will you fuffer this?

Rom. And you, the Mafter Rogue, the Coward Rafcal,
I fhall be with you fuddenly,

Nov. jun. Pontalier,
If I fhould ftrike him, I know I fhall kill him:
And therefore I would have thee beat him, for
He's good for nothing elfe.

Lilad. His Back
Appears to me, as it would tire a Beadle.
And then he has a knotted Brow, would bruife
A court-like Hand to touch it.

Aymer. He looks like
A Currier when his Hide's grown dear.

Pont. Take heed he curry not fome of you.

Nov. jun. Gads me! he's angry.

Rom. I break no Jefts, but I can break my Sword
About your Pates. 　　　　　　　　　　*Enter*

Enter Charalois *and* Beaumont.

Lilad. Here's more.

Aymer. Come let's be gone !
We are beleaguer'd.

Nov. jun. Look, they bring up their Troops.

Pont. Will you fit down with this Difgrace ?
You are abus'd moft grofly.

Lilad. I grant you, Sir, we are ; and you would have
Stay, and be more abus'd.

Nov. jun. My Lord, I'm forry
Your Houfe is fo inhofpitable, we muft quit it.

     [*Exeunt. Manent* Charalois, Romont.

Char. Pr'ythee, Romont, what caus'd this Uproar ?

Rom. Nothing.
They laugh'd, and us'd their fcurvy Wits upon me.

Char. Come, 'tis thy jealous Nature : But I wonder
That you, which are an honeft Man, and worthy,
Should fofter this Sufpicion. No Man laughs,
No one can whifper, but thou apprehend'ft
His Conference and his Scorn reflects on thee.
For my Part, they fhould fcoff their thin Wits out,
So I not heard them ; beat me, not being there.
Leave, leave thefe Fits to confcious Men, to fuch
As are obnoxious to thofe foolifh Things
As they can gibe at.

Rom. Well, Sir !

Char. Thou art known
Valiant without Defect, rightly defin'd,
Which is (as fearing to do Injury,
As tender to endure it) not a Brabbler,
A Swearer.

Rom. Pifh, pifh ! What needs this, my Lord ?
If I be known none fuch, how vainly you
Do caft away good Counfel ? I have lov'd you,
And yet muft freely fpeak : So young a Tutor
Fits not fo old a Soldier as I am.
And I muft tell you, 'twas in your Behalf

        I grew

I grew enrag'd thus; yet had rather die
Than open the great Caufe a Syllable further.

   Char. In my Behalf? Wherein hath *Charalois*
Unfitly fo demean'd himfelf, to give
The leaft Occafion to the loofeft Tongue
To throw Afperfions on him? Or fo weakly
Protected his own Honour, as it fhould
Need Defence from any but himfelf?
They're Fools that judge me by my outward Seeming;
Why fhould my Gentlenefs beget Abufe?
The Lion is not angry that does fleep,
Nor every Man a Coward that can weep.
For God's Sake fpeak the Caufe.

   Rom. Not for the World.
Oh! it will ftrike Difeafe into your Bones,
Beyond the Cure of Phyfick; drink your Blood,
Rob you of all your Reft, contract your Sight,
Leave you no Eyes but to fee Mifery,
And of your own; nor Speech, but to wifh thus,
Would I had perifh'd in the Prifon's Jaws,
From whence I was redeem'd! 'Twill wear you old,
Before you have Experience in that Art,
That caufes your Affliction.

   Char. Thou doft ftrike
A deathful Coldnefs to my Heart's high Heat,
And fhrink'ft my Liver like the *Calenture*.
Declare this Foe of mine, and Life's, that like
A Man I may encounter and fubdue it.
It fhall not have one fuch Effect in me,
As thou denounceft: With a Soldier's Arm,
If it be Strength, I'll meet it: If a Fault
Belonging to my Mind, I'll cut it off
With mine own Reafon, as a Scholar fhould.
—Speak, though it make me monftrous.

   Rom. I'll die firft.
Farewel! continue merry, and high Heaven
Keep your Wife chafte.

   Char. Hum!—Stay and take this Wolf
Out of my Breaft, that thou haft lodg'd there, or
For ever lofe me.   *Rom.*

Rom. Lofe not, Sir, yourfelf,;
And I will venture—fo the Door is faft.

[Locks the Door.

Now, noble *Charalois*, colle&t yourfelf;
Summon your Spirits; mufter all your Strength
That can belong to Man; fift Paffion
From ev'ry Vein, and, whatfoe'er enfues,
Upbraid not me hereafter, as the Caufe of
Jealoufy, Difcontent, Slaughter and Ruin:
Make me not Parent to Sin:—You will know
This Secret that I burn with.

Char. Devil on't,
What fhould it be? *Romont*, I hear you wifh
My Wife's Continuance of Chaftity.

Rom. There was no Hurt in that.

Char. Why? do you know
A Likelihood or Poffibility unto the contrary?

Rom. I know it not, but doubt it; thefe the Grounds.
The Servant of your Wife now, young *Novall*,
The Son unto your Father's Enemy
(Which aggravates my Prefumption the more)
I have been warn'd of, touching her; nay, feen them
Tie Heart to Heart, one in another's Arms,
Multiplying Kiffes, as if they meant
To 'pofe Arithmetic, or whofe Eyes would
Be firft burnt out with gazing on the other's.
I faw their Mouths engender, and their Palms
Glew'd, as if Love had lock'd them; their Words flow
And melt each others, like two circling Flames,
Where Chaftity, like a Phœnix, methought, burn'd,
But left the World nor Afhes, nor an Heir.
Why ftand you filent thus? What cold dull Flegm,
As if you had no Drop of Choler mix'd
In your whole Conftitution, thus prevails,
To fix you now thus ftupid, hearing this?

Char. You did not fee 'em on my Couch within,
Like *George* a Horfe-back, on her, nor a-bed?

Rom. No.

Char. Ha! ha!

Rom.

Rom. Laugh you ? E'en so did your Wife,
And her indulgent Father,
  Char. They were wise.
Would'st ha' me be a Fool ?
  Rom. No, but a Man.
  Char. There is no Dram of Manhood to suspect,
On such thin airy Circumstance as this
Mere Compliment and Courtship. Was this Tale
The hideous Monster which you so conceal'd ?
Away, thou curious Impertinent,
And idle Searcher of such lean nice Toys !
Go, thou seditious Sower of Debate !
Fly to such Matches, where the Bridegroom doubts :
He holds not Worth Enough to countervail
The Virtue and the Beauty of his Wife.
Thou buzzing Drone, that 'bout my Ears dost hum,
To strike thy rankling Sting into my Heart,
Whose Venom, Time nor Medicine could asswage.
Thus do I put thee off, and, confident
In mine own Innocency and Desert,
Dare not conceive her so unreasonable,
To put *Novall* in Balance against me,
An Upstart, cram'd up to the Height he has.
Hence, Busybody ! thou'rt no Friend to me,
That must be kept to a Wife's Injury.
  Rom. Is't possible ?—Farewel, fine, honest Man !
Sweet temper'd Lord, adieu ! What Apoplexy
Hath knit Sense up ? Is this *Romont's* Reward ?
Bear Witness, the great Spirit of thy Father,
With what a healthful Hope I administer
This Potion that hath wrought so virulently !
I not accuse thy Wife of Act, but would
Prevent her Precipice to thy Dishonour,
Which now thy tardy Sluggishness will admit !
Would I had seen thee grav'd with thy great Sire,
Ere live to have Mens marginal Fingers point
At *Charalois*, as a lamented Story.
An Emperor put away his Wife for touching
Another Man ; but thou wouldst have thine tasted

And

And keep her, I think, Phoh! I am a Fire
To warm a dead Man, that wafte out myfelf.
Blood—What a Plague, a Vengeance, is't to me,
If you will be a Cuckold ? Here I fhew
A Sword's Point to thee ; this Side you may fhun,
Or that, the Peril; if you will run on,
I cannot help it.

   Char. Didft thou never fee me
Angry, *Romont ?*
   Rom. Yes, and purfue a Foe
Like Lightning.
   Char. Pr'ythee fee me fo no more.
I can be fo again.—Put up thy Sword,
And take thyfelf away, left I draw mine.
   Rom. Come, fright your Foes with this, Sir! I am
        your Friend,
And dare ftand by you thus.
   Char. Thou'rt not my Friend ;
Or being fo, thou'rt mad.—I muft not buy
Thy Friendfhip at this Rate ; had I juft Caufe,
Thou know'ft I durft purfue fuch Injury
Through Fire, Air, Water, Earth, nay, were they all
Shuffled again to *Chaos*; but there's none.
Thy Skill, *Romont*, confifts in Camps, not Courts.
Farewel, uncivil Man ! let's meet no more.
Here our long Web of Friendfhip I untwift.
Shall I go whine, walk pale, and lock my Wife
For nothing, from her Birth's free Liberty,
That open'd mine to me ? Yes ; if I do ——
The Name of Cuckold, then, dog me with Scorn.
I am a *Frenchman*, no *Italian* born.   *[Exit.*
   Rom. A dull *Dutch* rather :—Fall and cool my Blood!
Boil not in Zeal of thy Friend's Hurt fo high,
That is fo low, and cold himfelf in't ! Woman,
How ftrong art thou ! how eafily beguil'd !
How thou doft rack us by the very Horns !
Now Wealth, I fee, change Manners, and the Man.
Something I muft do mine own Wrath to affuage,
And note my Friendfhip to an After-age.   *[Exit.*

ACT IV.   SCENE I.

Enter Novall *jún. as newly dreſſed, a Taylor, Barber, Perfumer,* Liladam, Aymer, *Page.*

Nov.jun. MEND this a little:—Pox! thou haſt burnt me.   Oh! fie upon't!—O lard! he has made me ſmell, for all the World, like a Flax, or a red-headed Woman's Chamber: Powder, Powder, Powder.

Perf. Oh, ſweet Lord!

[Novall *ſits in a Chair, Barber orders his Hair, Perfumer gives Powder, Taylor ſets his Cloaths.*

Page. That's his Perfumer.

Tayl. Oh, dear Lord!

Page. That's his Taylor.

Nov. jun. Monſieur *Liladam! Aymer!* how allow you the Model of theſe Cloaths?

Aymer. Admirably, admirably; oh ſweet Lord! aſ-ſuredly it's Pity the Worms ſhould eat thee.

Page. Here's a fine Cell; a Lord, a Taylor, a Per-fumer, a Barber, and a Pair of Monſieurs: Three to three, as little Wit in the one, as Honeſty in the other. S'foot I'll into the Country again, learn to ſpeak Truth, drink Ale, and converſe with my Father's Tenants; here I hear nothing all Day, but—upon my Soul! as I am a Gentleman, and an honeſt Man!

Aymer. I vow and affirm, your Taylor muſt needs be an expert Geometrician; he has the Longitude, Lati-tude, Altitude, Profundity, every Dimenſion of your Body, ſo exquiſitely.—Here's a Lace laid as directly, as if Truth were a Taylor.

Page. That were a Miracle.

Lilad. With a Hairs Breadth's Error, there's a Shoul-der-Piece cut, and the Baſe of a Pickadille [6] in *punƐo.*

---

[6] A Pickadil *(Dutch)* the Hem about the Skirt of a Garment.

Aymer.

Aymer. You are right, Monfieur! his Veftments fit as if they grew upon him; or Art had wrought 'em on the fame Loom, as Nature fram'd his Lordfhip; as if your Taylor were deeply read in Aftrology, and had taken Meafure of your honourable Body, with a *Jacob*'s Staff, an *Epbimerides.*

Taylor. I am bound t'ye, Gentlemen!

Page. You are deceiv'd; they'll be bound to you: You muft remember to truft 'em none.

Nov. jun. Nay, 'faith, thou art a reafonable, neat Artificer, give the Devil his Due.

Page. I, if he would but cut the Coat according to the Cloth ftill.

Nov. jun. I now want only my Miftrefs's Approbation, who is, indeed, the moft polite punctual Queen of Dreffing in all *Burgundy.* Pah, and makes all other young Ladies appear as if they came from board laft Week out of the Country; is't not true, *Liladam?*

Lilad. True, my Lord! as if any Thing your Lordfhip could fay, could be otherwife then true.

Nov. jun. Nay, O my Soul, 'tis fo, what fouler Object in the World, than to fee a young, fair, handfome Beauty, unhandfomely dighted and incongruently accouter'd; or a hopeful Chevalier, unmethodically appointed, in the external Ornaments of Nature? For, even as the Index tells us the Contents of Stories, and directs to the particular Chapters; even fo does the outward Habit and fuperficial Order of Garments, (in Man or Woman) give us a Tafte of the Spirit, and demonftratively Point (as it were a manual Note from the Margin) all the internal Quality, and Habiliment of the Soul; and there cannot be a more evident, palpable, grofs Manifeftation of poor, degenerate, dunghilly Blood, and Breeding, than a rude, unpolifh'd, diforder'd and flovenly Outfide.

Page. An admirable Lecture! oh, all you Gallants, that hope to be faved by your Cloaths, edify, edify!

Aymer. By the Lard, fweet Lard! thou deferv'ft a Penfion o'the State.

Page.—Oth' Taylors, two fuch Lords were able to
fpread Taylors o'er the Face of a whole Kingdom.

Nov. jun. 'Pox a this Glafs! it flatters.—I could find
in my Heart to break it.

Page. O, fave the Glafs, my Lord! and break their
Heads: They are the greater Flatterers, I affure you.

Aymer. Flatters, detracts, impairs.—Yet, put it by,
Left thou, dear Lord, *Narciffus*-like, fhould doat
Upon thyfelf, and die; and rob the World
Of Nature's Copy, that fhe works Form by.

Lilad. Oh! that I were the Infanta Queen of *Europe!*
Who but thyfelf, fweet Lord, fhould marry me!

Nov. jun. I marry? Were there a Queen o'th' World,
   not I.
Wedlock? No Padlock, Horfe-Lock, I wear Spurs
                                        [*He capers.*
To keep it off my Heels; yet, my *Aymer!*
Like a free, wanton Jennet i'th' Meadows,
I look about, and neigh, take Hedge and Ditch,
Feed in my Neighbour's Paftures; pick my Choice
Of all their fair-mane'd Mares: But married once,
A Man is ftak'd, or poun'd, and cannot graze
Beyond his own Hedge.

Enter Pontalier, *and* Malotin.

Pont. I have waited, Sir!
Three Hours to fpeak with you, and take it not well,
Such Magpies are admitted, whilft I dance
Attendance.

Lilad. Magpies? What d'ye take me for?

Pont. A long Thing with a moft unpromifing Face.

Aymer. I'll ne'er afk him what he takes me for.

Malot. Do not, Sir!
For he'll go near to tell you.

Pont. Art not thou a Barber-Surgeon?

Barb. Yes, Sirrah! why?

Pont. My Lord is forely troubled with two Scabs.

Lilad. Aymer. Humph——

Pont. I prythee, cure him of 'em.

                                        Nov.

Nov. jun. Pifh! no more;
Thy Gall fure's overthrown: Thefe are my Council,
And we were now in ferious Difcourfe.

Pont. Of Perfume and Apparel. Can you rife,
And fpend five Hours in Dreffing-Talk with thefe?

Nov. jun. Thould'ft have me be a Dog: Up, ftretch,
        and fhake,
And ready for all Day.

Pont. Sir! would you be
More curious in preferving of your Honour
Trim, 'twere more manly.   I am come to wake
Your Reputation from this Lethargy
You let it fleep in; to perfuade, importune,
Nay, to provoke you, Sir! to call to Account
This Colonel *Romont,* for the foul Wrong,
Which, like a Burthen, he hath laid on you,
And, like a drunken Porter, you fleep under.
'Tis all the Town-Talk, and, believe, Sir,
If your tough Senfe perfift thus, you're undone,
Utterly loft; you will be fcorn'd and baffled
By every Lacquey; feafon now your Youth
With one brave Thing, and it fhall keep the Odour
Even to your Death, beyond; and on your Tomb,
Scent like fweet Oils and Frankincenfe: Sir! this Life
Which once you fav'd, I ne'er fince counted mine;
I borrow'd it of you, and now will pay it;
I tender you the Service of my Sword
To bear your Challenge; if you'll write, your Fate.
I'll make mine own: What e'er betide you, I,
That have liv'd by you, by your Side will die.

Nov. jun. Ha! ha! would'ft ha' me challenge poor
        Romont:
Fight with clofe Breeches? Thou may'ft think I dare
        not.
Do not miftake me, Coze I'm very valiant;
But Valour fhall not make me fuch an Afs.
What Ufe is there of Valour, now-a-days?
'Tis fure, or to be kill'd, or to be hang'd.
Fight thou as thy Mind moves thee; 'tis thy Trade:

Thou

Thou haſt nothing elſe to do. Fight with *Romont?*
No, I'll not fight under a Lord.

Pont. Farewell, Sir! I pity you.
Such loving Lords walk their dead Honour's Graves,
For no Companions fit, but Fools and Knaves.
Come *Malotin.*   [*Exeunt* Pontalier, Malotin.

Enter Romont.

Lilad. 'Sfoot, *Colbrand,* the low Giant.
Aymer. He has brought a Battle in his Face, let's go.
Page. Colbrand, d'ye call him? He'll make ſome of
you ſmoak, I believe.
Rom. By your Leave, Sirs!
Aymer. Are you a Conſort? [7]
Rom. D'ye take me for
A Fidler? y'are deceiv'd:—Look, I'll pay you.

                                 [*Kicks 'em.*

Page. It ſeems he knows you one, he bumfiddles you
ſo.
Lilad. Was there ever ſo baſe a Fellow?
Aymer. A Raſcal!
Lilad. A moſt uncivil Groom!
Aymer. Offer to kick a Gentleman in a Nobleman's
Chamber? A Pox o' your Manners.
Lilad. Let him alone, let him alone, thou ſhalt loſe
thy Arm, Fellow! if we ſtir againſt thee, hang us.
Page. 'Sfoot, I think they have the better on him,
though they be kick'd, they talk ſo.
Lilad. Let's leave the mad Ape.
Nov. jun. Gentlemen!
Lilad. Nay, my Lord! we will not offer to diſhonour
you ſo much, as to ſtay by you, ſince he's alone.

7 Aym. *Are you a Conſort,* &c. *i. e.* Come you here to be play'd
on.—Thus in *Romeo,*
   Tyb. Mercutio, thou conſort'ſt with *Romeo——*
  Mer. Conſort! what doſt thou make us Minſtrel, if thou make
Minſtrels of us, look to hear nothing but Diſcords, &c.
                                      Act 3, Scene 1.
                                        Nov.

Nov. jun. Hark you.

Aymer. We doubt the Cause, and will not disparage you, so much as to take your Lordship's Quarrel in Hand. Plague on him, how he has crumpled our Bands.

Page, I'll e'en away with 'em, for this Soldier beats Man, Woman, and Child.

                         [*Exeunt all but* Novall *and* Romont.

Nov. jun. What mean you, Sir? My People.——

Rom. Your Boy's gone,   [*Locks the Door.*
And Door's lock'd,—yet for no Hurt to you,
But privacy: Call up your Blood again, Sir!
Be not afraid, I do beseech you, Sir!
And therefore, come, without more Circumstance,
Tell me how far the Passages have gone
'Twixt you, and your fair Mistress *Beaumelle.*
Tell me the Truth, and, by my Hope of Heaven,
It never shall go farther.

Nov. jun. Tell you? Why, Sir?
Are you my Confessor?

Rom. I will be your Confounder, if you do not.
                         [*Draws a Pocket Dagger,*
Stir not, nor spend your Voice.

Nov. jun. What will you do?

Rom. Nothing but line your Brain-pan, Sir! with
    Lead,
If you not satisfy me suddenly,
I'm desperate of my Life, and command yours.

Nov. jun. Hold! hold! I'll speak. I vow to Heaven
and you,
She's yet untouch'd, more than her Face and Hands,
I cannot call her innocent; for, I yield,
On my sollicitous Wrongs she consented,
Where Time and Place met Opportunity
To grant me all Requests.

Rom. But, may I build
On this Assurance?

Nov. jun. As upon your Faith. ·

Rom. Write this, Sir! nay, you muſt.

                              [Draws Inkhorn and Paper.

Nov. jun. Pox of this Gun.

Rom. Withall, Sir! you muſt ſwear, and put your
    Oath

Under your Hand, (ſhake not) ne'er to frequent
This Lady's Company ; nor ever ſend
Token, or Meſſage, or Letter, to incline
This (too much prone already) yielding Lady,

Nov. jun. 'Tis done, Sir!

Rom. Let me ſee, this firſt is right ;
And here you wiſh a ſudden Death may light
Upon your Body, and Hell take your Soul,
If ever more you ſee her, but by Chance,
Much leſs allure her.   Now, my Lord! your Hand.

Nov. jun. My Hand to this ?

Rom. Your Heart elſe, I aſſure you.

Nov. jun. Nay, there 'tis.

Rom. So, keep this laſt Article
Of your Faith given, and 'ſtead of Threat'nings, Sir!
The Service of my Sword and Life is yours :
But not a Word of it,—'tis Fairies Treaſure ;
Which, but reveal'd, brings on the Blabbers Ruin.
Uſe your Youth better, and this excellent Form
Heav'n hath beſtow'd upon you.   So, good Morrow to
        your Lordſhip.   *[Exit.*

Nov. jun. Good Devil to your Rogueſhip. No Man's
    ſafe.——

I'll have a Cannon planted in my Chamber,
Againſt ſuch roaring Rogues.

             Enter Bellapert.

Bellap. My Lord, away!——
The Coach ſtays : Now have your Wiſh, and judge,
If I have been forgetful.

Nov. jun. Ha !

Bellap. D'ye ſtand
Humming and hawing now?   *[Exit.*
                                     Nov.

Nov. jun. Sweet Wench, 1 come.
Hence Fear,
I fwore,—that's all one; my next Oath I'll keep
That I did mean to break, and then 'tis quit.
No Pain is due to Lover's Perjury:
If *Jove* himfelf laugh at it, fo will I.　　[*Exit* Novall.

SCENE II.

Enter Charalois, Beaumont.

Beaum. I grieve for the Diftafte
Though I have Manners,
Not to inquire the Caufe fall'n out between
Your Lordfhip and *Romont.*
　Char. I love a Friend,
So long as he continues in the Bounds
Prefcrib'd by Friendfhip; but, when he ufurps
Too far what is proper to myfelf,
And puts the Habit of a Governor on,
I muft and will preferve my Liberty.
But fpeak of fomething elfe, this is a Theme
I take no Pleafure in: What's this *Aymer.*
Whofe Voice for Song, and excellent Knowledge in
The chiefeft Parts of Mufick, you beftow
Such Praifes on?
　Beaum. He is a Gentleman,
(For fo his Quality fpeaks him) well receiv'd
Among our greateft Gallants; but yet holds
His main Dependance from the young Lord *Novall.*
Some Tricks and Crotchets he has in his Head,
As all Muficians have, and more of him
I dare not author: But, when you have heard him,
I may prefume, your Lordfhip fo will like him,
That you'll hereafter be a Friend to Mufick.
　Char. I never was an Enemy to't, *Beaumont*;
Nor yet do I fubfcribe to the Opinion
Of thofe old Captains, that thought nothing mufical,
But Cries of yielding Enemies, Neighing of Horfes,
Clafhing

Clashing of Armour, loud Shouts, Drums, and Trum-
　pets :
Nor, on the other Side, in Favour of it,
Affirm the World was made by musical Discord,
Or that the Happiness of our Life consists
In a well vary'd Note upon the Lute :
I love it to the Worth of it, and no farther.
—But, let us see this Wonder.

　Beaum. He prevents my calling of him.

Enter Aymer.

　Aymer. Let the Coach be brought
To the Back Gate, and serve the Banquet up:
My good Lord *Charalois !* I think my House
Much honour'd in your Presence.

　Char. To have Means
To know you better, Sir, has brought me hither
A willing Visitant ; and you'll crown my Welcome
In making me a Witness to your Skill,
Which, crediting from others, I admire.

　Aymer. Had I been one Hour sooner made acquainted
With your Intent, my Lord, you should have found me
Better provided : Now, such as it is,
Pray you grace with your Acceptance.

　Beaum. You are modest.

　Aymer. Begin the last new Air.

　Char. Shall we not see them ?

　Aymer. This little Distance from the Instruments
Will to your Ears convey the Harmony
With more Delight.

　Char. I'll not contend.

　Aymer. Y'are tedious, —
By this Means shall I with one Banquet please
Two Companies, those within, and these Gulls here.

　　　　　　　[*Musick, and a Song above.*
　Beaumel. within. Ha! ha! ha!
　Char. How's this? It is my Lady's Laugh, most cer-
　tain ——

　　　　　　　　　　　　　　　　　　　　When

When I firſt pleas'd her, in this merry Language,
She gave me Thanks.

   Beaum. How like you this?

   Char. 'Tis rare,——

Yet I may be deceiv'd, and ſhould be ſorry,
Upon uncertain Suppoſitions, raſhly
To write myſelf in the black Liſt of thoſe
I have declaim'd againſt, and to *Romont.*

   Aymer. I would he were well off.——Perhaps your
        Lordſhip

Likes not theſe ſad Tunes : I have a new Song,
Set to a lighter Note, may pleaſe you better ;
'Tis call'd *The Happy Huſband.*

   Char. Pray ſing it.

Song below. At the End of the Song, Beaumelle *within.*

   Beaumel. Ha! ha! 'tis ſuch a Groom.——

   Char. Do I hear this,

And yet ſtand doubtful ?   [*Exit* Charalois.

   Aymer. Stay him!—I am undone,

And they diſcover'd.

   Beaum. What's the Matter ?

   Aymer. Ah !

That Women, when they're well pleas'd, cannot hold,
But muſt laugh out.

Enter Novall, *jun.* Charalois, Beaumelle, Bellapert.

   Nov. jun. Help! ſave me! Murther ! Murther !

   Bellap. Undone forever !

   Char. Oh, my Heart !

Hold yet a little.—Do not hope to 'ſcape
By Flight, it is impoſſible : Though I might
On all Advantage take thy Life, and juſtly ;
This Sword, my Father's Sword, that ne'er was drawn
But to a noble Purpoſe, ſhall not now
Do th' Office of a Hangman ; I reſerve it
To right mine Honour, not for a Revenge
So poor, that though with thee it ſhould cut off
Thy Family, with all that are ally'd

                    To

To thee in Luſt, or Baſeneſs, 'twere ſtill ſhort of
All Terms of Satisfaction.—Draw.

Nov. jun. I dare not:
I have already done you too much Wrong
To fight in ſuch a Cauſe.

Char. Why, dar'ſt thou neither
Be honeſt, Coward ? nor yet valiant, Knave ?
In ſuch a Cauſe come, do not ſhame thyſelf ;
Such whoſe Blood's Wrongs, or Wrong done to them-
　　ſelves
Could never heat, are yet in the Defence
Of their Whores, daring.—Look on her again.
You thought her worth the Hazard of your Soul,
And yet ſtand doubtful, in her Quarrel, to
Venture your Body.

Beaum. No, he fears his Cloaths
More than his Fleſh.

Char. Keep from me :—Guard thy Life ;
Or, as thou haſt liv'd like a Goat, thou ſhalt
Die like a Sheep.

Nov. jun. Since there's no Remedy,
Deſpair of Safety now in me prove Courage.

　　　　　　　　　　[*They fight. Novall is ſlain.*

Char. How ſoon weak Wrong's o'erthrown ! Lend
　　　me your Hand,
Bear this to the Caroch—Come, you have taught me
To ſay, you muſt, and ſhall : I wrong you not ;
Y'are but to keep him Company you love.
—Is't done ? 'tis well.—Raiſe Officers ! and take Care,
All you can apprehend within the Houſe
May be forth-coming. Do I appear much mov'd ?

Beaum. No, Sir.

Char. My Griefs are now thus to be borne ;
Hereafter I'll find Time and Place to mourn.

　　　　　　　　　　　　　　[*Exeunt.*

SCENE

SCENE III,

Enter Romont, Pontalier.

Pont. I was bound to feek you, Sir!
Rom. And, had you found me
In any Place but in the Street, I fhould
Have done,—nor talk'd to you. Are you the Captain?
The hopeful *Pontalier?* whom I have feen
Do in the Field fuch Service, as then made you
Their Envy that commanded, here at Home
To play the Parafite to a gilded Knave,
And, it may be, the Pander?
    Pont. Without this,
I come to call you to Account, for what
Is paft already. I by your Example
Of Thankfulnefs to the dead General,
By whom you were rais'd, have practis'd to be fo
To my good Lord *Novall*, by whom I live;
Whofe leaft Difgrace, that is, or may be offer'd,
With all the Hazard of my Life and Fortunes,
I will make good on you, or any Man,
That has a Hand in't; and, fince you allow me
A Gentleman and a Soldier, there's no Doubt
You will except againft me.   You fhall meet
With a fair Enemy; you underftand
The Right I look for, and muft have.
    Rom. I do;
And with the next Day's Sun you fhall hear from me.
                               [*Exeunt.*

SCENE IV.

Enter Charalois *with a Cafktt*, Beaumelle, Beaumont.

    Char. Pray bear this to my Father; at his Leifure
He may pérufe it: But with your beft Language
Intreat his inftant Prefence.   You have fworn
Not to reveal what I have done.
                                 Beaum.

Beaum. Nor will I — but —

Char. Doubt me not. By Heaven, I will do nothing
But what may ftand with Honour.—Pray you leave me
                                [*Ex.* Beaumont.
To my own Thoughts.—If this be to me, rife:
                                [Beaumel. *kneels.*
I am not worthy the looking on, but only
To feed Contempt and Scorn ; and that, from you
Who with the Lofs of your fair Name have caus'd it,
Were too much Cruelty.

    Beaumel. I dare not move you
To hear me fpeak. I know my Fault is far
Beyond Qualification, or Excufe ;
That 'tis not fit for me to hope, or you
To think of Mercy; only I prefume
To intreat you would be pleas'd to look upon
My Sorrow for it, and believe, thefe Tears
Are the true Children of my Grief, and not
A Woman's Cunning.

    Char. Can you, *Beaumelle,*
Having deceived fo great a Truft as mine,
Though I were all Credulity, hope again
To get Belief ? No, no ; if you look on me
With Pity, or dare practife any Means
To make my Sufferings lefs, or give juft Caufe
To all the World, to think what I muft do,
Was call'd upon by you, ufe other Ways ;
Deny what I have feen, or juftify
What you have done ; and, as you defperately
Made Shipwreck of your Faith to be a Whore,
Ufe th' Arms of fuch a one, and fuch Defence ;
And multiply the Sin, with Impudence.
Stand boldly up, and tell me to my Teeth,
That you have done but what's warranted
By great Examples, in all Places where
Women inhabit : Urge your own Deferts,
Or Want in me of Merit : Tell me, how
Your Dow'r from the low Gulf of Poverty,
Weigh'd up my Fortunes to what now they are :
That I was purchas'd by your Choice, and Practice

                                         To

To shelter you from Shame, that you might sin
As boldly as securely; that poor Men
Are married to those Wives that bring them Wealth;
One Day their Husbands, but Observers ever:
That when by this proud Usage you have blown
The Fire of my just Vengeance to the Height,
I then may kill you; and yet say, 'twas done
In Heat of Blood, and after die myself,
To witness my Repentance.

    Beaumel. O my Fate!
That never would consent that I should see
How worthy thou wert both of Love and Duty
Before I lost you; and my Misery made
The Glass, in which I now behold your Virtue!
While I was good, I was a Part of you,
And of two, by the virtuous Harmony
Of our fair Minds, made one: But, since I wander'd
In the forbidden Labyrinth of Lust,
What was inseparable, is by me divided.
With Justice, therefore, you may cut me off,
And from your Memory wash the Remembrance
That e'er I was; like to some vicious Purpose
Within your better Judgment, you repent of,
And study to forget.

    Char. O *Beaumelle*!
That you can speak so well, and do so ill!
But you had been too great a Blessing, if
You had continu'd chaste: See how you force me
To this, because mine Honour will not yield
That I again should love you.

    Beaumel. In this Life
It is not fit you should: Yet you shall find,
Though I was bold enough to be a Strumpet,
I dare not yet live one: Let those fam'd Matrons
That are canoniz'd worthy of our Sex,
Transcend me in their Sanctity of Life,
I yet will equal them in dying nobly,
Ambitious of no Honour after Life,
But that, when I am dead, you will forgive me.

                                 Char.

Char. How Pity ſteals upon me! ſhould I hear her
                                  [*Knock within.*
But ten Words more, I were loſt.—One knocks, go in.
                                [*Exit* Beaumelle.
That to be merciful ſhould be a Sin!

Enter Rochfort.

O, Sir, moſt welcome! Let me take your Cloak,
I muſt not be deny'd.—Here are your Robes,
As you love Juſtice, once more put them on.
There is a Cauſe to be determin'd of,
That does require ſuch an Integrity
As you have ever us'd.—I'll put you to
The Trial of your Conſtancy and Goodneſs;
And look that you, that have been Eagle-ey'd
In other Mens Affairs, prove not a Mole
In what concerns yourſelf. Take you your Seat,
I will before you preſently.   [*Exit.*
    Roch. Angels guard me!
To what ſtrange Tragedy does this Deſtruction
Serve for a Prologue?

Enter Charalois *with* Novall's *Body*, Beaumelle, *and* Beaumont.

    Char. So, ſet it down before
The Judgment Seat, and ſtand you at the Bar:
For me, I am the Accuſer.
    Roch. Novall ſlain?
And *Beaumelle*, my Daughter, in the Place
Of one to be arraign'd?
    Char. O, are you touch'd?
I find that I muſt take another Courſe.
                      [*He Hoodwinks* Rochfort.
Fear nothing; I will only blind your Eyes,
For Juſtice ſhould do ſo, when 'tis to meet
An Object that may ſway her equal Doom
From what it ſhould be aim'd at.—Good my Lord!
A Day of Hearing.   *Roch.*

Roch. It is granted, ſpeak—You ſhall have Juſtice.

Char. I then here accuſe,
Moſt equal Judge, the Priſoner, your fair Daughter,
For whom I ow'd ſo much to you : Your Daughter,
So worthy in her own Parts, and that Worth
Set forth by yours, to whoſe ſo rare Perfeƈtions,
Truth witneſs with me, in the Place of Service
I almoſt paid idolatrous Sacrifice,
To be a falſe Adultreſs.

Roch. With whom ?

Char. With this *Novall*, here dead.

Roch. Be well advis'd,
And ere you ſay Adultreſs again,
Her Fame depending on it, be moſt ſure
That ſhe is one.

Char. I took them in the Aƈt.
I know no Proof beyond it.

Roch. O my Heart !

Char. A Judge ſhould feel no Paſſions.

Roch. Yet, remember
He is a Man, and cannot put off Nature.
What Anſwer makes the Priſoner ?

Beaumel. I confeſs
The Faƈt I am charg'd with, and yield myſelf
Moſt miſerably guilty.

Roch. Heaven take Mercy
Upon your Soul, then : It muſt leave your Body.——
Now free mine Eyes : I dare unmov'd look on her,
And fortify my Sentence with ſtrong Reaſons.
Since that the politick Law provides, that Servants,
To whoſe Care we commit our Goods, ſhall die,
If they abuſe our Truſt ; what can you look for,
To whoſe Charge this moſt hopeful Lord gave up
All he receiv'd from his brave Anceſtors,
Or he could leave to his Poſterity ?
His Honour, wicked Woman ! in whoſe Safety
All this Life's Joys and Comforts were lock'd up,
With thy Luſt, a Thief hath now ſtoln from him ;
And therefore——

VOL. II.   R   *Char.*

Char. Stay, juſt Judge.—May not what's loſt
By her own Fault (for I am charitable,
And charge her not with many) be forgotten
In her fair Life hereafter?

Roch. Never, Sir!
The Wrong that's done to the chaſte married Bed,
Repentant Tears can never expiate;
And be aſſur'd, to pardon ſuch a Sin,
Is an Offence as great as to commit it.

Char. I may not then forgive her?

Roch. Nor ſhe hope it:
Nor can ſhe wiſh to live. No ſun ſhall riſe,
But ere it ſet, ſhall ſhew her ugly Luſt
In a new Shape, and every one more horrid:
Nay, even thoſe Prayers, which with ſuch humble
      Fervour
She ſeems to ſend up yonder, are beat back;
And all Suits, which her Penitence can proffer,
As ſoon as made, are with Contempt thrown
Off all the Courts of Mercy.

Char. Let her die then.   [*He kills her.*
Better prepar'd I am. Sure I could not take her,
Nor ſhe accuſe her Father, as a Judge
Partial againſt her.

Beaumel. I approve his Sentence,
And kiſs the Executioner: My Luſt
Is now run from me in that Blood, In which
It was begot and nouriſhed.   [*Dies.*

Roch. Is ſhe dead then?

Char. Yes, Sir, this is her Heart-Blood, is it not?
I think it be.

Roch. And you have kill'd her?

Char. True, and did it by your Doom.

Roch. But I pronounc'd it
As a Judge only, and a Friend to Juſtice,
And zealous in Defence of your wrong'd Honour,
Broke all the Ties of Nature; and caſt off
The Love and ſoft Affection of a Father.
I, in your Cauſe, put on a Scarlet Robe

Of red-dy'd Cruelty; but, in Return,
You have advanc'd for me no Flag of Mercy.
I look'd on you as a wrong'd Hufband; but
You clos'd your Eyes againft me, as a Father.
O *Beaumelle!* my Daughter!
 Char. This is Madnefs.
 Roch. Keep from me.—Could not one good Thought
  rife up,
To tell you that fhe was my Age's Comfort,
Begot by a weak Man, and born a Woman,
And could not, therefore, but partake of Frailty?
Or wherefore did not Thankfulnefs ftep forth,
To urge my many Merits, which I may
Object unto you, fince you prove ungrateful;
Flinty-hearted *Charalois?*
 Char. Nature does prevail above your Virtue.
 Roch. No; it gives me Eyes,
To pierce the Heart of your Defign againft me.
I find it now; it was my 'State was aim'd at,
A nobler Match was fought for, and the Hours
I liv'd, grew tedious to you: My Compaffion
Towards you hath render'd me moft miferable,
And foolifh Charity undone myfelf.
But there's a Heaven above, from whofe juft Wreak
No Mifts of Policy can hide Offenders.

  Enter Novall, *fen. with Officers.*

 Nov. fen. Force ope the Doors.—O Monfter! Canibal!
Lay hold on him — My Son! my Son!—O *Rochfort!*
'Twas you gave Liberty to this bloody Wolf
To worry all our Comforts.——But this is
No Time to quarrel; now give your Affiftance
For the Revenge.
 Roch. Call it a fitter Name.
—Juftice for innocent Blood.
 Char. Though all confpire
Againft that Life which I am weary of,
A little longer yet I'll ftrive to keep it,

To ·

To fhew, in Spite of Malice, and their Laws,
His Plea muft fpeed, that hath an honeft Caufe.

[*Exeunt.*

ACT V.   SCENE I.

Enter Liladam, *Taylor, Officers.*

Lilad. WHY, 'tis both moft unconfcionable, and
untimely,
T' arreft a Gallant for his Cloaths, before
He has worn them out: Befides, you faid you afk'd
My Name in my Lord's Bond, but for me only,
And now you'll lay me up for't.   Do not think
The taking Meafure of a Cuftomer
By a Brace of Varlets, though I rather wait
Never fo patiently, will prove a Fafhion
Which any Courtier or Inns-of-Court Man
Would follow willingly.
Taylor. There I believe you.
But, Sir! 1 muft have prefent Monies, or
Affurance, to fecure me when I fhall ——
Or I will fee to your coming forth.
Lilad. Plague on't!
You have provided for my Entrance in:
That coming forth you talk of, concerns me.
What fhall I do? You've done me a Difgrace
In the Arreft, but more in giving Caufe
To all the Street to think I cannot ftand
Without thefe two Supporters for my Arms:
Pray you, let them loofe me: For their Satisfaction
I will not run away.
Taylor. For theirs you will not;
But for your own you would: Look to him, Fellows!
Lilad. Why do you call them Fellows? Do not
Your Reputation fo, as you are merely   [wrong

A

A Taylor, faithful, apt to believe in Gallants.
You're a Companion at a ten Crown Supper
For Cloth of Bodkin, and may with one Lark
Eat up three Manchets, and no Man obferve you,
Or call your Trade in Queftion for't, But, when
You ftudy your Debt-Book, and hold Correfpondence
With Officers of the Hanger, and leave Swordmen,
The Learned conclude, the Taylor and Serjeant
In the Expreffion of a Knave are thefe
To be fynonymous. Look, therefore, to it!
And let us part in Peace. I would be loth
You fhould undo yourfelf.

Enter Old Novall, *and* Pontalier.

Taylor. To let you go
Were the next Way. But, fee! here's your old Lord;
Let him but give his Word I fhall be paid,
And you are free.
Lilad. S'lid! I'll put him to't:
I can be but denied: or—what fay you?
His Lordfhip owing me three Times your Debt;
If you arreft him at my Suit, and let me
Go run before, to fee the Action enter'd,
'Twould be a witty Jeft.
Taylor. I muft have Earneft.—
I cannot pay my Debts fo.
Pont. Can your Lordfhip
Imagine, while I live, and wear a Sword,
Your Son's Death fhall be unreveng'd?
Nov. fen. I know not
One Reafon why you fhould not do like others:
I am fure, of all the Herd that fed upon him,
I cannot fee in any, now he's gone,
In Pity, or in Thankfulnefs, one true Sign
Of Sorrow for him.
Pont. All his Bounties yet
Fell not in fuch unthankful Ground: 'Tis true,
He had Weakneffes, but fuch, as few are free from.

And,

And, though none footh'd them lefs than I, for now
To fay that I forefaw the Dangers, that
Would rife from cherifhing them, were but untimely,
I yet could wifh, the Juftice that you feek for
In the Revenge, had been trufted to me,
And not the uncertain Iffue of the Laws :
'T has robb'd me of a noble Teftimony
Of what I durft do for him.—But, however,
My forfeit Life redeem'd by him, though dead,
Shall do him Service.

   Nov. fen. As far as my Grief
Will give me Leave, I thank you.'

   Lilad. Oh, my Lord !
Oh my good Lord ! deliver me from thefe Furies.

   Pont. Arrefted ? This is one of them, whofe bafe
And abject Flattery help'd to dig his Grave :
He is not worth your Pity, nor my Anger.—
Go to the Bafket, and Repent.

   Nov. fen. Away !—I only know now to hate thee
I will do nothing for thee.   [deadly :

   Lilad. Nor you, Captain ?

   Pont. No, to your Trade again ; put off this Cafe,
It may be, the difcovering what you were
When your unfortunate Mafter took you up,
May move Compaffion in your Creditor.
Confefs the Truth.

             [*Exit* Novall, *fen. and* Pontalier.

   Lilad. And, now I think on't better,
I will, Brother, your Hand ! your Hand, fweet Brother.
I'm of your Sect, and my Gallantry but a Dream,
Out of which thefe two fearful Apparitions
Againft my Will have wak'd me.   This rich Sword
Grew fuddenly out of a Taylor's Bodkin ;
Thefe Hangers from my Vails and Fees in Hell ;
And, whereas now this Beaver fits, full often
A thrifty Cap, compos'd of Broad-cloth Lifts,
Near-'kin unto the Cufhion where I fat
Crofs-leg'd, and yet ungarter'd, hath been feen,
Our Breakfafts, famous for the butter'd Loaves,

                    I have

I have with Joy been oft acquainted with;
And therefore ufe a Confcience, though it be
Forbidden in our Hall towards other Men,
To me that, as I have been, will again
Be of the Brotherhood.

Officer. I know him now:
He was a 'Prentice to *Le Robe* at *Orleance.*

Lilad. And from thence brought by my young Lord,
    now dead,
Unto *Dijon*; and with him, till this Hour,
Hath been receiv'd here for a compleat Monfieur.
Nor wonder at it; for but Tythe our Gallants,
Even thofe of the firft Rank, and you will find
In every ten, one, peradventure two,
That fmell rank of the dancing School, or Fiddle,
The Pantofle or Preffing-iron:—But hereafter
We'll talk of this. I will furrender up
My Suits again; there cannot be much Lofs.
'Tis but the turning of the Lace, with one
Addition more you know of, and what wants
I will work out.

Taylor. Then here our Quarrel ends:
The Gallant is turn'd Taylor, and all Friends. [*Exeunt.*

SCENE II.

Enter Romont, Beaumont.

Rom. You have them ready.

Beaum. Yes; and they will fpeak
Their Knowledge in this Caufe, when thou thinkft fit
To have them call'd upon.

Rom. 'Tis well; and fomething
I can add to their Evidence, to prove
This brave Revenge, which they would have call'd
    Murther,
A noble Juftice.

Beaum. In this you exprefs
(The Breach, by my Lord's Want of you, new made up)
A faithful Friend.

R 4

Beaum.

Rom. That Friendfhip's rais'd on Sand,
Which every fudden Guft of Difcontent,
Or Flowing of our Paffions, can change,
As if it ne'er had been :—But do you know
Who are to fit on him?

Beaum. Monfieur *Du Croy*,
Affifted by *Charmi*.

Rom. The Advocate,
That pleaded for the Marfhal's Funeral,
And was check'd for it by *Novall*.

Beaum. The fame.

Rom. How fortunes that?

Beaum. Why, Sir, my Lord *Novall*,
Being the Accufer, cannot be the Judge;
Nor would grieve *Rochfort*, but Lord *Charalois*
(However he might wrong him by his Power,)
Should have an equal Hearing.

Rom. By my Hopes
Of *Charalois*'s Acquittal, I lament
That reverend old Man's Fortune.

Beaum. Had you feen him,
As to my Grief I have, now promife Patience,
And, e'er it was believ'd, though fpake by him
That never break his Word, enrag'd again
So far as to make War upon thofe Hairs,
Which not a barbarous *Scythian* durft prefume
To touch, but with a fuperftitious Fear,
As fomething facred;—and then curfe his Daughter;
But with more frequent Violence himfelf,
As if he had been guilty of her Fault,
By being incredulous of your Report,
You would not only judge him worthy Pity,
But fuffer with him.—But here comes the Prifoner,

Enter Charalois, *with Officers.*

I dare not ftay to do my Duty to him;
Yet, reft affur'd, all poffible Means in me
To do him Service, keeps you Company.

Rom.

Rom. It is not doubted.   [*Exit* Beaumont.

Char. Why, yet, as I came hither,
The People, apt to mock Calamity,
And tread on the opprefs'd, made no Horns at me, .
Though they are too familiar :—I deferve them.
And, knowing too what Blood my Sword hath drunk,
In Wreak of that Difgrace, they yet forbear
To fhake their Heads, or to revile me for
A Murtherer; they rather all put on
(As for great Loffes the old *Romans* us'd)
A general Face of Sorrow, waited on
By a fad Murmur breaking through their Silence,
And no Eye but was readier with a Tear
To witnefs 'twas fhed for me, than I could
Difcern a Face made up with Scorn againft me.
Why fhould I then, though for unufual Wrongs
I chofe unufual Means to right thofe Wrongs,
Condemn myfelf, as over-partial
In my own Caufe.—*Romont ?*

Rom. Beft Friend, well met!
By my Heart's Love to you, and join to that
My Thankfulnefs that ftill lives to the dead,
I look upon you now with more true Joy,
Then when I faw you married.

Char. You have Reafon
To give you Warrant for't. My falling off
From fuch a Friendfhip, with the Scorn that anfwered
Your too prophetick Counfel, may well move you
To think your meeting me, going to my Death,
A fit Encounter for that Hate which juftly
I have deferv'd from you.

Rom. Shall I ftill, then,
Speak Truth, and be ill underftood?

Char. You are not.
I'm confcious I have wrong'd you, and allow me
Only a moral Man to look on you,
Whom foolifhly I have abus'd and injur'd,
Muft of Neceffity be more terrible to me,
Than any Death the Judges can pronounce

From

From the Tribunal which I am to plead at.

   Rom. Paffion tranfports you.

   Char. For what I have done
To my falfe Lady, or *Novall*, I can
Give fome apparent Caufe; but, touching you,
In my Defence, Child-like, I can fay nothing,
But I am forry for't; a poor Satisfaction!
And yet, miftake me not; for it is more
Then I will fpeak, to have my Pardon fign'd
For all I ftand accus'd of.

   Rom. You much weaken
The Strength of your good Caufe, fhould you but
    think,
A Man for doing well could entertain
A Pardon, were it offer'd. You have given
To blind and flow pac'd Juftice, Wings, and Eyes,
To fee, and overtake Impieties,
Which from a cold Proceeding had receiv'd
Indulgence or Protection.

   Char. Think you fo?

   Rom. Upon my Soul, nor fhould the Blood you
    challenge
And took to cure your Honour, breed more Scruple
In your foft Confcience, than if your Sword
Had been fheath'd in a Tygrefs, or She-Bear,
That in their Bowels would have made your Tomb.
To injure Innocence is more than Murther:
But when inhuman Lufts tranfform us, then
As Beafts, we are to fuffer, not like Men,
To be lamented. Nor did *Charalois* ever
Perform an Act fo worthy the Applaufe
Of a full Theatre of perfect Men,
As he hath done in this: The Glory got
By overthrowing outward Enemies,
Since Strength and Fortune are main Sharers in it,
We cannot, but by Pieces, call our own:
But, when we conquer our inteftine Foes,
Our Paffions bred within us, and of thofe
The moft rebellious Tyrant, powerful Love,

Our Reason suffering us to like no longer
Than the fair Object, being good, deserves it,
That's a true Victory; which, were great Men
Ambitious to atchieve, by your Example
Setting no Price upon the Breach of Faith,
But Loss of Life, 'twould fright Adultery
Out of their Families, and make Lust appear
As loathsome to us in the first Consent,
As when 'tis waited on by Punishment.

Char. You have confirm'd me. Who would love a
    Woman
That might enjoy, in such a Man, a Friend?
You've made me know the Justice of my Cause,
And mark'd me out the Way, how to defend it.

Rom. Continue to that Resolution constant,
And you shall, in Contempt of their worst Malice,
Come off with Honour.—Here they come.

Char. I am ready.

SCENE III.[1]

Enter Du Croy, Charmi, Rochfort, Novall *sen.* Pontalier, Beaumont.

Nov. sen. See, equal Judges, with what Confidence
The cruel Murtherer stands, as if he would
Out-face the Court and Justice!

Roch. But look on him,
And you shall find (for still methinks I do,
Though Guilt hath dy'd him black) something good in
    him,
That may perhaps work with a wiser Man,
Than I have been, again to set him free
And give him all he has.

[1] Scene 3. The ensuing Scene is most finely wrote, as is indeed
the whole Act. The Misfortunes of the good old generous *Rochfort*,
and the pious *Charalois*'s continued Round of Sorrows must be very affecting to every Heart, that is capable of being touched with Pity and
Tenderness.

Charmi.

Charmi. This is not well.
I would you had liv'd fo, my Lord! that I,
Might rather have continu'd your poor Servant,
Than fit here as your Judge.

Du Croy. I am forry for you.

Roch. In no Act of my Life I have deferv'd
This Injury from the Court, that any here
Should thus uncivily ufurp on what
Is proper to me only.

Du Croy. What Diftafte
Receives my Lord?

Roch. You fay you are forry for him:
A Grief in which I muft not have a Partner:
'Tis I alone am forry, that I rais'd
The Building of my Life, for feventy Years,
Upon fo fure a Ground, that all the Vices,
Practis'd to ruin Man, though brought againft me,
Could never undermine, and no Way left
To fend thefe grey Hairs to the Grave with Sorrow,
Virtue, that was my Patronefs, betray'd me:
For, entring, nay, poffeffing, this young Man,
It lent him fuch a powerful Majefty
To grace whate'er he undertook, that freely
I gave myfelf up with my Liberty,
To be at his difpofing: Had his Perfon,
Lovely I muft confefs, or far fam'd Valour,
Or any other feeming Good, that yet
Holds a near Neighbourhood with Ill, wrought on me,
I might have borne it better: But, when Goodnefs
And Piety itfelf in her beft Figure
Were brib'd to my Deftruction, can you blame me,
Though I forget to fuffer like a Man,
Or rather act a Woman?

Beaum. Good my Lord!

Nov. fen. You hinder our Proceeding,

Charmi. And forget
The Parts of an Accufer.

Beaum. 'Pray you, remember
To ufe the Temper, which to me you promis'd.

Roch.

Roch. Angels themfelves muft break, *Beaumont!* that
    promife,
Beyond the Strength and Patience of Angels.
But I have done :—My good Lord! pardon me
A weak old Man ; and pray add to that
A miferable Father ; yet be careful
That your Compaffion of my Age, nor his,
Move you to any Thing, that may mif-become
The Place on which you fit.
    Charmi. Read the Indictment.
    Char. It fhall be needlefs ; I myfelf, my Lords!
Will be my own Accufer, and confefs
All they can charge me with ; nor will I fpare
To aggravate that Guilt with Circumftance
They feek to load me with : Only I pray,
That, as for them you will vouchfafe me Hearing,
I may not be, deny'd it for myfelf,
When I fhall urge by what unanfwerable Reafons
I was compell'd to what I did, which yet,
Till you have taught me better, I repent not.
    Roch. The Motion's honeft.
    Charmi. And 'tis freely granted.
    Char. Then I confefs, my Lords! that I ftood bound,
When, with my Friends, ev'n Hope itfelf had left me,
To this Man's Charity for my Liberty ;
Nor did his Bounty end there, but began :
For, after my Enlargement, cherifhing
The Good he did, he made me Mafter of
His only Daughter, and his whole Eftate :
Great Ties of Thankfulnefs, I muft acknowledge,
Could any one, freed by you, prefs this further ?
But yet confider, my moft honour'd Lords !
If to receive a Favour, make a Servant,
And Benefits are Bonds to tie the Taker
To the imperious Will of him that gives,
There's none but Slaves will receive Courtefies,
Since they muft fetter us to our Difhonours.
Can it be call'd Magnificence in a Prince,
To pour down Riches, with a liberal Hand,

Upon

Upon a poor Man's Wants, if that muſt bind him,
To play the ſoothing Paraſite to his Vices?
Or any Man, becauſe he ſav'd my Hand,
Preſume my Head and Heart are at his Service?
Or, did I ſtand engag'd to buy my Freedom
(When my Captivity was honourable)
By making myſelf here, and Fame hereafter,
Bondſlaves to Men's Scorn, and calumnious Tongues?
Had his fair Daughter's Mind been like her Feature,
Or, for ſome little Blemiſh, I had ſought
For my Content elſewhere, waſting on others
My Body, and her Dowry; my Forehead then
Deſerv'd the Brand of baſe Ingratitude:
But if obſequious Uſage, and fair Warning
To keep her worth my Love, could not preſerve her
From being a Whore, and yet no cunning one,
So to offend, and yet the Fault kept from me——
What ſhould I do? Let any free-born Spirit
Determine truly, if that Thankfulneſs,
Choice Form, with the whole World given for a Dowry,
Could ſtrengthen ſo an honeſt Man with Patience,
As with a willing Neck to undergo
The inſupportable Yoke of Slave or Wittal.

 Charmi. What Proof have you ſhe did play falſe, beſides
Your Oath?

 Char. Her own Confeſſion to her Father.
I aſk him for a Witneſs.

 Roch. 'Tis moſt true.
I would not willingly blend my laſt Words
With an Untruth.

 Char. And then to clear myſelf,
That his great Wealth was not the Mark I ſhot at,
But that I held it, when fair *Beaumelle*
Fell from her Vertue, like the fatal Gold
Which *Brennus* took from *Delphos*, whoſe Poſſeſſion
Brought with it Ruin to himſelf and Army.
Here's one in Court, *Beaumont*, by whom I ſent
All Grants and Writings back, which made it mine,

Before

Before his Daughter dy'd by his own Sentence,
As freely, as, unask'd, he gave it to me.
　Beaum. They are here to be seen.
　Charmi. Open the Casket.——
Peruse that Deed of Gift.
　Rom. Half of the Danger
Already is discharg'd : The other Part
As bravely, and you are not only free,
But crown'd with Praise for ever.
　Du Croy. 'Tis apparent.
　Charmi. Your 'State, my Lord, again is yours.
　Roch. Not mine ;
I am not of the World : If it can prosper,
(And yet, being justly got, I'll not examine
Why it should be so fatal) do you bestow it
On pious Uses : I'll go seek a Grave.
And yet, for Proof, I die in Peace, your Pardon
I ask ; and, as you grant it me, may Heaven,
Your Conscience, and these Judges, free you from
What you are charg'd with.　So, farewell, for ever.——
　　　　　　　　　　　　　　　　[*Exit* Rochfort.
　Novall sen. I'll be mine own Guide.　Passion, nor
　　Example
Shall be my Leaders.　I have lost a Son,
A Son, grave Judges, I require his Blood
From his accursed Homicide.
　Charmi. What Reply you,
In your Defence for this ?
　Char. I but attended
Your Lordship's Pleasure.——For the Fact, as of
The former, I confess it ; but with what
Base Wrongs I was unwillingly drawn to it,
To my few Words there are some other Proofs
To witness this for Truth.　When I was married
(For there I must begin) the slain *Novall*
Was to my Wife, in Way of our *French* Courtship,
A most devoted Servant ; but yet aimed at
Nothing but Means to quench his wanton Heat,
His Heart being never warm'd by lawful Fires

　　　　　　　　　　　　　　　　　　　　As

As mine was, Lords; and though, on thefe Prefump-
    tions,
Join'd to the Hate between his Houfe and mine,
I might, with Opportunity and Eafe,
Have found a Way for my Revenge, I did not;
But ftill he had the Freedom as before,
When all was mine; and, told that he abus'd it
With fome unfeemly Licence, by my Friend,
My approv'd Friend, *Romont*, I gave no Credit
To the Reporter, but reprov'd him for it,
As one uncourtly and malicious to him.
What could I more, my Lords? Yet, after this,
He did continue in his firft Purfuit,
Hotter then ever, and at length obtained it;
But, how it came to my moft certain Knowledge,
For the Dignity of the Court, and my own Honour,
I dare not fay.

    Nov. fen. If all may be believ'd
A paffionate Prifoner fpeaks; who is fo foolifh
That durft be wicked, that will appear guilty?
No, my grave Lords: In his Impunity
But give Example unto jealous Men
To cut the Throats they hate, and they will never
Want Matter or Pretence for their bad Ends.

    Charmi. You muft find other Proofs, to ftrengthen thefe
But mere Prefumptions.——

    Du Croy. Or we fhall hardly
Allow your Innocence.

    Char. All your Attempts
Shall fall on me, like brittle Shafts on Armour,
That break themfelves; or like Waves againft a Rock,
That leave no Sign of their ridiculous Fury
But Foam and Splinters; my Innocence like thefe
Shall ftand triumphant, and your Malice ferve
But for a Trumpet to proclaim my Conqueft:
Nor fhall you, though you do the worft Fate can,
How e'er condemn, affright an honeft Man.

    Rom. May it pleafe the Court, I may be heard.

Nov. fen. You come not
To rail again ? But do——You ſhall not find
Another *Rochfort*.

Rom. In *Novall* I cannot.
But I come furniſhed with what will ſtop
The Mouth of his Conſpiracy againſt the Life
Of innocent *Charalois*.   Do you know this Character ?

Nov. fen. Yes, 'tis my Son's.

Rom. May it pleaſe your Lordſhips, read it,
And you ſhall find there, with what Vehemency
He did ſolicit *Beaumelle* ; how he had got
A Promiſe from her to enjoy his Wiſhes ;
How after he abjur'd her Company,
And yet——(but that 'tis fit I ſpare the Dead)
Like a damn'd Viilain, as ſoon as recorded,
He brake that Oath ;——to make this manifeſt,
Produce his Bawds and her's.

Enter Aymer, Florimel, Bellapert.

Charmi. Have they took their Oaths ?

Rom. They have, and, rather than endure the Rack,
Confeſs the Time, the Meeting, nay the Act ;
What would you more ? Only this Matron made
A free Diſcovery to a good End ;
And therefore I ſue to the Court, ſhe may not
Be plac'd in the black Liſt of the Delinquents.

Pont. I ſee by this, *Novall*'s Revenge needs me ;
And I ſhall do.——

Charmi. 'Tis evident——

Nov. fen. That I
Till now was never wretched : Here's no Place
To curſe him or my Stars.   [*Exit* Novall *fen.*

Charmi. Lord *Charalois* !
The Injuries you have ſuſtain'd, appear
So worthy of the Mercy of the Court,
That, notwithſtanding you have gone beyond
The Letter of the Law, they yet acquit you.

Pont. But, in *Novall*, I do condemn him——thus.
                                    [*Stabs him.*

Char. I'm flain.

Rom. Can I look on? Oh, murd'rous Wretch!
Thy Challenge now I anfwer.—So die with him.

[*Stabs* Pontalier.

Charmi. A Guard! difarm him!

Rom. I yield up my Sword
Unforc'd—Oh, *Charalois!*

Char. For Shame, *Romont!*
Mourn not for him, that dies, as he hath liv'd;
Still conftant and unmov'd: What's fall'n upon me,
Is by Heav'ns Will; becaufe I made myfelf
A Judge in my own Caufe without their Warrant:—
But he, that lets me know thus much in Death,
With all good Men—forgive me.   [*Dies.*

Pont. I receive
The Vengeance, which my Love not built on Virtue,
Has made me worthy of,   [*Dies.*

Charmi. We're taught
By this fad Precedent, how juft foever
Our Reafons are to remedy our Wrongs,
We're yet to leave them to their Will and Power,
That to that Purpofe have Authority.
For you, *Romont,* although in your Excufe
You may plead, what you did, was in Revenge
Of the Difhonour done unto the Court:
Yet, fince from us you had not Warrant for it,
We banifh you the State: For thefe, they fhall,
As they are found guilty or innocent,
Or be fet free, or fuffer Punifhment.   [*Exeunt.*

F I N I S.

THE

EMPEROR of the EAST.

A

TRAGI - COMEDY.

As it hath been divers Times acted, at the *Black-Fryers*, and *Globe* Play-Houfes, by the King's Majefty's Servants. 1632.

WRITTEN

By PHILIP MASSINGER.

To the Right Honourable, and my Especial Good Lord,

JOHN Lord MOHUN,

Baron of OKEHAMPTON, &c.

My Good Lord,

L ET my Presumption in stiling you so (having never deserved it in my Service) from the Clemency of your noble Disposition, find Pardon. The Reverence due to the Name of Mohun, *long since honoured in three Earls of* Somerset, *and eight Barons of* Munster, *may challenge from all Pens a deserved Celebration. And the rather in respect those Titles were not purchased, but conferred, and continued in your Ancestors, for many virtuous, noble, and still living Actions; nor ever forfeited, or tainted, but when the Iniquity of those Times laboured the Depression of approved Goodness, and in wicked Policy held it fit that Loyalty and Faith, in taking Part with the true Prince, should be degraded and mulcted. But this admitting no farther Dilation in this Place, may your Lordship please, and with all possible Brevity to understand, the Reasons why I am, in humble Thankfulness, ambitious to shelter this Poem under the Wings of your Honourable Protection. My worthy Friend, Mr.* Aston Cockain, *your Nephew, to my extraordinary Content, deliver'd to me, that your Lordship, at your vacant Hours, sometimes vouchsafed to peruse such Trifles of mine as have passed the Press, and not alone warranted them in your gentle Suffrage, but disdained not to bestow a Remembrance of your Love, and intended Favour to me. I profess to the World, I was exalted with the Bounty, and with good Assurance, it being so rare in this Age to meet with one Noble Name, that, in Fear to be censured of Levity and Weakness, dares express itself a Friend or Patron to contemn'd Poetry.**

---

* That this noble Lord not only favoured Poetry, but wrote himself, appears from S r *Aston Cockain's* Letter to his Lordship in Verse. See *Cockain's* Poems, Page 80.

S 3

Having

Having, therefore, no Means elfe left me to witnefs the Obligation, in which I ftand moft willingly bound to your Lordfhip, I offer this Tragi-Comedy to your gracious Acceptance, no Way defpairing, but that with a clear Afpect, you will deign to receive it (it being an Induction to my future Endeavours) and that in the Lift of thofe, that to your Merit truly admire you, you may defcend to number

Your Lordfhip's

Faithful Honourer,

PHILIP MASSINGER.

PROLOGUE at the BLACK-FRYERS.

BUT that imperious Cuftom warrants it,
Our Author with much Willingnefs would omit
This Preface to his new Work. He hath found
(And fuffer'd for't) many are apt to wound
His Credit in this Kind : and, whether he
Exprefs himfelf fearful, or peremptory,
He cannot 'fcape their Cenfures who delight
To mifapply whatever he fhould write.
'Tis his hard Fate. And though he will not fue,
Or bafely beg fuch Suffrages, yet to you
Free, and ingenuous Spirits, he doth now,
In me prefent his Service, with his Vow
He hath done his beft ; and, though he cannot glory
In his Invention, (this Work being a Story,
Of reverend Antiquity) he doth hope
In the Proportion of it, and the Scope,
You may obferve fome Pieces drawn like one
Of a ftedfaft Hand, and with the whiter Stone
To be mark'd in your fair Cenfures.   More than this
I am forbid to promife, and it is

With

With the moſt 'till you confirm it: ſince we know
Whate'er the Shaft be, Archer, or the Bow
From which 'tis ſent, it cannot hit the White
Unleſs your Approbation guide it right.

PROLOGUE at COURT.

AS ever (Sir) you lent a gracious Ear
To oppreſs'd Innocence, now vouchſafe to hear
A ſhort Petition. At your Feet, in me,
The Poet kneels, and to your Majeſty
Appeals for Juſtice. What we now preſent,
When firſt conceiv'd, in his Vote and Intent,
Was ſacred to your Pleaſure ; in each Part
With his beſt of Fancy, Judgment, Language, Art,
Faſhion'd, and form'd ſo, as might well, and may
Deſerve a Welcome, and no vulgar Way.
He durſt not (Sir) at ſuch a ſolemn Feaſt
Lard his grave Matter with one ſcurrilous Jeſt ;
But labour'd that no Paſſage might appear,
But what the Queen without a Bluſh might hear :
And yet this poor Work ſuffer'd by the Rage,
And Envy of ſome *Cato's* of the Stage :
Yet ſtill he hopes, this Play, which then was ſeen
With ſore Eyes, and condemn'd out of their Spleen,
May be by you, the ſupreme Judge, ſet free,
And rais'd above the Reach of Calumny.

Dramatis

Dramatis Personæ.

THEODOSIUS the Younger.

PAULINUS, a Kinsman to the Emperor.
PHILANAX, Captain of the Guard.
PATRIARCH.
TIMANTUS,
CHRYSAPIUS, } Eunuchs of the Emperor's Chamber.
GRATIANUS,
CLEON, a Traveller, Friend to PAULINUS.
Informer.
Projector.
Master of the Manners.
Mignion of the Suburbs.
Countryman.
Chirurgeon.
Empirick.

PULCHERIA, the Protectress.
ATHENAIS, a strange Virgin; after, the Empress.
ARCADIA,
FLACCILLA, } the young Sisters of the Emperor.

Servants.
Mutes.

The Scene, Constantinople.

THE

THE

EMPEROR of the EAST.

ACT I. SCENE I.*

Paulinus, Cleon.

Paulinus.

IN your fix Years Travel, Friend, no doubt,
you've met with,
  Many, and rare Adventures, and obferv'd
  The Wonders of each Climate, varying in
The Manners, and the Men, and fo return,
For the future Service of your Prince and Country,
In your Underftanding better'd.

 Cleon. Sir, I have made oft
The beft Ufe in my Power, and hope my Gleanings,
After the full Crop others reap'd before me,
Shall not, when I am call'd on, altogether
Appear unprofitable : Yet I left
The Miracle of Miracles in our Age
At home behind me ; every where abroad
Fame with a true, though prodigal Voice, deliver'd
Such Wonders of *Pulcheria* the Princefs,
To the Amazement, nay, Aftonifhment rather
Of fuch as heard it, that I found not one,
In all the States and Kingdoms that I pafs'd through,
Worthy to be her fecond.

 * The Plot of this Play is founded on the Hiftory of *Theodofius* the younger. See *Socrates*, Lib. 7. *Theodoret*, L. 5, &c.

Paul.

Paul. She, indeed, is
A perfect Phœnix, and difdains a Rival.
Her infant Years, as you know, promis'd much:
But grown to Ripenefs fhe tranfcends, and makes
Credulity her Debtor. I will tell you
In my blunt Way, to entertain the Time
Until you have the Happinefs to fee her,
How in your Abfence fhe hath borne herfelf,
And with all poffible Brevity, though the Subject
Is fuch a fpacious Field, as would require
An Abftract of the pureft Eloquence
(Deriv'd from the moft famous Orators
The Nurfe of Learning, *Athens*, fhew'd the World)
In that Man, that fhould undertake to be
Her true Hiftorian.

Cleon. In this you fhall do me
A fpecial Favour.

Paul. Since *Arcadius*' Death,
Our late great Mafter, the Protection of
The Prince his Son, the fecond *Theodofius*,
By a general Vote and Suffrage of the People;
Was to her Charge affign'd, with the Difpofure
Of his fo many Kingdoms. For his Perfon,
She hath fo train'd him up in all thofe Arts
That are both great and good, and to be wifhed
In an Imperial Monarch, that the Mother
Of the *Gracchi*, grave *Cornelia* (*Rome* ftill boafts of)
The wife *Pulcheria* but nam'd, muft be
No more remember'd. She, by her Example,
Hath made the Court a kind of Academy,
In which true Honour is both learn'd, and practis'd,
Her private Lodgings a chafte Nunnery,
In which her Sifters, as Probationers, hear
From her their Sovereign Abbefs, all the Precepts
Read in the School of Virtue.

Cleon. You amaze me.

Paul. I fhall, ere I conclude: For here the Wonder
Begins, not ends. Her Soul is fo immenfe,
And her ftrong Faculties fo apprehenfive,
To fearch into the Depth of deep Defigns,

And

And of all Natures, that the Burthen, which
To many Men were infupportable,
To her is but a gentle Exercife,
Made by the frequent Ufe familiar to her.

    Cleon. With your good Favour, let me interrupt you.
Being as fhe is in every Part fo perfect,
Methinks that all Kings of our Eaftern World
Should become Rivals for her.

    Paul. So they have;
But to no Purpofe. She, that knows her Strength
To rule, and govern Monarchs, fcorns to wear
On her free Neck the fervile Yoke of Marriage.
And for one loofe Defire, envy itfelf
Dares not prefume to taint her. *Venus'* Son [1]
Is blind indeed, when he but gazes on her.
Her Chaftity being a Rock of Diamonds,
With which encounter'd, his Shafts fly in Splinters,
His flaming Torches in the living Spring
Of her Perfections, quench'd: And, to crown all;
She's fo impartial when fhe fits upon
The high Tribunal, neither fway'd with Pity,
Nor aw'd by Fear, beyond her equal Scale,
That 'tis not Superftition to believe
Aftrea once more lives upon the Earth,
Pulcheria's Breaft her Temple.

    Cleon. You have given her
An admirable Character.

    Paul. She deferves it,
And fuch is the commanding Power of Virtue,
That from her vicious Enemies it compels
Pæans of Praife as a due Tribute to her.

                    [*Solemn loud Mufick.*

    Cleon. What means this folemn Mufick?
    Paul. It ufhers

[1] ————— Venus *Son*
    Is blind indeed, &c.
And thus *Shakespear* in *Criolanus*
————— Chafte as the Ificle
  That's curdled by the Froft from pureft Snow,
  And hangs on *Dian*'s Temple.
                    Act 5. Scene 3.
                       The

The Emperor's Morning-Meditation,
In which *Pulcheria* is more then affiftant.
'Tis worth your Obfervation, and you may
Colleƈt from her Expence of Time this Day,
How her Hours for many Years have been difpos'd of.
 Cleon. I am all Eyes and Ears.

 Enter after a Strain of Mufick, Philanax, Timantus,
  Patriarch, Theodofius, Pulcheria, Flaccilla, Arca-
  dia, *followed by* Chryfapius *and* Gratianus, *Informer,*
  Servants, Officers.

 Pulcb. Your Patience, Sir.
Let thofe corrupted Minifters of the Court,
Which you complain of, our Devotions ended,
Be cited to appear. For the Ambaffadors
Who are importunate to have Audience,
From me you may affume them, that To-morrow
They fhall in publick kifs the Emperor's Robe,
And we in private with our fooneft Leifure
Will give 'em Hearing. Have you efpecial Care too
That free Accefs be granted unto all
Petitioners. The Morning wears.—Pray you on, Sir ;
Time loft is ne'er recover'd.
   [*Exeunt* Theodofius, Pulcheria, *and the Train.*
 Paul. Did you note
The Majefty fhe appears in ?
 Cleon. Yes, my good Lord ;
I was ravifh'd with it.
 Paul. And then with what Speed
She orders her Difpatches, not one daring
To interpofe ; the Emperor himfelf
Without Reply, putting in Aƈt whatever
She pleas'd t' impofe upon him.
 Cleon. Yet there were fome
That in their fullen Looks rather confeffed
A forc'd Conftraint to ferve her, than a Will
To be at her Devotion : What are they ?
 Paul. Eunuchs of the Emperor's Chamber, that re-
  pine
The Globe and awful Scepter fhould give Place

Unto

Unto the Diftaff, for as fuch they whifper
A Woman's Government, but dare not, yet,
Exprefs themfelves.
  Cleon. From whence are the Ambaffadors
To whom fhe promis'd Audience?
  Paul. They are
Employ'd by divers Princes, who defire
Alliance with our Emperor, whofe Years now,
As you fee, write him Man. One would advance
A Daughter to the Honour of his Bed;
A fecond, his fair Sifter: To inftruct you
In the Particulars would afk longer Time ·
Than my own Defigns give Way to. I have Letters
From fpecial Friends of mine, that to my Care
Commend a ftranger Virgin, whom this Morning
I purpofe to prefent before the Princefs:
If you pleafe, you may accompany me.
  Cleon. I'll wait on you.   [*Exeunt.*

S C E N E II.

Informer, Officers bringing in the Projector, the Suburbs Mignion, the Mafters of the Habit and Manners.

  Informer. Why fhould you droop, or hang your work-
      ing Heads?
No Danger is meant to you; pray, bear up,
For aught I know you're cited to receive
Preferment due to your Merits.
  Projector. Very likely:
In all the Projects I have read and practis'd,
I never found one Man compell'd to come
Before the Seat of Juftice, under Guard,
To receive Honour.
  Informer. No? It may be, you are
The firft Example. Men of Qualities,
As I've deliver'd you to the Protectrefs,
Who knows how to advance them, can't conceive
A fitter Place to have their Virtues publifh'd,

                                                    Than

Than in open Court. Could you hope that the Princefs,
Knowing your precious Merits, will reward 'em
In a private Corner? No; you know not yet
How you may be exalted.

   Suburbs Minion. To the Gallows.

   Informer. Fie
Nor yet deprefs'd to the Gallies; in your Names
You carry no fuch Crimes: Your fpecious Titles
Cannot but take her—Prefident of the Projectors!
What a Noife it makes? The Mafter of the Habit!
How proud would fome one Country be that I know
To be your firft Pupil? Minion of the Suburbs,
And now and then admitted to the Court,
And honour'd with the Stile of Squire of Dames,
What Hurt is in it? One Thing I muft tell you,
As I am the State-fcout, you may think me an Informer,

   Mafter of the Habit. They are Synonimous.

   Informer. Conceal nothing from her
Of your good Parts, 'twill be the better for you;
Or if you fhould, it matters not, fhe can conjure,
And I am her ubiquitary Spirit,
Bound to obey her—You have my Inftructions,
Stand by, here's better Company.

   Enter Paulinus, Cleon, Athenais, *with a Petition.*

   Athen. Can I hope, Sir,
Oppreffed Innocence fhall find Protection,
And Juftice among Strangers, when my Brothers,
Brothers of one Womb, by one Sire begotten,
Trample on my Afflictions?

   Paul. Forget them,
Remembring thofe may help you.

   Athen. They have rob'd me
Of all Means to prefer my juft Complaint
With any promifing Hope to gain a Hearing,
Much lefs Redrefs: Petitions not fweetned
With Gold, are but unfavory, oft refufed;
Or, if receiv'd, are pocketed, not read.

A

A Suitor's fwelling Tears by the glowing Beams
Of cholerick Authority are dry'd up,
Before they fall; or, if feen, never pitied.
What will become of a forfaken Maid?
My flatt'ring Hopes are too weak to encounter
With my ftrong Enemy, Defpair, and 'tis
In vain t' oppofe her.

    Cleon. Cheer her up; fhe faints, Sir.

    Paul. This argues Weaknefs, though your Brothers
      were
Cruel beyond Expreffion, and the Judges
That fentenc'd you, corrupt; you fhall find here
One of your own Fair Sex to do you right,
Whofe Beams of Juftice, like the Sun, extend
Their Light and Heat to Strangers, and are not
Municipal, or confin'd.

    Athen. Pray you do not feed me
With airy Hopes, unlefs you can affure me
The great *Pulcheria* will defcend to hear
My miferable Story, it were better
I died without her Trouble.

    Paul. She is bound to it
By the fureft Chain, her natural Inclination
To help th' afflicted; nor fhall long Delays
(More terrible to miferable Suitors
Then quick Denials) grieve you. Dry your fair Eyes;
This Room will inftantly be fanctify'd
With her blefs'd Prefence; to her ready Hand
Prefent your Grievances, and reft affur'd
You fhall depart contented.

    Athen. You breathe in me
A fecond Life.

    Informer. Will your Lordfhip pleafe to hear
Your Servant a few Words?

    Paul. Away, you Rafcal!
Did I ever keep fuch Servants?

    Informer. If your Honefty
Would give you Leave, it would be for your Profit.

                                    Paul.

Paul. To make Ufe of an Informer? Tell me in what
Can you advantage me?

Informer. In the firſt Tender
Of a freſh Suit never beg'd yet,

Paul. What's your Suit, Sir?

Informer. 'Tis feaſible:—Here are three arrant Knaves
Diſcover'd by my Art:

Paul. And thou the Arch-knave;
The great devour the lefs:

Informer. And with good Reaſon;
I muſt eat one a Month, I cannot live elſe,

Paul. A notable Cannibal? But, ſhould I hear thee,
In what do your Knaves concern me?

Informer. In the begging
Of their Eſtates.

Paul. Before they are condemn'd?

Informer. Yes, or arraign'd, your Lordſhip may ſpeak
too late elſe.
They are your own, and I will be content
With the fifth Part of a Share.

Paul. Hence, Rogue!

Informer. Such Rogues
In this Kind will be heard, and cheriſh'd too.
Fool that I was to offer ſuch a Bargain.
To a ſpic'd Conſcience Chapman—But I care not;
What he diſdains to taſte others will ſwallow.

[*Loud Muſick.*

Enter Theodoſius, Pulcheria, *and the Train.*

Cleon. They are returned from the Temple.

Paul. See, ſhe appears;
What think you now?

Athen. A cunning Painter, thus,
Her Veil ta'n off, and awful Sword and Balance
Laid by would picture Juſtice.

Pulch. When you pleaſe,
You may intend thoſe royal Exerciſes
Suiting your Birth, and Greatneſs: I will bear

The

The Burthen of your Cares, and, having purged
The Body of your Empire of ill Humours,
Upon my Knees furrender it.

 Chryf. Will you ever
Be aw'd thus like a Boy ?

 Grat. And kifs the Rod
Of a proud Miftrefs ?

 Timan. Be what you were born, Sir.

 Phila. Obedience and Majefty never lodg'd
In the fame Inn.

 Theod. No more ; he never learned
The right Way to command, that ftop'd his Ears
To wife Directions.

 Pulch. Read o'er the Papers
I left upon my Cabinet ; two Hours hence
I will examine you.

 Flac. We fpend our Time well.
Nothing but praying, and poring on a Book ;
It ill agrees with my Conftitution, Sifter.

 Arcad. Would I had been born fome mafq'uing Lady's Woman,
Only to fee ftrange Sights, rather than live thus.

 Flac. We are gone, forfooth ; there is no Remedy,
  Sifter.   [*Exeunt* Arcadia *and* Flaccilla.

 Grat. What hath his Eye found out ?

 Timan. 'Tis fix'd upon
That Stranger Lady.

 Chryf. I am glad, yet, that
He dares look on a Woman.

   [*All this Time the Informer kneeling to* Pulcheria,
    and delivering Papers.]

 Theod. Philanax,
What is that comely Stranger ?

 Phila. A Petitioner.

 Chryf. Will you hear her Cafe, and difpatch her in
  your Chamber ?
I'll undertake to bring her.

Theod. Bring me to
Some Place where I may look on her Demeanour.
—'Tis a lovely Creature!

Chryf. There's fome Hope in this, yet.
[*Exeunt* Theodofius, Patriarch, *and the Train.*

Pulch. No, you have done your Parts:

Paul. Now Opportunity courts you,
Prefer your Suit.

Athen. As low as Mifery
Can fall, for Proof of my Humility,.
A poor diftreffed Virgin bows her Head,
And lays hold on your Goodnefs, the laft Altar
Calamity can fly to for Protection.
Great Minds erect their never-failing Trophies
On the firm Bafe of Mercy; but to triumph
Over a Suppliant, by proud Fortune captiv'd,
Argues a Baftard Conqueft—'tis to you
I fpeak, to you, the fair and juft *Pulcheria,*
The Wonder of the Age, your Sexes Honour;
And, as fuch, deign to hear me. As you have
A Soul moulded from Heaven, and do defire .
To have it made a Star there, make the Means
Of your Afcent to that Celeftial Height
Virtue wing'd with brave Action. They draw near
The Nature, and the Effence of the Gods,
Who imitate their Goodnefs.

Pulch. If you were
A Subject of the Empire, which your Habit
In every Part denies——

Athen. O fly not to
Such an Evafion; whate'er I am,
Being a Woman, in Humanity
You are bound to right me, though the Difference
Of my Religion may feem to exclude me
From your Defence (which you'd have confin'd)
The moral Virtue, which is general,
Muft know no Limits—By thefe bleffed Feet
That pace the Paths of Equity, and tread boldly
On the ftiff Neck of tyrannous Oppreffion,.

By

By thefe Tears by which I bathe 'em, I conjure you
With Pity to look on me.
   Pulch. Pray you rife.
And, as you rife, receive this Comfort from me.
Beauty fet off with fuch fweet Language never
Can want an Advocate; and you muft bring
More than a Guilty Caufe if you prevail not.
Some Bufinefs long fince thought upon, difpatched,
You fhall have Hearing, and, as far as Juftice
Will warrant me, my beft Aids.
   Athen. I do defire
No ftronger Guard; my Equity needs no Favour.
   Pulch. Are thefe the Men?
   Projector. We were, an't like your Highnefs.
The Men, the Men of Eminence, and Mark,
And may continue fo, if it pleafe your Grace.
   Mafter. This Speech was well projected.   [*Afide.*
   Pulch. Does your Confcience
(I will begin with you) whifper unto you
What here you ftand accus'd of? Are you named
The Prefident of Projectors?
   Informer. Juftify it, Man,
And tell her in what thou'rt ufeful.
   Project. That's apparent;
And, if you pleafe, afk fome about the Court,
And they will tell you too my rare Inventions,
They owe their Bravery, perhaps Means to purchafe,
And cannot live without me. I, alas!
Lend out my labouring Brains to Ufe, and fometimes
For a Drachma in the Pound,—the more the Pity.
I am all Patience, and endure the Curfes
Of many, for the Profit of one Patron.
   Pulch. I do conceive the reft—What is the Second?
   Informer. The Mignion of the Suburbs.
   Pulch. What hath he
To do in *Conftantinople?*
   Mign. I fteal in now and then,
As I am thought ufeful; marry, there I am call'd
The Squire of Dames, or Servant of the Sex,
        T 2   And

And by the Allowance of fome fportful Ladies
Honour'd with that Title.

    Pulch. Spare your Character,
You're here decipher'd—Stand by with your Compere.
What is the Third? A Creature I ne'er heard of;
The Mafter of the Manners, and the Habit?
You have a double Office.

    Mafter. In my Actions
I make both good; for by my Theorems
Which your polite, and terfer Gallants practife,
I refine the Court, and civilize
Their barbarous Natures. I have, in a Table
With curious Punctuality fet down
To a Hair's Breadth, how low a new-ftamp'd Courtier
May vail to a Country Gentleman, and, by
Gradation, to his Merchant, Mercer, Draper,
His Linen-Man, and Taylor.

    Pulch. Pray you, difcover
This hidden Myftery.

    Mafter. If the 'forefaid Courtier
(As it may chance fometimes) find not his Name
Writ in the Citizens Books with a State-Hum
He may falute 'em after three Days waiting:
But, if he owe them Money, that he may
Preferve his Credit, let him, in Policy, never
Appoint a Day of Payment; fo they may hope ftill:
But, if he be to take up more, his Page
May attend 'em at the Gate, and ufher 'em
Into his Cellar, and when they are warm'd with Wine,
Conduct 'em to his Bedchamber, and though then
He be under his Barber's Hands, as foon as feen,
He muft ftart up to embrace 'em, vail thus low;
Nay, though he call 'em Coufins, 'tis the better,
His Dignity no Way wrong'd in't.

    Paul. Here's a fine Knave!

    Pulch. Does this Rule hold without Exception, Sirrah,
For Courtiers in general?

    Mafter. No, dear Madam;
For one of the laft Edition, and for him

                                                     I

I have compos'd a Dictionary, in which
He is instructed, how, when, and to whom
To be proud or humble; at what Times of the Year
He may do a good Deed for itself, and that is
Writ in Dominical Letters; all Days else
Are his own, and of those Days the several Hours
Mark out, and to what Use.

Pulch. Shew us your Method;
I'm strangely taken with it.

Master. 'Twill deserve
A Pension, I hope. First a strong Cullis
In his Bed, to heighten Appetite: Shuttle cock,
To keep him in Breath, when he rises; Tennis-Courts
Are chargeable, and the riding of great Horses
Too boist'rous for my young Courtier; let the old ones
I think not of, use it; next his Meditation
How to court his Mistress, and that he may seem witty,
Let him be furnish'd with confederate Jests
Between him and his Friend, that, on Occasion,
They may vent 'em mutually: What his Pace and Garb
Must be in the Presence, then the Length of his Sword,
The Fashion of the Hilt — what the Blade is
It matters not, 'twere Barbarism to use it,
Unless to shew his Strength upon an Andiron;
So, the sooner broke, the better.

Pulch. How I abuse
This precious Time! Projector, I treat first
Of you and your Disciples; you roar out,
All is the King's, his Will above his Laws:
And that fit Tributes are too gentle Yokes
For his poor Subjects; whisp'ring in his Ear,
If he would have their Fear, no Man should dare
To bring a Sallad from his Country Garden,
Without the paying Gabel; kill a Hen,
Without Excise: and that, if he desire
To have his Children, or his Servants wear
Their Heads upon their Shoulders, you affirm,
In Policy, 'tis fit the Owner should
Pay for 'em by the Poll; or, if the Prince want

A

A prefent Sum, he may command a City
Impoffibilities, and for Non-performance
Compel it to fubmit to any Fine
His Officers fhall impofe. Is this the Way
To make our Emperor happy? Can the Groans
Of his Subjects yield him Mufick? Muft his Threfholds
Be wafh'd with Widow's and wrong'd Orphan's Tears,
Or his Power grow contemptible?

    Project. I begin
To feel myfelf a Rogue again.

    Pulch. But you are
The Squire of Dames, devoted to the Service
Of gamefome Ladies, the hidden Myftery
Difcover'd, their clofe Bawd; thy flavifh Breath
Fanning the Fires of Luft, the Go-between
This Female and that wanton Sir; your Art
Can blind a jealous Hufband, and, difguis'd
Like a Millener or Shoemaker, convey
A Letter in a Pantofle or Glove
Without Sufpicion : nay, at his Table,
In a Cafe of Pick-tooths. You inftruct 'em how
To parley with their Eyes, and make the Temple
A Mart of Loofenefs; to difcover all
Thy fubtile Brokages, were to teach in Publick,
Thofe private Practices, which are, in Juftice,
Severely to be punifh'd.

    Mignion. I am caft :
A Jury of my Patroneffes cannot quit me.

    Pulch. You are Mafter of the Manners, and the Habit;
Rather the Scorn of fuch as would live Men,
And not, like Apes, with fervile Imitation
Study prodigious Fafhions. You keep
Intelligence abroad, that may inftruct
Our giddy Youth at Home what new-found Fafhion
Is now in Ufe, fwearing he's moft complete
That firft turns Monfter. Know, Villains, I can thruft
This Arm into your Hearts, ftrip off the Flefh
That covers your Deformities, and fhew you
In your own Nakednefs. Now, though the Law

Call

Call not your Follies Death, you are for ever
Banifh'd my Brother's Court.—Away with em ;   .
I will hear no Reply.

[*Exeunt Informer, Officers, Prifoners.*

The Curtains drawn above, Theodofius *and his Eunuchs*
    difcovered.   )*,*

  Paul. What think you now ?
  Cleon. That I am in a Dream ; or that I fee
A fecond *Pallas.*
  Pulch. Thefe remov'd, to you
I clear my Brow. Speak without Fear, fweet Maid,
Since with a mild Afpect, and ready Ear,
I fit prepar'd to hear you.
  Athen. Know, great Princefs,
My Father, though a *Pagan,* was admired
For his deep Search into thofe hidden Studies,
Whofe Knowledge is deny'd to common Men :
The Motion, with the divers Operations
Of the Superior Bodies, by his long
And careful Obfervation, were made
Familiar to him ; all the fecret Virtues
Of Plants, and Simples, and in what Degree
They were ufeful to Mankind, he could difcourfe of :
In a Word, conceive him as a Prophet honour'd
In his own Country. But being born a Man,
It lay not in him to defer the Hour
Of his approaching Death, though long foretold :
In this fo fatal Hour he call'd before him
His two Sons, and myfelf, the dearest Pledges
Lent him by Nature, and with his Right Hand
Bleffing our feveral Heads, he thus began :
  Chryf. Mark his Attention.
  Phila. Give me Leave to mark too.
  Athen. If I could leave my Underftanding to you,
It were fuperfluous to make Divifion
Of whatfoever elfe I can bequeath you :
But, to avoid Contention, I allot
     T 4   An

An equal Portion of my Poſſeſſions
To you my Sons; but, unto thee, my Daughter,
My Joy, my Darling (pardon me, though I
Repeat his Words, if my prophetic Soul
Ready to take her Flight, can truly gueſs at
Thy future Fate, I leave thee ſtrange Aſſurance
Of the Greatneſs thou art born to, unto which
Thy Brothers ſhall be proud to pay their Service,

    Paul. And all Men elſe that honour Beauty.

    Theod. Ha!

    Athen. Yet, to prepare thee for that certain Fortune,
And that I may from preſent Wants defend thee,
I leave ten thouſand Crowns —— which ſaid, being call'd
To th' Fellowſhip of our Deities, he expir'd,
And with him all Remembrance of the Charge
Concerning me, left by him to my Brothers.

    Pulch. Did they detain your Legacy?

    Athen. And ſtill do.
His Aſhes were ſcarce quiet in his Urn,
When, in Deriſion of my future Greatneſs,
They thruſt me out of Doors, denying me
One ſhort Night's Harbour,

    Pulch. Weep not.

    Athen. I deſire,
By your Perſuaſion, or commanding Power,
The Reſtitution of mine own; or that,
To keep my Frailty from Temptation,
In your Compaſſion of me, you would pleaſe
I, as a Handmaid, may be entertain'd
To do the meaneſt Offices to all ſuch
As are honour'd in your Service.

    Pulch. Thou art welcome,
What is thy Name?

    Athen. The forlorn *Athenais.*

    Pulch. The Sweetneſs of thy Innocence ſtrangely
      takes me.

              [*Takes her up and kiſſes her.*
Forget thy Brothers Wrongs; for I will be
In my Care a Mother, in my Love a Siſter to thee;

                        And,

And, were it poſſible thou could'ſt be won
To be of our Belief——

Paul. May it pleaſe your Excellence,
That is an eaſy Taſk, I, though no Scholar,
Dare undertake it; clear Truth cannot want
Rhetorical Perſuaſions,

Pulch. 'Tis a Work,
My Lord, will well become you.—Break up the Court;
May your Endeavours proſper.

Paul. Come, my Fair One;
I hope, my Convert.

Athen. Never: I will die
As I was born.

Paul. Better you ne'er had been. [*Exeunt.*

Phila. What does your Majeſty think of?—— The
Maid's gone.

Theod. She's wond'rous fair, and in her Speech ap-
Pieces of Scholarſhip. [pear'd

Chryſ. Make Uſe of her Learning
And Beauty together; on my Life, ſhe will be proud
To be ſo converted.

Theod. From foul Luſt Heav'n guard me. [*Exeunt.*

The End of the Firſt Act.

✠✠✠✠✠✠✠✠✠✠✠✠✠✠✠✠✠✠✠✠✠✠✠

ACT II.   SCENE I.

Philanax, Timantus, Chryſapius, Gratianus.

Phila. WE only talk, when we ſhould do.
Timan. I'll ſecond you;
Begin, and when you pleaſe.

Grat. Be conſtant in it.

Chryſ. That Reſolution which grows cold To-day,
Will freeze To-morrow.

Grat. 'Slight, I think ſhe'll keep him
Her Ward for ever, to herſelf ingroſſing

The

The Difpofition of all the Favours
And Bounties of the Empire.

   Chryf. We, that by
The Nearnefs of our Service to his Perfon,
Should raife this Man, or pull down that, without
Her Licence, hardly dare prefer a Suit,
Or, if we do, 'tis crofs'd.——

   Phila. You are troubled for
Your proper Ends; my Aims are high and honeft.
The Wrong that's done to Majefty I repine at:
I love the Emperor, and 'tis my Ambition
To have him know himfelf, and to that Purpofe
I'll run the Hazard of a Check.

   Grat. And I
The Lofs of my Place.

   Timan. I will not come behind,
Fall what can fall.

   Chryf. Let us put on fad Afpects
To draw him on; charge home, we'll fetch you off,
Or lie dead by you.

        Enter Theodofius.

   Theod. How's this? Clouds in the Chamber,
And the Air clear abroad!

   Phila. When you, our Sun,
Obfcure your glorious Beams, poor we, that borrow
Our little Light from you, cannot but fuffer
A general Eclipfe.

   Timan. Great Sir, 'tis true;
For, 'till you pleafe to know, and be yourfelf,
And freely dare difpofe of what's your own
Without a Warrant, we are falling Meteors,
And not fix'd Stars.

   Chryf. The pale-fac'd Moon, that fhould
Govern the Night, ufurps the Rule of Day,
And ftill is at the Full, in Spite of Nature,
And will not know a Change.

   Theod. Speak you in Riddles?

                       I am

I am no *Oedipus*, but your Emperor,
And as fuch would be inftructed.

   Phila. Your Command
Shall be obey'd : 'Till now, I never heard you
Speak like yourfelf ; and may that Power, by which
You are fo, ftrike me dead, if what I fhall
Deliver, as a faithful Subject to you,
Hath Root, or Growth from Malice, or bafe Envy
Of your Sifter's Greatnefs, I could honour in her
A Power fubordinate to yours ; but not
As 'tis predominant.

   Timan. Is it fit that fhe,
In her Birth your Vaffal, fhould command the Knees
Of fuch as fhould not bow but to yourfelf ?

   Grat. She with Security walks upon the Heads
Of the Nobility ; the Multitude,
As to a Deity, offering Sacrifice
For her Grace and Favour.

   Chryf. Her proud Feet ev'n wearied
With the Kiffes of Petitioners.

   Grat. While you,
To whom alone fuch Reverence is proper,
Pafs unregarded by her.

   Timan. You have not, yet,
Been Mafter of one Hour of your whole Life.

   Chryf. Your Will and Faculties kept in more Awe
Than fhe can do her own.

   Phila. And as a Bondman,
(O let my Zeal find Grace, and Pardon from you,
That I defcend fo low) you are defign'd
To this or that Employment, fuiting well
A private Man, I grant, but not a Prince,
To be a perfect Horfeman, or to know
The Words of the Chace ; or a fair Man of Arms,
Or to be able to pierce to the Depth,
Or write a Comment on th' obfcureft Poets,
I grant are Ornaments ; but your main Scope
Should be to govern Men to guard your own,
If not enlarge your Empire.

                                   Chryf.

Chryſ. You are built up
By th' curious Hand of Nature to revive
The Memory of *Alexander*, or by
A proſperous Succeſs in your brave Actions,
To rival *Cæſar*.

Timan. Rouze yourſelf, and let not
Your Pleaſures be a Copy of her Will.

Phila. Your Pupil Age is paſt, and manly Actions
Are now expected from you.

Grat. Do not loſe
Your Subjects Hearts.

Timan. What is't to have the Means
To be magnificent, and not exerciſe
The boundleſs Virtue ?

Grat. You confine yourſelf
To that which ſtrict Philoſophy allows of,
As if you were a private Man.

Timan. No Pomp,
Or glorious Shows of Royalty, rend'ring it
Both lov'd, and terrible.

Grat. 'Slight, you live, as it
Begets ſome Doubt, whether you have, or not,
Th' Abilities of a Man.

Chryſ. The Firmament
Hath not more Stars than there are ſeveral Beauties
Ambitious at the Height to impart their dear,
And ſweeteſt Favours to you.

Grat. Yet you have not
Made Choice of one, of all the Sex, to ſerve you,
In a phyſical Way of Courtſhip.

Theod. But that I would not
Begin the Expreſſion of my being a Man,
In Blood, or ſtain the firſt white Robe I wear
Of Abſolute Power, with a ſervile Imitation
Of any tyrannous Habit, my juſt Anger
Prompts me to make you in your Suff'rings feel,
And not in Words to inſtruct you, that the Licence
Of the looſe and ſaucy Language you now practiſed,
Hath forfeited your Heads.

Grat.

Grat. How's this ?   [*Aside.*

Phila. I know not
What the Play may prove; but I assure you that
I do not like the Prologue.   [*Aside.*

Theod. O the miserable
Condition of a Prince ! who, though he vary
More Shapes than *Proteus* in his Mind, and Manners,
He cannot win an universal Suffrage
From the many-headed Monster, Multitude.
Like *Æsop*'s foolish Frogs, they trample on him,
As a senseless Block, if his Government be easy:
And, if he prove a Stork, they croak, and rail
Against him as a Tyrant.—I'll put off
That Majesty, of which you think I have
Nor Use, nor Feeling ; and, in arguing with you,
Convince you with strong Proofs of common Reason,
And not with Absolute Power, against which, Wretches,
You are not to dispute.   Dare you, that are
My Creatures, by my prodigal Favours fashion'd,
Presuming on the Nearness of your Service,
Set off with my familiar Acceptance,
Condemn my Obsequiousness to the wise Directions
Of an incomparable Sister, whom all Parts
Of our World, that are made happy in Knowledge
Of her Perfections, with Wonder gaze on?
And yet you, that were only born to eat
The Blessings of our Mother Earth, that are
Distant but one Degree from Beasts (since Slaves
Can claim no larger Privilege) that know
No farther than your sensual Appetites
Or wanton Lust have taught you, undertake
To give your Sovereign Laws to follow that
Your Ignorance marks out to him ?   [*Walks by.*

Grat. How were we
Abus'd in our Opinion of his Temper !   [*Aside.*

Phil. We had forgot 'tis found in Holy Writ,
That Kings Hearts are inscrutable.   [*Aside.*

Timan. I ne'er read it ;
My Study lies not that Way.   [*Aside.*
                                                        Phila.

Phila. By his Looks
The Tempeft ftill increafes.   [*Afide.*

Theod. Am I grown
So ftupid in your Judgments, that you dare
With fuch Security offer Violence
To Sacred Majefty? Will you not know
The Lion is a Lion, though he fhew not
His rending Paws, or fill th' affrighted Air
With the Thunder of his Roarings?———You blefs'd
      Saints!
How am I trenched on? Is that Temperance
So famous in your cited *Alexander,*
Or *Roman Scipio* a Crime in me?
Cannot I be an Emperor, unlefs
Your Wives and Daughters bow to my proud Lufts?
And 'caufe I ravifh not their faireft Buildings
And fruitful Vineyards, or what is deareft,
From fuch as are my Vaffals, muft you conclude
I do not know the awful Power, and Strength
Of my Prerogative? Am I clofe-handed,
Becaufe I fcatter not among you that
I muft not call mine own? Know, you Court-leeches,
A Prince is never fo magnificent
As when he's fparing to enrich a Few
With th' Injuries of Many. Could your Hopes
So grofly flatter you, as to believe
I was born and train'd up as an Emperor, only
In my Indulgence to give Sanctuary,
In their unjuft Proceedings, to the Rapine
And Avarice of my Grooms?

   Phila. In the true Mirror
Of your Perfections, at length we fee
Our own Deformities.

   Timan. And not once daring
To look upon that Majefty we now flighted ——

   Chryf. With our Faces thus glu'd to the Earth, we
Your gracious Pardon.   [beg

   Grat. Offering our Necks
To be trod on, as a Punifhment for our late

                                        Pre-

Prefumption, and a willing Teftimony
Of our Subjection.
 Theod. Deferve our Mercy
In your better Life hereafter, you fhall find,
Though in my Father's Life I held it Madnefs
To ufurp his Power, and in my Youth difdain'd not
To learn from the Inftructions of my Sifter.
I'll make it good to all the World, I am
An Emperor; and ev'n this Inftant grafp
The Scepter, my rich Stock of Majefty
Entire, no Scruple wafted.
 Phila. If thefe Tears
I drop, proceed not from my Joy to hear this,
May my Eye-balls follow 'em.
 Timan. I will fhew myfelf
By your fudden Metamorphofis transform'd
From what I was.
 Grat. And ne'er prefume to afk
What fits not you to give.
 Theod. Move in that Sphere,
And my Light with full Beams fhall fhine upon you.
Forbear this flavifh Courtfhip; tis to me
In a kind idolatrous.
 Phila. Your gracious Sifter.

Enter Pulcheria *and Servant.*

 Pulch. Has he converted her?
 Serv. And, as fuch, will
Prefent her, when you pleafe.
 Pulch. I am glad of it.
Command my Dreffer to adorn her with
The Robes that I gave Order for.
 Serv. I fhall.
 Pulch. And let thofe precious Jewels I took laft
Out of my Cabinet, if't be poffible,
Give Luftre to her Beauties; and, that done,
Command her to be near us.
Serv.

Serv. 'Tis a Province
I willingly embrace.   [*Exit Servant.*

Pulch. O, my dear Sir,
You have forgot your Morning Task, and therefore
With a Mother's Love I come to reprehend you,
But it shall be gently.

Theod. 'Twill become you, though
You said with reverent Duty. Know hereafter,
If my Mother liv'd in you, howe'er her Son,
Like you she were my Subject.

Pulch. How?

Theod. Put off
Amazement; you will find it. Yet I'll hear you
At Distance, as a Sister, but no longer
As a Governess, I assure you.

Grat. This is put home.   [*Aside.*

Timan. Beyond our Hopes.   [*Aside.*

Phila. She stands, as if his Words
Had powerful Magick in 'em.   [*Aside.*

Theod. Will you have me
Your Pupil ever? The Down on my Chin
Confirms I am a Man, a Man of Men,
The Emperor, that knows his Strength.

Pulch. Heav'n grant
You know it not too soon.

Theod. Let it suffice
My Wardship's out. If your Design concerns us
As a Man, and not a Boy, with our Allowance
You may deliver it.

Pulch. A strange Alteration!
But I will not contend.   [*Aside.*] Be as you wish, Sir,
Your own Disposer; uncompell'd I cancel
All Bonds of my Authority.   [*Kneels.*

Theod. You in this
Pay your due Homage; which perform'd, I thus
Embrace you as a Sister, no Way doubting
Your Vigilance for my Safety as my Honour;
And what you now come to impart, I rest
Most confident, points at one of them.

                                            Pulch.

Pulcb. At both,
And not alone the prefent, but the future
Tranquility of your Mind : Since in the Choice
Of her, you are to heat with holy Fires,
And make the Confort of your Royal Bed, .
The certain Means of glorious Succeffion,
With the true Happinefs of our human Being,
Are wholly comprehended.

Theod. How ? A Wife ?
Shall I become a Votary to *Hymen,*
Before my Youth hath facrific'd to *Venus?*
'Tis fomething with the foonefl—Yet, to fhew,
In Things indifferent, I am not averfe
To your wife Counfels, let me firft furvey
Thofe Beauties, that, in being a Prince, I know
Are Rivals for me. You will not confine me
To your Election ; I muft fee, dear Sifter
With mine own Eyes.

Pulcb. 'Tis fit, Sir—Yet, in this,
You may pleafe to confider, abfolute Princes
Have, or fhould have, in Policy, lefs free Will
Then fuch as are their Vaffals. For you muft,
As you are an Emperor, in this high Bufinefs,
Weigh with due Providence, with whom Alliance
May be moft ufeful for the Prefervation
Or your Increafe of Empire.

Theod. I approve not
Such Compofitions for our moral Ends,
In what is in itfelf divine, nay more,
Decreed in Heav'n. Yet, if our Neighbour Princes,
Ambitious of fuch nearnefs, fhall prefent
Their deareft Pledges to me (ever referving
The Caution of mine own Content) I'll not
Contemn their courteous Offers.

Pulcb. Bring in the Pictures. [*Two Pictures brought in.*
Theod. Muft I then judge the Subftances by the Sha-
dows ?
The Painters are moft envious, if they want
.Good Colours for Preferment. Virtuous Ladies

Love this Way to be flatter'd, and accuse
The Workman of Detraction, if he add not
Some Grace they cannot truly call their own.
Is't not so, *Gratianus?* You may challenge
Some Interest in the Science.

   Grat. A Pretender
To the Art, I truly Honour, and subscribe
To your Majesty's Opinion.

   Theod. Let me see——
Cleanthe, Daughter to the King of *Epirus,*
Ætatis suæ, the fourteenth: Ripe enough,
And forward too, I assure you. Let me examine
The Symmetries. If Statuaries could
By the Foot of *Hercules* set down punctually
His whole Dimensions, and the Countenance be
The Index of the Mind, this may instruct me,
With th' Aids of that I've read touching this Subject,
What she is inward. The Colour of her Hair,
If it be, as this does Promise, pale, and faint,
And not a glitt'ring white. Her brow, so so.
The Circles of her Sight, too much contracted;
Juno's fair Cow-eyes by old *Homer* are
Commended to their Merit; here's a sharp Frost,
I' th' Tip of her Nose, which by the Length assures me
Of Storms at Midnight, if I fail to pay her
The Tribute she expects.—I like her not:
What is the other?

   Chrys. How hath he commenc'd
Doctor in this so sweet and secret Art,
Without our Knowledge?   [*Aside.*

   Timan. Some of his forward Pages
Have robbed us of the Honour.   [*Aside.*

   Phila. No such Matter;
He has the Theory only, not the Practic.   [*Aside.*

   Theod. Amasia, Sister to the Duke of *Athens;*
Her Age eighteen, descended lineally
From *Theseus,* as by her Pedigree
Will be made apparent—Of his lusty Kindred,
And lose so much Time? 'Tis strange!—As I live, she
     hath   A

A Philofophical Afpeƈt : There is
More Wit than Beauty in her Face, and, when
I court her, it muſt be in Tropes, and Figures,
Or ſhe will cry abſurd. She will have her Clenches
To cut off any Fallacy I can hope
To put upon her, and expeƈt I ſhould
Ever conclude in Syllogiſms, and thoſe true ones
In parte & toto, or ſhe'll tire me with
Her tedious Elocutions in the Praiſe
Of the Increaſe of Generation, for which
Alone the Sport, in her Morality,
Is good and lawful, and to be often practis'd
For fear of miſſing.—Fie on't, let the Race
Of *Theſeus* be match'd with *Ariſtotles*,
I'll none of her.

 Pulch. You are curious in your Choice, Sir,
And hard to pleaſe; yet, if that your Conſent
May give Authority to it, I'll preſent you
With one, that, if her Birth, and Fortunes anſwer
The Rarities of her Body, and her Mind,
Detraƈtion durſt not tax her.

 Theod. Let me ſee her,
Though wanting thoſe Additions, which we can
Supply from our own Store : it is in us
To make Men rich, and noble; but, to give
Legitimate Shapes and Virtues, does belong
To the Great Creator of 'em, to whoſe Bounties
Alone 'tis proper, and in this diſdains
An Emperor for his Rival.

 Pulch. I'applaud
This fit Acknowledgment, ſince Princes then
Grow leſs than common Men, when they contend
With Him, by whom they are ſo.

 Enter Paulinus, Cleon, Athenais *newly habited.*

 Theod. I confeſs it.
 Pulch. Not to hold you in Suſpence, Behold the Virgin
    U 2   Rich

Rich in her natural Beauties, no War borrowing
Th' adulterate Aids of Art. Peruſe her better;
She's worth your ſerious View.

    Phila. I am amaz'd too:
I never ſaw her Equal.

    Grat. How his Eye
Is fix'd upon her!

    Timan. And, as ſhe were a Fort,
He'd ſuddenly ſurprize, he meaſures her
From the Baſes to the Battlements.

    Chryſ. Ha! now I view her better,
I know her; 'tis the Maid that, not long ſince,
Was a Petitioner; her Bravery
So alters her, I had forgot her Face.

    Phila. So has the Emperor.

    Paul. She holds out yet,
And yields not to th' Aſſault.

    Cleon. She's ſtrongly guarded
In her Virgin Bluſhes.

    Paul. When you know, fair Creature,
It is the Emperor that honours you
With ſuch a ſtrict Survey of your ſweet Parts,
In Thankfulneſs you cannot but return
Due Reverence for the Favour.

    Athen. I was loſt
In my Aſtoniſhment at the glorious Object,
And yet reſt doubtful whether he expects,
Being more then Man, my Adoration
(Since ſure there is Divinity about him:)
Or will reſt ſatisfy'd, if my humble Knees
In Duty thus bow to him.

    Theod. Ha! it ſpeaks.

    Pulch. She is no Statue, Sir,

    Theod. Suppoſe her one,
And that ſhe had nor Organs, Voice, nor Heat,
Moſt willingly I would reſign my Empire,
So it might be to After-times recorded
That I was her *Pygmalion*, though, like him,
I doated on my Workmanſhip, without Hope too

                                Of

Of having *Cytherea* fo propitious
To my Vows, or Sacrifice, in her Compaffion
To give it Life or Motion.

   Pulch. Pray you, be not rap'd fo,
Nor borrow from imaginary Fiction
Impoffible Aids.　She's Flefh and Blood, I affure you;
And, if you pleafe to honour her in the Trial,
And be your own Security, as you'll find
I fable not, fhe comes in a noble Way
To be at your Devotion.

   Chryf. 'Tis the Maid
I offer'd to your Highnefs; her chang'd Shape
Conceal'd her from you :

   Theod. At the firft I knew her;
And a fecond Firebrand *Cupid* brings, to kindle
My Flames almoft put out : I am too cold,
And play with Opportunity.——May I tafte, then,
The Nectar of her Lip ?——I do not give it
The Praife it merits: Antiquity is too poor
To help me with a Simile to exprefs her.
Let me drink often from this living Spring,
To nourifh new Invention.

   Pulch. Do not furfeit
In over-greedily devouring that
Which may without Satiety feaft you often.
From the Moderation in receiving them,
The choiceft Viands do continue pleafing
To the moft curious Palates.　If you think her
Worth your Embraces, and the fovereign Title
Of the *Grecian* Emprefs——

   Theod. If? How much you fin,
Only to doubt it; the Poffeffion of her
Makes all, that was before moft precious to me,
Common, and cheap in this you've fhown yourfelf
A provident Protectrefs.　I already
Grow weary of the abfolute Command
Of my fo numerous Subjects, and defire
No Sov'reignty but here, and write down gladly
A Period to my Wifhes.

Pulch. Yet, before
It be too late, confider her Condition;
Her Father was a *Pagan*, fhe herfelf
A new-converted Chriftian.

    Theod. Let me know
The Man to whofe religious Means I owe
So great a Debt.

    Paul. You are advanc'd too high, Sir,
To acknowledge a Beholdingnefs, 'tis difcharg'd,
And I, beyond my Hopes, rewarded, if
My Service pleafe your Majefty.

    Theod. Take this Pledge
Of our affured Love.   Are there none here
Have Suits to prefer? On fuch a Day as this
My Bounty's without Limit.   O my deareft,
I will not hear thee fpeak ; whatever in
Thy Thoughts is apprehended, I grant freely.
Thou would'ft plead thy Unworthinefs ; by thyfelf
The Magazine of Felicity, in thy Lownefs
Our Eaftern Queens, at their full Height, bow to thee,
And are, in their beft Trim, thy Foils and Shadows.
Excufe the Violence of my Love, which cannot
Admit the leaft Delay.   Command the Patriarch
With Speed to do his Holy Office for us,
That, when we are made one——

    Pulch. You muft forbear, Sir;
She is not yet baptiz'd.

    Theod. In the fame Hour
In which fhe is confirmed in our Faith,
We mutually will give away each other,
And both be Gainers ; we'll hear no Reply
That may divert us.   On

    Pulch. You may, hereafter,
'Pleafe to remember to whofe Furtherance
You owe this Height of Happinefs.

    Athen. As I was
Your Creature when I firft petition'd you,
I will continue fo, and you fhall find me,

                       Though

Though an Emprefs, ftill your Servant.
[*All exit but* Philanax, Gratianus, *and* Timantus.
Grat. Here's a Marriage
Made up o' th' fudden!
Phila. I repine not at
The fair Maid's Fortune—though I fear the Princefs
Had fome peculiar End in't.
Timan. Who's fo fimple
Only to doubt it?
Grat. It is too apparent,
She hath prefer'd a Creature of her own,
By whofe Means fhe may ftill keep to herfelf
The Government of the Empire.
Timan. Whereas if
The Emperor had efpous'd fome Neighbour Queen,
Pulcheria, with all her Wifdom, could not
Keep her Preheminence.
Phila. Be It as it will,
'Tis not now to be alter'd,—Heaven, I fay,
Turn all to th' beft!
Grat. Are we come to praying again?
Phil. Leave thy Prophanenefs
Grat. Would it leave me.
I am fure I thrive not by it.
Timan. Come to the Temple.
Grat. Ev'n where you will—I know not what to
think on't.

The End of the Second Act.

❧❧❧ ❧❧❧ ❧❧❧ ❧❧❧ ❧❧❧ ❧❧❧ ❧❧❧ ❧❧❧ ❧❧❧ ❧❧❧ ❧❧❧

A C T III. S C E N E I.

Paulinus, Philanax.

Paul. **N**OR this, nor th' Age before us, ever look'd
on
The like Solemnity.

U 4   *Phila.*

Phila. A fudden Fever
Kept me at home. Pray you, my Lord, acquaint me
With the Particulars.

Paul. You may prefume,
No Pomp, nor Ceremony could be wanting,
Where there was Privilege to command, and Means
To cherifh rare Inventions.

Phila. I believe it;
But the Sum of all, in brief.

Paul. Pray you fo take it;
Fair *Athenais*, not long fince a Suitor,
And almoft in her Hopes forfaken, firft
Was chrift'ned, and the Emperor's Mother's Name,
Eudoxia, as he will'd, impos'd upon her:
Pulcheria, the ever matchlefs Princefs,
Affifted by her reverend Aunt *Maria*,
Her God-mothers.

Phila. And who the Mafculine Witnefs?

Paul. At the new Emprefs' Suit I had the Honour:
—For which I muft ever ferve her.

Phila. 'Twas a Grace,
With Juftice you may boaft of.

Paul. The Marriage follow'd,
And, as 'tis faid, the Emperor made bold
To turn the Day to Night; for to Bed they went
As foon as they had din'd, and there are Wagers
Laid by fome merry Lords, he hath already
Begot a Boy upon her.

Phila. That is yet
To be determin'd of; but I am certain,
A Prince, fo foon in his Difpofition alter'd,
Was never heard nor read of.

Paul. But of late,
Frugal and fparing, now nor Bounds, nor Limits
To his magnificent Bounties. He affirm'd,
Having receiv'd more Bleffings by his Emprefs
Then he could hope, in Thankulnefs to Heaven
He cannot be too prodigal to others,

What-

Whatever's offer'd to his Royal Hand
He figns without perufing it.

Phila. I am here
Injoin'd to free all fuch as lie for Debt,
The Creditors to be paid out of his Coffers.

Paul. And I all Malefactors that are not
Convicted, or for Treafon or foul Murther;
Such only are excepted;

Phila. 'Tis a rare Clemency!

Paul, Which we muft not difpute, but put in Practice.

[*Exeunt.*

SCENE II.

Loud Mufick, Shouts within: Heaven preferve the Empe-
ror, Heaven blefs the Emprefs. Then in State, Chry-
fapius, *Patriarch.* Paulinus, Theodofius, Athenais,
Pulcheria, *her two young Sifters bearing up* Athenais's
Train, followed by Philanax, Gratianus, Timantus,
Suitors, prefenting Petitions, the Emperor fealing them.
Pulcheria *appears troubled.*

Pulch. Sir, by your own Rules of Philofophy
You know Things violent laft not.   Royal Bounties
Are great, and gracious while they are difpens'd
With Moderation; but, when their Excefs
In giving Giant-Bulks to others, take from
The Prince's juft Proportion, they lofe
The Names of Virtues, and, their Natures chang'd,
Grow the moft dangerous Vices

Theod. In this, Sifter,
Your Wifdom is not circular; they that fow
In narrow Bounds, cannot expect, in Reafon,
A Crop beyond their Ventures, what I do
Difperfe, I lend, and will with Ufury
Return unto my Heap.   I only then
Am rich, and happy (though my Coffers found
With Emptinefs) when my glad Subjects feel,
Their Plenty and Felicity is my Gift;

And

And they will find, when they with Cheerfulnefs
Supply not my Defects, I being the Stomach
To th' politick Body of the State, the Limbs
Grow fuddenly faint and feeble.   I could urge
Proofs of more Finenefs in their Shape and Language;
But none of greater Strength.—Diffuade me not;
What we will, we will do; yet, to affure you
Your Care does not offend us, for an Hour,
Be happy in the Converfe of my beft
And deareft Comfort—May you pleafe to licenfe
My Privacy fome few Minutes?   [*To* Athenais.
 Athen. Licenfe, Sir?
I have no Will, but is deriv'd from yours,
And that ftill waits upon you; nor can I
Be left with fuch Security with any,
As with the gracious Princefs, who receives
Addition, though fhe be all Excellence,
In being ftil'd your Sifter.
 Theod. O fweet Creature!
Let me be cenfur'd fond, and too indulgent,
Nay, though they fay uxorious, I care not;
Her Love, and fweet Humility exact
A Tribute far beyond my Power to pay
Her matchlefs Goodnefs. [*Afide.*[Forward.
      [*Exeunt* Theodofius *and the Train.*
 Pulch. Now you find
Your dying Father's Prophecy, that foretold
Your prefent Greatnefs, to the full accomplifh'd.
For the poor Aids, and Furtherance I lent you,
I willingly forget.
 Athen. Ev'n that binds me
To a more ftrict Remembrance of the Favour;
Nor fhall you, from my foul Ingratitude,
In any Circumftance, ever find Caufe
T'upbraid me with your Benefit.
 Pulch. I believe fo.
Pray you give us Leave—What now I muft deliver
Under the deepeft Seal of Secrecy,

          Though

Though it be for your Good, will give Affurance
Of what is look'd for, if you not alone
Hear, but obey my Counfels.

Athen. They muft be
Of a ftrange Nature, if with zealous Speed
I put 'em not in Practice.

Pulch. 'Twere Impertinence
To dwell on Circumftances, fince the Wound
Requires a fudden Cure; efpecially
Since you, that are the happy Inftrument
Elected to it, though young in your Judgment
Write far above your Years, and may inftruct
Such as are more experienc'd.

Athen. Good Madam,
In this I muft oppofe you, I am well
Acquainted with my Weaknefs, and it will not
Become your Wifdom, by which I am rais'd
To this titulary Height, that fhould correct
The Pride, and overweening of my Fortune,
To play the Parafite to it, in afcribing
That Merit to me, unto which I can
Pretend no Intereft—Pray you, excufe
My bold Simplicity, and to my Weight
Defign me where you pleafe, and you fhall find
In my Obedience, I am ftill your Creature.

Pulch. 'Tis nobly anfwer'd, and I glory in
The Building I have rais'd. Go on, fweet Lady,
In this your virtuous Progrefs.—But to the Point;
You know, nor do I envy it, you have
Acquir'd that Power, which, not long fince, was mine,
In governing the Emperor, and muft ufe
The Strength you hold in the Heart of his Affections,
For his private, as the publick Prefervation,
To which there is no greater Enemy,
Than his exorbitant Prodigality,
Howe'er his Sycophants, and Flatterers call it,
Royal Magnificence; and, though he may
Urge what's done for your Honour, muft not be

Curb'd

Curb'd, or be controul'd by you, you cannot in
Your Wifdom but conceive, if that the Torrent
Of his violent Bounties be not ftop'd, or leffen'd,
It will prove moft pernicious.   Therefore, Madam,
Since 'tis your Duty, as you are his Wife,
To give him faving Counfels, and, in being
Almoft his Idol, may command him to
Take any Shape you pleafe, with a powerful Hand,
To ftop him in his Precipice to Ruin.

   Atben. Avert it, Heaven!

   Pulcb. Heaven is moft gracious to you, Madam,
In chufing you to be the Inftrument
Of fuch a pious Work.   You fee he figns
What Suit foever is prefer'd, not once
Enquiring what it is, yielding himfelf
A Prey to all.   I would, therefore, have you, Lady,
As I know you will, to advife him, or command him,
As he would reap the Plenty of your Favours,
To ufe more Moderation in his Bounties;
And that, before he gives, he would confider,
The what, to whom, and wherefore.

   Atben. Do you think
Such Arrogance, or Ufurpation, rather,
Of what is proper, and peculiar
To ev'ry private Hufband, and much more
To him an Emperor, can rank with th' Obedience
And Duty of a Wife? Are we appointed
In our Creation (let me reafon with you)
To rule, or to obey? Or, 'caufe he loves me
With a kind Impotence; muft I tyrannize
Over his Weaknefs? Or abufe the Strength,
With which he arms me, to his Wrong? Or, like
A proftituted Creature, merchandize
Our mutual Delight for Hire? Or to
Serve mine own fordid Ends? In vulgar Nuptials
Priority is exploded, though there be
A Difference in the Parties; and fhall I,
His Vaffal, from Obfcurity, rais'd by him

To this so eminent Light, * presume t' appoint him
To do, or not to do, this, or that ? When Wives
Are well accommodated by their Husbands
With all Things both for Use, and Ornament,
Let them fix there, and never dare to question
Their Wills or Actions.   For myself, I vow,
Though now my Lord would rashly give away
His Scepter, and Imperial Diadem,
Or if there could be any Thing more precious,
I would not cross it ;—but I know this is
But a Trial of my Temper, and as such
I do receive it; or, if't be otherwise,
You are so subtil in your Arguments,
I dare not stay to hear them.

    Pulch. Is't ev'n so ?
I've Power o'er these, yet, and command their Stay,
To hearken nearer to me.

    1 *Sister.* We are charg'd
By the Emperor, our Brother, to attend
The Empress' Service.

    2 *Sister.* You are too mortify'd, Sister,
(With Reverence I speak it) for young Ladies
To keep you Company.   I am so tir'd
With your tedious Exhortations, Doctrines,
Uses of your religious Morality,
That, for my Health-sake, I must take the Freedom
To enjoy a little of those pretty Pleasures
That I was born to.

    1 *Sister.* When I come to your Years,
I'll do as you do; but, till then, with your Pardon,
I'll lose no more Time.   I have not learn'd to dance yet,
Nor sing, but Holy Hymns, and those to vile Tunes too;
Nor to discourse, but of Schoolmens Opinions.
How shall I answer my Suitors ? Since, I hope,
Ere long I shall have many, without Practice

    * *To this so eminent Light.*

  Thus we read in the old Copies, which I have here follow'd, tho'
I think it ought to be

    To this so eminent Height.

       , **To**

To write, and speak something that's not deriv'd
From the Fathers of Philosophy.

   2 *Sister*. We shall shame
Our Breeding, Sister, if we should go on thus.

   1 *Sister*. 'Tis for your Credit, that we study
How to converse with Men; Women with Women
Yields but a barren Argument.

   2 *Sister*. She frowns——
But you'll protect us, Madam?

   Athen. Yes, and love
Your sweet Simplicity.

   1 *Sister*. All young Girls are so,
'Till they know the Way of't.

   2 *Sister*. But, when we are enter'd,
We shall on a good round Pace.

   Athen. I'll leave you, Madam.

   1 *Sister*. And we; our Duties with you.

              [*Exeunt* Athenais *and the young Ladies.*

   Pulch. On all Hands
Thus slighted? No Way left? Am I grown stupid
In my Invention? Can I make no Use
Of the Emperor's Bounties?——Now 'tis thought: within
     there.

Enter Servant.

   Serv. Madam.

   Pulch. It shall be so:—Nearer; your Ear
Draw a Petition to this End.

   Serv. Besides
The Danger to prefer it, I believe
'Twill ne'er be granted.

   Pulch. How's this? Are you grown,
From a Servant, my Director? Let me hear
No more of this. Dispatch, I'll master him

                [*Exit Servant.*

At his own Weapon.

                   Enter

Enter Theodofius, Favorinus, Philanax, Timantus,
Gratianus.

Theod. .Let me underſtand it,
If yet there be ought wanting that may perfect
A general Happineſs.
Favor. The People's Joy
In Seas of Acclamations flow in
To wait on yours.
Phila. Their Love with Bounty levied,
Is a ſure Guard : Obedience, forc'd from Fear,
Paper Fortification, which in Danger
Will yield to the Impreſſion of a Reed,
Or of itſelf fall off.
Theod. True, *Philanax.*
And by that certain Compaſs we reſolve
To ſteer our Barque of Government.

Enter Servant with the Petition.

Pulch. 'Tis well.
Theod. My deareſt, and my all-deſerving Siſter,
As a Petitioner kneel? It muſt not be.
Pray you, riſe; although your Suit were half my Em-
pire,
'Tis freely granted.
Pulch. Your Alacrity
To give hath made a Beggar; yet, before
My Suit is by your ſacred Hand and Seal
Confirm'd, 'tis neceſſary you peruſe
The Sum of my Requeſt.
Theod. We will not wrong
Your Judgment, in conceiving what 'tis fit
For you to aſk, and us to grant, ſo much,
As to proceed with Caution, give me my Signet,
With Confidence I ſign it, and here vow
By my Father's Soul, but with your free Conſent,
It is irrevocable.
Timantus.

Timan. What if fhe now
Calling to Memory, how often we
Have crofs'd her Government, in Revenge hath made
Petition for our Heads?

Grat. They muft even off, then;
No Ranfom can redeem us.

Theod. Let thofe Jewels
So highly rated by the *Perfian* Merchants
Be bought, and as a Sacrifice from us
Prefented to *Eudoxia*, fhe being only
Worthy to wear 'em. I am angry with
The unrefiftable Neceffity
Of my Occafions, and important Cares,
That fo long keep me from her.

                  [Exeunt Theodofius *and the Train.*

Pulch. Go to the Emprefs,
And tell her on the fudden, I am fick,
And do defire the Comfort of a Vifit,
If fhe pleafe to vouchfafe it.   From me ufe
Your humbleft Language.——But, when once I have her

                         [Exit Servant.

In my Poffeffion, I will rife, and fpeak
In a higher Strain: Say it raife Storms, no matter.
Fools judge by the Event, my Ends are honeft. *[Exeunt.*

SCENE III.

Theodofius, Timantus, Philanax.

Theod. What is become of her? Can fhe that carries
Such glorious Excellence of Light about her,
Be any where conceal'd?

Phila. We have fought her Lodgings,
And all we can learn from the Servants, is,
She by your Majefty's Sifters waited on,
The Attendance of her other Officers,
By her exprefs Command, deny'd,——

Theod. Forbear
Impertinent Circumftances,—whither went fhe? Speak.

                              Phila.

Phila. As they guefs, to the Laurel Grove.

Theod. So flightly guarded!
What an Earthquake I feel in me! and, but that
Religion affures the contrary,
The Poets Dreams of luftful Fawns, and Satyrs,
Would make me fear I know not what.

Enter Favorinus.

Favor. I have found her,
And it pleafe your Majefty.

Theod. Yes, it doth pleafe me.
But why return'd without her?

Favor. As fhe made
Her fpeedieft Approaches to your Prefence,
A Servant of the Princefs's, *Pulcheria,*
Encounter'd her. What 'twas he whifper'd to her
I'm ignorant; but, hearing it, fhe ftarted,
And will'd me to excufe her Abfence from you
The third Part of an Hour.

Theod. In this fhe takes
So much of my Life from me; yet, I'll bear it
With what Patience I may; fince 'tis her Pleafure,
Go back, my *Favorinus*, and intreat her
Not to exceed a Minute.

Timant. Here's ftrange Fondnefs!   [*Exeunt.*

SCENE IV.

Pulcheria. *Servants.*

Pulch. You're certain fhe will come?

Serv. She is already
Enter'd your outward Lodgings.

Pulch. No Train with her?

Serv. Your Excellency's Sifters only.

Pulch. 'Tis the better.
See the Doors ftrongly guarded, and deny
Accefs to all, but with our fpecial Licence:

Why doft thou ftay ? Shew your Obedience ;
Your Wifdom now is ufelefs.   [*Exeunt Servants.*

Enter Athenais, Arcadia, Flaccilla.

Flac. She is fick, fure ;
Or, in fit Reverence to your Majefty,
She had waited you at the Door,
 Arcad. 'Twould hardly be

        [Pulcheria *walking by.*
Excus'd, in civil Manners, to her Equal :
But with more Difficulty to you, that are
So far above her.
 Athen. Not in her Opinion ;
She hath been too long accuftom'd to Command
T' acknowledge a Superior.
 Arcad. There fhe walks.
 Flac. If fhe be not fick of the Sullens, I fee not
The leaft Infirmity in her.
 Athen. This is ftrange !
 Arcad. Open your Eyes : The Emprefs.——
 Pulch. Reach that Chair :
Now, fitting thus at Diftance, I'll vouchfafe
To look upon her.
 Arcad. How, Sifter ? Pray you awake.
Are you in your Wits ?
 Flac. Grant, Heaven, your too much Learning
Does not conclude in Madnefs.
 Athen. You intreated
A Vifit from me.
 Pulch. True, my Servant us'd
Such Language : But now, as a Miftrefs, I
Command your Service.
 Athen. Service ?
 Arcad. She's ftark mad, fure.
 Pulch. You'll find I can difpofe of what's mine own
Without a Guardian.
 Athen. Follow me.—I will fee you
When your frantick Fit is o'er. I do begin
To be of your Belief.
          Pulch.

Pulch. It will deceive you.
Thou ſhalt not ſtir from hence.—Thus, as mine own,
I ſeize upon thee.
Flac. Help, help! Violence
Offer'd to the Empreſs' Perſon!
Pulch. 'Tis in vain :
She was an Empreſs once ; but, by my Gift :
Which, being abus'd, I do recall my Grant.
You are read in Story ; call to Remembrance
What the great *Hector*'s Mother, *Hecuba*,
Was to *Ulyſſes*, *Ilium* ſack'd.
Athen. A Slave.
Pulch. To me thou art ſo.
Athen. Wonder and Amazement
Quite overwhelm me : How am I transform'd ?
How have I loſt my Liberty ?

                              [*Knocking without.*

Enter Servant.

Pulch. Thou ſhalt know
Too ſoon, no Doubt.—Who's that, with ſuch Rudeneſs
Beats at the Door ?
Serv. The Prince *Paulinus*, Madam,
Sent from the Emperor to attend upon
The gracious Empreſs.
Arcad. And who is your Slave now ?
Flac. Siſter, repent in Time, and beg Pardon
For your Preſumption.
Pulch. — It is reſolv'd :
From me return this Anſwer to *Paulinus* ;
She ſhall not come ; ſhe's mine ; the Emperor hath
No Intereſt in her.   [*Exit Servant.*
Athen. Whatſoe'er I am,
You take not from your Power o'er me, to yield
A Reaſon for this Uſage.
Pulch. Though my Will is
Sufficient to add to thy Affliction,
Know, Wretched Thing, 'tis not thy Fate, but Folly
Hath made thee what thou art : 'Tis ſome Delight

                      X 2

To urge my Merits to one so ungrateful;
Therefore with Horror hear it. —When thou wert
Thrust as a Stranger from thy Father's House,
Expos'd to all Calamities that Want
Could throw upon thee; thine own Brothers' Scorn,
And in thy Hopes, as by the World, forsaken,
My Pity, the last Altar that was left thee;
I heard thy *Syren* Charms, with Feeling heard them,
And my Compassion made mine Eyes vie Tears
With thine, dissembling Crocodile! and when Queens
Were emulous for thy Imperial Bed,
The Garments of thy Sorrows cast aside,
I put thee in a Shape as would have forc'd
Envy from *Cleopatra*, had she seen thee,
Then, when I knew my Brother's Blood was warm'd
With youthful Fires, I brought thee to his Presence;
And how my deep Designs, for thy Good plotted,
Succeeded to my Wishes, is apparent,
And needs no Repetition.

   Athen. I am conscious
Of your so many, and unequal'd Favours,
But find not how I may accuse myself
For any Facts committed, that with Justice
Can raise your Anger to this Height against me.

    Pulch. Pride and Forgetfulness would not let thee
       see that,
Against which now thou canst not close thine Eyes.
What Injury could be equal to thy late
Contempt of my good Counsel, when I urg'd
The Emperor's prodigal Bounties, and intreated
That you would use your Power to give 'em Limits,
Or, at the least, a due Consideration
Of such as su'd, and for what, ere he sign'd it?
In Opposition, you brought against me
Th' Obedience of a Wife, that Ladies were not,
Being well accommodated by their Lords,
To question, but much less to cross, their Pleasures;
Nor would you, though the Emperor were resolv'd
To give away his Scepter, hinder it,

                       Since

Since 'twas done for your Honour, covering with
Falfe Colours of Humility your Ambition.

Atben. And is this my Offence?

Pulcb. As wicked Counfel
Is ftill moft hurtful unto thofe that give it;
Such as deny to follow what is good,
In Reafon, are the firft that muft repent it.
When I pleafe, you fhall hear more; in the mean Time,
Thank your own wilful Folly that hath chang'd you
From an Emprefs to a Bondwoman.

Theod. Force the Doors:
Kill thofe that dare refift.

Enter Theodofius, Paulinus, Philanax, Chryfapius,
Gratianus.

Atben. Dear Sir, redeem me.

Flac. O fuffer not, for your own Honour's fake,
The Emprefs, you fo late lov'd, to be made
A Prifoner in the Court.

Arcad. Leap to his Lips,
You'll find them the beft Sanctuary.

Flac. And try, then,
What Intereft my reverend Sifter hath
To force you from 'em.

Theod. What ftrange May game's this?
Though done in Sport, how ill this Levity
Becomes your Wifdom?

Pulcb. I am ferious, Sir,
And have done nothing but what you in Honour,
And as you are yourfelf an Emperor,
Stand bound to juftify.

Theod. Take heed; put not thefe
Strange Trials on my Patience.

Pulcb. Do not you, Sir,
Deny your own Act; as you are a Man,
And ftand on your own Bottom, 'twill appear
A childifh Weaknefs to make void a Grant,
Sign'd by your Sacred Hand and Seal, and ftrengthen'd

With

With a religious Oath, but with my Licence
Never to be recall'd.   For some few Minutes
Let Reason rule your Paffion, and in this,

          [Delivers the Deed.

Be pleas'd to read my Intereft.   You will find, there,
What you in me call Violence, is Juftice,
And that I may make Ufe of what's mine own,
According to my Will.   'Tis your own Gift, Sir;
And what an Emperor gives, fhould ftand as firm
As the Celeftial Poles upon the Shoulders
Of *Atlas*, or his Succeffor in that Office
The great *Alcides*.

 Theod. Miferies of more Weight,
Than 'tis feign'd they fupported, fall upon me!
What hath my Rafhnefs done? In this Tranfaction
Drawn in exprefs and formal Terms, I have
Giv'n and confign'd into your Hands, to ufe
And obferve, as you pleafe, my dear *Eudoxa*.
It is my Deed, I do confefs it is,
And, as I am myfelf, not to be cancell'd:
But yet you may fhew Mercy—and you will,
When you confider that there is no Beauty
So perfect in a Creature, but is foil'd
With fome unbefeeming Blemifh.   You have labour'd
To build me up a complete Prince; 'tis granted:
Yet, as I am a Man, like other Monarchs,
I have Defects and Frailties; my Facility,
To fend Petitioners with pleas'd Looks from me,
Is all I can be charg'd with, and it will
Become your Wifdom, (fince 'tis in your Power)
In Charity to provide, I fall no further
Or in my Oath, or Honour.

 Pulch. Royal Sir,
This was the Mark I aim'd at, and I glory
At the length, you fo conceive it: 'Twas a Weaknefs
To meafure by your own Integrity
The Purpofes of others.   I have fhewn you,
In a true Mirror, what Fruit grows upon
The Tree of hoodwink'd Bounty, and what Dangers

             Preci-

Precipitation in the managing
Your great Affairs produceth.

Theod. I embrace it
As a grave Advertifement, and vow hereafter
Never to fign Petitions at this Rate.

Pulch. For mine, fee, Sir, 'tis cancel'd; on my Knees
I re-deliver what I now begg'd from you.

　　　　　　　　　　　　　　　[*Tears the Deed.*

She is my fecond Gift.

Theod. Which if I part from
'Till Death divorce us ——　　　　[*Kiffing* Athenais.

Athen. So, Sir ——

Theod. Nay, Sweet, chide not:
I am punifh'd in thy Looks; defer the reft,
'Till we're more private.

Pulch. I afk Pardon too,
If, in my perfonated Paffion, I
Appear'd too harfh and rough.

Athen. 'Twas gentle Language,
What I was then confider'd.

Pulch. O dear Madam,
It was Decorum in the Scene.

Athen. This Trial,
When I was *Athenais,* might have pafs'd;
But, as I am the Emprefs ——

Theod. Nay, no Anger,
Since all Good was intended.

　　　　　[*Exeunt* Theodofius, Athenais, Arcadia, Flaccilla.

Pulch. Building on
That certain Bafe, I fear not what can follow.

　　　　　　　　　　　　　　　[*Exit* Pulcheria.

Paul. Thefe are ftrange Devices, *Philanax.*

Phila. True, my Lord.
May all turn to the beft!

Grat. The Emperor's Looks
Promis'd a Calm.

Chryf. But the vex'd Emprefs' Frowns
Prefag'd a fecond Storm.

Paul. I am fure I feel one

　　　　　　　　X 4　　　　　　　　　　　In

In my Leg already.

Phila. Your old Friend, the Gout?

Paul. My forc'd Companion, *Philanax.*

Chryſ. To your Reſt.

Paul. Reſt, and forbearing Wine, with a temperate
    Diet,
Though many Mountebanks pretend the Cure of't,
I've found my beſt Phyſicians.

Phila. Eaſe to your Lordſhip.   [*Exeunt.*

The End of the Third Act.

A C T IV. S C E N E I.

Athenais, Chryſapius.

Athen, MAKE me her Property?
              Chryſ. Your Majeſty
Hath juſt Cauſe of Diſtaſte; and your Reſentment
Of the Affront in the Point of Honour cannot
But meet a fair Conſtruction.

Athen. I have only
The Title of an Empreſs, but the Power
Is, by her, raviſh'd from me. She ſurveys
My Actions as a Governeſs, and calls
My not obſerving all that ſhe directs,
Folly, and Diſobedience.

Chryſ. Under Correction,
With Grief I've long obſerv'd it; and, if you
Stand pleas'd to ſign my Warrant, I'll deliver
In my unfeign'd Zeal, and Deſire to ſerve you,
(Howe'er I run the Hazard of my Head for't,
Should it arrive at the Knowledge of the Princeſs)
Not alone, the Reaſons why Things are thus carried,
But give into your Hands the Power to clip
The Wings of her Command.

                              Athen.

Atben. Your Service this Way
Cannot offend me.

Chryf. Be you pleas'd to know, then,
(But ftill with Pardon, if I am too bold)
Your too much Sufferance imps the broken Feathers
Which carry her to this proud Height, in which
She with Security foars, and ftill tow'rs o'er you :
But, if you would employ the Strengths you hold
In the Emperor's Affections, and remember
The Orb you move in fhould admit no Star elfe,
You never would confefs the managing
Of State Affairs to her alone are proper,
And you fit by a Looker on,

Atben. I would not,
If it were poffible I could attempt
Her Diminution, without a Taint
Of foul Ingratitude in myfelf.

Chryf. In this
The Sweetnefs of your Temper does abufe you ;
And you call that a Benefit to yourfelf
Which fhe for her own Ends confer'd upon you.
'Tis yielded fhe gave Way to your Advancement :
But for what Caufe ? that fhe might ftill continue
Her Abfolute Sway and Swing o'er the whole State ;
And that fhe might to her Admirers vaunt,
The Emprefs was her Creature, and the Giver
To be prefer'd before the Gift.

Atben. It may be.

Chryf. Nay, 'tis moft certain : Whereas, would you
            pleafe
In a true Glafs to look upon yourfelf,
And view without Detraction your own Merits,
Which all Men wonder at, you would find that Fate,
Without a fecond Caufe, appointed you
To the fupremeft Honour.   For the Princefs,
She hath reign'd long enough, and her Remove
Will make your Entrance free to the Poffeffion
Of what you were born to ; and, but once refolve
To build upon her Ruins, leave the Engines

                                    That

That muſt be us'd to undermine her Greatneſs
To my Proviſion.

Athen. I thank your Care :
But a Deſign of ſuch Weight muſt not be
Raſhly determin'd of ; it will exaɛt
A long and ſerious Conſultation from me,
In the mean Time, *Chryſapius*, reſt aſſur'd
I live your thankful Miſtreſs.   [*Exit* Athenais.

Chryſ. Is this all ?
Will the Phyſick that I miniſter'd work no further ?
I've play'd the Fool ; and, leaving a calm Port,
Embark'd myſelf on a rough Sea of Danger.
In her Silence lies my Safety, which how can I
Hope from a Woman ?—But the Die is thrown,
And I muſt ſtand the Hazard.

     Enter Theodoſius, Philanax, Timantus, Gratianus,
              Huntſmen.

     Theod. Is *Paulinus*
So tortur'd with his Gout ?

     Phila. Moſt miſerably, Sir.
And it adds much to his Affliɛtion, that
The Pain denies him Power to wait upon
Your Majeſty.

     Theod. I pity him.——He is
A wond'rous honeſt Man, and what he ſuffers,
I know, will grive my Empreſs.

     Timan. He, indeed, is
Much bound to her gracious Favour.

     Theod. He deſerves it ;
She cannot find a Subjeɛt upon whom
She better may confer it.—Is the Stag
Safe lodg'd ?

     Grat. Yes, Sir, and the Hounds and Huntſmen ready.

     Phila. He will make you royal Sport. He is a Deer,
Of ten, at the leaſt.

                              Enter

Enter Countryman with an Apple.

Grat. Whither will this Clown?

Timan. Stand back.

Count. I would zee the Emperor. Why fhould you Courtiers
Scorn a poor Countryman? We zweat at the Plough
To vill your Mouths, you and you Curs might ftarve, elfe.
We prune the Orchards, and you cranch the Fruit;
Yet ftill y'are fnarling at us.

Theod. What's the matter?

Count. I would look on thy fweet Face.

Timan. Unmannerly Swain!

Count. Zwain? Though I am a Zwain, I have a Heart, yet,
As ready to do Service for my Leg,
As any Princock, Peacock of you all.
Zookers!. had I one of you zingle, with this Twig
I would fo veeze you.

Timan. Will your Majefty
Hear this rude Language?

Theod. Yes, and hold it as
An Ornament, not a Blemifh. O *Timantus!*
Since that dread Power by whom we are, difdains not
With an open Ear to hear Petitions from us,
Eafy Accefs in us, his Deputies,
To the meaneft of our Subjects, is a Debt
Which we ftand bound to pay.

Count. By my Granam's Ghoft
'Tis a wholefome Zaying; our Vicar could not mend it
In the Pulpit on a Zunday.

Theod. What's their Suit Friend?

Count. Zute? I would laugh at that. Let the Court
, beg from thee,
What the poor Country gives. I bring a Prefent
To thy good Grace, which I can call mine own,
And look not, like thefe gay Volk, for a Return

Of

Of what they venture. Have I giv'nt you, ha!
  Chryſ. A perilous Knave.
  Count. Zee here a dainty Apple.   [*Preſents the Apple.*
Of mine own grafting; zweet and zownd, I aſſure thee.
  Theod. It is the faireſt Fruit I ever ſaw.
Thoſe golden Apples in the *Heſperian* Orchards
So ſtrangely guarded by the watchful Dragon,
As they requir'd great *Hercules* to get 'em;
Nor thoſe with which *Hippomenes* deceiv'd,
Swift-footed *Atalanta,* when I look
On this, deſerve no Wonder. You behold
The poor Man, and his Preſent, with Contempt:
I to their Value prize both; He, that could
So aid weak Nature, by his Care and Labour,
As to compel a Crabtree-ſtock to bear
A precious Fruit of this large Size and Beauty,
Would by his Induſtry change a petty Village
Into a populous City, and from that
Erect a flouriſhing Kingdom. Give the Fellow,
For an Encouragement to his future Labours,
Ten *Attick* Talents.
  Count. I will weary heaven
With my Prayers for your Majeſty.   [*Exit Countryman.*
  Theod. Philanax,
From me preſent this Rarity to the rareſt
And beſt of Women. When I think upon
The boundleſs Happineſs that from her flows to me
In my Imagination I am rap'd
Beyond myſelf.——But I forget our Hunting,
To the Foreſt for the Exerciſe of my Body;
But for my Mind, 'tis wholly taken up
In the Contemplation of her matchleſs Virtues.   [*Exeunt.*

SCENE II.

Athenais, Pulcheria, Arcadia, Flaccilla.

Athen. You ſhall know there's a Difference between us.
Pulch. There was, I'm certain, not long ſince, when
    you   Kneel'd

Kneel'd a Petitioner to me; then you were happy
To be near my Feet; and do you hold it, now,
As a Difparagement that I fide you, Lady?

Athen. Since you refpect me only as I was,
What I am fhall be remember'd.

Pulch. Does the Means
I practis'd, to give good and faving Counfels
To th' Emperor, and your new ftamp'd Majefty
Still ftick in your Stomach?

Athen. 'Tis not yet digefted,
In troth it is not. Why, good Governefs,
Though you are held for a grand Madam, and yourfelf
The firft that overprize it, I ne'er took
Your Words for *Delphian* Oracles, nor your Actions
For fuch Wonders as you make 'em,—there is one,
When fhe fhall fee her Time, as fit and able
To be made Partner of the Emperor's Cares,
As your wife felf, and may with Juftice challenge
A nearer Intereft.—You have done your Vifit,
So, when you pleafe, you may leave me.

Pulch. I'll not bandy
Words with your Mightinefs, proud one, only this,
You carry too much Sail for your fmall Bark;
And that, when you leaft think upon't, may fink you,
[*Exit* Pulcheria.

Flac. I am glad fhe's gone.

Arcad. I fear'd fhe would have read
A tedious Lecture to us.

Enter Philanax *with the Apple.*

Phila. From the Emperor.
This rare Fruit to the rareft.

Athen. How, my Lord?

Phila. I ufe his Language, Madam; and that Truft,
Which he impos'd on me, difcharg'd, his Pleafure
Commands my prefent Service. [*Exit* Philanax.

Athen. Have you feen
So fair an Apple?

Flac.

Flac. Never.

Arcad. If the Tafte

Anfwer the Beauty.

Athen. Prettily beg'd ;—you fhould have it ;
But that you eat too much cold Fruit, and that
Changes the frefh Red in your Cheeks to Palenefs.

Enter Servant.

I've other Dainties for you ; you come from
Paulinus ; how is't with that truly noble,
And honeft Lord ? My Witnefs at the Fount ;
In a Word, the Man to whofe blefs'd Charity
I owe my Greatnefs. How is't with him ?

Serv. Spiritly,
In his Mind ; but, by the raging of his Gout,
In his Body much diftemper'd ; that you pleas'd
To inquire his Health, took off much from his Pain ;
His glad Looks did confirm it.

Athen. Do his Doctors
Give him no Hope ?

Serv. Little ; they rather fear,
By his continual burning, that he ftands
In danger of a Fever.

Athen. To him again,
And tell him that I heartily wifh it lay
In me to eafe him, and from me deliver
This choice Fruit to him ; you may fay to that
I hope it will prove phyfical.

Serv. The good Lord
Will be o'erjoy'd with the Favour.

Athen. He deferves more.   [*Exeunt.*

SCENE III.

Paulinus brought in a Chair, Chirurgeon.

Chirurg. I've done as much as Art can do, to ftop
The violent Courfe of your Fit, and I hope you feel it.
How does your Honour?   *Paul.*

Paul. At some Eafe, I thank you:
I would you could affure Continuance of it,
For the Moiety of my Fortune.

    Chirurg. If I could cure
The Gout, my Lord, without the Philofopher's Stone
I fhould foon purchafe, it being a Difeafe,
In poor Men very rare, and in the rich
The Cure impoffible, your many Bounties
Bid me prepare you for a certain Truth,
And to flatter you, were difhoneft.

    Paul. Your plain dealing
Deferves a Fee. Would there were many more fuch
Of your Profeffion. Happy are poor Men;
If fick with the Excefs of Heat or Cold,
Caus'd by neceffitous Labour, not loofe Surfeits
They, when fpare Diet, or kind Nature fail
To perfect their Recovery, foon arrive at
Their Reft in Death; but, on the contrary,
The Great and Noble are expos'd as Preys
To the Rapine of Phyficians; and they,
In ling'ring out what is remedilefs,
Aim at their Profit, not the Patients Health.
A thoufand Trials and Experiments
Have been put upon me, and I forc'd to pay dear
For my Vexation; but I am refolv'd,
(I thank your honeft Freedom) to be made
A Property no more for Knaves to work on.
—What have you there?

Enter Cleon *with a Parchment Roll.*

    Cleon. The Triumphs of an Artfman
O'er all Infirmities, made authentical
With the Names of Princes, Kings and Emperors
That were his Patients.

    Paul. Some Empirick.

    Cleon. It may be fo; but he fwears, within three Days
He will grub up your Gout by th' Roots, and make
      you able

To

To march ten Leagues a Day in compleat Armour,

Paul. Impossible.

Cleon. Or, if you like not him——

Chirurg. Hear him, my Lord, for your Mirth; I will take Order,

They shall not wrong you.

Paul. Usher in your Monster.

Cleon. He is at hand, march up: Now speak for yourself.

Enter Empirick.

Empir. I come not, Right Honourable, to your Presence, with any base and sordid End of Reward; the Immortality of my Fame is the White I shoot at, the Charge of my most curious and costly Ingredients defray'd, amounting to some seventeen thousand Crowns—a Trifle in respect of Health—writing your noble Name in my Catalogue, I shall acknowledge myself amply satisfy'd.

Chirurg. I believe so.

Empir. For your own Sake, I most heartily wish, that you had now all the Diseases, Maladies and Infirmities upon you, that were ever remember'd by old *Galen, Hippocrates,* or the later, and more admired *Paracelsus.*

Paul. For your good Wish, I thank you.

Empir. Take me with you, I beseech your good Lordship. I urg'd it, that your Joy, in being certainly and suddenly free from them, may be the greater, and my not to be parallel'd Skill the more remarkable. The Cure of the Gout's a Toy, without Boast be it said; my Cradle-practice, the Cancer, the Fistula, the Dropsy, Consumption of Lungs and Kidneys, Hurts in the Brain, Heart, or Liver, are Things worthy my Opposition; but in the Recovery of my Patients I ever overcome them.—But to your Gout——

Paul. I, marry, Sir; that cur'd, I shall be apter To give Credit to the rest.

Empir.

Empir. Suppose it done, Sir.

Chirur. And the Means you use, I beseech you.

Empir. I will do it in the plaineſt Language, and diſcover my Ingredients.   Firſt, my *boteni Terebinthina*, of *Cypris*, my Manna, *ros cælo*, coagulated with *vetulos ovorum*, vulgarly Yolks of Eggs, with a little Cyath, or Quantity of my potable Elixir, with ſome few Scruples of Saſſafras and Guacum, ſo taken every Morning and Evening, in the Space of three Days, purgeth, cleanſeth, and diſſipateth the inward Cauſes of the virulent Tumor.

Paul. Why do you ſmile?

Chirur. When he hath done, I will reſolve you.

Empir. For my exterior Applications, I have theſe Balſumunguentulums, extracted from Herbs, Plants, Roots, Seeds, Gums, and a Million of other Vegetables, the principal of which are Uliſſipona, or Serpentaria, Sophia, or Herba Conſolidarum, Parthenion, or Commanilla Romana, Mumia tranſmarina, mixed with my plumbum Philoſophorum, and mater metallorum, *cum oſſa paraleli, eſt univerſale medicamentum in podagra.*

Cleon. A conjuring Balſamum,

Empir. This applied warm upon the pained Place, with a feather of Struthio cameli, or a Bird of Paradiſe, which is every where to be had, ſhall expulſe this tartarous, viſcous, anatheos, and malignant Dolor.

Chirur. An excellent Receipt! but does your Lordſhip Know what it is good for?

Paul. I would be inſtructed.

Chirur. For the Gonorrhœa, or, if you will hear it In a plainer Phraſe, the Pox.

Empir. If it cure his Lordſhip
Of that, by the Way, I hope, Sir, 'tis the better.
My Medicine ſerves for all Things, and the Pox, Sir,
Though falſely nam'd the Sciatica, or Gout,
Is the more Catholick Sickneſs.

Paul. Hence with the Raſcal!
Yet hurt him not; he makes me ſmile, and that

Frees him from Punishment.

                      [They thrust off the Empirick.

   Chirur. Such Slaves as this
Render our Art contemptible,

              Enter Servant.

   Serv. My good Lord——
   Paul. So soon return'd ?
   Serv. And with this Present from
Your great, and gracious Miftress, with her Wifhes
It may prove phyfical to you.
   Paul. In my Heart
I kneel, and thank her Bounty.   Dear Friend *Cleon*,
Give him the Cup-board of Plate in the next Room
For a Reward.   *[Exeunt* Cleon *and the Servant.*
Moft glorious Fruit ; but made
More precious by her Grace and Love that fent it.
To touch it only, coming from her Hand,
Makes me forget all Pain.   A Diamond
Of this large Size, though it would buy a Kingdom,
Hew'd from the Rock, and laid down at my Feet,
Nay, though a Monarch's Gift, will hold no Value,
Compar'd with this—And yet, ere I prefume
To tafte it, though, fans Queftion, it is
Some heavenly Reftorative, I in Duty
Stand bound to weigh my own Unworthinefs.
Ambrofia is Food only for the Gods ;
And not by human Lips to be prophan'd.
I may adore it as fome holy Relique,
Deriv'd from thence, but impious to keep it
In my Poffeffion ; the Emperor only
Is worthy to enjoy it.—Go, good *Cleon*,

             Enter Cleon.

(And ceafe this Admiration at this Object)
From me prefent this to my Royal Mafter,
I know it will amaze him, and excufe me

                            That

That I am not myfelf the Bearer of it.
That I fhould be lame now, when with Wings of Duty
I fhould fly to the Service of this Emprefs!
Nay, no Delays, good *Cleon.*
    Cleon. I am gone, Sir.   [*Exeunt.*

SCENE IV.

Theodofius, Chryfapius, Timantus, Gratianus.

    Chryf. Are you not tir'd, Sir?
    Theod. Tir'd? I muft not fay fo,
However, though I rode hard. To a Huntfman,
His Toil is his Delight, and to complain
Of Wearinefs, would fhew as poorly in him,
As if a General fhould grieve for a Wound,
Receiv'd upon his Forehead, or his Breaft,
After a glorious Victory, lay by
Thefe Accoutrements for the Chafe.

Enter Pulcheria.

    Pulch. You are well return'd, Sir,
From your Princely Exercife.
    Theod. Sifter, to you
I owe the Freedom, and the Ufe of all
The Pleafures I enjoy. Your Care provides
For my Security, and the Burthen, which
I fhould alone fuftain, you undergo,
And, by your painful Watchings, yield my Sleeps
Both found, and fure. How happy am I in
Your Knowledge of the Art of Government!
And, credit me, I glory to behold you
Difpofe of great Defigns, as if you were
A Partner, and no Subject of my Empire.
    Pulch. My Vigilance, fince it hath well fucceeded,
I'm confident, you allow of—yet it is not
Approv'd by all.

                        Theod.

Theod. Who dares repine at that
Which hath our Suffrage?

Pulch. One that too well knows
The Strength of her Abilities can better
My weak Endeavours.

Theod. In this you reflect
Upon my Emprefs?

Pulch. True; for, as fhe is
The Confort of your Bed, 'tis fit fhe fhare in
Your Cares, and abfolute Power.

Theod. You touch a String
That founds but harfhly to me, and I muft
In a Brother's Love advife you, that hereafter
You would forbear to move it. Since fhe is
In her pure felf a Harmony of fuch Sweetnefs,
Compos'd of Duty, chafte Defires, her Beauty
(Though it might tempt a Hermit from his Beads)
The leaft of her Endowments. I am forry
Her holding the firft Place, fince that the fecond
Is proper to yourfelf, calls on your Envy.
She err? It is impoffible in a Thought,
And, much more, fpeak, or do what may offend me.
In other Things, I would believe you, Sifter:
But, though the Tongues of Saints and Angels tax'd her
Of any Imperfection, I fhould be
Incredulous,

Pulch. She is, yet, a Woman, Sir.

Theod. The Abftract of what's excellent in the Sex:
But to their Mulcts, and Frailties a mere Stranger:
—I'll die in this Belief.

Enter Cleon *with the Apple.*

Cleon. Your humbleft Servant,
The Lord *Paulinus*, as a Witnefs of
His Zeal and Duty to your Majefty,
Prefents you with this Jewel.

· *Theod.* Ha!

Cleon. It is
Preferr'd by him——

Theod.

Theod. Above his Honour?

Cleon. No, Sir;
I would have said his Patrimony.

Theod. 'Tis the same.

Cleon. And he intreats, since Lameness may excuse
His not presenting it himself, from me
(Though far unworthy to supply his Place)
You would vouchsafe to accept it.

Theod. Farther off;
You've told your Tale: Stay you for a Reward?
—Take that.   [*Strikes him.*

Pulch. How's this?

Chrys. I never saw him mov'd thus.

Theod. We muft not part fo, Sir—A Guard upon him.

Enter Guard.

Theod. May I not vent my Sorrows in the Air,
Without Difcovery? Forbear the Room!
                    [*They all go afide.*
Yet be within Call—What an Earthquake I feel in me! [3]
And on the fudden my whole Fabrick totters.
My Blood within me turns, and through my Veins
Parting with natural Redness I difcern it,
Chang'd to a fatal Yellow.   What an Army
Of hellifh Furies in the horrid Shapes
Of Doubts, and Fears, charge on me! Rife to my
     Refcue,
Thou ftout Maintainer of a chafte Wife's Honour,
The Confidence of her Virtues; be not fhaken
With the Wind of vain Surmifes; much lefs fuffer
The Devil Jealoufy to whifper to me
My curious Obfervation of that

[3] —— *What an Earthquake I feel in me*
     And on the fudden, &c.

Though *Shakefpear* is peculiar excellent in the Paffion of Jealoufy,
yet in my Opinion there are fome Flights of a *Maffinger* fo truly
Original, that if he does not equal that immortal Bard, he comes the
neareft to him of all our other dramatic Writers.

Y 3   I

I muſt no more remember.—Will it not be?
Thou uninvited Gueſt, ill-manner'd Monſter,
I charge thee, leave me! wilt thou force me to
Give Fuel to that Fire I would put out?
The Goodneſs of my Memory proves my Miſchief,
And I would ſell my Empire, could it purchaſe
The dull Art of Forgetfulneſs.—Who waits there?

   Timan. Moſt Sacred Sir.

   Theod. Sacred, as 'tis accurs'd,
Is proper to me.   Sirrah, upon your Life,
Without a Word concerning this, command

                        [*Exit* Timantus.

Eudoxia to come to me.—Would I had
Ne'er known her by that Name, my Mother's Name!
Or that, for her own Sake, ſhe had continued
Poor *Athenais* ſtill!—No Intermiſſion?
Wilt thou ſo ſoon torment me? Muſt I read
Writ in the Table of my Memory,
To warrant my Suſpicion, how *Paulinus*
(Though ever thought a Man averſe to Women)
Firſt gave her Entertainment? Made her Way
For Audience to my Siſter; then I did
Myſelf obſerve how he was raviſh'd with
The gracious Delivery of her Story,
(Which was, I grant, the Bait that firſt took me, too)
She was his Convert; what the Rhetorick was
He us'd, I know not, and, ſince ſhe was mine,
In private, as in publick, what a Maſs
Of Grace and Favours hath ſhe heap'd upon him!
And but to-day this fatal Fruit—She's come.

     Enter Timantus, Athenais, Flaccilla, Arcadia.

Can ſhe be guilty?

   Athen. You ſeem troubl'd, Sir;
My Innocence makes me bold to aſk the Cauſe,
That I may eaſe you of it.—No ſalute
After four long Hours Abſence?

   Theod. Prythee, forgive me.

                        [*Kiſſes her.*
                        Methinks

Methinks I find *Paulinus* on her Lips,
And the fresh *Nectar* that I drew from thence
Is on the sudden pal'd [*Aside.*] How have you spent
Your Hours since I last saw you?

Athen. In the Converse
Of your sweet Sisters.

Theod. Did not *Philanax*,
From me, deliver you an Apple?

Athen. Yes, Sir;
Heaven! how you frown! Pray you, talk of something
    else:
Think not of such a Trifle.

Theod. How! a Trifle?
Does any Toy from me presented to you,
Deserve to be so slighted? Do you value
What's sent, and not the Sender?—From a Peasant
It had deserv'd your Thanks.

Athen. And meets from you, Sir
All possible Respect.

Theod. I priz'd it, Lady,
At a higher Rate than you believe, and would not
Have parted with it, but to one I did
Prefer before myself.

Athen. It was, indeed,
The fairest that I ever saw.

Theod. It was?
And it had Virtues in it, my *Eudoxia*,
Not visible to the Eye.

Athen. It may be so, Sir,

Theod. What did you with it,—tell me punctually;
I look for a strict Accompt.

Athen. What shall I answer?

Theod. Do you stagger? Ha!

Athen. No, Sir, I have eaten it.
It had the pleasant Taste. I wonder that
You found it not in my Breath.

Theod. I'faith I did not,
And it was wond'rous strange.

Athen. Pray you, try again.
        Y 4

                                Theod.

Theod. I find no Scent of't here.   You play with me,
You have it ſtill ?

Athen. By your ſacred Life, and Fortune,
An Oath I dare not break, I've eaten it.   •

Theod. Do you know how this Oath binds ?

Athen. Too well, to break it.

Theod. That ever Man to pleaſe his brutiſh Senſe
Should ſlave his Underſtanding to his Paſſions,
And, taken with ſoon fading White and Red
Deliver up his credulous Ears to hear
The Magick of a *Syren,* and from theſe
Believe there ever was, is, or can be
More than a ſeeming Honeſty in bad Woman,

Athen. This is ſtrange Language, Sir.

Theod. Who waits? Come all.
—Nay, Siſter not ſo near ; being of the Sex,
I fear you are infected to,

Pulch. What mean you ?

Theod. To ſhow you a Miracle, a Prodigy
Which *Afric* never equal'd :—Can you think ⁴
This Maſter-piece of Heaven, this precious Vellam,
Of ſuch a Purity, and Virgin Whiteneſs,
Could be deſign'd to have Perjury, and Whoredom
In Capital Letters writ upon't?

Pulch. Dear Sir,

Theod. Nay, add to this, an Impudence beyond
All proſtituted Boldneſs.   Art not dead, yet?
Will not the Tempeſts in thy Conſcience rend thee
As ſmall as Atoms ? That there may no Sign
Be left, thou ever wert ſo ? Wilt thou live
'Till thou art blaſted with the dreadful Lightning
Of pregnant and unanſwerable Proofs,

4 ———— *Can you think*
   This Maſter-piece of Heaven, &c.
Thus in *Othello.*
        Was this fair Paper, this moſt goodly Book
        Made to write Whore upon ?

                              Act 4. Scene 9.

                                          Of

Of thy adulterous twines? Die yet, that I
With my Honour may conceal it.

   Athen. Would, long since,
The *Gorgon* of your Rage had turn'd me Marble.
Or, if I have offended——

   Theod. If!—good Angels!—
But I am tame. Look on this dumb Accuser.

                                      [*Shewing the Apple.*

   Athen. Oh, I am lost!   [*Aside.*

   Theod. Did ever Cormorant
Swallow his Prey and then digest it whole,
As she hath done this Apple? *Philanax,*
As 'tis, from me presented it. The good Lady
Swore she had eaten it; yet, I know not how,
It came intire unto *Paulinus'* Hands,
And I from him receiv'd it; sent in Scorn
Upon my Life, to give me a close Touch,
That he was weary of thee. Was there nothing
Left thee to fee him, to give Satisfaction
To thy insatiate Lust, but what was sent
As a dear Favour from me? How have I sin'd
In my Dotage on this Creature? But to her
I've liv'd, as I was born, a perfect Virgin.
Nay, more, I thought it not enough to be
True to her Bed, but that I must feed high,
To strengthen my Abilities to cloy
Her rav'nous Appetite, little suspecting
She would desire a Change.

   Athen. I never did, Sir.

   Theod. Be dumb; I will not waste my Breath in taxing
Thy base Ingratitude. How I have rais'd thee,
Will by the World be, to thy Shame, spoke often.
But for that Ribawd, who held in my Empire
The next Place to myself, so bound unto me
By all the Ties of Duty, and Allegiance
He shall pay dear for't, and feel what it is
In a Wrong of such high Consequence to pull down,
His Lord's slow Anger on him. *Philanax,*
He's troubl'd with the Gout; let him be cur'd

                                      With

With a violent Death, and in the other World,
Thank his Phyſician.

    Phila. His Cauſe unheard, Sir?

    Pulch. Take Heed of Raſhneſs.

    Theod. Is what I command,
To be diſputed?

    Phila. Your Will ſhall be done, Sir:
But that I am the Inſtrument——

    Theod. Do you murmur?

                       [*Exit* Philanax *with the Guard.*
What couldſt thou ſay, if that my Licence ſhould
Give Liberty to thy Tongue? Thou would'ſt die? I am
       not [Athenais *kneeling,* points to Theodoſius *Sword.*
So to be reconcil'd.—See me no more:
The Sting of Conſcience ever gnawing on thee,
A long Life be thy Puniſhment.   [*Exit* Theodoſius.

    Flac. O ſweet Lady.
How I could weep for her!

    Arcad. Speak, dear Madam, ſpeak.
Your Tongue, as you are a Woman, while you live,
Should be ever moving; at the leaſt, the laſt Part
That ſtirs about you.

    Pulch. Though I ſhould, ſad Lady,
In Policy rejoice, you as a Rival
Of my Greatneſs are remov'd, Compaſſion,
Since I believe you innocent, commands me
To mourn your Fortune; credit me I will urge
All Arguments I can alledge that may
Appeaſe the Emperor's Fury.

    Arcad. I will grow too,
Unto my Knees, unleſs he bid me riſe,
And ſwear he will forgive you.

    Flac. And repent too:
All this Pother for an Apple?

                   [*Exeunt* Pulcheria, Arcadia, Flaccilla.
    Chryſ. Hope, dear Madam,
And yield not to Deſpair. I'm ſtill your Servant,
And never will forſake you; though a-while
You leave the Court, and City, and give Way

                                To

To th' violent Paffions of the Emperor.
Repentance in his Want of you will foon find him.
In the mean Time I'll difpofe of you, and omit
No Opportunity that may invite him
To fee his Error.

 Athen. Oh!   [*Wringing her Hands.*
 Chryf. Forbear, for Heav'n's Sake:

The End of the Fourth Act.

ACT V. SCENE I.

Philanax, Paulinus, *Guard, Executioners.*

Paul. THis is moft barbarous! how have you loft
    All Feeling of Humanity, as Honour,
In your Confent alone, to have me us'd thus?
But to be, as you are a Looker on,
Nay, more, a principal Actor in't 'the Softnefs
Of your former Life confider'd) almoft turns me
Into a fenfelefs Statue.

 Phila. Would, long fince,
Death, by fome other Means, had made you one,
That you might be lefs fenfible of what
You have, or are to fuffer.

 Paul. Am to fuffer?
Let fuch, whofe Happinefs, and Heaven, depend
Upon their prefent Being, fear to part with
A Fort, they cannot long hold; mine to me is
A Charge that I am weary of, all Defences
By Pain, and Sicknefs batter'd;—yet, take heed,
Take heed, Lord *Philanax*, that, for private Spleen,
Or any falfe conceived Grudge againft me,
(Since in one Thought of Wrong to you, I am
Sincerely innocent) you do not that
My Royal Mafter muft in Juftice punifh,

If

If you pafs to your own Heart thorough mine,
The Murther, as it will come out, difcover'd.

 Phila. I murther you, my Lord? Heav'n witnefs for me
With the reftoring of your Health, I wifh you
Long Life, and Happinefs : For myfelf, I am
Compell'd to put in Execution that
Which I would fly from ; 'tis the Emperor,
The high incenfed Emperor's Will commands
What I muft fee perform'd.

 Paul. The Emperor?
Goodnefs, and Innocence guard me! Wheels, nor Racks
Can force into my Memory, the Remembrance
Of the leaft Shadow of Offence, with which
I ever did provoke him ; though belov'd,
(And yet the People's Love is fhort, and fatal)
I never courted popular Applaufe ;
Feafted the Men of Action, or labour'd
By prodigal Gifts to draw the needy Soldier,
The Tribunes, or Centurions to a Faction,
Of which I would rife up the Head againft him.
I hold no Place of Strength, Fortrefs or Caftle
In my Command, that can give Sanctuary
To Mal-contents, or countenance Rebellion.
I've built no Palaces to face the Court,
Nor do my Follower's Bravery fhame his Train ;
And, though I cannot blame my Fate for Want,
My competent Means of Life deferves no Envy.
In what, then, am I dangerous?

 Phila. His Difpleafure
Reflects on none of thofe Particulars
Which you have mention'd, though fome jealous Princes
In a Subject cannot brook 'em.

 Paul. None of thefe?
In what, then, am I worthy his Sufpicion?
But it may, nay it muft be, fome Informer,
To whom my Innocence appear'd a Crime,
Hath poifon'd his late good Opinion of me.
'Tis not to die, but, in the Cenfure of
So good a Mafter, guilty, that afflicts me.

Phila.

Phila. There is no Remedy.

Paul. No ?—I have a Friend, yet,
Could the Strictness of your Warrant give way to it,
To whom the State I stand in now deliver'd,
That by fair Intercession for me would
So far prevail, that, my Defence unheard,
I should not, innocent or guilty, suffer,
Without a fit Distinction.

Phila. These false Hopes,
My Lord, abuse you. What Man, when condemn'd,
Did ever find a Friend ? or who dares lend
An Eye of Pity to that Star-crofs'd Subject
On whom his Sovereign frowns ?

Paul. She that dares plead
For Innocence without a Fee ; the Emprefs,
My great and gracious Miftrefs.

Phila. There's your Error.
Her many Favours, which you hop'd should make you
Prove your Undoing. She, poor Lady, is
Banish'd for ever from the Emperor's Prefence,
And his confirm'd Sufpicion, to his Wrong,
That you have been over-familiar with her,
Dooms you to Death. I know you underftand me.

Paul. Over-familiar ?

Phila. In sharing with him
Thofe fweet and fecret Pleafures of his Bed,
Which can admit no Partner.

Paul. And is that
The Crime for which I am to die ? Of all
My num'rous Sins, was there not one of Weight
Enough to fink me, if he borrow'd not
The Colour of a Guilt I never faw,
To paint my Innocence in a deform'd
And monftrous Shape ? But that it were prophane
To argue Heav'n of Ignorance, or Injuftice,
I now should tax it. Had the Stars that reign'd
At my Nativity fuch curfed Influence,
As not alone to make me miferable,
But, in the Neighbourhood of her Goodnefs to me,

To

To force Contagion upon a Lady,
Whofe purer Flames were not inferior
To theirs, when they fhine brighteft ? To die for her,
Compar'd with what fhe fuffers, is a Trifle.
By her Example warn'd, let all great Women
Hereafter throw Pride and Contempt on fuch
As truly ferve 'em, fince a Retribution
In lawful Courtefies, is now ftil'd Luft,
And to be thankful to a Servant's Merits
Is grown a Vice, no Virtue.

    Phila. Thefe Complaints
Are to no Purpofe : Think on the long Flight
Your better Part muft make.

    Paul. She is prepar'd :
Nor can the freeing of an Innocent
From the Emperor's furious Jealoufy hinder her.
It fhall out, 'tis refolv'd, but to be whifper'd
To you alone. What a folemn Preparation
Is made here to put forth an Inch of Taper
In itfelf almoft extinguifh'd ? Mortal Poifon ?
The Hangman's Sword, the Haltar ?

    Phila. 'Tis left to you
To make Choice of which you pleafe.

    Paul. Any will ferve
To take away my Gout and Life together.
I would not have the Emperor imitate
Rome's Monfter, *Nero,* in that cruel Mercy
He fhew'd to *Seneca.* When you have difcharg'd
What you are trufted with, and I have giv'n you
Reafons beyond all Doubt or Difputation,
Of the Emprefs's and my Innocence ; when I am dead,
(Since 'tis my Mafter's Pleafure, and High Treafon
In you not to obey it) I conjure you,
By the Hopes you have of Happinefs hereafter,
Since mine in this World are now parting from me,
That you would win the young Man to Repentance
Of the Wrong done to his chafte Wife *Eudoxia*,
And if perchance he fhed a Tear for what

                                         In

In his Rafhnefs he impos'd on his true Servant,
So it cure him of future Jealoufy,
'Twill prove a precious Balfam, and find me
When I am in my Grave.—Now, when you pleafe,
For I am ready.

Phila. His Words work ftrangely on me,
And I would do — but I know not what to think on't.

[*Exeunt.*

SCENE II.

Pulcheria, Flaccilla, Arcadia, Timantus, Gratianus,
Chryfapius.

Pulch. Still in his fullen Mood? No Intermiffion
Of his melancholy Fit?

Timan. It rather, Madam,
Increafes, than grows lefs.

Grat. In the next Room
To his Bed-Chamber, we watch'd; for he by Signs
Gave us to underftand, he would admit
Nor Company, nor Conference.

Pulch. Did he take
No Reft, as you could guefs?

Chryf. Not any, Madam;
Like a *Numidian* Lion, by the Cunning
Of the defp'rate Huntfman, taken in a Toil,
And forc'd into a fpacious Cage, he walks
About his Chamber, we might hear him gnafh
His Teeth in Rage; which open'd, hollow Groans
And Murmurs iffu'd from his Lips, like Winds
Imprifon'd in the Caverns of the Earth
Striving for Liberty; and fometimes throwing
His Body on his Bed, then on the Ground,
And with fuch Violence, that we more than fear'd
And ftill do, if the Tempeft of his Paffions
By your Wifdom be not laid, he will commit
Some Outrage on himfelf.

Pulch. His better Angel,

I hope,

I hope, will ſtay him from ſo foul a Miſchief;
Nor ſhall my Care be wanting.

   Timan. Twice I heard him
Say, Falſe *Eudoxia!* how much art thou
Unworthy of theſe Tears! Then ſigh'd, and ſtraighc
Roar'd out, *Paulinus!* was his gouty Age
To be prefer'd before my Strength and Youth?
Then groan'd again, ſo many Ways expreſſing
Th' Afflictions of a tortur'd Soul, that we,
Who wept in vain for what we could not help,
Were Sharers in his Suff'rings.

   Pulch. Though your Sorrow
Is not to be condemn'd, it takes not from
The Burthen of his Miſeries. We muſt practiſe
With ſome freſh Object to divert his Thoughts
From that they're wholly fix'd on.

   Chryſ. Could I gain
The Freedom of Acceſs, I would preſent him
                             [*A Paper deliver'd.*
With this Petition. Will your Highneſs pleaſe
To look upon it: You will ſoon find there
What my Intents and Hopes are.

Enter Theodoſius.

   Grat. Ha! 'tis he.

   Pulch. Stand cloſe,
And give way to his Paſſions: 'tis not ſafe
To ſtop them in their violent Courſe, before
They've ſpent themſelves.

   Theod. I play the Fool, and am
Unequal to myſelf; Delinquents are
To ſuffer, not the Innocent. I have done
Nothing, which will not hold Weight in the Scale
Of my impartial Juſtice; neither feel
The Worm of Conſcience upbraiding me
With one black Deed of Tyranny; wherefore, then,
Should I torment myſelf? Great *Julius* would not
                                     Reſt

Reſt ſatisfy'd that his Wife was free from Faἀt,
But, only for Suſpicion of a Crime,
Su'd a Divorce ; nor was this *Roman* Rigour
Cenſur'd as cruel : And ſtill the wife *Italian*,
That knows the Honour of his Family
Depends upon the Purity of his Bed
For a Kiſs, nay, wanton Look, will plough up Miſchief,
And ſow the Seeds of his Revenge in Blood.
And ſhall I, to whoſe Power the Law's a Servant,
That ſtands accomptable to none, for what
My Will calls an Offence, being compell'd,
And on ſuch Grounds to raiſe an Altar to
My Anger; though, I grant, 'tis cemented
With a looſe Strumpet's and Adulterer's Gore,
Repent the Juſtice of my Fury ? No,
I ſhould not : Yet ſtill my Exceſs of Love,
Fed high in the Remembrance of her choice
And ſweet Embraces, would perſuade me that
Connivance, or Remiſſion of her Fault,
Made warrantable by her true Submiſſion
For her Offence, might be excuſable,
Did not the Cruelty of my wounded Honour
With an open Mouth deny it.
  Pulch. I approve of
Your good Intention, and I hope 'twill proſper.
                                            [*To* Chryſapius.
—He now ſeems calm. Let us upon our Knees
Encompaſs him. Moſt Royal Sir ——
  Flac. Sweet Brother ——
  Arcad. As you're our Sovereign, by the Ties of Nature
You're bound to be a Father in your Care
To us poor Orphans.
  Timant. Shew Compaſſion, Sir,
Unto yourſelf.
  Grat. The Majeſty of your Fortune
Should fly above the Reach of Grief.
  Chryſ. And 'tis
Impair'd, if you yield to it.

Theod. Wherefore pay you [6]
This Adoration to a finful Creature ?
I'm Flefh and Blood, as you are ; fenfible
Of Heat and Cold ; as much a Slave unto
The Tyranny of my Paffions, as the meaneft
Of my poor Subjects.   The proud Attributes
(By oil-tongu'd Flattery impos'd upon us)
As Sacred, Glorious, High, Invincible,
The Deputy of Heaven, and in that
Omnipotent, with all falfe Titles elfe
Coin'd to abufe our Frailty, though compounded,
And by the Breath of Sycophants apply'd,
Cure not the leaft Fit of an Ague in us.
We may give poor Men Riches ; confer Honours
On Undefervers ; raife, or ruin fuch
As are beneath us, and, with this puff'd up,
Ambition would perfuade us to forget
That we are Men : But He that fits above us,

[6] *Wherefore pay you*
    This Adoration to a finful Creature ?

Thefe Reflections are very beautiful and juft.   In *Shakefpear* we
have many of the like Kind, thus in *Richard* II. the unfortunate
King fays,

———————— Within the hollow Crown
That rounds the mortal Temples of a King,
Keeps Death his Court.   And there the Antic fits,
Scoffing his State, and grinning at his Pomp ;
Allowing him a Breath, a little Scene
To monarchize, be fear'd, and kill with Looks :
Infufing him with felf and vain Conceit,
As if this Flefh which walls about our Life,
Were Brafs impregnable : And humour'd thus,
Comes at the laft, and with a little Pin
Bores through his Caftle Walls, and farewel King !
Cover your Heads, and mock not Flefh and Blood
With folemn Rev'rence : Throw away Refpect,
Tradition, Form, and ceremonious Duty ;
For you have but miftook me all this while :
I live on Bread like you ; feel Want like you ;
Tafte Grief, want Friends like you : Subjected thus,
How can you fay to me, I am a King ?
                              Act IV. Scene 4.

                                        And

And to whom, at our utmoſt Rate, we are
But Pageant Properties, derides our Weakneſs.
In me, to whom you kneel, 'tis moſt apparent.
Can I call back Yeſterday, with all their Aids
That bow unto my Scepter? Or reſtore
My Mind to that Tranquillity and Peace
It then enjoy'd?—Can it make *Eudoxia* chaſte?
Or vile *Paulinus* honeſt?

Pulch. If I might,
Without Offence, deliver my Opinion ——
Theod. What would you ſay?
Pulch. That, on my Soul, the Empreſs
Is innocent.

Chryſ. The good *Paulinus* guiltleſs.
Grat. And this ſhould yield you Comfort.
Theod. In being guilty
Of an Offence, far, far tranſcending that
They ſtand condemn'd for. Call you this a Comfort,
Suppoſe it could be true? A Corroſive rather;
Not to eat our dead Fleſh, but putrify
What yet is found. Was Murther ever held
A Cure for Jealouſy? or the crying Blood
Of Innocence, a Balm to take away
Her feſt'ring Anguiſh?—As you do deſire
I ſhould not do a Juſtice on myſelf,
Add to the Proofs by which *Paulinus* fell,
And not take from 'em; in your Charity
Sooner believe that they were falſe, than I
Unrighteous in my Judgment? Subjects Lives
Are not their Prince's Tennis-Balls to be bandy'd
In Sport away. All that I can endure
For them, if they were Guilty, is an Atom
To the Mountain of Affliction I pull'd on me,
Should they prove innocent.

Chryſ. For your Majeſty's Peace
I more than hope they were not. The falſe Oath
Took by the Empreſs, and for which ſhe can
Plead no Excuſe, convicted her, and yields
A ſure Defence for your Suſpicion of her.

Z 2   And

And yet, to be refolv'd, fince ftrong Doubts are
More grievous, for the moft Part, than to know
A certain Lofs.——

    Theod. 'Tis true, *Chryfapius* ;
Were there a poffible Means.

    Chryf. 'Tis offer'd to you,
If you pleafe to embrace it.   Some few Minutes
Make Truce with Paffion ; and but read, and follow
What's there projeéted, you fhall find a Key
Will make your Entrance eafy to difcover
Her fecret Thoughts ; and then, as in your Wifdom
You fhall think fit, you may determine of her,
And reft confirm'd, whether *Paulinus* died
A Villain, or a Martyr.

    Theod. It may do ;
Nay, fure it muft : Yet, howfoever it fall,
I am moft wretched ; which Way in my Wifhes
I fhould fafhion the Event, I'm fo diftraéted
I cannot yet refolve of.—Follow me ;
Though in my Name, all Names are comprehended,
I muft have Witneffes, in what Degree
I have done Wrong, or fuffer'd.

    Pulch. Hope the beft, Sir.   [*Exeunt.*

SCENE III.

A fad Song.   Athenais *in Sack-cloth* ; *her Hair loofe.*

    Athen. *WHY* art thou *flow, thou* Reft *of* Trouble,
           Death,
      To ftop a Wretch's Breath,
  That calls on thee, and offers her fad Heart
      . *A Prey unto thy Dart ?*
  I am ncr young, nor fair ; *be, therefore, bold.*
      Sorrow hath made me old,
  Deform'd, and wrinkled ; *all that I can crave,*
      Is Quiet in my Grave.
  Such as live happy, hold Long Life a Jewel ;
      But to me thou art cruel ;

                             If

If thou end not my tedious Misery,
And I soon cease to be.
Strike, and strike home, then; Pity unto me,
In one short Hour's Delay is Tyranny.

Thus, like a dying Swan, to a sad Tune
I sing my own Dirge; would a Requiem follow,
Which in my Penitence I despair not of,
(This brittle Glass of Life already broken
With Misery) the long and quiet Sleep
Of Death would be most welcome.—Yet, before
We end our Pilgrimage, 'tis fit that we
Should leave Corruption, and foul Sins behind us.
But with wash'd Feet, and Hands, the Heathens dare not
Enter their prophane Temples; and for me
To hope my Passage to Eternity
Can be made easy, 'till I have shook off
The Burthen of my Sins in free Confession,
Aided with Sorrow, and Repentance for 'em,
Is against Reason. 'Tis not laying by
My royal Ornaments, or putting on
This Garment of Humility and Contrition;
The throwing Dust and Ashes on my Head;
Long Fasts to tame my proud Flesh, that can make
Attonement for my Soul; that must be humbled,
All outward Signs of Penitence, else, are useless.
Chrysapius did assure me, he would bring me
A holy Man, from whom (having discover'd
My secret, crying Sins) I might receive
Full Absolution.—And he keeps his Word.

Enter Theodosius, *like a Friar, with* Chrysapius.

Welcome, most Reverend Sir! upon my Knees
I entertain you,
   Theod. Noble Sir, forbear
The Place; The sacred Office that I come for
                        [*Exit* Chrysapius.
Commands all Privacy.—My penitent Daughter,
                       Be

Be careful, as you wish Remission from me,
That, in Confession of your Sins, you hide not
One Crime, whose pond'rous Weight, when you would
    make
Your Flights above the Firmament, may sink you.
A foolish Modesty in concealing aught
Is now far worse than Impudence to profess,
And justify your Guilt; be, therefore, free:
So may the Gates of Mercy open to you.

Athen. First then, I ask a Pardon, for my being
Ingrateful to Heav'n's Bounty.

Theod. A good Entrance.

Athen. Greatness comes from Above; and I, rais'd
    to it
From a low Condition, sinfully forgot
From whence it came, and, looking on myself
In the false Glass of Flattery, I receiv'd it
As a Debt due to my Beauty, not a Gift
Or Favour from the Emperor.

Theod. 'Twas not well.

Athen. Pride waited on Unthankfulness, and no more
Rememb'ring the Compassion of the Princess,
And the Means she us'd to make me what I was,
Contested with her, and with sore Eyes seeing
Her greater Light, as it dimm'd mine, I practis'd
To have it quite put out.

Theod. A great Offence;
But, on Repentance, not unpardonable.
Forward.

Athen. O Father!—what I now must utter,
I fear, in the Delivery will destroy me,
Before you have absolv'd me.

Theod. Heav'n is gracious,
Out with it.

Athen. Heav'n commands us to tell Truth.
Yet I, most sinful Wretch — forswore myself.

Theod. On what Occasion?

Athen. Quite forgetting that
An innocent Truth can never stand in need

Of a guilty Lie, being on the fudden afk'd
By the Emperor, my Hufband, for an Apple
Prefented by him, I fwore I had eaten it;
When my griev'd Confcience too well knows, I fent it
To comfort fick *Paulinus*, being a Man,
I truly lov'd and favour'd.
Theod. A cold Sweat,
Like the Juice of Hemlock, bathes me.   [*Afide.*
Atben. And from this
A furious Jealoufy getting Poffeffion
Of the good Emperor's Heart, in his Rage he doom'd
The innocent Lord to die, my Perjury
The fatal Caufe of Murder.
Theod. Take heed, Daughter,
You niggle not with your Confcience, and Religion, [7]
In ftiling him an Innocent from your Fear,
And Shame to accufe yourfelf. The Emperor
Had many Spies upon you, faw fuch Graces,
Which Virtue could not warrant, fhowr'd upon him;
Glances in publick, and more liberal Favours
In your private Chamber-meetings, making Way
For foul Adultery; nor could he be
But fenfible of the Compact pafs'd between you,
To the Ruin of his Honour.
Atben. Hear me, Father;
I look'd for Comfort; but, in this, you come
To add to my Afflictions.   ·
Theod. Caufe not you   ·
·Your own Damnation, in concealing that
Which may, in your Difcovery, find Forgivenefs.
Open your Eyes; fet Heaven, or Hell, before you,
In the revealing of the Truth, you fhall
Prepare a Palace for your Soul to dwell in,
Stor'd with Celeftial Bleffings; whereas, if

---

[7] Theod. *Take Heed, Daughter,*
    You niggle *not with your Confcience, and Religion.*
    The Word *niggle* I cannot find in any Dictionary, I am apt to think
it ought to be *Nifle,* which fignifies a Trifle, a Thing of little or no
Value.

You palliate your Crime, and dare beyond,
Playing with Lightning, in concealing it,
Expect a dreadful Dungeon, fill'd with Horror,
And never-ending Torments.

Atben. May they fall
Eternally upon me, and increase,
When that which we call Time hath lost its Name!
May Lightning cleave the Centre of the Earth,
And I fink quick, before you have abfolv'd me,
Into the bottomlefs Abyfs, if ever
In one unchafte Defire, nay, in a Thought
I wrong'd the Honour of the Emperor's Bed.
I do deferve, I grant more, than I fuffer,
In that, my Fervor and Defire to pleafe him,
In my holy Meditations, prefs'd upon me,
And would not be kept out, now to diffemble
(When I fhall fuddenly be infenfible
Of what the World fpeaks of me) were mere Madnefs:.
And, though you are incredulous, I prefume,
If, as I kneel now; my Eyes fwol'n with Tears,
My Hands heav'd up thus, my ftretch'd Heart-ftrings
      ready
To break afunder, my incenfed Lord
(His Storm of Jealoufy blown o'er) fhould hear me,
He would believe I lied not.

Theod. Rife, and fee him,   [*Difcovers himfelf.*
On his Knees, with Joy affirm it.

Atben. Can this be?

Theod. My Sifters, and the reft there,—all bear Wit-
      nefs.

Enter Pulcheria, Arcadia, Flaccilla, Chryfapius, Gra-
      tianus, Timantus, Philanax.

In freeing this incomparable Lady
From the Sufpicion of Guilt, I do
Accufe myfelf, and willingly fubmit
To any Penance, fhe in Juftice fhall
Pleafe to impofe upon me.

                                    Atben.

Atben. Royal Sir,
Your ill Opinion of me's foon forgiven.
  Pulcb. But how you can make Satisfaction to
The poor *Paulinus,* he being dead, in Reafon
You muft conclude impoffible.
  Theod. And in that
I am moft miferable : The Ocean
Of Joy, which in your Innocence flow'd high to me,
Ebbs in the Thought of my unjuft Command,
By which he died.   O *Philanax* (as thy Name
Interpreted fpeaks thee) thou haft ever been
A Lover of the King, and thy whole Life
Can witnefs thy Obedience to my Will,
In putting that in Execution, which
Was trufted to thee; fay but, yet, this once,
Thou haft not done what rafhly I commanded,
And that *Paulinus* lives, and thy Reward,
For not performing that which I enjoin'd thee,
Shall centuple whatever yet thy Duty,
Or Merit, challeng'd from me.
  Phila. 'Tis too late, Sir.
He's dead; and, when you know he was unable
To wrong you, in the Way that you fufpected,
You'll wifh it had been otherwife.
  Theod. Unable ?
  Phila. I am fure he was an Eunuch, and might fafely
Lie by a Virgin's Side; at four Years made one;
Though, to hold Grace with Ladies, he conceal'd it.
—The Circumftances, and the Manner how,
You may hear at better Leifure.
  Theod. How ! an Eunuch ?
The more the Proofs are, that are brought to clear thee,
My beft *Euaoxia,* the more my Sorrows.
  Atben. That I am innocent ?
  Theod. That I am guilty
Of Murther, my *Eudoxia.* I will build
A glorious Monument to his Memory;
And, for my Punifhment, live and die upon it, .
And never more converfe with Men.
                                        Enter

Enter Paulinus.

Paul. Live long, Sir!
May I do fo to ferve you! and, if that
I live does not difpleafe you, you owe for it
To this good Lord.
   Theod. Myfelf, and all that's mine.——
   Phila. Your Pardon is a Payment.
   Theod. I am rap'd
With Joy beyond myfelf. Now, my *Eudoxia*,
My Jealoufy puff'd away thus, in this Breath
I fcent the natural Sweetnefs.   [*Kiffes her.*
   Arcad. Sacred Sir,
I'm happy to behold this, and prefume,
Now you are pleas'd, to move a Suit, in which
My Sifter is join'd with me.
   Theod. Pr'ythee, fpeak it;
For I have vow'd to hear before I grant;
I thank your good Inftructions.   [*To* Pulcheria.
   Arcad. 'Tis but this, Sir.
We have obferv'd the falling out, and in,
Between the Hufband and the Wife fhews rarely;
Their Jars and Reconcilements ftrangely take us.
   Flac. Anger and Jealoufy that conclude in Kiffes
Is a fweet War, in footh.
   Arcad. We therefore, Brother,
Moft humbly beg you would provide us Hufbands,
That we may tafte the Pleafure of't.
   Flac. And with Speed, Sir;
For fo your Favour's doubled.
   Theod. Take my Word,
I will with all Convenience; and not blufh
Hereafter to be guided by your Counfels:
I will deferve your Pardon. *Philanax*
Shall be remember'd, and magnificent Bounties
Fall on *Chryfapius:* My Grace on all.

Let

Let *Cleon* be deliver'd and rewarded.
My Grace on all, which as I lend to you,
Return your Vows to Heaven, that it may pleafe
(As it is gracious) to quench in me
All future Sparks of burning Jealoufy.

F I N I S.

EPILOGUE.

EPILOGUE.

WE've Reafon to be doubtful, whether he,
On whom (forc'd to it by Neceffity)
The Maker did confer his Emperor's Part,
Hath giv'n you Satisfaction, in his Art
Of Action and Delivery ; 'tis fure Truth
The Burden was too heavy for his Youth *
To undergo.—But in his Will, we know,
He was not wanting, and fhall ever owe,
With his, our Service, if your Favours deign
To give him Strength, hereafter to fuftain
A greater Weight.   It is your Grace that can
In your Allowance of this, write him Man
Before his Time : which if you pleafe to do,
You make the Player and the Poet too.

---

* *The Burden was too heavy for his Youth.*

The Intent of this Epilogue is to apologize for fome young Actor
who performed the Part of the *Emperor*, and of whofe Abilities they
were fomething doubtful.

THE

MAID of HONOUR.

A

TRAGI-COMEDY.

As it hath been often prefented with good Allowance at the *Phœnix* in *Drury-Lane*, by the Queen's
Majefty's Servants. 1632.

WRITTEN

By PHILIP MASSINGER.

To my moſt honour'd Friends, Sir FRANCIS FOLIAMBE, Knt. and Bart. and to Sir THOMAS BLAND, Knt.

HAT you have been and continued ſo for many Years, ſince you vouchſafed to own me Patrons to me and my deſpiſed Studies, I cannot but with all humble Thankfulneſs acknowledge: And living, as you have done, inſeparable in your Friendſhip (notwithſtanding all Differences, and Suits in Law ariſing between you) I held it as impertinent, as abſurd, in the Preſentment of my Service in this Kind, to divide you. A free Confeſſion of a Debt in a meaner Man, is the ampleſt Satisfaction to his Superiors, and I heartily Wiſh, that the World may take Notice, and from myſelf, that I had not to this Time ſubſiſted, but that I was ſupported by your frequent Courteſies, and Favours. When your more ſerious Occaſions will give you Leave, you may pleaſe to peruſe this Trifle, and peradventure find ſomething in it that may appear worthy of your Protection. Receive it, I beſeech you, as a Teſtimony of his Duty, who, while he lives, reſolves to be

Truly and ſincerely devoted to your Service,

PHILIP MASSINGER.

Dramatis

Dramatis Personæ.

ROBERTO, King of *Sicily*.
FERDINAND, Duke of *Urbin*.
BERTOLDO, the King's natural Brother, a Knight of *Malta*.
GONZAGA, a Knight of *Malta*, General to the Dutchess of *Siena*.
ASTUTIO, a Counsellor of State.
FULGENTIO, the Minion of *Roberto*.
ADORNI, a Follower of *Camiola*'s Father.
AMBASSADOR, from the Duke of *Urbin*.
SIGNIOR SYLLI, a foolish Self-lover.
ANTHONIO, } Two rich Heirs, City-bred.
GASPARO, }
PIERIO, a Colonel to *Gonzaga*.
RODERIGO, } Captains to *Gonzaga*.
IACOMO, }
DRUSO, } Captains to Duke *Ferdinand*.
LIVIO, }
PAULO, a Priest, *Camiola*'s Confessor.

AURELIA, Dutchess of *Siena*.
CAMIOLA, the Maid of Honour.
CLARINDA, her Woman.
Scout, Soldiers, Servants, Gaoler, Dwarf, Mutes.

THE

THE
MAID of HONOUR.

ACT I. SCENE I.

The Presence Chamber.

Astutio, Adorni.

Adorni.

GOOD Day to your Lordship!

Astutio. Thanks, *Adorni.*

Adorni. May I presume to ask if the Ambassador
Employ'd by *Ferdinand*, the Duke of *Urbin*,
Hath Audience this Morning?

Enter Fulgentio.

Astutio. 'Tis uncertain,
For, though a Counsellor of State, I am not
Of the Cabinet Counsel. But there's one, if he please,
That may resolve you.

Adorni. I will move him Sir.

Fulgen. If you've a Suit, shew Water, I am blind, else.

Adorni. A Suit, yet of a Nature, not to prove
The Quarry that you hawk for: If your Words
Are not like *Indian* Wares, and every Scruple,
To be weigh'd and rated, one poor Syllable,
Vouchsaf'd in Answer of a fair Demand,
Cannot deserve a Fee.

Fulgen. It feems you're ignorant;
I neither fpeak, nor hold my Peace, for nothing:
And yet, for once, I care not if I anfwer
One fingle Queftion, *gratis.*

Adorni. I much thank you.
Hath the Ambaffador Audience, Sir, To-day?

Fulgen. Yes.

Adorni. At what Hour?

Fulgen. I promis'd not fo much.
A Syllable you begg'd; my Charity gave it.
Move me no further.   [*Exit* Fulgentio.

Aftutio. This you wonder at?
With me, 'tis ufual.

Adorni. Pray you, Sir, what is he?

Aftutio. A Gentleman, yet no Lord. He hath fome
    Drops
Of the King's Blood running in his Veins, deriv'd
Some ten Degrees off. His Revenue lies
In a narrow Compafs, the King's Ear; and yields him
Every Hour a fruitful Harveft: Men may talk
Of three Crops in a Year in the *Fortunate Iflands.*
Or Profit made by Wool: But, while there are Suitors,
His Sheep-fheering, nay, fhaving to the quick
Is in every Quarter of the Moon, and conftant.
In the Time of truffing a Point, he can undo,
Or make a Man. His Play or Recreation
Is to raife this up, or pull down that; and, though
He never yet took Orders, makes more Bifhops
In *Sicily,* than the Pope himfelf.

    Enter Bertoldo, Gafparo, Anthonio, *a Servant.*

Adorni. Moft ftrange!

Aftutio. The Prefence fills. He in the *Malta* Habit
Is the natural Brother of the King—a By-blow.

Adorni. I underftand you.

Gafp. 'Morrow to my Uncle.

Anth. And my late Guardian. But at length I have
The Reigns in my own Hands.

                           Aftutio.

Aſtutio. Pray you uſe 'em well,
Or you'll too late repent it.

Bert. With this Jewel
Preſented to *Camiola*, prepare
This Night a Viſit for me. I ſhall have [*Exit Servant.*
Your Company, Gallants, I perceive, if that
The King will hear of War.

Antb. Sir, I have Horſes
Of the beſt Breed in *Naples*, fitter far
To break a Rank, then crack a Lance, and are
In their Career of ſuch incredible Swiftneſs
They out-ſtrip Swallows.

Bert. And ſuch may be uſeful
To run away with, ſhould we be defeated.
You're well provided, Signior?

Antb. Sir, excuſe me.
All of their Race by Inſtinct know a Coward,
And ſcorn the Burthen. They come on like Lightning;
Founder'd in a Retreat.

Bert. By no means back 'em;
Unleſs you know your Courage ſympathize
With the daring of your Horſe.

Antb. My Lord, this is bitter.

Gaſp. I will raiſe me a Company of Foot;
And, when at puſh of Pike I am to enter
A Breach, to ſhew my Valour, I have brought me
An Armour Cannon-proof.

Bert. You will not leap, then,
O'er an Out-work in your Shirt?

Gaſp. I do not like
Activity that Way.

Bert. You had rather ſtand
A Mark to try their Muſkets on?

Gaſp. If I do
No Good, I'll do no Hurt.

Bert. 'Tis in you, Signior,
A Chriſtian Reſolution, and becomes you;
But I will not diſcourage you.

Antb.

Anth. You are, Sir,
A Knight of *Malta*, and, as I have heard,
Have ferv'd againft the *Turk*.

Bert. 'Tis true.

Anth. Pray you, fhew us
The Difference between the City-Valour,
And Service in the Field.

Bert. 'Tis fomewhat more
Then roaring in a Tavern, or a Brothel,
Or to fteal a Lanthorn from a fleeping Watch;
Then burn their Halberts; or, fafe-guarded by
Your Tenant's Son's, to carry away a Maypole
From a Neighbour-Village. You will not find, there,
Your Mafters of Dependencies to take up
A drunken Brawl, or, to get you the Names
Of valiant Chevaliers, Fellows that will be,
For a Cloak with thrice-dy'd Velvet, and a caft Suit,
Kick'd down the Stairs. A Knave with half a Breech,
        there,
And no Shirt (being a Thing-fuperfluous,
And worn out of his Memory) if you bear not
Yourfelves both in, and upright with a provant Sword,
Will flafh your Scarlets, and your Plufh a new Way;
Or with the Hilts thunder about your Ears
Such Mufick, as will make your Worfhips dance
To the doleful Tune of *Lachryma*,

Gafp. I muft tell you,
In private, as you are my princely Friend,
I do not like fuch Fidlers.

Bert. No? They are ufeful
For your Imitation; I remember you,
When you came firft to the Court, and talk'd of nothing
But your Rents, and your Entradas, [1] ever chiming

                                            The

---

[1] *Your Rents and your Entradas.*
Thus it ftands in the old Copies, the Senfe of which I take to be
    Your Rents and your *Comings in.*

                                            The

The Golden Bells in your Pockets, you believ'd
The taking of the Wall, as a Tribute due to
Your gaudy Cloaths.; and could not walk at Midnight
Without a caufelefs Quarrel, as if Men
Of coarfef Outfides were in Duty bound
To fuffer your Affronts: But, when you had been
Cudgel'd well, twice or thrice, and from the Doctrine
Made profitable Ufes, you concluded
The Sov'reign Means to teach irregular Heirs
Civility, with Conformity of Manners,
Were, two or three found Beatings.

 Antb. I confefs
They did much Good upon me.

 Gafp. And on me;—the Principles that they read were
  found

 Bert. You'll find
The like Inftructions in the Camp.

 Aftutio. The King——

A Flourifh.

Enter Roberto, Fulgentio, Ambaffador, *Attendants.*

 Rober. We fit prepared to hear.

 Ambaff. Your Majefty
Hath been long fince familiar, I doubt not,
With th' defp'rate Fortunes of my Lord; and Pity
O' th' much that your Confederate hath fuffer'd
(You being his laft Refuge) may perfuade you
Not alone to compaffionate, but to lend
Your Royal Aids, to ftay him in his Fall
To certain Ruin. He, too late, is confcious
That his Ambition to encroach upon
His Neighbour's Territories, with the Danger of

The Word *Entradas* I am apt to think is falfe, and that it ought to
be *Intrado* from the *Spanifh,* which fignifies the coming-in, *i. e.* into
any Place.

Thus *Shakefpear* in *Henry* 5th.

  What are thy Rents? What are thy Comings in?

           His

His Liberty, nay, his Life, hath brought in Queftion
His own Inheritance : But Youth and Heat
Of Blood, in your Interpretation, may
Both plead, and meditate for him. I muft grant it
An Error in him, being deny'd the Favours
Of the fair Princefs of *Siena* (though
He fought her in a noble Way) t' endeavour
To force Affection, by Surprifal of
Her principal Seat, *Siena,*

   Rober. Which now proves
The Seat of his Captivity, not Triumph.
Heav'n is ftill juft. [a]

   Ambaff. And yet that Juftice is
To be with Mercy temper'd, which Heav'n's Deputies

---

[a] Rober. *Heav'n is ftill juft*
  Ambaff. *And yet that Juftice is*
    To be with Mercy temper'd.

This is a very beautiful Paffage, and not lefs fo for being bor-
rowed from Religion. After the Ambaffador of the Duke of *Urbin*
had reprefented the Misfortunes of his Mafter, *Roberto* fays, that *Heaven is ftill juft*——"juft in punifhing the Ambitious." The Ambaffador anfwers, that "the Juftice of Heaven is tempered with Mercy,
which he, as Heaven's Deputy, ftands bound to minifter." This is a
fine Addrefs to the King's Paffions. He would reprefent the Mercy of
Heaven as infinite, and extended to all in Diftrefs : And how then
can the King refufe Mercy, when the Deity has fhewed his to all Men,
even to the King himfelf ? If this could not raife in him Sentiments of
Compaffion, yet furely the Thoughts of his being Heaven's Deputy
fhould. He was obliged by his Office to fhew Mercy as the Deity had
done, and to relieve as many of the Miferable as he could, becaufe
Heaven had relieved all Men. *Shakefpear* has very happily exprefs'd
this Thought in his *Meafure* for *Meafure. Angelo* fays to *Yfabella*

   Your Brother is a Forfeit of the Law,
   And you but wafte your Words.

 Ifab. Alas! alas!
   Why, all the Souls that are, were forfeit once,
   And he that might the 'Vantage beft have took,
   Found out the Remedy. How would you be,
   If he which is the top of Judgment, fhould
   But judge you as you are ? Oh! think on that;
   And Mercy then will breathe within your Lips,
   Like Man new made.

                      Act 2. Scene 7.

Stand bound to minifter. The injur'd Dutchefs
By Reafon taught, as Nature, could not, with
The Reparation of her Wrongs, but aim at
A brave Revenge; and my Lord feels too late
That Innocence will find Friends. The great *Gonzaga*,
The Honour of his Order—(I muft praife
Virtue, though in an Enemy) He whofe Fights
And Conquefts hold one Number, rallying up
Her fcatter'd Troops, before we could get Time
To victual, or to man the conquer'd City,
Sat down before it; and, prefuming that
'Tis not to be reliev'd, admits no Parley,
Our Flags of Truce hung out in vain: Nor will he
Lend an Ear to Compofition, but exacts
With th' rend'ring up the Town, the Goods, and Lives
Of all within the Walls, and of all Sexes
To be at his Difcretion.

   Rober. Since Injuftice
In your Duke meets this Correction, can you prefs us,
With any feeming Argument of Reafon,
In foolifh Pity to decline his Dangers,
To draw 'em on Our Self? Shall We not be
Warn'd by his Harms? The League, proclaim'd be-
     tween us,
Bound neither of us farther than to aid
Each other, if by foreign Force invaded;
And fo far in my Honour I was ty'd.
But, fince, without our Counfel, or Allowance,
He hath took Arms, with his good Leave, he muft
Excufe us, if we fteer not on a Rock
We fee, and may avoid. Let other Monarchs
Contend to be made glorious by proud War,
And with the Blood of their poor Subjects purchafe
Increafe of Empire, and augment their Cares
In keeping that which was by Wrongs extorted,
Gilding unjuft Invafions with the trim
Of glorious Conquefts; We, that would be known
The Father of our People in our Study
And Vigilance for their Safety, muft not change

Their Plough-fhares into Swords, and force them from
The fecure Shade of their own Vines to be
Scorch'd with the Flames of War, or, for our Sport,
Expofe their Lives to Ruin.

    Ambaff. Will you, then,
In his Extremity forfake your Friend ?

    Rober. No ; but preferve Our Self.

    Bert. Cannot the Beams
Of Honour thaw your icy Fears ?

    Rober. Who's that ?

    Bert. A kind of Brother, Sir ; howe'er, your Sub-
      ject,
Your Father's Son, and one who blufhes that
You are not Heir to his brave Spirit, and Vigour,
As to his Kingdom.

    Rober. How's this ?

    Bert. Sir, to be
His living Chronicle, and to fpeak his Praife,
Cannot deferve your Anger.

    Rober. Where's your Warrant
For this Prefumption ?

    Bert. Here, Sir, in my Heart.
Let Sycophants, that feed upon your Favours,
Stile Coldnefs in you Caution, and prefer
Your Eafe before your Honour ; and conclude
To eat and fleep fupinely, is the End
Of Human Blefsings : I muft tell you, Sir,
Virtue, if not in Action, is a Vice, [3]
And, when we move not forward, we go backward ;

---

    [3] —— *I muft tell you, Sir,*
      Virtue, if not in Action, is a Vice.

The Poets have many Paffages fimilar to this.   Thus *Shakefpear*

    —— If our Virtues
    Did not go forth of us, 'twere all alike
    As if we had them not.

            Meafure for *Meafure*, Act 1. Scene 2.

And *Horace* tells us, Virtue concealed is of little Confequence,

    Paulum fepultæ diftat inertiæ
    Celata virtus.

                               · Nor

Nor is this Peace (the Nurfe of Drones, and Cowards)
Our Health, but a Difeafe.

Gafp. Well urg'd, my Lord.

Anth. Perfect what is fo well begun.

Ambaff. And bind
My Lord your Servant.

Rober. Hare·brain'd Fool! What Reafon
Canft thou infer to make this Good?

Bert. A thoufand,
Not to be contradicted. But confider
Where your Command lies? 'Tis not, Sir, in *France,*
Spain, Germany, Portugal, but in *Sicily*;
An Ifland, Sir. Here are no Mines of Gold
Or Silver to enrich you; No Worm fpins
Silk in her Womb, to make Diftinction
Between you and a Peafant, in your Habits.
No Fifh lives near our Shores, whofe Blood can dye
Scarlet, or Purple; all that we poffefs,
With Beafts we have in common :. Nature did
Defign us to be Warriors, and to break through
Our Ring the Sea, by which we are environ'd;
And we by Force muft fetch in what is wanting,
Or precious to us. Add to this, we are
A populous Nation, and increafe fo faft,
That, if we by our Providence are not fent
Abroad in Colonies, or fall by the Sword,
Not *Sicily* (though now it were more fruitful
Than when 'twas ftil'd the Granary of great *Rome)*
Can yield our num'rous Fry Bread : We muft ftarve.
Or eat up one another.

Adorni. The King hears
With much Attention.   [*Afide.*

Aftutio. And feems mov'd with what
Bertoldo hath deliver'd.   [*Afide.*

Bert. May you live long, Sir,
The King of Peace, fo you deny not us
The Glory of the War; let not our Nerves
Shrink up with Sloth, nor, for want of Employment,
Make younger Brothers Thieves : 'Tis their Sword, Sir,
                                      Muft

Muſt ſow and reap their Harveſt. If Examples
May move you more than Arguments, look on *Eng-*
            land, 4
The Empreſs of the *European* Iſles,
And unto whom alone ours yields Precedence,
When did ſhe flouriſh ſo, as when ſhe was
The Miſtreſs of the Ocean? Her Navies
Putting a Girdle round about the World,
When the *Iberian* quak'd, her Worthies nam'd;
And the fair *Fleur de Lis* grew pale, ſet by
The Red Roſe and the White. Let not our Armour
Hung up, or our unrigg'd *Armada* make us
Ridiculous to the late poor Snakes our Neighbours
Warm'd in our Boſoms, and to whom again
We may be terrible; while we ſpend our Hours
Without Variety, confin'd to Drink,
Dice, Cards, or Whores. Rouze us, Sir, from the
            Sleep
Of Idleneſs, and redeem our mortgag'd Honours.
Your Birth, and juſtly, claims my Father's Kingdom;
But his heroic Mind deſcends to me:
—I will confirm ſo much.
    Adorni. In his Looks he ſeems
To break ope *Janus'* Temple.
    Aſtutio. How theſe Younglings
Take Fire from him!
    Ador. It works an Alteration
Upon the King.
    Anth. I can forbear no longer:
War, War, my Sovereign!
    Fulgen. The King appears
Reſolv'd, and does prepare to ſpeak.

---

4 ———— *Look on* England,
    The Empreſs of European *Iſles.*

All our old Poets have celebrated their Country, neither is *Meſ-
ſinger* wanting: As the Paſſages ſimilar to this are well known, I ſhall
forbear ſetting them down here.

                                            Rober.

Rober. Think not
Our Counsel's built upon so weak a Base,
As to be overturn'd, or shaken with
Tempestuous Winds of Words. As I, my Lord,
Before resolv'd you, I will not engage
My Person in this Quarrel, neither press
My Subjects to maintain it: Yet, to shew
My Rule is gentle, and that I've Feeling of
Your Master's Sufferings, since these Gallants, weary
Of the Happiness of Peace, desire to taste
The bitter Sweets of War, we do consent
That, as Adventurers, and Volunteers
(No Way compell'd by us) they may make Trial
Of their boasted Valours.

   Bert. We desire no more.

   Rober. 'Tis well ; and, but my Grant in this, expect
      not
Assistance from me. Govern as you please
The Province you make Choice of ; for, I vow
By all Things sacred, if that thou miscarry
In this rash Undertaking, I will hear it
No otherwise than as a sad Disaster,
Fall'n on a Stranger ; nor will I esteem
That Man my Subject, who, in thy Extremes,
In Purse or Person aids thee. Take your Fortune:
You know me ; I have said it. So, my Lord,
You have my whole Answer.

   Ambass. My Prince pays
In me his Duty.

   Rober. Follow me, *Fulgentio,*
And you, *Astutio.*   [*Exeunt* Roberto, Fulgentio,
                    Astutio, *Attendants.*

   Gasp. What a Frown he threw,
At his Departure, on you.

   Bert. Let him keep
His Smiles for his State-Catamite ; I care not.

   Anth. Shall we aboard To-night ?

   Ambass. Your Speed, my Lord,
Doubles the Benefit.

                               Bert.

Bert. I have a Bufinefs
Requires Difpatch. — Some two Hours hence I'll meet
    you.   [*Exeunt.*

SCENE II.

Camiola's *Houfe.*

Signior Sylli, *walking fantaftically before, followed by*
Camiola *and* Clarinda.

Camiola. Nay, Signior, this is too much Ceremony
In my own Houfe.

Sylli. What's gracious abroad,
Muft be in Private practis'd.

Clar. For your Mirth-fake
Let him alone, he has been all this Morning
In Practice with a peruk'd Gentleman-Ufher,
To teach him his true Amble and his Poftures,
         [Sylli *walking by, and practifing his Poftures.*
When he walks before a Lady.

Sylli. You may, Madam,
Perhaps, believe that I in this ufe Art,
To make you doat upon me by expofing
My more than moft rare Features to your View.
But I, as I have ever done, deal fimply;
A Mark of fweet Simplicity, ever noted
I' th' Family of the *Syllies.* Therefore, Lady,
Look not with too much Contemplation on me;
If you do, you are i' th' Suds.

Camiola. You are no Barber?

Sylli. Fie! no, not I; but my good Parts have drawn
More loving Hearts out of fair Ladies Bellies,
Than the whole Trade have done Teeth.

Camiola. Is't poffible?

Sylli. Yes, and they live too; marry, much condoling
The Scorn of their *Narciffus,* as they call me,
Becaufe I love myfelf.

Camiola. Without a Rival.
What Philtres or Love-powders do you ufe

                                 To

To force Affection ? I fee nothing in
Your Perfon; but I dare look on, yet keep
My own poor Heart ftill.

 Sylli. You are warn'd — be arm'd;
And do not lofe the Hope of fuch a Hufband,
In being too foon enamour'd.

 Clar. Hold in your Head,
Or you muft have a Martingale.

 Sylli. I have fworn.
Never to take a Wife, but fuch a one
(O may your Ladyfhip prove fo ftrong!) as can
Hold out a Month againft me.

 Camiola. Never fear it;
Tho' your beft taking Part, your Wealth, were trebled,
I would not woo you, But, fince in your Pity
You pleafe to give me Caution, tell me what
Temptations I muft fly from.

 Sylli. The firft is,
That your ne'er hear me fing; for I'm a Syren.
If you obferve, when I warble, the Dogs howl,
As ravifh'd with my Ditties, and you will
Run mad to hear me.

 Camiola. I will ftop my Ears,
And keep my little Wits.

 Sylli. Next, when I dance,
And come aloft, thus, caft not a Sheep's Eye
Upon the Quiv'ring of my Calf.

 Camiola. Proceed, Sir.

 Sylli. But on no Terms (for 'tis a main Point) dream
   not
O' th' Strength of my Back, though 'twill bear a Burthen
With any Porter.

 Camiola. I mean not to ride you.

 Sylli. Nor I your little Ladyfhip, 'till you have
Perform'd the Covenant.—Be not taken with
My pretty Spider-Fingers; nor my Eyes,
That twinkle on both Sides.

 Camiola. Was there ever fuch   *[One knocks.*
A Piece of Motley heard of! —Who's that; you may
   fpare   The

The Catalogue of my Dangers.   [*Exit* Clarinda.

Sylli. No, good Madam;
I have not told you half.

Camiola. Enough, good Signior;
If I eat more of such Sweet-meats, I shall surfeit.

Enter Clarinda.

Who is't?

Clar. The Brother of the King.

Sylli. Nay, start not.
The Brother of the King! Is he no more?
Were it the King himself, I'd give him Leave
To speak his Mind to you, for I'm not jealous;
And, to assure your Ladyship of so much,
I'll usher him in, and, that done—hide myself.

[*Exit* Sylli.

Camiola. Camiola, if ever, now be constant:
This is, indeed, a Suitor, whose sweet Presence,
Courtship, and loving Language, would have stagger'd
The chaste *Penelope*; and, to increase
The Wonder, did not Modesty forbid it,
I should ask that from him, he sues to me for.
And yet my Reason, like a Tyrant, tells me
I must nor give, nor take it.

Enter Sylli *and* Bertoldo.

Sylli. I must tell you,
You lose your Labour. 'Tis enough to prove it,
Signior *Sylli* came before you; and you know,
First come, first serv'd: Yet, you shall have my Coun-
            tenance
To parley with her; and I'll take special Care
That none shall interrupt you.

Bert. You are courteous.

Sylli. Come, Wench, wilt thou hear Wisdom?

[*Steps aside.*

Clar. Yes, from you, Sir.

Bert.

Bert. If forcing this sweet Favour from your Lips,

[*Kisseth her.*

Fair Madam, argue me of too much Boldness
When you are pleas'd to understand, I take
A parting Kiss, if not excuse, at least
'Twill qualify th' Offence.

Camiola. A parting Kiss, Sir?
What Nation, envious of the Happiness
Which *Sicily* enjoys in your sweet Presence,
Can buy you from her? or what Climate yield
Pleasures transcending those which you enjoy here,
Being both belov'd and honour'd? the North-Star
And Guider of all Hearts, and, to sum up
Your full Accompt of Happiness in a Word,
The Brother of the King.

Bert. Do you, alone,
And with an unexampled Cruelty,
Enforce my Absence, and deprive me of
Those Blessings, which you with a polish'd Phrase
Seem to insinuate that I do possess,
And yet tax me as being guilty of
My wilful Exile? What are Titles to me?
Or Popular Suffrage? or my Nearness to
The King in Blood? or fruitful *Sicily*,
Though it confess'd no Sovereign but myself;
When you, that are the Essence of my Being,
The Anchor of my Hopes, the real Substance
Of my Felicity, in your Disdain
Turn all to fading and deceiving Shadows?

Camiola. You tax me without Cause.

Bert. You must confess it.
But, answer Love with Love, and seal the Contract
In the uniting of our Souls, how gladly
(Though now I were in Action, and assur'd,
Following my Fortune, that plum'd Victory
Would make her glorious Stand upon my Tent)
Would I put off my Armour, in my Heat
Of Conquest, and, like *Anthony*, pursue
My *Cleopatra*! Will you yet look on me

With

With an Eye of Favour?

Camiola. Truth bear Witnefs for me,
That, in the Judgment of my Soul, you are
A Man fo abfolute, and circular
In all thofe wifh'd-for Rarities, that may take
A Virgin captive, that, though at this Inftant
All fcepter'd Monarchs of our Weftern World
Were Rivals with you, and *Camiola* worthy
Of fuch a Competition, you alone
Should wear the Garland.

Bert. If fo, what diverts
Your Favour from me?

Camiola. No Mulct in yourfelf;
Or in your Perfon, Mind, ot Fortune.

Bert. What then?

Camiola. The Confcioufnefs of mine own Wants.——
              Alas! Sir, [5]
We are not Parallels; but, like Lines divided,
Can ne'er meet in one Center. Your Birth, Sir,
(Without Addition) were an ample Dowry
For one of fairer Fortunes; and this Shape,
Were you ignoble, far above all Value:
To this fo clear a Mind, fo furnifh'd with
Harmonious Faculties, moulded from Heaven,
That, though you were *Therfites* in your Features,
Of no Defcent, and *Irus* in your Fortunes,
Ulyffes like, you'd force all Eyes and Ears
To love, but feen; and, when heard, wonder at
Your matchlefs Story. But, all thefe bound up
Together in one Volume, give me Leave
With Admiration to look upon 'em;
But not prefume, in my own flatt'ring Hopes,
I may, or can, enjoy 'em.

---

5 ———— *Alas! Sir,*
We are not Parallels; but, like Lines divided,
Can ne'er meet in one Center.

This feems badly expreffed. Parallels are the only Lines that
cannot meet in a Center; for all Lines divided with any Angle towards each other, muft meet fomewhere, if continued both Ways.

                                                Bert.

Bert. How you ruin
What you would feem to build up! I know no
Difparity between us; you're an Heir
Sprung from a noble Family; fair, rich, young,
And ev'ry Way my Equal.

  Camiola. Sir, excufe me,[6]
One airy with Proportion, ne'er difclofes
The Eagle and the Wren: Tiffue and Frize,
In the fame Garment, monftrous: But, fuppofe
That what's in you exceffive, were diminifh'd,
And my Defert fupply'd, the ftrongeft Bar,
Religion, ftops our Entrance. You are, Sir,
A Knight of *Malta*, by your Order bound
To a fingle Life: You cannot marry me;
And, I affure myfelf, you are too noble
To feek me (though my Frailty fhould confent)
In a bafe Path.

  Bert. A Difpenfation, Lady,
Will eafily abfolve me.

  Camiola. O take heed, Sir!
When what is vow'd to Heav'n is difpens'd with,
To ferve our Ends on Earth, a Curfe muft follow,
And not a Bleffing.

  Bert. Is there no Hope left me?

  Camiola. Nor to myfelf, but is a Neighbour to
Impoffibility. True Love fhould walk
On equal Feet; in us it does not, Sir.
But reft affur'd, excepting this, I fhall be
Devoted to your Service.

Bert. And this is your
Determinate Sentence ?

Camiola. Not to be revok'd.

Bert. Farewel, then, faireſt Cruel ! All Thoughts in
Of Women periſh ! Let the glorious Light   [me
Of noble War extinguiſh Love's divine 'aper,
That only lends me Light to ſee my Folly !
Honour, be thou my ever living Miſtreſs,
And fond Affection as thy Bond-ſlave ſerve thee !

　　　　　　　　　　　　　　[*Exit* Bertoldo.

Camiola. How ſoon my Sun is ſet ! He being abſent,
Never to riſe again ! What a fierce Battle
Is fought between my Paſſions !—Methinks
We ſhould have kiſs'd at Parting.

Sylli. I perceive
He has his Anſwer.—Now muſt I ſtep in
To comfort her. You have found, I hope, ſweet Lady,
Some Difference between a Youth of my Pitch,
And this Bug-bear *Bertoldo.* Men are Men,
The King's Brother is no more : Good Parts will do it,
When Titles fail.—Deſpair not ; I may be
In Time entreated.

Camiola. Be ſo now, to leave me.
Lights for my Chamber.—O my Heart !

　　　　　　　　　　　　　[*Exeunt* Camiola *and* Clarinda.

Sylli. She now,
I know, is going to Bed to ruminate
Which Way to glut herſelf upon my Perſon ;
But, for my Oath-ſake, I will keep her hungry ;
And, to grow full myſelf, I'll ſtrait to Supper.

　　　　　　　　　　　　　　　　　　[*Exit.*

The End of the Firſt Act.

✖✖✖✖✖✖✖✖✖✖✖✖✖✖✖✖✖✖✖✖✖✖✖✖

ACT II. SCENE I.

The Palace at Palermo.

Roberto, Fulgentio, Aſtutio.

Rober. EMbarq'd To-night, do you ſay ?
   Fulgen. I ſaw him aboard, Sir.
Rober. And without taking of his Leave ?
Aſtutio. 'Twas ſtrange !
Rober. Are we grown ſo contemptible ?
Fulgen. 'Tis far from me, Sir, to add Fuel to your
   Anger,
That in your ill Opinion of him burns
Too hot already ; elſe, I ſhould affirm
It was a groſs Neglect.
 Rober. A wilful Scorn
Of Duty and Allegiance ; you give it
Too fair a Name.—But we ſhall think on't. Can you
Gueſs what the Numbers were that follow'd him
In his deſperate Action ?
 Fulgen. More than you think, Sir.
All ill-affected Spirits in *Palermo,*
Or to your Government, or Perſon, with
The turbulent Sword-men ; ſuch, whoſe Poverty forc'd
To wiſh a Change, are gone along with him ; ['em
Creatures devoted to his Undrtakings,
In Right or Wrong, and, to expreſs their Zeal,
And Readineſs to ſerve him, ere they went,
Prophanely took the Sacrament on their Knees,
To live and die with him.
 Rober. O moſt impious !
Their Loyalty to us forgot ?
 Fulgen. I fear ſo.
 Aſtutio. Unthankful as they are !
 Fulgen. Yet this deſerves not

On

One troubled Thought in you, Sir ; with your Pardon
I hold that their Remove from hence makes more
For your Security, than Danger.
   Rober. True ;
And, as I'll fashion it, they shall feel it too.
Astutio, you shall presently be dispatch'd
With Letters writ, and sign'd with our own Hand,
To the Dutchess of *Siena,* in Excuse
Of these Forces sent against her. , If you spare
An Oath to give it Credit, that we never
Consented to it, swearing for the King,
Though false, it is no Perjury.
   Astutio. I know it.
They are not fit to be State Agents, Sir,
That, without Scruple of their Conscience cannot
Be prodigal in such Trifles.
   Fulgen. Right, *Astutio.*
   Rober. You must, beside, from us take some In-
     structions,
To be imparted, as you judge 'em useful,
To the General *Gonzaga.* Instantly
Prepare you for your Journey.
   Astutio. With the Wings
Of Loyalty and Duty   [*Exit* Astutio.
   Fulgen. I am bold to put your Majesty in Mind—
   Rober. Of my Promise,
And Aids, to further you in your am'rous Project
To the fair and rich *Camiala :* There's my Ring ;
Whatever you shall say that I intreat,
Or can command by Pow'r, I will make good.
   Fulgen. -Ever your Majesty's Creature.
   Rober. Venus prove propitious to you !
                    [*Exit* Roberto.
   Fulgen. All sorts to my Wishes.
Bertoldo was my Hindrance. He remov'd,
I now will court her in the Conqu'ror's Stile ;
" Come, see, and overcome."——Boy !

Enter Page.

Page. Sir, your Pleafure!

Fulgen. Hafte to *Camiola* ; bid her prepare
An Entertainment fuitable to a Fortune
She could not hope for. Tell her, I vouchfafe
To honour her with a Vifit.

Page. 'Tis a Favour
Will make her proud.

Fulgen. I know it.

Page. I am gone, ·Sir.   *[Exit Page.*

Fulgen. Entreaties fit not me ; a Man in Grace
May challenge Awe, and Privilege, by his Place.
              [Exit Fulgentio.

S C E N E II.

Camiola's *Houfe.*

Sylli, Adorni, Clarinda.

Adorni. So melancholick, fay you ?

Clar. Never given
To fuch Retirement.

Adorni. Can you guefs the Caufe ?

Clar. If it hath not its Birth, and Being, from
The brave *Bertoldo's* Abfence, I confefs
'Tis paft my Apprehenfion.

Sylli. You are wide ;
The whole Field wide. I, in my Underftanding,
Pity your Ignorance.—Yet, if you will
Swear to conceal it, I will let you know
Where her Shoe wrings her.

Clar. I vow, Signior,
By my Virginity.

Sylli. A perilous Oath,
In a Waiting-Woman of Fifteen! and is, indeed,
A Kind of Nothing.

Adorni. I'll take one of Something,

         . If

If you pleafe to minifter it.

   Sylli. Nay, you fhall not fwear :
I had rather take your Word ; for, fhould you vow,
Damn me, I'll do this, you are fure to break.

   Adorni. I thank you, Signior ; but refolve us ——

   Sylli. Know, then,
Here walks the Caufe. She dares not look upon me ;
My Beauties are fo terrible, and enchanting,
She can't endure my Sight.

   Adorni. There I believe you.

   Sylli. But the Time will come (be comforted) when
      I will
Put off this Vizor of Unkindnefs to her,
And fhew an amorous and yielding Face :
And, until then, though *Hercules* himfelf
Defire to fee her, he had better eat
His Club than pafs her Threfhold ; for I'll be
Her *Cerberus* to guard her,

   Adorni. A good Dog !

   Clar. Worth twenty Porters.

Enter Page.

   Page. Keep you Open Houfe, here ?
No Groom t' attend a Gentleman ? O, I fpy one.

   Sylli. He means not me, I am fure.

   Page. You, Sirrah ! Sheep's-head,
With a Face cut on a Cat-ftick, Do you hear ?
You Yeoman-Phewterer, [7] conduct me to
The Lady of the Manfion ; or my Poignard
Shall difembogue thy Soul.

   Sylli. O terrible !
Difembogue ? I talk'd of *Hercules*, and here is one
Bound up in *decimo-fexto*.

   Page. Anfwer, Wretch.

---

   [7] *You, Yeoman-Phewterer.* i. e. You Journeyman.——In the *Picture*,
Act 5. Scene 1. we find the fame Expreffion varied: It is there
Yeoman Phenterer.

                                   Sylli.

Sylli. Pray you, little Gentleman, be not so furious;
The Lady keeps her Chamber.

Page. And we present?
Sent in an Embassy to her? But here is
Her Gentlewoman, Sirrah! hold my Cloak,
While I take a Leap at her Lips. Do it and neatly;
Or having first tripp'd up thy Heels, I'll make
Thy Back my Footstool. [*Page kisses* Clarinda.

Sylli. *Tamerlane* in little!
Am I turn'd *Turk?* What an Office am I put to!

Clar. My Lady, gentle Youth, is indispos'd.

Page. Though she were dead and buried, only tell her,
The great Man in the Court, the brave *Fulgentio,*
Descends to visit her, and it will raise her
Out of the Grave for Joy.

Enter Fulgentio.

Sylli. Here comes another!
The Devil, I fear in his Holiday Cloaths.

Page. So soon!
My Part is at an End then. Cover my Shoulders;
When I grow great, thou shalt serve me.

Fulgen. Are you, Sirrah,
An Implement of the House?

Sylli. Sure he will make
A Joint-stool of me!

Fulgen. Or, if you belong
To the Lady of the Place, command her hither.

Adorni. I do not wear her Livery; yet acknowledge
A Duty to her. And as little bound
To serve your peremptory Will, as she is
To obey your Summons. 'Twill become you, Sir,
To wait her Leisure; then, her Pleasure known,
You may present your Duty.

Fulgen. Duty, Slave?
I'll teach you Manners.

Adorni. I'm past Learning; make not
A Tumult in the House.

Fulgen.

Fulgen. Shall I be brav'd thus?   [*They draw.*
Sylli. O I am dead! and now I fwoon.
Clar. Help! Murther!   [*Falls on his Face.*
Page. Recover, Sirrah! the Lady's here.

Enter Camiola.

Sylli. Nay, then
I am alive again, and I'll be valiant.
    Camiola. What Infolence is this?   *Adorni* Hold,
Hold, I command you.
    Fulgen. Saucy Groom!
    Camiola. Not fo, Sir;
However, in his Life, he had Dependance
Upon my Father; he is a Gentleman
As well born as yourfelf. Put on your Hat.
    Fulgen. In my Prefence, without Leave?
    Sylli. He has mine, Madam?
    Camiola. And I muft tell you, Sir, and in plain Lan-
        guage,
Howe'er your glitt'ring Outfide promife Gentry,
The Rudenefs of your Carriage and Behaviour
Speaks you a coarfer Thing.
    Sylli. She means a Clown, Sir:
I am her Interpreter, for want of a better.
    Camiola. I am a Queen in mine own Houfe; nor muft
        you
Expect an Empire here.
    Sylli. Sure, I muft love her
Before the Day, the pretty Soul's fo valiant.
    Camiola. What are you? And what would you with
        me?
    Fulgen. Proud one,
When you know what I am, and what I came for,
And may, on your Submiffion, proceed fo,
You in your Reafon muft repent the Coarfenefs
Of my Entertainment.
    Camiola. Why, fine Man, what are you?

                      Fulgen.

Fulgen. A Kinſman of the King's.

Camiola. I cry you Mercy !
For his Sake, not your own.   But, grant you are ſo,
'Tis not impoſſible, but a King may have
A Fool to's Kinſman,—no Way meaning you, Sir.

Fulgen. You have heard of *Fulgentio.*

Camiola. Long ſince, Sir;
A Suit-broker in Court.   He has the worſt
Report, among good Men, I ever heard of,
For Bribery and Extortion : In their Prayers
Widows and Orphans curſe him for a Canker
And Caterpiller in the State.   I hope, Sir,
You're not the Man ;   much leſs employ'd by him
As a Smock-agent to me.

Fulgen. I reply not
As you deſerve, being aſſur'd you know me,
Pretending Ignorance of my Perſon, only
To give me a Taſte of your Wit: 'Tis well and courtly;
I like a ſharp Wit well.

Sylli. I can't endure it !
Nor any of the *Syllies.*

Fulgen. More I know too,
This harſh Induction muſt ſerve as a Foil
To the well-tun'd Obſervance and Reſpect
You will hereafter pay me, being made
Familiar with my Credit with the King,
And that contain your Joy I deign to love you.

Camiola. Love me ? I am not rap'd with't.

Fulgen. Hear't again.
I love you honeſtly—Now you admire me.

Camiola. I do, indeeed, it being a Word ſo ſeldom
Heard from a Courtier's Mouth, But, pray you, deal
          plainly,
Since you find me ſimple, what might be the Motives
Inducing you to leave the Freedom of
A Batchelor's Life, on your ſoft Neck to wear,
The ſtubborn Yoke of Marriage ? And, of all
The Beauties in *Palermo*, to chooſe me,
Poor me ? That is the main Point you muſt treat of.

Fulgen.

Fulgen. Why, I will tell you. Of a little Thing
You are a pretty Piece, indifferently fair too;
And like a new rigg'd Ship both tight, and y'are
Well trufs'd to bear. Virgins of Giant Size
Are Sluggards at the Sport: But, for my Pleafure,
Give me a neat well-timber'd Gamefter like you;
Such need no Spurs,—the Quicknefs of your Eye
Affures an active Spirit.

Camiola. You're pleafant, Sir;
Yet I prefume that there was one Thing in me
Unmention'd yet, that took you more than all
Thofe Parts you have remember'd.

Fulgen. What?

Camiola. My Wealth, Sir.

Fulgen. You are i'th' right; without that, Beauty is *
A Flower worn in the Morning, at Night trod on:
But, Beauty, Youth, and Fortune meeting in you,
I will vouchfafe to marry you.

Camiola. You fpeak well;
And, in Return, excufe me, Sir, if I
Deliver Reafons why, upon no Terms,
I'll marry you; I fable not.

Sylli. I'm glad
To hear this; I began to have an Ague. [*Afide.*

Fulgen. Come, your wife Reafons.

Camiola. Such as they are, pray you, take them.
Firft, I am doubtful whether you are a Man,
Since, for your Shape trim'd up in a Lady's Dreffing,
You might pafs for a Woman: Now I love
To deal on Certainties. And, for the Fairnefs
Of your Complexion, which you think will take me,
The Colour, I muft tell you, in a Man
Is weak and faint, and never will hold out
If put to Labour. Give me the lovely brown.

* ———— *Beauty is*
A Flower worn in the Morning, at Night trod on.
This Thought is happily exprefs'd by Mr. *Gay* in the fixth Air of
the *Beggar's Opera.*

Act 1. Scene 7.
A

A thick curl'd Hair of the fame Dye; broad Shoulders;
A brawny Arm full of Veins; a Leg without
An artificial Calf;—I fufpect yours;
But let that pafs.

Sylli. She means me, all this while,
For I have every one of thofe good Parts,
O *Sylli!* fortunate *Sylli!*

Camiola. You are mov'd, Sir.

Fulgen. Fie! no; go on.

Camiola. Then, as you are a Courtier,
A grac'd one too, I fear you have been too forward:
And fo much for your Perfon.   Rich you are,
Devilifh rich, as 'tis reported, and fure have
The Aids of *Satan's* little Fiends to get it;
And what is got upon his Back, muft be
Spent you know where; the Proverb's ftale.   One Word
     more,
And I have done.

Fulgen. I'll eafe you of the Trouble,
Coy, and difdainful.

Camiola. Save me, or elfe he'll beat me.

Fulgen. No, your own Folly fhall; and, fince you
     put me
To my laft Charm, look upon this, and tremble.
                         [*Shews the King's Ring.*

Camiola. At the Sight of a fair Ring? The King's, I
     take it:
I have feen him wear the like: If he hath fent it
As a Favour to me——

Fulgen. Yes, 'tis very likely;
His dying Mother's Gift, priz'd at his Crown.
By this he does command you to be mine;
By his Gift you are fo:—You may, yet, redeem all.

Camiola. You are in a wrong Account ftill.   Though
     the King may
Difpofe of my Life and Goods, my Mind's mine own,
And never fhall be your's. The King (Heav'n blefs him!)
Is good and gracious, and, being in himfelf
Abftemious from bafe and goatifh Loofenefs,

                                        Will

Will not compel, againſt their Wills, chaſte Maidens,
To dance in his Minion's Circles. I believe,
Forgetting it, when he waſh'd his Hands, you ſtole it
With an Intent to awe me. But you are cozen'd;
I'm ſtill myſelf, and will be.

Fulgen. A proud Haggard,
And not to be reclaim'd! Which of your Grooms,
Your Coachman, Fool, or Footman, Miniſters
Night-phyſick to you?

Camiola. You're foul-mouth'd,

Fulgen. Much fairer
Than thy black Soul; and ſo I will proclaim thee.——

Camiola. Were I a Man, thou durſt not ſpeak this.

Fulgen. Heaven
So proſper me, as I reſolve to do it
To all Men, and in every Place,—ſcorn'd by
A Tit of Ten-pence? [*Exit* Fulgentio *and his Page.*

Sylli. Now I begin to be valiant:
Nay, I will draw my Sword. O for a Butcher! [9]
Do a Friend's Part; 'Pray you, carry him the Length
  of 't.
I give him three Years and a Day, to match my Toledo;
And then we'll fight like Dragons.

Adorni. Pray, have Patience.

Camiola. I may live to have Vengeance: My *Bertoldo*
Would not have heard this.

Adorni. Madam.——

Camiola. 'Pray you, ſpare
Your Language; Pr'thee Fool, make me merry:

Sylli. That is my Office, ever.

---

[9] ———— *O for a Butcher!*
Do a Friends Part, &c.

This is a true Picture of a Fop. He is here drawn in his proper
Features—A Coward. Nothing could be more abjectly fearful, than
this our Bravado, when in Danger: But, now his Enemy is gone, he
ſwaggers about moſt courageouſly. *Now I begin to be valiant; nay, I
will draw my Sword. O for a Butcher!* The bloody cruel Temper of
one: He wiſhes he could act like one of them. Then turning to
Adorni with the ſame intrepid Reſolution, he ſays, *Do a Friend's Part;
pray you, carry him the Length of 't,* &c.

Adorni.

Adorni. I muſt do,
Not talk; this glorious Gallant ſhall hear from me. [10]
[*Exeunt.*

SCENE III.

The Caſtle at Siena.

The Chambers diſcharg'd.   A Flouriſh, as to an Aſſault.
    Gonzaga, Pierio, Roderigo, Jacomo, *Soldiers.*

Gonz. IS the Breach made aſſaultable ?
Pierio.   Yes, and the Moat
Fill'd up ; the Cannoneer hath done his Parts,
We may enter ſix a-breaſt.
    Roder. There's not a Man
Dares ſhew himſelf upon the Wall.
    Jacomo. Defeat not
The Soldiers hoped-for Spoil.
    Pierio. If you, Sir,
Delay the Aſſault, and the City be given up
To your Diſcretion, you in Honour cannot
Uſe the Extremity of War, but, in
Compaſſion to 'em, you to us prove cruel.
    Jacomo. And an Enemy to yourſelf.
    Roder. A Hindrance to
The brave Revenge you've vow'd.
    Gonz. Temper your Heat,
And loſe not, by too ſudden Raſhneſs, that
Which, be but Patient, will be offer'd to you.
Security uſhers Ruin ; proud Contempt
Of an Enemy, three Parts vanquiſh'd, with Deſire

[10] The foregoing Scene we ſtill find is a perfect Repreſentation of *the Inſolence of Office.* Power inebriates: But few have Strength to bear i'. It turns the Heads of the *many*, and makes them think their Station is a Protection for whatever they ſay or do. They have a cer-tain Self-ſufficiency that bears them out in every Thing ; even like *Fulgentio* againſt good Manners and Virtue: They think like him that whatever their Soul luſteth after they can attain it ; that *there is no Man they cannot bribe—and no Woman they cannot lie with.*

And

And Greedinefs of Spoil, hath often wrefted
A certain Victory from the Conqu'ror's Gripe.
Difcretion is the Tutor of the War,
Valour the Pupil; and, when we command
With Lenity, and our Direction's follow'd
With Chearfulnefs, a profp'rous End muft crown
Our Works well undertaken.

Roder. Ours are finifh'd.

Pierio. If we make Ufe of Fortune.

Gonz. Her falfe Smiles
Deprive you of your Judgments. The Condition
Of our Affairs exacts a double Care,
And like bifronted *Janus*, we muft look
Backward, as forward. Though a flatt'ring Calm
Bids us urge on, a fudden Tempeft rais'd,
Not fear'd, much lefs expected, in our Rear
May foully fall upon us, and diftract us
To our Confufion.

Enter Scout.

Our Scout! what brings
Thy ghaftly Looks, and fudden Speed?

Scout. Th' Affurance
Of a new Enemy.

Gonz. This I fore-faw, and fear'd.
What are they? Know'ft thou?

Scout. They are, by their Colours,
Sicilians, bravely mounted, and the Brightnefs
Of their rich Armours doubly gilded with
Reflection of the Sun.

Gonz. From *Sicily?*
The King in League! No War proclaim! 'Tis foul:
But this muft be prevented, nor difputed.
Ha! how is this? Your Oftrich plumes, that, but
E'n now, like Quills of Porcupines feem'd to threaten
The Stars, drop at the Rumour of a Shower?
And like to captive Colours fweep the Earth?
Bear up; but, in great Dangers, greater Minds

Are

Are never proud.   Shall a few loofe Troops, untrain'd
But in a cuftomary Oftentation
Prefented as a Sacrifice to your Valours,
Caufe a Dejection in you?
   Pierio. No Dejection.
   Roder. However ftartl'd, where you lead, we'll follow.
   Gonz. 'Tis bravely faid. We will not ftay their Charge,
But meet 'em Man to Man, and Horfe to Horfe.
Pierio, in our Abfence hold our Place,
And with our Footmen, and thofe fickly Troops,
Prevent a Sally.   I in mine own Perfon,
With part of the Cavalry, will bid
Thefe Hunters welcome to a bloody Breakfaft:
But I lofe Time.
   Pierio. I'll to my Charge.   [*Exit* Pierio.
   Gonz. And we
To ours: I'll bring you on.
   Jacomo. If we come off,
It's not amifs; if not, my 'State is fettl'd.
                       [*Exeunt, Alarm.*

SCENE IV.
Siena.
Ferdinand, Drufo, Livio *above.*

   Ferd. No Aids from *Sicily?* Hath Hope forfook us?
And that vain Comfort to Affliction, Pity,
By our vow'd Friend, deny'd us? We can nor live,
Nor die, with Honour: Like Beafts in a Toil
We wait the Leifure of the bloody Hunter,
Who is not fo far reconcil'd unto us,
As in one Death to give a Period
To our Calamities; but, in delaying
The Fate we cannot fly from, ftarv'd with Wants,
We die this Night, to live again To-morrow,
And fuffer greater Torments.
   Drufo. There is not
Three Day's Provifion for every Soldier,
At an Ounce of Bread a Day, left in the City.
                            Liv.

Liv. To die the Beggar's Death, with Hunger made
Anatomies while we live, cannot but crack
Our Heart-ftrings with Vexation.
　Ferd. Would they would break,　·
Break altogether! How willingly, like *Cato*, ''
Could I tear out my Bowels, rather than
Look on the Conqueror's infulting Face;
But that Religion, and the horrid Dream
To be fuffer'd in th' other World, denies it.
What News with thee?

Enter Soldier.

　Sold. From the Turret of the Fort,
By the rifing Clouds of Duft, through which, likeLight-
　·　ning
TheSplendour of bright Arms fometimes break through,
I did defcry fome Forces making towards us;
And, from the Camp, as emulous of their Glory,
The General, (for I know him by his Horfe)
And bravely feconded, encounter'd 'em.
Their Greetings were too rough for Friends; their Swords,
And not their Tongues, exchanging Courtefies.
By this the main Battalias are join'd;
And, if you pleafe to be Spectators of
The horrid Iffue, I will bring you where,
As in a Theatre, you may fee their Fates
In purple Gore prefented.

''　————— *How willingly, like* Cato,
　　　Could I, &c.

Ferdinand in the midft of his Misfortunes, could willingly murder
himfelf like *Cato*; but that he was reftrained by Religion. *Shakefpear*
makes *Hamlet* reafon in the fame Manner: And, indeed, nothing can
fupport a refolute Mind labouring under Afflictions without any Hope
of Relief, and make him bear them rather than put an End to them,
but the Thoughts of an *hereafter*—The Thoughts of running into
greater and more lafting Miferies, to avoid leffer. Pity but *Cato* could
have reafoned and acted like *Ferdinand* and *Hamlet*: He would have
been not lefs a Patriot—the more a Hero; and would then have better deferved to be prefented upon an *Englifh* Stage.

Ferd.

Ferd. Heav'n, if yet
Tho art appeas'd for my Wrong done to *Aurelia*, }
Take Pity of my Miferies !—Lead the Way, Friend.

[*Exeunt.*

SCENE V.

Before the Caftle of Siena.

A long Charge, after a Flourifh for Victory.

Gonzaga, Jacomo, Roderigo *wounded.* Bertoldo, Gafparo, Anthonio, *Prifoners.*

Gonz. We have 'em yet, though they coft us dear.
This was
Charg'd home, and bravely follow'd. Be to yourfelves
True Mirrors to each other's·Worth ; and, looking
With noble Emulation on his Wounds
(The glorious Liv'ry of triumphant war)

[*To* Jacomo *and* Roderigo.

Imagine thefe with equal Grace appear
Upon yourfelf. The bloody Sweat you've fuffer'd
In this laborious, nay, toilfome Harveft,
Yields a rich Crop of Conqueft, and the Spoil,
Moft precious Balfam to a Soldier's Hurts,
Will eafe and cure 'em. Let me look upon

[*To* Gafparo *and* Anthonio.

The Prifoners Faces. Oh, how much transform'd
From what they were! O *Mars!* were thefe Toys fa-
fhion'd
To undergo the Burthen of thy Service ?
The Weight of their defenfive Armour bruis'd
Their weak, effem'nate Limbs, and would have forc'd 'em
In a hot day without a Blow to yield.

Anth. This Infultation fhews not manly in you.

Gonz. To men I had forborn it ; you are Women,
Or, at the beft, loofe Carpet-knights. What Fury
Seduc'd you to exchange your Eafe in Court
For Labour in the Field ? Perhaps, you thought

To charge, through Duft and Blood, an armed Foe,
Was but like graceful running at the Ring
For a wanton Miftrefs' Glove, and the Encounter
A foft Impreffion on her Lips.　But you
Are gaudy Butterflies, and I wrong myfelf
In parl'ing with you.

　Gafp. Væ *victis!* now we prove it.

　Roder. But here's one fafhion'd in another Mould,
And made of tougher Metal.

　Gonz. True; I owe him
For this Wound bravely given.

　Bert. O that Mountains
Were heap'd upon me, that I might expire
A Wretch no more remember'd!

　Gonz. Look up, Sir.
To be o'ercome deferves no Shame.　If you
Had fal'n ingloriously, or could accufe
Your want of Courage in Refiftance, 'twere
To be lamented: But, fince you perform'd
As much as could be hop'd for from a Man,
(Fortune his Enemy) you wrong yourfelf
In this Dejection.　I am honour'd in
My Victory o'er you; but to have thefe
My Prifoners, is, in my true Judgment, rather
Captivity than a triumph.　You fhall find
Fair Quarter from me, and your many Wounds
(Which I hope are not mortal) with fuch Care
Look'd to, and cur'd, as if your neareft Friend
Attended on you.

　Bert. When you know me better,
You will make void this Promife: Can you call me
Into your Memory?

　Gonz. The brave *Bertoldo!*
A Brother of our Order! by St. *John,*
(Our holy Patron) I am more amaz'd,
Nay, thunderftruck, with thy Apoftacy,
And *Præcipice* from the moft folemn Vows
Made unto Heaven, when this, the glorious Badge
Of our Redeemer was conferr'd upon thee

By

By the great Mafter, then if I had feen
A reprobate *Jew*, an Atheift, *Turk*, or *Tartar*
Baptiz'd in our Religion.

Bert. This I look'd for,
And am refolv'd to fuffer.

Gonz. Fellow-Soldiers,
Behold this Man, and, taught by his Example,
Know that, 'tis fafer far to play with Lightning,
Than trifle in Things facred.—In my Rage.   [*Weeps*.
I fhed thefe at the Funeral of his Virtue,
Faith and Religion—why, I will tell you;
He was a Gentleman, fo train'd up, and fafhion'd
For noble Ufes, and his Youth did Promife
Such Certainties, more than Hopes, of great Atchieve-
            ments,
As, if the Chriftian World had ftood oppos'd
Againft the *Ottoman* Race to try the Fortune
Of one Encounter, this *Bertoldo* had been,
For his Knowledge to direct, and matchlefs Courage
To execute, without a Rival, by
The Votes of good Men chofen General,
As the prime Soldier, and moft deferving,
Of all that wear the Crofs; which now, in Juftice,
I thus tear from him,

Bert. Let me die with it
Upon my Breaft.

Gonz. No; by this, thou wert fworn
On all Occafions, as a Knight, to guard
Weak Ladies from Oppreffion, and never
To draw thy Sword againft 'em; whereas thou,
In Hope of Gain or Glory, when a Princefs,
And fuch a Princefs as *Aurelia* is,
Was difpoffefs'd by Violence, of what was
Her true Inheritance, againft thine Oath,
Hafte to thy uttermoft labour'd to uphold
Her falling Enemy. But thou fhalt pay
A heavy Forfeiture, and learn too late,

Valour,

Valour, employ'd in an ill Quarrel, turns [12]
To Cowardice, and Virtue then puts on
Foul Vice's Vizard. This is that which cancels
All Friendship's Bands between us,—Bear 'em off;
(I will hear no Reply) and let the Ransom
Of these, for they are yours, be highly rated.
In this I do but right, and let it be
Stil'd Justice, and not wilful Cruelty. *[Exeunt.*

The End of the Second Act.

ACT III. SCENE I.

Before the Walls of Siena.

Gonzaga, Astutio, Roderigo, Jacomo.

Gonz. WHAT I have done, Sir, by the Law of
Arms
I can, and will, make good.
Astutio. I've no Commission
To expostulate the Act. These Letters speak
The King my Master's Love to you, and his
Vow'd Service to the Dutchess, on whose Person
I am to give Attendance.
Gonz. At this Instant,
She's at *Pienza:* You may spare the Trouble
Of riding thither; I have advertized her
Of our Success, and on what humble Terms
Siena stands : Though presently I can
Possess it, I defer it, that she may

[12] *Valour, employ'd in an ill Quarrel, turns
To Cowardice, &c.*

The *Greeks* and *Romans* were so fond of this Thought, that they
have adopted it into their Languages, and made the same Word stand
for Valour and the right Use of it. 'Αρετη is Courage and Virtue. So
Virtus, in *Latin.*—But the *Greeks* and *Romans* are no longer imitated!
Enter

Enter her own, and, as fhe pleafe, difpofe of
The Prifoners and the Spoil.

Aftutio. I thank you, Sir.
I' the mean Time, if I may have your Licence,
I have a Nephew, and one once my Ward ;
For whofe Liberties and Ranfoms, I would gladly
Make Compofition.

Gonz. They are, as I take it,
Call'd *Gafparo* and *Anthonio*,

Aftutio. The fame, Sir.

Gonz. For them you muft treat with thefe : But, for
        Betoldo,
He is mine own : If the King will ranfom him,
He pays down fifty thoufand Crowns ; if not,
He lives and dies my Slave,

Aftutio. Pray you a Word——
The King will rather thank you to detain him,
Than give one crown to free him.

Gonz. At his Pleafure.
I'll fend the Prifoners under Guard : My Bufinefs
Calls me another Way.   [*Exit* Gonzaga.

Aftutio. My Service waits you.
Now, Gentlemen, do not deal like Merchants with me,
But noble Captains ; you know, in great Minds,
Poffe, & nolle, nobile.

Roder. Pray you, fpeak
Our Language.

Jacomo. I find not, in my Commiffion,
An Officer's bound to fpeak or underftand
More than his Mother-tongue.

Roder. If he fpeak that
After Midnight, 'tis remarkable.

Aftutio. In plain Terms, then,
Anthonio is your Prifoner ; *Gafparo*, yours.

Jacomo. You are i' the right.

Aftutio. At what Sum do you rate
Their feveral Ranfoms.

Roder. I muft make my Market
As the Commodity coft me.

C c 3   *Aftu.*

Aftutio. As it coft you ?
You did not buy your Captainfhip ? Your Defert,
I hope, advanc'd you.

Roder. How ? It well appears
You are no Soldier.   Defert in thefe Days ?
Defert may make a Serjeant to a Colonel,
And it may hinder him from rifing higher ;
But, if it ever get a Company
(A Company ; pray you, mark me) without Money,
Or private Service done for the General's Miftrefs,
With a Commendatory Epiftle from her,
I will turn Lancepefade.

Jacomo. Pray you, obferve, Sir :
I ferv'd two 'Prenticefhips, juft fourteen Year,
Trailing the puiffant Pike ; and half fo long
Had the Right-hand File ; and I fought well, 'twas
     faid, too :
But I might have ferv'd, and fought, and ferv'd till
     Doomfday,
And ne'er have carried a Flag, but for the Legacy
A buckfome widow, of threefcore, bequeath'd me,
And that too, my Back knows, I labour hard for,
But was better paid.

Aftutio. Y're merry with yourfelves ;
But this is from the Purpofe.

Roder. To the Point then.
Pris'ners are not ta'en every Day ; and, when
We have 'em, we muft make the beft Ufe of 'em,
Our Pay is little to the Part we fhould bear,
And that fo long a coming, that 'tis fpent
Before we have it, and hardly wipes off Scores
At the Tavern, and th' Ordinary.

Jacomo. You may add too,
Our Sport took up on Truft.

Roder. Peace, thou Smock-vermin !
Difcover Commanders Secrets ? In a Word, Sir,
We have enquir'd, and find our Pris'ners rich :
Two thoufand Crowns a-piece, our Companies coft us ;
And fo much each of us will have, and that
In prefent Pay,   *Jacomo.*

Jacomo. It is too little : Yet,
Since you have faid the Word, I am content;
But will not go a Gazet lefs. [13]
Aftutio. Since you are not
To be brought lower, there is no evading :
I'll be your Pay-mafter.
Roder. We defire no better.
Aftutio. But not a Word of what's agreed between us,
°Till I have fchool'd my Gallants.
Jacomo. I am dumb, Sir.

Enter a Guard: Bertoldo, Anthonio, Gafparo, *in Irons.*

Bert. And where remov'd now ? Hath the Tyrant
   found out
Worfe·Ufage for us?
Antb. Worfe it cannot be.
My Greyhound has frefh Straw, and fcrapes in his Ken-
   nel;
But we have neither.
Gafp. Did I ever think
To wear fuch Garters on filk Stockings ? Or
That my too curious Appetite, that turn'd
At the Sight of Godwits, Pheafant, Partridge, Quails
Larks, Wood-cocks, collar'd Salmon, as coarfe Diet,
Would leap at a mouldy Cruft ?
Antb. And go without it;
So oft as I do ? Oh ! how have I jeer'd
The City Entertainment. A huge Shoulder
Of glorious Ram Mutton, feconded
With a Pair of tame Cats, or Conies, a Crab-tart
With a worthy Loin of Veal, and valiant Capon,
Mortify'd to grow tender.—Thefe I fcorn'd
From their plentiful Horn of Abundance, though in-
   vited :

[13] *But will not go a Gazet lefs.*

From the Word *Gazetta*, a Farthing, *Maffinger* makes Ufe of the
fame Word, and to the fame Purpofe, in the firft Scene of the *Guardian.*

But

But now I could carry my own Stool to a Tripe, *
And call their Chitterlings Charity, and bless the Founder.

   Bert. O that I were no farther sensible
Of my Miseries than you are! You, like Beasts,
Feel only Stings of Hunger, and complain not
But when you're empty : But your narrow Souls
(If you have any) cannot comprehend
How insupportable the Torments are,
Which a free and noble Soul, made Captive, suffers:
Most miserable Men! and what am I, then,
That envy you? Fetters, though made of Gold,
Express base Thraldom, and all Delicates
Prepar'd by *Median* Cooks for Epicures,
When not our own, are bitter; Quilts, fill'd high
With Gossemore and Roses, cannot yield
The Body soft Repose, the Mind kept waking
With Anguish and Affliction.

   Astutio. My good Lord——
   Bert. This is no Time, nor Place for Flatt'ry, Sir:
Pray you, stile me, as I am, a Wretch, forsaken
Of the World, as myself.

   Astutio. I would it were
In me to help you.

   Bert. If that you want Power, Sir,
Lip-Comfort cannot cure me.—Pray you, leave me
To mine own private Thoughts.

   Astutio. My valiant Nephew!   [*Walks by.*
And my more than warlike Ward! I am glad to see you
After your glorious Conquests. Are these Chains
Rewards for your good Service? If they are,
You should wear 'em on your Necks (since they are
   massey)
Like Aldermen of the Ward.

   Anth. You jeer us too.
   Gasp. Good Uncle, name not (as you are a Man of
   Honour)

---

  * A Mistake of the Proverb, Bring your Cheer.

                             That

That fatal Word of War; the very Sound of't
Is more dreadful than a Cannon.

Anth. But redeem us
From this Captivity, and I'll vow hereafter
Never to wear a Sword, or cut my Meat
With a Knife that has an Edge or Point. I'll ftarve firft.

Gafp. I will cry Brooms or Cat's Meat in *Palermo*;
Turn Porter, carry Burthens; any Thing,
Rather than live a Soldier.

Aftutio. This fhould have
Been thought upon before. At what Price, think you,
Your two wife Heads are rated?

Anth. A Calve's Head is
More worth than mine; I'm fure it had more Brains in't,
Or I had ne'er come here.

Roder. And I will eat it
With Bacon, if I have not fpeedy Ranfom.

Anth. And a little Garlick too, for your own Sake,
'Twill boil in your Stomach, elfe.   [Sir:

Gafp. Beware of mine,
Or th' Horns may choak you. I am marry'd, Sir.

Anth. You fhall have my Row of Houfes near the
        Palace.

Gafp. And my Villa.—All——

Anth. All that we have.   [*To* Aftutio.

Aftutio. Well, have more Wit hereafter: For this
You're ranfom'd.   [Time

Jacomo. Off with their Irons.

Roder. Do, do:
If you are ours again, you know your Price.

Anth. Pray you, difpatch us: I fhall ne'er believe
I am a Freeman, 'till I fet my Foot
In *Sicily* again, and drink *Palermo*,
And in *Palermo* too.

Aftutio. The Wind fits fair,
You fhall aboard To-night: With the rifing Sun
You may touch upon the Coaft. But take your Leaves
Of the late General, firft.

Gafp. I will be brief.

Anth.

Anth. And I.—My Lord, Heaven keep you.

Gaſp. Yours, to uſe

In the Way of Peace ; but, as your Soldiers, never.

Anth. A Pox of War! No more of War !

Bert. Have you

   [*Exeunt* Roderigo, Jacomo, Anthonio, Gaſparo.

Authority to looſe their Bonds, yet leave

The Brother of your King, whoſe Worth diſdains

Compariſon with ſuch as theſe, in Irons ?

If Ranſom may redeem them, I have Lands,

A Patrimony of mine own aſſign'd me

By my deceaſed Sire, to ſatisſy

Whate'er can be demanded for my Freedom.

 Aſtutio. I wiſh you had, Sir ; but the King, who
   yields

No Reaſon for his Will, in his Diſpleaſure

Hath ſeiz'd on all you had ; nor will *Gonzaga,*

Whoſe Priſ'ner now you are, accept of leſs

Than fifty thouſand Crowns.

 Bert. I find it now,

That Miſery ne'er comes alone. But, grant

The King is yet inexorable, Time

May work him to a Feeling of my Suff'rings.

I've Friends, that ſwore their Lives and Fortunes were

At my Devotion, and among the reſt

Yourſelf, my Lord, when, forfeited to the Law

For a foul Murther, and in cold Blood done,

I made your Life my Gift, and reconcil'd you

To this incenſed King, and got your Pardon.

—Beware Ingratitude. I know you're rich,

And may pay down the Sum.

 Aſtutio. I might, my Lord ;

But, pardon me.

 Bert. And will *Aſtutio* prove, then, ¹⁴

To pleaſe a paſſionate Man, the King's no more,

            Falſe

¹⁴ Bert. *And will* Aſtutio *prove, then,*
 To pleaſe a paſſionate Man, &c.

Bertoldo's Reaſoning is ſtrong, though, at firſt Sight, not very
clear : " Will *Aſtutio* break through all his Obligations to me, to
              pleaſe

Falfe to his Maker·and his Reafon, which
Commands more than I afk ? O Summer-Friendfhip,
Whofe flatt'ring Leaves that fhadow'd us in
Our Profperity, with the leaft Guft drop off
In th' Autumn of Adverfity ! How like
A Prifon is to a Grave! When dead, we are
With folemn Pomp brought thither; and our Heirs,
(Mafking their Joy in falfe, diffembled Tears)
Weep o'er the Hearfe ; but Earth no fooner covers
The Earth brought thither, but they turn away
With inward Smiles, the Dead no more remember'd.
So, enter'd in a Prifon.——

Aftutio. My Occafions
Command me hence, my Lord.

Bert. Pray you, leave me, do ;
And tell the cruel King, that I will wear
Thefe Fetters 'till my Flefh and they are one
Incorporated Subftance. In myfelf,
As in a Glafs, I'll look on human Frailty,
And curfe the Height of Royal Blood : fince I,
In being born near to *Jove*, am near his Thunder.

[*Exit* Aftutio.

Cedars once fhaken with a Storm, their own
Weight grubs their Roots out.—Lead me where you
   pleafe ;
I am his, not Fortune's Martyr, and will die
The great Example of his Cruelty

[*Exit with the Guard.*

pleafe a paffionate Mad man, for the King is no more, he is one?
Will *Aftutio* prove falfe to his Maker, and deaf to his own Reafon, which
commands, in Return for the Benefits received of me, more than I
afk ? furely he cannot. " But, feeing the courtly *Aftutio* unmoved
with thefe generous Sentiments, *Bertoldo* breaks out into that beautiful Defcription which follows :

—— *O Summer-Friendfhip,* &c.

SCENE

SCENE II.

A Grove near the Palace at Palermo.

Adorni. He undergoes my Challenge, and contemns
And threatens me with the late Edict made   [it,
'Gainft Duellifts, that Altar Cowards fly to. [15]
But I, that am engag'd, and nourifh in me
A higher Aim than fair *Camiola* dreams of,
Muft not fit down thus.   In the Court I dare not
Attempt him; and in Publick, he's fo guarded
With a Herd of Parafites, Clients, Fools and Suitors,
That a Mufket cannot reach him.——My Defigns
Admit of no Delay.   This is her Birth-day,
Which with a fit and due Solemnity
Camiola celebrates; and on it, all fuch
As love or ferve her, ufually prefent
A tributary Duty.   I'll have fomething
To give, if my Intelligence prove true,
Shall find Acceptance.   I'm told, near this Grove
Fulgentio every Morning makes his Markets
With his Petitioners.   I may prefent him
With a fharp Petition.——Ha! 'tis he: my Fate
Be ever blefs'd for't

Enter Fulgentio.

Fulgen. Command fuch as wait me,
Not to prefume, at the leaft for half an Hour,
To prefs on my Retirements.
   Page. I will fay, Sir, you are at your Prayers,

---

[15] *'Gainft Duellifts, then, &c.*

Fulgentio put up his Challenge, and, inftead of accepting it,
threatened him with the Law againft Duels.   This *Adorni* would
reprefent as bafe Treatment.   A Man of Courage he fuppofes would
not have taken the Advantage of fuch a Law.   *That Altar,* that
was a Sanctuary Cowards only would fly to.   The Senfe here
plainly requires the Alteration I have made of *that* for *then,* which
in the former Reading was fcarce intelligible.

Fulgen.

Fulgen. That will not find Belief;
Courtiers have fomething elfe to do.—Be gone, Sir.
Challeng'd! 'tis well. And by a Groom! ftill better.
Was this Shape made to fight? I have a Tongue, yet,
Howe'er no Sword, to kill him; and what Way,
This Morning I'll refolve of. [*Exit* Fulgentio.
Adorni. I fhall crofs
Your Refolution, or fuffer for you. [*Exit* Adorni.

SCENE III.

Camiola's *Houfe.*

Camiola: *divers Servants with Prefents.*

Sylli, Clarinda.

Sylli. What are all thefe?
Clar. Servants with feveral Prefents,
And rich ones too.
  1 Serv. With her beft Wifhes, Madam,
Of many fuch Days to you, the Lady *Petula*
Prefents you with this Fan.
  2 Serv. This Diamond
From your Aunt *Honoria.*
  3 Serv. This Piece of Plate
From your Uncle, old *Vincentio,* with your Arms
Graven upon it.
Camiola. Good Friends, they are too
Munificent in their Love, and Favour to me.
Out of my Cabinet return fuch Jewels
As this directs you, for your Pains;—and yours;—
Nor muft you be forgotten. Honour me
With the drinking of a Health.
  1 Serv. Gold, on my Life!
  2 Serv. She fcorns to give bafe Silver.
  3 Serv. Would fhe had been
Born every Month in the Year!
  1 Serv. Month? every Day.
  2 Serv. Shew fuch another Maid,

                                        3 Serv.

3 Serv. All Happiness wait you.

Sylli. I'll see your Will done.

[*Exeunt* Sylli, Clarinda, *Servants.*

Enter Adorni *wounded.*

Camiola. How! *Adorni* wounded?

Adorni. A Scratch got in your Service, else not worth
Your Observation; I bring not, Madam,
In Honour of your Birth-day, antique Plate,
Or Pearl, for which the savage *Indian* dives
Into the Bottom of the Sea; nor Diamonds
Hewn from steep Rocks with Danger: Such as give
To those that have what they themselves want, aim at
A glad Return with Profit: Yet, despise not
My Off'ring at the Altar of your Favour;
Nor let the Lowness of the Giver lessen
The Height of what's presented. Since it is
A precious Jewel, almost forfeited,
And, dim'd with Clouds of Infamy, redeem'd,
And, in its natural Splendor, with Addition,
Restor'd to the true Owner.

Camiola. How is this?

Adorni. Not to hold you in Suspense, I bring you,
    Madam,
Your wounded Reputation cur'd, the Sting
Of virulent Malice, fest'ring your fair Name,
Pluck'd out and trod on. That proud Man, that was
Deny'd the Honour of your Bed, yet durst
With his untrue Reports strumpet your Fame,
Compell'd by me, hath giv'n himself the Lye,
And in his own Blood wrote it.—You may read
Fulgentio subscrib'd.

Camiola. I am amaz'd!

Adorni. It does deserve it, Madam. Common Service
Is fit for Hinds, and the Reward proportion'd
To their Conditions. Therefore, look not on me
As a Follower of your Father's Fortunes, or
One that subsists on yours.—You frown! my Service

Merits

Merits not this Aspect.

Camiola. Which of my Favours,
I might say Bounties, hath begot, and nourish'd
This more then rude Presumption ? Since you had
An Itch to try your desp'rate Valour, wherefore
Went you not to the War ? Couldst thou suppose
My Innocence could ever fall so low
As to have Need of thy rash Sword to guard it
Against malicious Slander ? O how much
Those Ladies are deceiv'd and cheated, when
The Clearness and Integrity of their Actions
Do not defend themselves, and stand secure
On their own Bases ? Such as in a Colour
Of seeming Service give Protection to 'em,
Betray their own Strengths. Malice, scorn'd, puts out
Itself; but argu'd, gives a kind of Credit
To a false Accusation. In this,
This your most memorable Service, you believ'd
You did me right; but you have wrong'd me more
In your Defence of my undoubted Honour,
Than false *Fulgentio* could.

Adorni. I am sorry, what
Was so well intended, is so ill receiv'd.

Enter Clarinda.

Yet, under your Correction, you wish'd
Bertoldo had been present.

Camiola. True, I did:
But he and you, Sir, are not Parallels,
·Nor must you think yourself so.

···*Adorni.* I am what
You'll please to have me.

Camiola. If *Bertoldo* had
Punish'd *Fulgentio*'s Insolence, it had shown
His Love to her, whom in his Judgment he
Vouchsafe to make his Wife; a Height, I hope,
Which you dare not aspire to. The same Actions
Suit not all Men alike :—But I perceive

Repentance

Repentance in your Looks. For this Time, leave me
I may forgive, perhaps forget, your Folly,
Conceal yourfelf till this Storm be blown over.¦
You will be fought for; yet, for my Eftate
          [*Gives him her Hand to kifs.*
Can hinder it, fhall not fuffer in my Service.

Adorni. This is fomething, yet, though I mifs'd the
      Mark I fhot at.   [*Exit* Adorni.

Camiola. This Gentleman is of a noble Temper;
And I too harfh, perhaps, in my Reproof:
Was I not, *Clarinda?*

Clar. I am not to cenfure
Your Actions, Madam: but there are a thoufand
Ladies, and of good Fame, in fuch a Caufe,
Would be proud of fuch a Servant.

Camiola. It may be;

      Enter a Servant.

Let me offend in this Kind.
Why uncall'd for?

Serv. The Signiors, Madam, *Gafparo* and *Anthonio,*
(Selected Friends of the renown'd *Bertoldo*)
Put afhore this Morning.

Camiola. Without him?

Serv. I think fo.

Camiola. Never think more, then.

Serv. They have been at Court.
Kifs'd the King's Hand; and, their firft Duties done
To him, appear ambitious to tender
To you their fecond Service.

Camiola. Wait 'em hither.   [*Exeunt Servant.*
Fear, do not rack me! Reafon, now, if ever,
Hafte with thy Aids, and tell me, fuch a Wonder
As my *Bertolda* is, with fuch Care fafhion'd,
Muft not, nay, cannot, in Heav'ns Providence.

                              Enter

Enter Anthonio, Gafparo, *Servant.*

So foon mifcarry; pray you, forbear; e'er you
Take the Privilege, as Strangers, to falute me,
(Excufe my Manners) make me firft underftand,
How it is with *Bertoldo?*
Gafp. The Relation
Will not, I fear, deferve your Thanks.
Anth. I wifh
Some other fhould inform you.
Camiola. Is he dead?
You fee, though with fome Fear, I dare enquire it.
Gafp. Dead? Would that were the worft, a Debt
    were paid then,
Kings in their Birth owe Nature.
Camiola. Is their aught
More terrible than Death?
Anth. Yes, to a Spirit
Like his; cruel Imprifonment, and that
Without the Hope of Freedom.
Camiola. You abufe me:
The Royal King cannot, in Love to Virtue
(Though all Springs of Affeñction were dry'd up)
But pay his Ranfom.
Gafp. When you know what 'tis,
You will think otherwife—No lefs will do it
Then fifty thoufand Crowns.
Camiola. A petty Sum;
The Price weigh'd with the Purchafe; fifty thoufand?
To the King 'tis nothing. He, that can fpare more
To his Minion for a Mafque, cannot but ranfom
Such a Brother at a Million—You wrong
The King's Magnificence.
Anth. In your Opinion;
But 'tis moft certain. He does not alone
In himfelf refufe to pay it; but forbids
All other Men.
Camiola. Are you fure of this?

Gasp. You may read
The Edict to that Purpose, publish'd by him:
That will resolve you.

Camiola. Possible? Pray you, stand off;
If I do not mutter Treason to myself,
My Heart will break: Yet I will not curse him; [*Aside.*
He is my King—The News you have deliver'd,
Makes me weary of your Company: we'll salute
When we meet next. I'll bring you to the Door.
—Nay, pray you, no more Compliments.

Gasp. One Thing more,
And that's substantial: Let your *Adorni*
Look to himself.

Anth. The King is much incens'd
Against him, for *Fulgentio.*

Camiola. As I am
For your Slowness to depart.

Both. Farewel, sweet Lady!

[*Exeunt* Gasparo, Anthonio.

Camiola. O more then impious Times! when not alone
Subordinate Ministers of Justice are
Corrupted and seduc'd, but Kings themselves
(The greater Wheels by which the lesser move)
Are broken or disjointed! could it be, else,
A King, to sooth his politick Ends, should so far
Forsake his Honour, as at once to break
Th' Adamant Chains of Nature and Religion,
To bind up Atheism, as a Defence [16]
To his dark Counsels? Will it ever be?
That to deserve too much is dangerous,
And Virtue, when too eminent, a Crime?
Must She serve Fortune still? Or, when stripp'd of
Her gay, and glorious Favours, lose the Beauties
Of her own natural Shape? O my *Bertoldo!*
Thou only Sun in Honours Sphere, how soon
Art thou eclips'd and darken'd! not the Nearness

---

[16] *To bind up Atheism,* &c.
This appears to me to be false; I would read,
To *bring* up Atheism, &c.

Art

Of Blood prevailing on the King; nor all
The Benefits to the gen'ral Good difpens'd
Gaining a Retribution! but that
To owe a Courtefy to a fimple Virgin
Would take from the deferving, I find in me
Some Sparks of Fire, which, fann'd with Honours
　Breath,
Might rife into a Flame, and in Men darken
Their ufurp'd Splendor. Ha! my Aim is high,
And, for the Honour of my Sex, to fall fo,
Can never prove inglorious.—'Tis refolv'd :
Call in *Adorni*.
　Clar. I am happy in
Such Employment, Madam. 　　　[*Exit* Clarinda.
　Camiola. He's a Man,
I know, that at a reverend Diftance loves me,
And fuch are ever faithful. What a Sea
Of melting Ice I walk on! what ftrange Cenfures
Am I to undergo! but good Intents
Deride all future Rumours.

　　　Enter Clarinda *and* Adorni.

　Adorni. I obey
Your Summons, Madam.
　Camiola. Leave the Place, *Clarinda* :
One Woman, in a Secret of fuch Weight,
Wife Men may think too much. Nearer, *Adorni*.
　　　　　　　　　[*Exit* Clarinda.
I warrant it with a Smile.
　Adorni. I cannot afk
Safer Protection, what's your Will ?
　Camiola. To doubt
Your ready Defire to ferve me, or prepare you
With the Repetition of former Merits,
Would in my Diffidence, wrong you: But I will,
And without Circumftance, in the Truft that I
Impofe upon you, free you from Sufpicion.
　Adorni. I fofter none of you.
　Camiola. I know you do not,
You are *Adorni*, by the Love you owe me.——
　　　　　　D d 2　　　　　　　　*Adorni.*

Adorni. The fureſt Conjuration.

Camiola. Take me with you.——
Love born of Duty; but advance no further.
You are, Sir, as I ſaid, to do me Service,
To undertake a Taſk, in which your Faith,
Judgment, Diſcretion—in a Word, your all
That's good, muſt be engag'd; nor muſt you ſtudy,
In the Execution, but what may make
For th' Ends I aim at.

Adorni. They admit no Rivals.

Camiola. You anſwer well.—You have heard of *Ber-*
    toldo's
Captivity? and the King's Neglect? the Greatneſs
Of his Ranſom, fifty thouſand Crowns, *Adorni*;
Two Parts of my Eſtate.

Adorni. To what tends this?

Camiola. Yet I ſo love the Gentleman (for to you
I will confeſs my Weakneſs) that I purpoſe,
Now, when he is forſaken by the King,
And his own Hopes, to ranſom, and receive him
Into my Boſom as my lawful Huſband,
                    [*Adorni ſtarts, and ſeems troubled.*
Why change you Colour?

Adorni. 'Tis in Wonder of
Your Virtue, Madam.

Camiola. You muſt, therefore, to
Siena for me, and pay to *Gonzaga*
This Ranſom for his Liberty; you ſhall
Have Bills of Exchange along with you. Let him ſwear
A ſolemn Contract to me, for you muſt be
My principal Witneſs, if he ſhould—But why
Do I entertain theſe Jealouſies? You will do this?

Adorni. Faithfully, Madam.—But not live long after.
                                [*Aſide.*
Camiola. One Thing I had forgot.—Beſides his Free-
He may want Accommodations; furniſh him [dom,
According to his Birth. And from *Camiola*
Deliver this Kiſs, printed on your Lips [*Kiſſes him.*
Seal'd on his Hand.—You ſhall not ſee my Bluſhes;
                                I'll

I'll inftantly difpatch you.   [*Exit* Camiola.
Adorni. I'm half-hang'd
Out of the Way, already.—Was there ever
Poor Lover fo employ'd againft himfelf
To make Way for his Rival ? I muft do it :
Nay, more, I will. If Loyalty can find
Recompence beyond Hope, or Imagination,
Let it fall on me in the other World, ·
As a Reward ; for, in this, I dare not hope it. [*Exit*.

The End of the Third Act.

A C T IV.   S C E N E I.

The Camp.

Gonzaga, Pierío, Roderigo, Jacomo.

Gonz. YOu've feiz'd upon the Citadel, and difarm'd
        All that could make Refiftance ? ·
Pierio. Hunger |had
Done that, before we came ; nor was the Soldier
Compell'd to feek for Prey ; the famifh'd Wretches,
In Hope of Mercy, as a Sacrifice offer'd
All that was worth the taking.
Gonz. You proclaim'd,
On Pain of Death, no Violence· fhould be offer'd
To any Woman ?
Roder. But it needed not ;
For Famine had fo humbled 'em, and took off
The Care of their Sex's Honour, that there was not
So coy a Beauty in the Town, but would   ·
For half·a mouldy Bifket fell herfelf
To a poor Befognion, and without fhrieking.
Gonz. Where is the Duke of *Urbin?*
Jacomo. Under Guard,
As you directed.

Gonz. See the Soldiers fet
In Rank, and File ; and, as the Dutchefs paffes,
Bid 'em vail their Enfigns ; and charge 'em, on their
Not to cry Whores. [*Lives,*
Jacomo. The Devil cannot fright 'em
From their military Licence ; though they know
They are her Subjects, and will part with Being,
To do her Service ; yet, fince fhe's a Woman,
They will touch at her Breech with their Tongues —
 and that is all
That they can hope for. [*A Shout, and a general*
 Cry within, Whores ! Whores !
Gonz. O the Devil ! they are at it.
Hell ftop their bawling Throats.—Again ! make up
And cudgel them into Jelly.
Roder. To no Purpofe,
Though their Mothers were there,
They would have the fame Name for 'em. [*Exeunt.*

S C E N E II.

Before the Walls of Siena.

Roderigo, Jacomo, Pierio, Gonzaga, Aurelia *(under
 a Canopy).* Aftutio *prefents her with Letters. Loud
 Mufick. She reads the Letters.*

Gonz. I do befeech your Highnefs not to afcribe
To th' Want of Difcipline, the barbarous Rudenefs
Of the Soldier, in his Prophanation of
Your facred Name and Virtues.
Aurelia. No, Lord General,
I've heard my Father fay oft, 'twas a Cuftom,
Ufual i' th' Camp ; nor are they to be punifh'd
For Words, that have in Fact deferv'd fo well.
Let the one excufe the other.
All. Excellent Princefs !
Aurelia. But for thefe Aids from *Sicily* fent againft us
To blaft our Spring of Conqueft in the Bud :
 I can-

I cannot find, my Lord Ambaſſador,
How we ſhould entertain't but as a Wrong,
With Purpoſe to detain us from our own ;
Howe'er the King endeavours, in his Letters,
To mitigate th' Affront.

Aſtutio. Your Grace, hereafter,
May hear from me ſuch ſtrong Aſſurances
Of his unlimited Deſires to ſerve you,
As will, I hope, drown in Forgetfulneſs
The Mem'ry of what's paſt.

Aurelia. We ſhall take Time
To ſearch the Depth of 't further, and proceed
As our Council ſhall direct us.

Gonz. We preſent you
With the Keys of the City ; all Lets are remov'd ;
Your Way is ſmooth and eaſy ; at your Feet
Your proudeſt Enemy falls.

Aurelia. We thank your Valours :
A Victory without Blood is twice atchiev'd,
And the Diſpoſure of it, to us tender'd,
The greateſt Honour. Worthy Captains, Thanks !
My Love extends itſelf to All.   [*A Guard made.*
            Aurelia *paſſes through 'em. Loud Muſick.*

Gonz. Make Way, there.   [*Exeunt.*

SCENE III.

A Priſon.

Bertoldo, *with a ſmall Book, in Fetters.* Jailor.

Bert. 'Tis here determin'd [17] (great Examples, arm'd
With Arguments, produc'd to make it good)
                           That

---

[17] *'Tis here determin'd,* &c.

This Soliloquy of *Bertoldo*'s is a very true Account of the Incon-
ſiſtency of the Stoicks. It was one of their favourite Maxims, that
Pain was not an Evil. Their wiſe Man was to be inſenſible ; and yet
no one bore Pain worſe than he. They could argue, with great Ap-
pearance of Reaſon, againſt ſuffering from Affliction ; but, when
they felt it, it was intolerable. They were mighty Heroes in Theory,

                                   but,

That neither Tyrants, nor the wrefted Laws ;
The People's frantick Rage, fad Exile, Want,
Nor, that which I endure, Captivity,
Can do a wife Man any Injury.
Thus *Seneca*, when he wrote it, thought.—But then
Felicity courted him ; his Wealth exceeding
A private Man's ; happy in the Embraces
Of his chafte Wife *Paulina* ; his Houfe full
Of Children, Clients, Servants, flatt'ring Friends,
Soothing his Lip-Pofitions, and created
Prince of the Senate, by the general Voice,
As his Pupil news Suffrage : Then, no Doubt,
He held, and did believe, this.   But no fooner
The Prince's Frowns, and Jealoufies had thrown him
Out of Security's Lap, and a Centurion
Had offer'd him what Choice of Death he pleas'd ;
But told him, Die he muft : when ftraight the Armour
Of his fo boafted Fortitude, fell off,
                        [*Throws away the Book.*
Complaining of his Frailty.   Can it, then,
Be cenfur'd womanifh Weaknefs in me, if,
Thus clogg'd with Irons, and the Period
To clofe up all Calamities deny'd me,
(Which was prefented *Seneca*) I wifh
I ne'er had Being ; at leaft, never knew
What Happinefs was ; or argue with Heav'ns Juftice,
Tearing my Locks, and in Defiance throwing
Duft in the Air ? or, falling on the Ground, thus
With my Nails and Teeth to dig a Grave, or rend
The Bowels of the Earth, my Step-mother,
And not a natural Parent ? or thus practife
To die, and, as I were infenfible,
Believe I had no Motion ?   [*Lies on his Face.*

but, in Practice, Cowards.   The great *Cleanthes* ftarved himfelf to
Death, becaufe of a little Inflammation in his Gums.   The Prince
of Patriots, *Cato*, chofe to die, becaufe he could not bear to fee
Cæfar : And *Seneca* puled and whined at Death with the moft womanifh Fear imaginable : Thefe were the Men who could demon-
ftrate that Pain was not an Evil !

                        Enter

Enter Gonzaga, Adorni, *Jailor.*

Gonz, There he is :
I'll not enquire by whom his Ranfom's paid,
I'm fatisfy'd that I have it ; nor allege
One Reafon to excufe his cruel Ufage,
As you may interpret it ; let it fuffice
It was my Will to have it fo.—He is yours, now,
Difpofe of him as you pleafe   [*Exit* Gonzaga.
   Adorni. Howe'er I hate him,
As one preferr'd before me, being a Man,
He does deferve my Pity.   Sir,—he fleeps,
Or is he dead ?- Would he were a Saint in Heaven ;
'Tis all the Hurt I wifh him.   But, I was not
                                   [*Kneels by him.*
Born to fuch Happinefs.—No, he breathes—Come near,
And, if 't be poffible, without his Feeling,
Take off his Irons.—So, now leave us private.
                              [*His Irons taken off.*
He does begin to ftir, and as tranfported   [*Exit Jailor,*
With a joyful Dream.—How he ftares ! and feels his
As yet uncertain, whether it can be   [*Legs,*
True or phantaftical.
   Bert. Minifters of Mercy,   .
Mock not Calamity.—Ha ! 'tis no Vifion !
Or, if it be, the happieft that ever
Appear'd to finful Flefh !—Who's here ? His Face
Speaks him *Adorni !* but fome glorious Angel,
Concealing its Divinity in his Shape,
Hath done this Miracle, it being not an Act
For wolvifh Man.   Refolve me, if thou look'ft for
Bent Knees in Adoration ?——
   Adorni. O forbear, Sir !
I am *Adorni,* and the Inftrument
Of your Deliverance ; but the Benefit
You owe another.
   Bert. If he has a Name,
As foon as fpoken, 'tis writ on my Heart,
I am his Bondman.   *Adorni,*

Adorni. To the Shame of Men,
This great Act is a Woman's.

Bert. The whole Sex
For her fake muſt be deify'd.   How I wander
In my Imagination, yet cannot
Gueſs who this Phœnix ſhould be!

Adorni. 'Tis *Camiola.*

Bert. Pray you ſpeak't again! there's Muſick in her
·   Name!

Once more, I pray you, Sir!

Adorni. Camiola,
The Maid of Honour.

Bert. Curs'd Atheiſt that I was,
Only to doubt it could be any other ;
Since ſhe alone, in th' Abſtract of herſelf,
That ſmall, but raviſhing Subſtance, comprehends
Whatever is, or can be wiſh'd, in the
Idea of a Woman.   O what Service,
Or Sacrifice of Duty, can I pay her,
If not to live, and die, her Charity's Slave ?
Which is reſolv'd already.

Adorni. She expects not
Such a Dominion o'er you : Yet, ere I
Deliver her Demands, give me your Hand :
On this, as ſhe enjoin'd me, with my Lips
I print her Love and Service, by me ſent you,

Bert. I am o'erwhelm'd with Wonder !

Adorni. You muſt now
(Which is the Sum of all that ſhe deſires)
By a ſolemn Contract bind yourſelf, when ſhe
Requires it, as a Debt due for your Freedom,
To marry her.

Bert. This does engage me further,
A Payment! an Increaſe of Obligation!
To marry her !—'twas my *nil ultra,* ever !
The End of my Ambition! O that now
The Holy Man, ſhe preſent, were prepar'd
To join our Hands, but with that Speed, my Heart
Wiſhes mine Eyes might ſee her.

Adoani,

Adorni. You muſt ſwear this.

Bert. Swear it ? Collect all Oaths and Imprecations,
Whoſe leaſt Breach is Damnation ; and thoſe
Miniſter'd to me in a Form more dreadful ;
Set Heav'n and Hell before me, I will take 'em :
Falſe to *Camiola ?* Never.—Shall I now
Begin my Vows to you ?

Adorni. I am no Churchman ;
Such a one muſt file it on Record. You are free ;
And, that you may appear like to yourſelf
(For ſo ſhe wiſh'd) there's Gold with which you may
Redeem your Trunks and Servants, and whatever
Of late you loft. I have found out the Captain
Whoſe Spoil they were.—His Name is *Roderigo.*

Bert. I know him.

Adorni. I have done my Part.

Bert. So much, Sir,
As I am ever yours for't. Now, methinks,
I walk in Air !—Divine *Camiola !*——
But Words cannot expreſs thee. I'll build to thee
An Altar in my Soul, on which I'll offer
A ſtill increaſing Sacrifice of Duty. [*Exit* Bertoldo.

Adorni. What will become of me now is apparent !
Whether a Poniard, or a Halter be
The neareſt Way to Hell (for I muſt thither,
After I've kill'd myſelf) is ſomewhat doubtful.
This *Roman* Reſolution of Self-Murther,
Will not hold Water, at the high Tribunal,
When it comes to be argu'd ; my good Genius
Prompts me to this Conſideration. He
That kills himſelf to avoid Miſery, fears it.
And, at the beſt, ſhews but a baſtard Valour.
This Life's a Fort committed to my Truſt,
Which I muſt not yield up, 'till it be forc'd.
—Nor will I. He's not valiant that dares die,
But he that boldly bears Calamity. [*Exit.*

SCENE

SCENE IV.

Siena.   *A Flourish.*

Pierio, Roderigo, Jacomo, Gonzaga, Aurelia, Ferdinand, Astutio. *Attendants.*

Aurelia. A Seat here for the Duke. It is our Glory
To overcome with Courtesies, not Rigour;
The lordly *Roman*, who held it the Height
Of human Happiness, to have Kings and Queens
To wait by his triumphant Chariot-wheels
In his insulting Pride, depriv'd himself
Of drawing near the Nature of the Gods,
Best known for such, in being merciful.
Yet, give me Leave, but still with gentle Language,
And with the Freedom of a Friend, to tell you,
To seek by Force, what Courtship could not win,
Was harsh, and never taught in *Love's* mild School.
Wise Poets feign, that *Venus'* Coach is drawn
By Doves and Sparrows, not by Bears and Tygers.

Ferd. I spare the Application,—In my Fortune
Heav'n's Justice hath confirm'd it; yet, great Lady,
Since my Offence grew from Excess of Love,
And not to be resisted, having paid too,
With Loss of Liberty, the Forfeiture
Of my Presumption, in your Clemency
It may find pardon.

Aurelia. You shall have just Cause
To say it hath. The Charge of the long Siege
Defray'd, and the Loss my Subjects have sustain'd
Made good, (since so far I must deal with Caution)
You have your Liberty.

Ferd. I could not hope for
Gentler Conditions.

Aurelia. My Lord *Gonzaga*,
Since my coming to *Siena*, I've heard much of
Your Pris'ner, brave *Bertoldo*.

Gonz.

Gonz. Such an one,
Madam, I had,
　　Aftutio. And have ftill, Sir, I hope.
　　Gonz. Your Hopes deceive you. — He is ranfom'd,
　　　　Madam.
　　Aftutio. By whom, I pray you, Sir?
　　Gonz. You had beft enquire
Of your Intelligencer: I am no Informer.
　　Aftutio. I like not this.　　　　　　　[*Afide.*
　　Aurelia. He is, as 'tis reported,
A goodly Gentleman, and of noble Parts,
A Brother of your Order.
　　Gonz. He was, Madam,
'Till he, againft his Oath, wrong'd you, a Princefs,
Which his Religion bound him from.
　　Aurelia. Great Minds,
For Trial of their Valours, oft maintain
Quarrels that are unjuft; yet without Malice;
And fuch a fair Conftruction I make of him.
I would fee that brave Enemy.
　　Gonz. My Duty
Commands me to feek for him.
　　Aurelia. Pray you do:
And bring him to our Prefence.　　[*Exit Gonzaga.*
　　Aftutio. I muft blaft
His Entertainment. [*Afide.*] May it pleafe your Ex-
　　cellency,
He is a Man debauch'd, and for his Riots
Caft off by th' King my Mafter; and that, I hope, is
A Crime fufficient.
　　Ferd. To you, his Subjects,
That like as your King likes——
　　Aurelia. But not to Us;
We muft weigh with our own Scale.

　　Enter Gonzaga, Bertoldo *richly habited,* Adorni.

This is he, fure!
How foon mine Eye had found him!—What a Port
　　　　　　　　　　　　　　　　　　　　　He

He bears! how well his Bravery becomes him!
A Pris'ner! nay, a Princely Suitor, rather!
But I'm too fudden.

Gonz. Madam, 'twas his Suit,
Unfent for, to prefent his Service to you,
Ere his Departure.

Aurelia. With what Majefty
He bears himfelf!

Aſtutio. The Devil, I think, fupplies him.
Ranfom'd? and thus rich, too!

Aurelia. You ill deferve

       [Bertoldo, *kneeling, kiſſes her Hand.*

The Favour of our Hand.—We are not well:
Give Us more Air.   [*She defcends fuddenly.*

Gonz. What fudden Qualm is this?

Aurelia. —That lifted yours againft me.

Bert. Thus, once more,
I fue for Pardon.

Aurelia. Sure his Lips are poifon'd,
And, through thefe Veins, force Paffage to my Heart,
Which is already feiz'd upon.   [*Aſide.*

Bert. I wait, Madam,
To know what your Commands are; my Defigns
Exact me in another Place.

  Aurelia. Before
You have our Licence to depart? If Manners,
Civility of Manners cannot teach you
T' attend our Leifure, I muft tell you, Sir,
That you are ftill our Prifoner; nor had you
Commiffion to free him.

Gonz. How's this, Madam?

Aurelia. You were my Subftitute, and wanted Power,
Without my Warrant, to difpofe of him.
I will pay back his Ranfom ten times over,
Rather than quit my Intereft.

Bert. This is
Againft the Law of Arms.

Aurelia. But not of Love: [*Aſide.*
Why, hath your Entertainment, Sir, been fuch

             In

In your Reſtraint, that, with the Wings of Fear,
You would fly from it ?
Bert. I know no Man, Madam,
Enamour'd of his Fetters, or delighting
In Cold or Hunger, or that would in Reaſon
Prefer Straw in a Dungeon, before
A Down Bed in a Palace.
Aurelia. How!—Come nearer;
Was his Uſage ſuch ?
Gonz. Yes; and it had been worſe,
Had I foreſeen this.
Aurelia. O thou miſ-ſhap'd Monſter !
In thee it is confirm'd, that ſuch as have
No Share in Nature's Bounties, know no Pity
To ſuch as have 'em. Look on him with my Eyes,
And anſwer then, whether this were a Man
Whoſe Cheeks of lovely Fulneſs ſhould be made
A Prey to meagre Famine ? or theſe Eyes,
Whoſe every Glance ſtore *Cupid*'s empty'd Quiver,
To be dim'd with tedious Watching ; or theſe Lips,
Theſe ruddy Lips, of whoſe freſh Colour, Cherries
And Roſes were but Copies, ſhould grow pale
For want of Nectar ? or theſe Legs that bear
A Burthen of more Worth, than is ſupported
By *Atlas*' weary'd Shoulders, ſhould be cramp'd
With the Weight of Iron ? Oh, I could dwell ever
On this Deſcription !
Bert. Is this in Deriſion,
Or Pity, of me ?
Aurelia. In your Charity
Believe me innocent. Now you are my Priſoner,
You ſhall have fairer Quarter ; you will ſhame
The Place where you have been, ſhould you now leave it
Before you are recover'd. I'll conduct you
To more convenient Lodgings, and it ſhall be
My Care to cheriſh you. Repine who dare ;
It is our Will. You'll follow me ?
Bert. To the Centre,
Such a *Sibylla* guiding me. [*Exeunt* Aurelia, Bertoldo.
Gonz.

Gonz. Who fpeaks firft?

Ferd. We ftand, as we had feen *Medufa*'s Head!

Pierio. I know not what to think, I'm fo amaz'd!

Roder. Amaz'd! I'm thunderftruck!

Jacomo. We are enchanted.

And this is fome Illufion.

Adorni. Heav'n forbid!

In dark Defpair, it fhews a Beam of Hope.

Contain thy Joy, *Adorni.*

Aftutio. Such a Princefs,

And of fo long experienc'd Refervednefs

Break forth, and on the fudden, into Flafhes

Of more than doubted Loofenefs!

Gonz. They come again,

—Smiling, as I live: His Arm circling her Waift —

—I fhall run mad:—Some Fury hath poffefs'd her.

If I fpeak, I may be blafted.   Ha!—I'll mumble

A Prayer or two, and crofs myfelf, and then,

Though the Devil fart Fire, have at him.

Enter Bertoldo *and* Aurelia.

Aurelia. Let not, Sir,

The Violence of my Paffions nourifh in you

An ill Opinion; or, grant my Carriage

Out of the Road, and Garb of private Women,

'Tis ftill done with Decorum.   As I am

A Princefs, what I do, is above Cenfure,

And to be imitated.

Bert. Gracious Madam,

Vouchfafe a little Paufe; for I am fo rap'd

Beyond myfelf, that, 'till I have collected

My fcatter'd Faculties, I cannot tender

My Refolution.

Aurelia. Confider of it,

I will not be long from you.

[Bertoldo *walking by,* mufing.

Gonz.

Gonz. Pray I cannot,
This curfed Object ftrangles my Devotion :
I muft fpeak, or I burft.   Pray you, fair Lady,
If you can n Courtefy, direct me to
The chafte *Aurelia.*

Aurelia. Are you blind ? Who are We ?

Gonz. Another kind of Thing.   Her Blo od was go
     vern'd
By her Difcretion, and not rul'd her Reafon :
The Reverence and Majefty of *Juno*
Shin'd in her Looks, and, coming to the Camp,
Appear'd a fecond *Pallas.*   I can fee
No fuch Divinities in you : If I
Without Offence may fpeak my Thoughts, you are,
As't were, a wanton *Helen.*

Aurelia. Good ; e'er long,
You fhall know me better.

Gonz. Why, if you are *Aurelia,*
How fhall I difpofe of the Soldier ?

Aftutio. May it pleafe you
To haften my Difpatch ?

Aurelia. Prefer your Suits
Unto *Bertoldo* ; we will give him Hearing,
And you'll find him your beft Advocate. [*Exit* Aurelia.

Aftutio. This is rare !

Gonz. What are we come to ?

Roder. Grown up in a Moment
A Favourite !

Ferd. He does take State already.

Bert. No, no, it cannot be !—yet, but *Camiola,*
There is no Stop between me and a Crown :
—Then my Ingratitude ! a Sin in which
All Sins are comprehended ! aid me, Virtue,
Or I am loft.   [*Afide.*

Gonz. May it pleafe your Excellence——
—Second me, Sir.

Bert. Then my fo horrid Oaths,
And hell-deep Imprecations made againft it.   [*Afide.*

Aftutio. The King, your Brother, will thank you for
th' Advancement
Of his Affairs——
Bert. And yet who can hold out
Againſt ſuch Batteries, as her Power and Greatneſs
Raiſe up againſt my weak Defences!   [*Afide.*
Gonz. Sir,

Enter Aurelia.

Do you dream waking ?—Slight, ſhe's here again.
Bert. Walks ſhe on woollen Feet!
Aurelia. You dwell too long
In your Deliberation, and come
With a Cripple's Pace to that which you ſhould fly to.
Bert. It is confeſs'd: Yet, why ſhould I, to win
From you, that hazard all to my poor nothing,
By falſe Play ſend you off a Loſer from me ?
I'm already too too much engag'd
To th' King my Brother's Anger; and who knows
But that his Doubts, and politick Fears, ſhould you
Make me his Equal, may draw War upon
Your Territories; were that Breach made up,
I ſhould with Joy embrace, what now I fear
To touch but with due Rev'rence.
Aurelia. That Hind'rance
Is eaſily remov'd.   I owe the King
For a Royal Viſit, which I ſtraight will pay him,
And having firſt reconcil'd you to his Favour,
A Diſpenſation ſhall meet with us,
Bert. I am wholly yours.
Aurelia. On this Book ſeal it.
Gonz. What Hand and Lip too? Then the Bargain's
sure,
You've no Employment for me ?
Aurelia. Yes, *Gonzaga*;
Provide a Royal Ship.
Gonz. A Ship? Saint *John!*
Whither are we bound, now ?

                                                    Aurelia.

Aurelia. You fhall know hereafter,
My Lord, your Pardon, for my too much trenching
Upon your Patience.

 Adorni. Camiola—   [*Whifpers to* Bertoldo,
Aurelia. How do you?

Bert. Indifpofed; but I attend you.   [*Exeunt.*

Adorni. The heavy Curfe that waits on Perjury,
And foul Ingratitude, purfue thee, ever!
Yet why from me this? In this Breach of Faith
My Loyalty finds Reward! what poifons him,
Proves Mithridate to me [12] I have perform'd
All fhe commanded punctually, and now,
In the clear Mirrour of my Truth, fhe may
Behold his Falfhood. O that I had Wings
To bear me to *Palermo!* this, once known,
Muft change her Love into a juft Difdain,
And work her to Compaffion of my Pain.   [*Exit.*

SCENE V.

Camiola's *Houfe.*

Sylli, Camiola, Clarinda, *at feveral Doors.*

Sylli. Undone! undone!—poor I, that whilome was
The Top and Ridge of my Houfe, am, on the fudden,
Turn'd to the pitifulleft Animal
O' th' Lineage of the *Syllies!*

 Camiola. What's the Matter?

Sylli. The King—break Girdle, break!

Camiola. Why, what of him?

Sylli. Hearing how far you doted on my Perfon,
Growng envious of my Happinefs, and knowing
His Brother, nor his Favourite *Fulgentio,*
Could get a Sheep's Eye from you, I being prefent,

---

  [12] ———— *What poifons him*
   Proves Mithridate to me, &c.

 Mithridate (called after its Inventor, *Mithridate,* King of *Pontus*) a
Confection, that is a fpecial Prefervative againft Poifon.

Is come himſelf a Suitor, with the Awl
Of his Authority to bore my Noſe,
And take you from me—Oh, oh, oh!

   Camiola. Do not roar ſo :
The King?

   Sylli. The King : Yet loving *Sylli* is not
So ſorry for his own, as your Misfortune ;
If the King ſhould carry you, or you bear him,
What a Loſer ſhould you be ? He can but make you
A Queen, and what a ſimple Thing is that
To th' being my lawful Spouſe. The World can never
Afford you ſuch a Huſband.

   Camiola. I believe you.
But how are you ſure the King is ſo inclin'd ?
Did not you dream this ?

   Sylli. With theſe Eyes I ſaw him
Diſmiſs his Train, and 'lighting from his Coach,
Whiſper *Fulgentio* in the Ear.

   Camiola. If ſo,
I gueſs the Buſineſs.

   Sylli. It can be no other
But to give me the Bob, that being a Matter
Of main Importance.—Yonder they are, I dare not

       Enter Roberto, Fulgentio.

Be ſeen, I am ſo deſperate ! if you forſake me,
Send me Word, that I may provide a Willow-Garland,
To wear, when I drown myſelf. O *Sylli,* O *Sylli.*
                    [*Exit crying.*

   Ful. It will be worth your Pains, Sir, to obſerve
The Conſtancy and Bravery of her Spirit.
Though great Men tremble at your Frowns, I dare
Hazard my Head, your Majeſty, ſet off
With Terror, cannot fright her.

   Rober. May ſhe anſwer
My Expectation.

   Fulgen. There ſhe is

   Cam. My Knees thus

                           Bent

Bent to the Earth (while my Vows are fent upward
For th' Safety of my Sov'reign) pay the Duty
Due for fo great an Honour, in this Favour
Done to your humbleft Hand-maid.

   Rober. You miftake me,
I come not (Lady) that you may report
The King, to do you Honour, made your Houfe *
(He being there) his Court; but to correct
Your ftubborn Difobedience.   A Pardon,
For that, could you obtain it, were well purchas'd
With this Humility.

   Camiola. A Pardon, Sir?
'Till I am confcious of an Offence,
I will not wrong my Innocence to beg one,
What is my Crime, Sir?

   Rober. Look on him I favour,
By your fcorn'd and neglected.

   Camiola. Is that all, Sir?

   Rober. No, Minion; though that were too much.
      How can you
Anfwer the fetting on your defp'rate Bravo
To murther him?

   Camiola. With your Leave, I muft not kneel, Sir,
While I reply to this: But thus rife up
In my Defence, and tell you as a Man
(Since when you are unjuft, the Deity
Which you may challenge as a King, parts from you)
'Twas never read in Holy Writ, or moral,
That Subjects on their Loyalty were oblig'd
To love their Sov'reign's Vices; your Grace, Sir,
To fuch an Undeferver is no Virtue.

   Fulgen. What think you now, Sir?

   Camiola. Say you fhould love Wine,
You being the King, and 'caufe I am your Subject,
Muft I be ever drunk? Tyrants, not Kings,
By Violence, from humble Vaffals force
The Liberty of their Souls.   I could not love him.

   * Courts make not Kings, but Kings Courts.

DENHAM.
E e 3
And

And to compel Affection, as I take it,
Is not found in your Prerogative.
  Rober. Excellent Virgin!
How I admire her Confidence!   [*Aside.*
  Camiola. He complains
Of Wrong done him : But, be no more a King,
Unlefs you do me right. Burn your Decrees,
And of your Laws and Statutes make a Fire
To thaw the frozen Numbnefs of Delinquents,
If he efcape unpunifh'd. Do your Edicts
Call it Death in any Man that breaks into
Another's Houfe to rob him, though of Trifles,
And fhall *Fulgentio*, your *Fulgentio* live ?
Who hath committed more than Sacrilege
In the Pollution of my clear Fame
By his malicious Slanders.
  Rober. Have you done this ?
Anfwer truly on your Life.
  Fulgen. In the Heat of Blood
Some fuch Thing I reported.
  Rober. Out of my Sight !
For I vow, if by true Penitence thou win not
This injur'd Lady to fue out thy Pardon,
Thy Grave is digg'd already.
  Fulgen. By my own Folly
I've made a fair Hand of't,   [*Exit* Fulgentio.
  Rober. You fhall know, Lady,
While I wear a Crown, Juftice fhall ufe her Sword
To cut Offenders off, though neareft to us.
  Camiola. I, now you fhew whofe Deputy you are,
If now I bathe your Feet with Tears, it cannot
Be cenfur'd Superftition.
  Rober. You muft rife.
Rife in our Favour, and Protection ever :   [*Kiffes her.*
  Camiola. Happy are Subjects! when the Prince is ftill
Guided by Juftice, not his paffionate Will.   [*Exeunt.*

The End of the Fourth Act.

A C T

ACT V.   SCENE I.

Camiola's House.

Camiola, Sylli.

Camiola. YOU see how tender I am of the Quiet
And Peace of your Affection, and what
great ones
I put off in your Favour.
  Sylli. You do wisely,
Exceeding wisely! and, when I have said,
I thank you for't, be happy.
  Camiola. And good Reason,
In having such a Blessing.
  Sylli. When you have it,
But the Bait is not yet ready.   Stay the Time,
While I triumph by myself.—King, by your Leave,
I have wip'd your royal Nose, without a Napkin,
You may cry Willow, Willow! for your Brother,
I'll only say go by.   For my fine Favourite,
He may graze where he please; his Lips may Water
Like a Puppies o'er a frumenty Pot, while *Sylli*
Out of his two-leav'd Cherry-stone Dish drinks *Nectar!*
I cannot hold out any longer; Heav'n forgive me,
'Tis not the first Oath, I have broke, I must take
A little for a Preparative. [*Offers to kiss and embrace her.*
  Camiola. By no Means.
If you forswear yourself we shall not prosper.
I'll rather lose my Longing.
  Sylli. Pretty Soul!
How careful it is of me! let me buss yet,
Thy little dainty Foot for't : That, I'm sure, is
Out of my Oath.
  Camiola. Why, if thou canst dispense with't
So far, I'll not be scrupulous ; such a Favour

My

My amorous Shoemaker fteals.

Sylli. O moft rare Leather !   [*Kiffes her Shoe often.*
I do begin at the loweft, but in time
I may grow higher.

Camiola. Fie! you dwell too long there ;
Rife, pry'thee, rife.

Sylli. O, I am up already.

Enter Clarinda *baftily.*

Camiola. How I abufe my Hours!—What news with
    thee, now ?

Clar. Off with that Gown, 'tis mine ; mine by your
    Promife :
Signior *Adorni* is return'd ! now upon Entrance ;
Off with it, off with it, Madam.

Camiola. Be not fo hafty :
When I go to Bed, 'tis thine.

Sylli. You have my grant too;
But, do you hear, Lacy, though I give Way to this,
You muft hereafter afk my Leave before
You part with Things of Moment.

Camiola. Very good ;
When I'm yours, I'll be govern'd.

Sylli. Sweet Obedience !

Enter Adorni.

Camiola. You're well return'd

Adorni. I wifh that the Succefs
Of my Service had deferv'd it.

Camiola. Lives *Bertoldo* ?

Adorni. Yes, and return'd with Safety.

Camiola. 'Tis not, then,
In the Rower of Fate to add to, or take from
My perfect Happinefs : And yet he fhould
Have made me his firft Vifit.

Adorni. So I think too ;
But he——

Sylli.

Sylli. Durſt not appear, I being preſent:
That's his Excuſe, I warrant you.

Camiola. Speak, where is he?
With whom? Who hath deſerv'd more from him? Or
Can be of equal Merit? In this
Do not except the King.

Adorni. He's at the Palace
With the Dutcheſs of *Siena.* One Coach brought 'em
    hither,
Without a third. He's very gracious with her,
You may conceive the reſt.

Camiola. My jealous Fears
Make me to apprehend.

Adorni. Pray you, diſmiſs
Signior Wiſdom, and I'll make relation to you
Of the Particulars.

Camiola. Servant, I would have you
To haſte unto the Court.

Sylli. I will out-run
A Footman for your Pleaſure.

Camiola. There obſerve
The Dutcheſs' Train and Entertainment.

Sylli. Fear not,
I will diſcover all that is of Weight
To the Liveries of her Pages, and her Footmen.
This is fit Employment for me. [*Exit* Sylli.

Camiola. Gracious with ·
The Duchefs! ſure, you ſaid ſo?

Adorni. I will uſe
All poſſible Brevity to inform you, Madam,
Of what was truſted to me, and diſcharg'd
With Faith and loyal Duty.

Camiola. I believe it;
You ranſom'd him, and ſupply'd his Wants—imagine
That is already ſpoken; and what Vows
Of Service he made to me, is apparent;
His Joy of me, and Wonder too perſpicuous;
Does not your Story end ſo?

Adorni. Would the End

Had

Had anſwered the Beginning—In a Word,
Ingratitude and Perjury at the Height,
Cannot expreſs him.

Camiola. Take heed.

Adorni. Truth is arm'd
And can defend itſelf. It muſt out, Madam.
I ſaw (the preſence full) the amorous Dutcheſs
Kiſs and embrace him, on his Part accepted
With equal Ardor, and their willing Hands
No ſooner jóin'd, but a Remove was publiſh'd,
And put in Execution.

Camiola. The Proofs are
Too pregnant.—*O Bertoldo !*

Adorni. He's not worth
Your ſorrow, Madam.

Camiola. Tell me, when you ſaw this,
Did not you grieve, as I do now, to hear it ?

Adorni. His Precipice from Goodneſs raiſing mine,
And ſerving as a Foil to ſet my Faith off,
I had little Reaſon.

Camiola. In this you confeſs
The Devilliſh Malice of your Diſpoſition.
As you were a Man, you ſtood bound to lament it,
And not in Flattery of your falſe Hopes
To glory in it.   When good Men purſue
The Path mark'd out by Virtue, the bleſſed Saints
With Joy look on it, and Seraphic Angels
Clap their celeſtial Wings in heav'nly Plaudits,
To ſee a Scene of Grace ſo well preſented,
The Fiends, and Men made up of envy, mourning ;
Whereas now, on the contrary, as far
As their Divinity can partake of Paſſion,
With me they weep, beholding a fair Temple ;
Built in *Bertoldo's* Loyalty, turn'd to Aſhes
By the Flames of his Inconſtancy, the damn'd
Rejoicing in the Object.—'Tis not well
In you, *Adorni.*

Adorni. What a temper dwells
In this rare Virgin,—Can you pity him   [*Aſide*

That

That hath fhewn none to you?

Camiola. I muft not be
Cruel by his Example, You, perhaps,
Expect now I fhould feek Recovery
Of what I have loft by Tears, and with bent Knees
Beg his Compaffion. No; my tow'ring Vertue,
From the Affurance of my Merit, fcorns
To ftoop fo low. I'll take a nobler Courfe,
And, confident in the Juftice of my Caufe,
(The King his Brother, and new Miftrefs Judges)
Ravifh him from her Arms—You have the Contract
In which he fwore to marry her?

Adorni. 'Tis here, Madam.   [Hufband,

Camiola. He fhall be, then, againft his will my
And when I have him, I'll fo ufe him—Doubt not,
But that, your Honefty being unqueftion'd;
This Writing with your Teftimony clears all.

Adorni. And buries me in the dark Mifts of Error.

Camiola. I'll prefently to Court, pray you, give Order
For my Coach.

Adorni. A Cart for me were fitter,
To hurry me to th' Gallows   [*Exit* Adorni.

Camiola. O falfe Men!
Inconftant! perjur'd! My good Angel, help me
In thefe my Extremities!

Enter Sylli.

Sylli. If you ever will fee a brave Sight,
Lofe it not now. *Bertoldo* and the Dutchefs
Are prefently to be married. There's fuch Pomp
And Preparation.

Camiola. If I marry, 'tis
This Day, or never.

Sylli. Why, with all my Heart;
Though I break this, I'll keep the next Oath I make,
And then it is quit.

Camiola. Follow me to my Cabinet;
You know my Confeffor, Father *Paulo?*

                                        Sylli.

Sylli. Yes : Shall he
Do the Feat for us ?
Camiola. I will give in Writing
Directions to him, and attire myfelf
Like a Virgin-bride, and fomething I will do
That fhall deferve Men's Praife and Wonder too.
Sylli. And I, to make all know I am not fhallow,
Will have my Points of Cochineal and Yellow. [*Exeunt,*

S C E N E II.

The Palace at Palermo.

Loud Mufick,

Roberto, Bertoldo, Aurelia, Aftutio, Gonzaga, Roderigo, Iacomo, Pierio, Bifhop, *with Attendants.*

Rober. Had your Divifion been greater, Madam,
Your Clemency, (the Wrong being done to you)
In Pardon of it, like the Rod of Concord,
Muft make a perfect Union, once more
With a brotherly Affection we receive you
Into our Favour, Let it be your Study
Hereafter to deferve this Bleffing, far
Beyond your Merit,
Bert. As the Princefs, Grace
To me is without Limit, my Endeavours
With all Obfequioufnefs to ferve her Pleafures
Shall know no Bounds ; nor will I, being made
Her Hufband, forget the Duty that
I owe her as a Servant,
Aureila. I expect not
But fair Equality, fince I well know,
If that Superiority be due,
'Tis not to me. When you are made my Confort,
All the Prerogatives of my high Birth cancell'd,
I'll practice the Obedience of a Wife,
And freely pay it. Queens themfelves, if they
Make Choice of their Inferiors, only aiming

To

To feed their ſenſual Appetites, and to reign
Over their Huſbands, in ſome Kind commit
Authoriz'd Whoredom , nor will I be guilty,
In my Intent of ſuch a Crime.

 Gonz. This done,
As it is promis'd, Madam, may well ſtand for
A Precedent to great Women : But, when once
The griping Hunger of Deſire is cloy'd,
(And the poor Fool, advanc'd, brought on his Knees)
Moſt of your Eagle-Breed, I'll not ſay all,
(Ever excepting you) challenge again,
What in hot Blood they parted from.

 Aurelia. You are ever
An Enemy of our Sex, but you, I hope, Sir,
Have better Thoughts.

 Bert. I dare not entertain
An ill one of your Goodneſs.

 Rober. To my Power
I will enable him, to prevent all Danger
Envy can raiſe againſt your Choice. One Word more
Touching the Articles.

   Enter Fulgentio, Camiola, Sylli, Adorni.

 Fulgen. In you alone
Lie all my Hopes; you can or kill or ſave me;
But pity in you will become you better,
(Though, I confeſs, in juſtice 'tis deny'd me)
Then too much Rigour.

 Camiola. I will make your Peace
As far as it lies in me ; but muſt firſt
Labour to right myſelf.

 Aurelia. Or add or alter
What you think fit. In him I have my all,
Heav'n make me thankful for him.

 Rober. On to the Temple.

 Camiola. Stay, Royal Sir, and, as you are a King,
Erect one here, in doing Juſtice to
An injur'd Maid.

         Aurelia.

Aurelia. How's this?

Bert. O I am Blasted!   [Promptness

Rober. I have giv'n some Proof, sweet Lady, of my
To do you Right, you need not, therefore, doubt me;
And rest assur'd. that, this great Work dispatch'd,
You shall have Audience and Satisfaction
To all you can demand.

Camiola. To do me Justice
Exacts your present Care, and can admit
Of no Delay.   If ere my Cause be heard,
In Favour of your Brother, you go on, Sir,.
Your Scepter cannot right me.   He's the Man,
The guilty Man, whom I accuse, and you
Stand bound in Duty, as you are Supreme,
To be impartial.   Since you are a Judge,
As a Delinquent look on him, and not
As on a Brother, Justice painted blind,
Infers, her Ministers are oblig'd to hear
The Cause and Truth, the Judge determine of it;
And not sway'd, or by Favour or Affection,
By a false Gloss, or wrested Comment, alter
The true Intent, and Letter of the Law.

Roder. Nor will I, Madam,

Aurelia. You seem troubled, Sir,

Gonz. His Colour changes too.

Camiola. The Alteration.
Grows from his Guilt.   The Goodness of my Cause
Begets such Confidence in me, that I bring
No hir'd Tongue to plead for me, that with gay
Rhetorical Flourishes may palliate
That which, stripp'd naked, will appear deform'd.
I stand here mine own Advocate; and my Truth,
Deliver'd in the plainest Language; will
Make good itself; nor will I, if the King
Give Suffrage to it, but admit of you,
My greatest Enemy, and this Stranger Prince,
To sit Assistants with him.

Aurelia. I ne'er wrong'd you..

Cam. In your Knowledge of the Injury; I believe it;
                                                   Nor

Nor will you in your Juſtice, when you are
Acquainted with my Intereſt in this Man
Which I lay claim to.

Rober. Let us take our Seats,
What is your Title to him ?

Camiola. By this Contract,
Seal'd ſolemnly before a reverend Man,
I challenge him for my Huſband.

Sylli. Ha! was I
Sent for the Frier, for this ? O *Sylli ! Sylli !*
Some Cordial, or I faint!

Rober. This Writing is
Authentical.

Aurelia. But done in Heat of Blood,
(Charm'd by her Flatt'ries, as, no doubt, he was)
To be diſpens'd with.

Ferd. Add this, if you pleaſe,
The Diſtance and Diſparity between
Their Births and Fortunes.

Camiola. What can Innocence hope for,
When ſuch as ſit her Judges, are corrupted !
Diſparity of Birth, or fortune, urge you ?
Or *Syren* Charms ? or, at his beſt, in me,
Wants to deſerve him ? Call ſome few Days back,
And, as he was, conſider him, and you
Muſt grant him my Inferior. Imagine
You ſaw him now in fetters, with his Honour,
His Liberty loſt ; with her black Wings Deſpair
Circling his Miſeries, and this *Gonzago*
Trampling on his Afflictions ; the great Sum
Propoſed for his Redemption ; the King
Forbidding Payment of it ; his near Kinſmen,
With his proteſting Followers and Friends,
Falling off from him ; by the whole World forſaken ;
Dead to all Hope, and buried in the Grave
Of his Calamities ; and then weigh duly
What ſhe deſerv'd (whoſe Merits now are doubted)
That as his better Angel in her Bounties
Appear'd unto him, his great Ranſom pay'd ;

His

His Wants; and with a prodigal Hand, fupply'd;
Whether, then, being my manumifed Slave,
He ow'd not himfelf to me?

    Aurelia. Is this true?

    Rober. In his Silence 'tis acknowledg'd.

    Gonz. If you want
A Witnefs to this Purpofe, I'll depofe it.

    Camiola. If I have dwelt too long on my Defervi
To this unthankful Man, pray you pardon me;
The Caufe requir'd it.   And, though now I add
A little, in my Painting to the Life
His barbarous Ingratitude, to deter
Others from Imitation, let it meet with
A fair Interpretation.   This Serpent,
Frozen to Numbnefs, was no fooner warm'd
In the Bofom of my Pity and Compaffion,
But, in Return, he ruin'd his Preferver,
The Prints, the Irons had made in his Flefh,
Still ulcerous; but all that I had done
(My Benefits in Sand, or Water written) [19]
As they had never been, no more remember'd:
And on what Ground, but his ambitious Hopes
To gain this Duchefs' Favour.

    Aurelia. Yes; the Object
(Look on it better, Lady) may excufe
The Charge of his Affection.

    Camiola. The Object?
In what? forgive me, Modefty, if I fay
You look upon your Form in the falfe Glafs
Of Flatt'ry and Self-love, and that deceives you.
That you were a Dutchefs, as I take it, was not
Character'd on your Face, and, that not feen,
For other Feature, make all thefe, that are
Experienc'd in Women, judges of 'em;
And, if they are not Parafites, they muft grant

---

[19] *My Benefits in Sand, or Water Written.*
Thus in *Shakefpear's Henry VIII.*
    Men's Evil Manners live in Brafs; their Virtues
    We write in Water.   ACT. IV.

                                    For

For Beauty without Art, though you ſtorm at it,
I may take the Right-Hand File.

Gonz. Well ſaid, I' faith!
I ſee fair Women on no Terms will yield
Priority in Beauty.

Camiola. Down, proud Heart!
Why do I riſe up in Defence of that,
Which, in my cheriſhing of it, hath Undone me!
No, Madam, I recant;—You are all Beauty,
Goodneſs and Virtue ; and poor I not worthy
As a Foil to ſet you off; Enjoy your Conqueſt;
But do not tyrannize. Yet, as I am
In my Lowneſs from your Height, you may look on me,
And in your Suffrage to me, make him know
That, though to all Men elſe I did appear
The Shame and Scorn of Women,²⁰ He ſtands bound
To hold me as her Maſter-piece.

Rober. By my Life,
You've ſhew'n yourſelf of ſuch an abjeƈt Temper,
So poor, and low-condition'd, as I grieve for
Your Nearneſs to me.

Ferd. I am chang'd in my
Opinion of you, Lady, and profeſs
The Virtues of your Mind, an ample Fortune
For an abſolute Monarch.

Gonz. Since you are reſolv'd
To damn yourſelf, in your forſaking of
Your noble Order for a Woman, do it   [meet not
For this. You may ſearch through the World, and
With ſuch another *Phænix.*

Aurelia. On the Sudden
I feel all Fires of Love quench'd in the Water

²⁰ —————— *I did appear,*
    The Shame and Scorn of Women.

This is the Reading of all the Old Copies, but I imagine it is falſe,
and that we ought to read.

    —————— *I did appear,*
    The Shame and Scorn of Nature.

What ſtrengthens this Suppoſition, is the Lines following, which
makes the Senſe entire.

Of Compaſſion.—Make your Peace; you have
My free Conſent; for here I do diſclaim
All Int'reſt in you: And, to further your
Deſires, fair Maid, compos'd of Worth and Honour,
The Diſpenſation procur'd by me,
Freeing *Bertoldo* from his Vow, makes Way
To your Embraces.

 Bert. Oh, how have I ſtray'd,
And wilfully, out of the noble Track
Mark'd me by Virtue! 'Till now, I was never
Truly a Priſoner. To excuſe my late
Captivity, I might allege the Malice
Of Fortune; you, that conquer'd me, confeſſing
Courage in my Defence was no Way wanting.
But now I have ſurrender'd up my Strengths
Into the Power of Vice, and on my Forehead
Branded with mine own Hand, in Capital Letters,
Diſloyal and ingrateful. Though barr'd from
Human Society, and hiſs'd into
Some Deſert ne'er yet haunted with the Curſes
Of Men and Women, ſitting as a Judge
Upon my guilty ſelf, I muſt confeſs
It juſtly falls upon me; and one Tear,
Shed in Compaſſion of my Suff'rings, more
Than I can hope for.

 Camiola. This Compunction
For th' Wrong that you have done me, tho' you ſhould
Fix here, and your true Sorrow move no farther,
Will, in reſpect I lov'd once, make theſe Eyes
Two Springs of Sorrow for you.

 Bert. In your Pity
My Cruelty ſhews more monſtrous: Yet I am not,
Though moſt ingrateful, grown to ſuch a Height
Of Impudence, as in my Wiſhes only
To aſk your Pardon. If, as now I fall
Proſtrate before your Feet, you will vouchſafe
To act your own Revenge, treading upon me
As a Viper eating through the Bowels of
Your Benefits, to whom, with Liberty,

I owe

I owe my Being, 'twill take from the Burthen
That now is infupportable.

Camiola. Pray you, rife ;
As I wifh Peace and Quiet to my Soul,
I do forgive you heartily. Yet, excufe me,
Though I deny myfelf a Blefling that,
By the Favour of the Dutchefs feconded,
With your Submiffion is offer'd to me,
Let not the Reafon I allege for't grieve you,
You have been falfe once.—I have done : and if,
When I am married (as this Day I will be)
As a perfect Sign of your Atonement with me,
You wifh me Joy, I will receive it for
Full Satisfaction of all Obligations
In which you ftand bound to me.

Bert. I will do it,
And, what's more, in Defpite of Sorrow, live
To fee myfelf undone, beyond all Hope
To be made up again.

Sylli. My Blood begins
To come to my Heart again.

Camiola. Pray you, Signior *Sylli,*
Call in the holy Frier. , He's prepar'd
For finifhing the Work.

Sylli. I knew I was
The Man. Heaven make me thankful !

Rober. Who is this ?

Aftutio. His Father was the Banker of *Palermo :*
And this the Heir of his great Wealth.—His Wifdom
Was not hereditary.

Sylli. Though you know me not,
Your Majefty owes me a round Sum ; I have
A Seal or two, to witnefs ; yet, if you pleafe
To wear my Colours, and dance at my Wedding,
I'll never fue you.

Rober. And I'll grant your Suit.

Sylli. Gracious *Madona,* noble General,
Brave Captains and my quondam Rivals wear 'em,

Since

Since I am confident you dare not harbour
A Thought, but that Way current.   [*Exit.*

Aurelia. For my Part
I cannot guefs the Iffue.

            Enter Sylli *with the Friar.*

Sylli. Do your Duty,
And with all Speed you can, you may difpatch us.

  Paulo. Thus, as a principal Ornament to the Church,
I feize her.

  All. How!

  Rober, So young, and fo religious!

  Paulo. She has forfook the World.

  Sylli. And *Sylli* too?
I fhall run mad.

  Rober. Hence with the Fool! Proceed, Sir.
                       [Sylli *thruft off.*

  Paulo. Look on this Maid of Honour, now
Truly honour'd in her Vow
She pays to Heaven: Vain Delight
By Day, or Pleafure of the Night,
She no more thinks of: This fair Hair
(Favours for great Kings to wear)
Muft now be fhorn. Her rich Array
Chang'd into a homely gray.
The Dainties, with which fhe was fed
And her proud Flefh pampered,
Muft not be tafted; from the Spring,
For Wine, cold Water we will bring,
And with fafting mortify
The Feafts of Senfuality.
Her Jewels, Beads; and fhe muft look
Not in a Glafs, but holy Book;
To teach her the ne'er erring Way
To Immortality. O may
She, as fhe purpofes to be
A child new born to Piety,
Perfevere in it, and good Men,

                                      With

With Saints and Angels, fay, Amen!
Camiola. This is the Marriage! this the Port to which
My Vows muft fteer me! Fill my fpreading Sails
With the pure Wind of your Devotions for me,
That I may touch the fecure Haven, where
Eternal Happinefs keeps her Refidence,
Temptations to Frailty never ent'ring.
I am dead to the World, and thus difpofe
Of what I leave behind me, and, dividing
My 'State into three Parts. I thus bequeath it.
The firft to the fair Nunnery, to which
I dedicate the laft, and better Part
Of my frail Life ; a fecond Portion
To pious Ufes ; and the third to thee,
Adorni, for thy true and faithful Service.
And, e'er I take my laft Farewel, with Hope
To find a Grant, my Suit to you is, that
You would, for my Sake, pardon this young Man,
And to his Merits love him, and no further.
    Rober. I thus confirm it.
                   [*Gives his Hand to* Fulgentio.
    Camiola. And, as e'er you hope,   [*To* Bertoldo.
Like me, to be made happy, I conjure you
To re-affume your Order ; and in fighting
Bravely againft the Enemies of our Faith
Redeem your mortgag'd Honour.
    Rober. I reftore this :——   [*The white Crofs.*
Once more Brothers in Arms.
    Bert. I'll live and die fo.
    Camiola. To you my pious Wifhes! And, to end
All Differences, Great Sir, I befeech you
To be an Arbitrator, and compound
The Quarrel, long continuing, between
The Duke and Dutchefs.
    Rober. I'll take it into
My fpecial Care.
    Camiola. I'm then at reft.—Now, Father,
Conduct me where you pleafe.
              [*Exeunt* Paulo *and* Camiola.
                     Rober.

Rober. She well deferves
Her Name, *The Maid of Honour!* May fhe ftand
To all Pofterity, a fair Example
For noble Maids to imitate! Since, to live
In Wealth and Pleafure, is common; but to part with
Such poifon'd Baits is rare, there being nothing
Upon this Stage of Life to be commended,
Though well begun, till it be fully ended.　　　*[Exeunt.*

We are now come to the Conclufion of *the Maid of Honour:* A Piece which in my Judgment does *Honour* to its Author, and well deferves to be prefented upon the *Englifh* Stage.

The END of the SECOND VOLUME.